STAKE NIGHT

Susan Archer

Credit for photography on the cover to Avis Girdler (avisphoto.com)

FOREWORD

Stake Night is the story of a single year in the glamorous and competitive world of show horses, where the rewards are large and so are the lengths to which people will go to win. For the owners, it is about wielding power through money in their quest to proudly hold the prestigious World Championship trophy. For the riders, it is about demonstrating technical skill and nerve by out-riding their competitors and maneuvering their horse in the frenetic ring so the judges notice it. For the trainers, it is about finding the key that makes your horse out-perform others that might actually be more talented and achieving the professional recognition that leads to new clients and financial security. For everyone, it is about settling scores and finding a way to win.

The central character is Jennifer, a young, relatively unknown trainer. She can't believe her luck when a rich client brings her the reigning world champion horse and tells Jennifer to prepare the horse for her timid daughter to ride. Jennifer quickly learns that this horse and rider are a dangerous and doomed combination, and she must move carefully to find an alternative that keeps her important client from leaving the barn and ruining Jennifer's chances to finally join the ranks of the most well-known and respected trainers.

ACKNOWLEDGEMENTS

Thank you to Avis Girdler, horse show photographer extraordinaire, for the beautiful image on the book cover. You can find more of her brilliant work at avisphoto.com. I also thank my kind and hilarious friend Lori Weis for her very helpful comments and edits. Her sense of humor, eye for detail and willingness to read and re-read a story about horse shows made this a better book. My artistic and tenacious friend Angie Eckdahl did a great job of fighting with fonts so that the cover is gorgeous. My trainer, Peter Palmer, patiently explained training methods that I over-simplified so that people like me could understand them. Finally, thank you to my wonderful, generous, thoughtful and encouraging husband who kept asking me how Stake Night was going. It would be gathering dust in the corner of my office if you hadn't persevered. I love you the most.

TABLE OF CONTENTS

CHAPTER 1

"And this year's winner of the Five Gaited World Championship is…" The tuxedo-clad announcer pauses dramatically and Marianne holds her breath, until he finally says "SS Toreador!" The crowd erupts in cheers and he continues, raising his voice so he can be heard over the noise in Freedom Hall, "SS Toreador is owned by Marianne Bartlett Smithson of Kentucky and is ridden and trained by Johnnie Stuart of Stuart Stables."

"Yes!" Marianne's relief and joy expel in a single word as she leaps to her feet and exchanges a long hug with her daughter, Blair, carefully protecting her makeup from rubbing off onto her tall daughter's white evening gown. She smiles and begins graciously accepting the congratulations of the cheering fans that surround her. Her face, recently smoothed with a mini-facelift, shows her happiness as the accomplishment begins to sink in. They won! They actually won the most coveted prize in the Saddlebred show horse industry! She joins the 40,000 horse show fans cheering and clapping as Johnnie Stuart rides her stunning chestnut gelding to the end of the show ring and dismounts, handing the reins of his sweaty horse to his groom with a cocky grin, and then raising his arms in victory.

The announcer emerges from the fancy white pergola encircled by colorful potted flowers in the center of the ring, adjusting his black tuxedo jacket with his left hand as he holds the microphone with his right. He quickly walks across the show ring towards Johnnie and the large group of presenters who are holding trophies, ribbons, and a blanket of red roses. As soon as he reaches them, he begins the traditional interview with the winning rider. "Johnnie. What can you tell us about this horse?"

"Well," Johnnie begins in his slow Kentucky drawl. "I can't use no fancy words, but I can just tell you that he tried his hardest out there and there wasn't no one could match him tonight. I couldn't be prouder of my horse. I've been dreaming about this win since I was 10 years old and it took me almost 35 years to find a horse that could deliver it."

1

As Marianne listens to her horse's trainer, it strikes her how little she trusts him. She recognizes his body language and tone as those he uses to disguise one of the most ambitious and focused minds in the Saddlebred show horse business.

Johnnie continues, "I recognized this horse was special the moment he hit the ground, even before his mama had a chance to clean him up and feed him. I turned him out in the paddock when he was one day old and watched him trot off. He was everything I expected him to be from that day forward."

The announcer interjects, "Can you tell us about your ride tonight?"

"Toreador hasn't been an easy horse to train, but tonight he did exactly what I asked him to do. I believe he showed everyone here that he was clearly the best. We deserve this $100,000 prize."

Marianne cringes. While she agrees that Toreador was the best horse tonight, the ring had been filled with talented horses and riders and she is embarrassed that Johnnie isn't acknowledging the other competitors. She leans over to her daughter and says under her breath, "I wish Johnnie had left his ego at the barn."

Blair nods slightly and raises a single perfectly arched eyebrow to signal her agreement. Her delicate features immediately return to their normally placid expression and both women return their attention to Johnnie.

The announcer is now asking about the horse's future. "What's next for SS Toreador?"

"I'm going to win the Stake Class at the Royal in November, and then give him a little time off. But I'll definitely be back here next year to defend our win and become repeat World Champions!" Johnnie ends his statement emphatically and the crowd applauds in appreciation.

Johnnie remounts Toreador for his victory pass, and Marianne makes eye contact with Blair and jerks her head towards the exit to indicate that she wants to leave. While her daughter quickly gathers her sequined handbag, Marianne steps into the aisle, carefully raising the hem of her lace evening gown. The people around them are also moving towards the exit and Marianne politely accepts their congratulations with a tight smile as the crowd siphons out of the box seats, into the concourse of Freedom Hall, and eventually, out into the warm August evening.

As soon as Marianne and Blair separate from the well-wishers that surround them, Marianne quietly says to Blair, "How dare that son of a bitch." Marianne emits waves of quiet, cold rage as she leads her daughter to their black Mercedes.

Blair wisely waits to comment until they are both sitting in the car. Marianne is taking deep breaths but hasn't yet started the ignition. "Mom, I think we have to go to the barn. We can't just leave. People will notice."

"What would they notice? To hear Johnnie Stuart tell it, he's the only one that had anything to do with my horse's success. You'd think that asshole was the one who'd been writing checks for the last nine years."

Blair attempts to calm her mother, "He probably just was caught up in the moment. He knows that you own Toreador…"

Marianne vehemently interrupts her daughter, "Damn right I do."

"You're right to be upset, but there isn't anything we can do about it. I think we need to make at least a token appearance at the barn or people will think that something is wrong. And I'd like to give Toreador a pat on the neck. We don't even have to talk to Johnnie. We just need to be seen." Blair's voice is faintly pleading.

Marianne takes several moments before she responds. "I guess you're right. We don't want to air any dirty laundry in this crowd. But let's be quick about it so I don't say something to Johnnie Stuart that I'll regret."

Both women open their car doors and carefully step back out into the humid night. The darkness of the parking lot is illuminated by the stabs of headlights of cars making their way out of the fairgrounds towards the Interstate. As they pick their way across the parking lot back towards the horse barns, they maneuver around crowds heading the opposite direction. A few people recognize Marianne and Blair and voice their congratulations as they pass.

Now that she has had a moment to calm down, Marianne's good manners are on full display as she replies, "Thank you. I thought the class was terrific. It was filled with several grand horses and tonight just happened to be Toreador's night."

Carefully avoiding random piles of horse manure in their high-heeled sandals, they enter the barn in which Stuart Stables has been housed throughout the entire week-long World Championship. Blair has to lean towards Marianne to hear her say, "Remember, no dawdling. I am in no mood to be nice to Johnnie."

There is a large group of people celebrating in the barn aisle. A champagne cork pops as they approach, accompanied by cheers, laughter, and applause. They hear Johnnie Stuart drawl, "Ya'll are just going to have to get used to paying more for Stuart Stable stock from now on. I'm looking forward to selling ya'll some expensive show horse prospects this fall."

Because of the loud and boisterous crowd, the women's arrival goes unnoticed and they stop at SS Toreador's stall before reaching the area where Johnnie is jubilantly holding court. There are three grooms in the stall, toweling the sweat off the large chestnut gelding and sponging liniment onto his legs. Blair immediately digs in her handbag and extracts a cellophane-wrapped red-and-white peppermint. She deliberately crinkles the paper as she unwraps it, hoping to interest the horse with the treat. As she extends it with a cautious "Good boy…" Toreador eyes her with hostility, tossing his head and laying his ears back to warn them against approaching. All three grooms step away from him warily, keeping their eyes on his hooves and teeth. Blair and Marianne quickly step back from the stall door, making sure they are safely out of his reach.

"He's not a very friendly horse, is he?" Blair says this almost curiously, as though she is trying to understand his reaction.

"Well, he hasn't had you around to make friends yet. When you start showing him, I'm sure it won't take him long to soften up. He'll be begging peppermints from you as soon as he hears your voice in the barn, just like all the other horses you've ever shown." Marianne says this with certainty. "I can't wait for you to show him. You will dominate the Amateur Class."

Blair hesitates and softly says, "Well, there's no hurry. He has a long career ahead of him. Wouldn't it be great if he could be one of the few horses that wins the World Championship two years in a row?"

Marianne doesn't reply as she is surrounded by new arrivals to the party who congratulate her on Toreador's win. A photographer for the *National Horseman*, a glossy industry magazine, arrives and invites Marianne and her well-wishers to pose for a picture. Marianne quickly removes her silver cosmetic compact from her bag and uses it to make sure her hair and makeup are still perfect while the others maneuver to join the group being photographed. This picture will almost certainly be in the centerfold of the next issue.

While waiting for the photographer to pose the photo, Marianne glances around for Blair and notices she is standing several yards down the aisle, chatting with Jennifer Hornig. As soon as she can extricate herself from her well-wishers, she joins them, intending to leave with Blair as quietly as they arrived. "Blair, let's get out of here."

Jennifer looks at her curiously, saying, "Congratulations on Toreador's win. He certainly did well out there. I thought his trot was the best I'd seen at the entire show."

"Thanks Jennifer," Marianne begins her well-rehearsed comments about what a strong class it had been when she feels a hand on her shoulder and turns to see Johnnie Stuart behind her.

"I was getting tired of talking to ugly old trainers like myself and came over to have a conversation with you beautiful ladies." Johnnie's eyes are bright and his voice is over-loud. It is clear that he is still experiencing an emotional high from his ride.

Jennifer notices the look of irritation that crosses Marianne's face and she moves quickly to cover what is becoming an awkward moment. "I was just congratulating Marianne. Toreador was spectacular."

Johnnie's grin broadens. "He worked just like I wanted him to." He cocks his head sideways at Jennifer and continues, "I imagine I'll be looking for another assistant now to help me get some new colts ready for prospective buyers over the winter. Why don't you and me sit down and talk about whether you might be a fit for that?"

Marianne's eyes move quickly from Johnnie to Jennifer as the pretty young woman leans away from Johnnie, obviously uncomfortable. Marianne interjects, "Now Johnnie, you know that Jennifer has a very busy training business of her own. She trains

5

Blair's pleasure horse at Beech Tree Farm and has been doing an excellent job for us. She has several clients and does very well."

Johnnie laughs lightly, his eyes not leaving Jennifer. "Oh. That's right. You're running your Dad's old place. I guess since I don't see you in the gaited classes, I'd forgotten that barn was still going." He hesitates and then adds with a smirk, "I don't pay much attention to those other divisions."

Jennifer's expression is a combination of annoyance and amusement. Everyone in the industry is aware of Johnnie's belief that trainers who specialize in pleasure horses are second-class citizens. Extricating herself from the awkward conversation, she says, "I have to get going. The truck is coming early tomorrow to take the horses back home and I still have to get the tack room packed up." She congratulates Marianne and Blair again and reconfirms Blair's riding lesson for the next week before retreating down the aisle.

Marianne turns to Johnnie and says, "That was unkind. She's a good trainer and everyone has to start somewhere."

"I was just trying to help. I don't know why so many trainers insist on struggling on their own, rather than being an assistant to those of us who know what we're doing." Then he goes on, insensitive to the fact that Jennifer is training Blair's horse, "At my place, she'd have the opportunity to work good horses. She ought to be thankful that I offered to consider her."

Another champagne cork pops in the rowdy crowd behind them before Marianne has a chance to reply. After the cheers quiet enough for them to be heard, Marianne and Blair use the opportunity to say their goodbyes and leave the barn.

CHAPTER 2

Johnnie Stuart checks his watch and realizes he still isn't tired although he has been up all night. He made the transition from champagne to coffee about an hour ago, when the celebration at Barn C of the Kentucky State Fairgrounds finally wound down. He swallows two Advil tablets and steps across the aisle to peer into SS Toreador's stall. The large chestnut gelding looks up from his hay and lays his ears back tightly against his head, signaling that he doesn't want to be interrupted. Although Toreador has a disagreeable personality, he works as hard in the show ring as any horse Johnnie has ever trained. In return, Johnnie ignores his misbehaviors outside of the ring. The grooms have learned to give the horse a wide berth and Johnnie routinely sedates him before the farrier or veterinarian arrives. He turns away from the stall and notices Jennifer coming down the alley towards him. As she gets closer, Johnnie notices that the attractive young woman looks worried and tense. He smiles at her and loudly says, "So did you decide you want to come work for me after all?"

Jennifer starts to talk before she reaches him, "Has Marianne called you this morning?"

"No. I wasn't expecting her to call. I imagine she's still sleeping." Johnnie responds in a slow drawl that disguises his growing curiosity.

"Did she tell you about her decision when you saw her last night?" By now, Jennifer has stopped walking towards him and stands in the corridor fidgeting with the halter she is holding.

Johnnie raises his eyebrows. "What decision?"

"On her way out last night she came by my stalls and told me that she wants me to take Toreador back to Beech Tree this morning. She told me that she wants me to get him ready for Blair to show next season."

"Pretty funny." Johnnie tries to absorb what Jennifer is saying. Even if Marianne still had the crazy idea of transitioning Toreador to an amateur class, why would she move him to a place like Jennifer's Beech Tree Farm?

7

"No, Johnnie. I'm dead serious. She was pretty upset. Maybe you should call her and sort it out. I'll go back to my stalls and hang out until I hear from you."

Johnnie's fingers shake as he dials his cell phone and Marianne answers without a greeting. "I'm glad you made it out of bed this morning. I expect you've heard the news that Toreador will be beginning his amateur career tomorrow."

Johnnie swallows hard, ignoring his racing heartbeat so that he can respond calmly. "Marianne, you can't be serious. Toreador is just now peaking. We need to make sure he's ready for Kansas City. We only have ten weeks before that show."

Marianne's tone is cold. "Well Johnnie, it is interesting that this morning it is 'we' when last night it was all about you. But I've made up my mind. Have Jose' take him down to Jennifer's stalls immediately."

"Marianne, please be reasonable." Johnnie's voice is pleading, "I bred this colt. I was there the night he foaled. I watched and waited for him to be ready to enter training. He's my horse!"

Marianne's voice shakes with the anger that has been building since last night. "It was obvious from your speech during the awards ceremony last night that you believe he is your horse. But in fact, he is my horse. I paid half a million dollars for him before he'd ever seen a show ring. I've paid his board, his training, his vet bills, his farrier bills, his acupuncturist, wraps, vitamins, masseuse, and every other cost you could possibly dream up. I've never complained or balked. So you can imagine that it surprised me a bit when you failed to so much as mention my name in your speech last night. It was typical of you, Johnnie. It was all about how you bred him, you saw his talent, you trained him, and you rode him." She takes a deep breath and then continues, gaining momentum, "Well, I'm here to remind you that you don't own him. Have Jose' take him to Jennifer or I'll call the sheriff. I will call her in fifteen minutes and she had better have his halter rope in her hand. And he'd better be standing on the end of that rope."

Johnnie hears the click of Marianne disconnecting the call. He slams his phone closed and sinks down to sit on the cement corridor to catch his breath.

CHAPTER 3

Kenny Rivers wakes slowly, emerging from sleep with a heaviness that he feels in every muscle and joint. At first he is disoriented and keeps his eyes closed, staying motionless as he tries to remember where he is. As the fog starts to clear from his head, he recognizes the sounds and smells of home and realizes that he is in his own bed rather than in a cheap hotel room that reeks of mildew and disinfectant. He smells bacon frying, opens his eyes and smiles. His kids are poking their heads around the edge of the bedroom door.

"He's awake! He's awake! Mommy! Daddy's awake!" Emily shrieks at the top of her four-year-old voice as she rushes over to jump on the bed. It looks like she has insisted on picking out her own clothes this morning. Her pink striped T-shirt and her purple-and-white polka-dotted leggings are a little girl's idea of fashion.

"Well, if he wasn't before, he is now." His son looks like Kenny, with dark eyes and hair and long legs that make Jeremy one of the tallest kids in his class. At only eight, he is already showing a talent for sarcasm, particularly where his little sister is concerned. Emily leaps onto the bed with her favorite stuffed animal, a purple horse named Princess Alexia, and chatters in her most excited voice, telling him that the horse's bridle is broken and he needs to fix it NOW. Jeremy approaches with more dignity than Emily, and gives his dad a big hug.

By now, Angela is leaning in the doorway, smiling at them all. "You're just in time for breakfast. We didn't think you were ever going to wake up so I pulled out my secret weapon – bacon! Kids, let your dad jump in the shower so we can all have breakfast together for the first time in more than a week." Before getting out of bed, Kenny returns Jeremy's hug and then reaches out to tickle his daughter until she is shrieking and breathless.

While in the shower, Kenny replays the events of the last week. The World's Championship Horse Show that finally ended late last night had been a seven-day marathon for the American Saddlebred Industry. More than one thousand horses, their trainers, grooms, breeders, and owners had converged on the Kentucky State

Fairgrounds in Louisville to compete for ribbons and bragging rights. Kenny and the other trainers worked themselves into states of nervous exhaustion, preparing and presenting horses in two performances a day for a solid week.

As he shuts the water off in the shower, the knob comes off in his hand. Angela has been complaining that their trailer is falling down around their ears and he had promised to do some maintenance as soon as the Louisville show was over. Well, it probably wouldn't be today. Even though he brought all the horses and tack home last night, he still has to put everything away. He hopes that Angela will understand and give him time to catch up on all the work in the barn that piled up while he was gone. He deliberately pushes his worries to the side and pastes on a smile as he sits down to breakfast.

He doesn't have to wait long for Angela to start with a seemingly innocent, "You came in so late last night that I didn't get a chance to hear all the details. How was the show?"

Kenny helps himself to several pancakes, reaching to put one on Emily's plate and says, "It was okay. Two of our clients won ribbons in their qualifying classes."

Angela pours syrup on Emily's pancake and begins to cut it in small pieces while the girl squirms in her chair. "Out of how many classes?"

Kenny darts a look at his wife and answers quietly, "Eight." Before she can respond, he continues, "It wasn't a great show for us."

Angela maintains a careful tone, "So what was the reaction?" She wants to know if any of the clients are unhappy.

Both parents are keeping their voices level and casual, but Jeremy detects the tension and his eyes follow their conversation as though he is watching a tennis match.

"It's hard to say," Kenny answers. "I think we probably got what we deserved, but it was still disappointing. Our clients are just over-matched at the World Championships. I should probably have done more to convince them not to go. It is expensive and stressful, and they don't have much to show for it."

Angela tries to hide her worry as she carefully asks, "Are they disappointed enough to go to another barn?"

10

Kenny looks directly at his wife and says very quietly, "Can we talk about this later? I know we can't afford to have anyone leave our barn. I'm doing everything I can to keep everyone happy and hold Riverside together until we can catch a break."

"No need to be so defensive. I'm just trying to understand where we stand." She glances at Jeremy, notices his worried expression, and deliberately brightens her voice as she changes the subject, "So, what's on your agenda today?"

He looks at her over the brim of his coffee cup. She is still as pretty as the day they married, with clear blue eyes and a long blond ponytail. Motherhood and the worries of making ends meet have made her less carefree recently, but she can still turn heads. "Well, I need a couple of hours to put all the stuff from the show away. Otherwise, it will be all screwed up when I try to use it the next time. And I need to order some feed and wash blankets and clean tack."

Angela hesitates, moves the remnants of her pancake around on her plate and carefully says, "It's Sunday. I was really hoping we could spend some time together as a family today. It seems like we haven't seen you in ages and Jeremy starts school in a week."

Without thinking, Kenny makes a rash promise. "Well, I was really hoping that we could go to the zoo tomorrow and maybe even have a picnic."

Emily immediately starts bouncing in her chair and screaming, "The zoo, the zoo! The BEARS, and the LIONS! Mommy! We're going to the ZOO!" Her long unbrushed hair gets in her face and she wipes it away with a hand that is sticky with syrup.

Jeremy pauses while he is reaching for the last piece of bacon, looks at his dad and says, "Really? Do you mean it?"

"Yes, I mean it. We'll even spend time at the Water Park." Now that he is committed, he might as well go all in. He takes advantage of Jeremy's distraction to grab the bacon off the platter and take a bite before putting the rest back on his son's plate.

Angela smiles brightly, "You have a deal. We'll help you today and we'll all take tomorrow off and go to the zoo."

Kenny leaves Angela to clean up the breakfast mess and walks across the driveway to the barn, wondering whether he has enough room on his credit card to buy zoo admissions for the family. As he enters the barn, the horses nicker. It is obvious they haven't been fed yet, even though the groom should have done it two hours ago. He feels guilty, knowing that he should have checked earlier since it isn't the first time Javier hasn't shown up to feed on a Sunday. Kenny wishes he could get more reliable help, but he can't pay enough to compete with the more successful barns. He begins feeding the eight impatient horses, checking their water, and turning on each horse's fan to keep the stalls tolerably cool in the Kentucky heat and humidity.

Six of the horses in the eight-stall barn belong to clients. The client horses are all more than nine years old, and have a variety of minor health issues that Kenny attends to every day. As he works through the morning routine, he thinks about his clients. They are all female, ranging in age from their late teens to over sixty, and they all adore their horses and get along with each other fairly well. He knows from his friends in other barns that there is often a lot of internal competition and in-fighting in a barn, but his clients seem to genuinely like each other.

The two remaining stalls contain two-year-old prospects he and Angela own and hope to sell for a reasonable profit. Angela has been getting them out of their stalls to walk them this week while he was gone. The week-long break in their training couldn't be helped, but he needs to give them a serious workout today. He wants to make sure they are advanced enough to get someone in paying decent money for them. With the price of feed, veterinarian and farrier bills, he can't afford to keep them through the winter.

After feeding, he heads to the trunks and crates in the storage shed, cleaning the tack, and carefully repacking the stall curtains so that they will be ready for the Kentucky State Pleasure Championships in a couple of weeks.

CHAPTER 4

Late Sunday morning, Eileen Miller patiently stands in line to hand her bags to the gate agent at the Louisville Airport. She looks crisp and cool despite the heat and chaos of the airport. The lines wind back and forth across the airport lobby and are full of people heading home from the week-long horse show. The crowd is primarily female, with a heavy proportion of young girls wearing horse-themed T-shirts. Most groups have piles of luggage that include hat carriers, suit bags, and even a few saddle trunks. Everyone looks fatigued, even the mother holding a tri-color ribbon, evidence that her daughter won a class during the last week.

Eileen tucks her expertly colored ash-blonde shoulder-length hair behind her ear and slowly works her way through the airport. Once she finally boards the flight and claims her window seat, she makes sure the straps of her Louis Vuitton bag are carefully tucked under the seat, reties her silk scarf and opens her water bottle.

A heavy-set woman about her age awkwardly settles into the seat next to her and introduces herself as soon as she catches Eileen's eye. "Hi. I'm Joanne. Were you here for the horse show?" Pausing barely long enough for Eileen to nod, she effuses, "Wasn't it fabulous? I'm so inspired." The woman oozes energy and enthusiasm, but perhaps it is attributable to the Venti-sized Starbucks cup that she is balancing.

Eileen pulls her Kindle out of the seat back pocket in an effort to dissuade Joanne from chatting, and politely answers, "Hi Joanne. I'm Eileen. And yes, I'm headed back home. The show was great but I'm definitely ready to be home."

Joanne misses the clue and gushes, "The show was amazing! We don't get crowds like this at our shows in Denver. We're often lucky to get anyone at all sitting in the stands. And people here dress up for the show! I had no idea! I felt like a hick from the sticks. And the stall decorations were amazing! I even saw one barn that had a pond with live ducks!"

Eileen grips her Kindle and keeps glancing at it, but finds herself loosening up as she soaks in some of Joanne's good mood. "Yes, some of the barns get carried away with their decorations. Our barn just focuses on a few hanging baskets of flowers and some curtains. I'd rather be noticed for the beautiful horses than the beautiful stalls. Do you have Saddlebreds?"

"Yes, I have one. But he is nothing at all like the ones I saw here. He is more of a backyard horse. I'd like to upgrade but I love him and can't afford two horses, especially if they're in training. Did you have a horse showing here?" Joanne talks fast, looking directly into Eileen's eyes. Although they are nearly the same age, all resemblance ends there. Joanne is wearing worn jeans, running shoes and a colorful T-shirt. Her gray hair is cut short and she has a round face, free of makeup.

"I am lucky enough to live around great trainers in Southern California. And I did have a horse here. He's a four-year-old gaited horse." Eileen smiles. Her beautiful chestnut stallion, Spy Master, had won the Junior Class in the Five-Gaited Division. Although he had looked good at the shows out west earlier in the summer, it had been a thrilling surprise to win his class this week. The competition in Kentucky is always very stiff and she is proud to take the trophy home to California.

"Wow! It's cool that you have a gaited horse. I've never even ridden the slow gait or rack. Is it really as smooth as it looks? Can all Saddlebreds be trained to rack?"

Eileen puts her Kindle aside and commits herself to the conversation with Joanne. "No, not all Saddlebreds can do five gaits. And of the subset of Saddlebreds that can do them, not all of them enjoy it. A horse needs to be happy and comfortable in order to show well in the ring and it is better to find the right division and class for each horse." As their conversation progresses, Eileen realizes that she is enjoying talking about Saddlebreds to someone that is really interested in learning more. At horse shows, she is usually surrounded by people that can recite bloodlines and show records and have very loud opinions about who the judge should reward with a first place ribbon.

As Joanne asks more questions about the gaits, Eileen struggles with describing how it feels to ride the lateral racking gait. "It is the most exciting gait I've ever ridden. Not only is it fast, but it is so comfortable. When it is done properly, your body sits in the saddle

14

almost as smoothly as at the walk, but you can feel and hear just how BUSY your horse is underneath you. His head is up, his ears are up, and he feels eager and animated and happy about doing his job." Eileen looks at Joanne and laughs. "You should come visit me in California sometime and we'll get you a ride on a gaited horse. It probably won't be Spy Master, though. He's too much for an amateur like you or me to handle."

"What? You don't ride your own horse?"

Eileen often gets this reaction from her friends. "Spy Master will be five years old next year. He will be too old for the Junior Class, but he's still a little wild. So I plan to have my trainer show him in the Stake Class and compete for the $100K prize. I don't want my trainer to have to worry about making him suitable for an amateur like me to ride. I'd rather give him every chance to beat a horse like Toreador."

Joanne's blue eyes are focused on Eileen, "Wow! That horse is amazing! The Stake Class last night was full of great horses. Do you think that Spy Master might have a chance to win it next year?"

Eileen shrugs, "I don't know. If everything goes right, he might have a chance. He's at a disadvantage because we're in California and we have to travel farther to get to shows, so I've considered moving him to a trainer in Kentucky to improve his chances. Once he retires from the show ring and starts his breeding career I'll almost certainly move him to Kentucky. There are more breeders there and it will increase his value as a breeding stallion."

"But wouldn't you miss him?"

"Well, it isn't realistic for me to think I'd ever show him. I can hold my own on a horse, but the Stake horses are almost always ridden by trainers. And Stallions are not always well-behaved, so it can be hard for an amateur to show them." Joanne sighs and then admits, "And it really starts to be about money for me. I need to give Spy Master his best opportunity to be a leading sire."

As the airplane begins the descent into Denver, Eileen and Joanne are chatting like old friends. "It was really great to meet you and I hope we can stay in touch," Joanne scribbles her email address on a piece of note paper and hands it to Eileen. "Best of luck to Spy Master! I'll be back in Louisville this time next year to cheer him on when he wins the gaited Stake!"

15

Eileen crosses her fingers and holds them up to show Joanne. "I hope to see that happen. Lots can go wrong between now and then."

The women separate on the concourse and Eileen hurries towards the connecting flight that will take her to LAX.

CHAPTER 5

It is nearly 9PM when Jennifer finishes all her chores at the barn and walks across the driveway to the small home her parents built when they first bought the property. She opens the door, noticing that it needs to be repainted, and stands back as Jelly, her boxer, rushes in ahead of her. He goes straight to his food dish and looks up at her expectantly. He is wagging his stubby tail and it is clear that he expects to be fed immediately. Jennifer laughs and quickly fills his bowl. "Calm down, Jelly. I know you're hungry! All of that running around at the barn is hard work!" She reaches down to pet the young dog and then speed-dials her mom as she rummages through her freezer looking for a frozen meal.

"Hi Honey!" Her mom answers cheerfully. Jennifer often wishes she had inherited her mother's perpetual optimism. Jennifer's first instinct is to analyze everything that can go wrong with every decision in her life while her Mom always assumes everything will work out for the best.

"Hi Mom. You'll never guess what happened." The Sunday after a show is always a day off for horses and grooms, so she has spent the day working alone, cleaning the tack room and doing some basic repairs that she's been putting off. It has given her time to process the fact that SS Toreador is now in her barn, and this is the first time she has shared the news with anyone.

"You won the lottery and met a handsome prince on your way back home with your winnings?"

Jennifer smiles and answers, "Well, not exactly. At least about the prince part, anyway." She takes a deep breath and says, "Marianne Smithson gave me Toreador to train."

"You're kidding!" Her mother is laughing and yelling into the phone. "That is the greatest news EVER! Congratulations! You actually have him in your barn right now?"

Jennifer uses one hand to remove her frozen meal from its box and says, "Yep. He came home on the truck with all the other horses this morning. But don't congratulate me yet. I peeked into his stall about a dozen times this afternoon and he seemed angrier each time. He doesn't act happy to be here. He actually glares at me."

"Oh honey. I'm sure he's just out of sorts about being someplace different. He'll settle in and calm down soon enough. Your customers will get him addicted to peppermints before you know it and then he'll be fine."

"Gosh, Mom, I hope you're right. Marianne told me to get Toreador ready for Blair to ride next season but Blair is so timid that even her pleasure horse intimidates her. I'm worried that it won't be possible to turn Toreador into a safe enough horse for her to show." Jennifer has been training horses in Simpsonville Kentucky for almost ten years and knows that matching horses to riders is difficult. She voices her real concern, "I hope Marianne didn't send Toreador to me just to spite Johnnie Stuart."

"Honey, she picked you because you are talented. If anyone can turn that horse into the right horse for Blair, it's you. And Marianne can trust you to give her the straight scoop along the way. You learned that from your Dad. From what I know of Johnnie Stuart, it will be a refreshing change for her to get an honest trainer."

"I hope you're right mom, but I'm worried that I don't know anything at all about this horse. Johnnie was so angry that there is no way he's going to tell me anything that can help me. I don't even know what kind of bit he wears!"

Her mom laughs. "Johnnie or the horse?"

Jennifer laughs along with her mom but then reverts to her serious tone, "It's a serious handicap to have to figure out a horse's secrets through trial and error. Each horse works very differently and basic equipment choices can make a significant difference in how well the horse performs. Toreador doesn't strike me as the tolerant type. I don't imagine he'll give me many chances to figure out what he likes. I just wish Daddy were here to help me. He'd know what to do." Jennifer's dad had been a successful Saddlebred trainer until his fatal heart attack shortly after Jennifer graduated from college and joined him at Beech Tree. She still finds herself wanting to ask him questions about the horses and the business.

Her mom sighs. "I know you miss him. I do too. But you've been doing this for ten years now and you have good instincts. Just go slow and don't do anything dangerous. You can't afford to get hurt."

Like most trainers, Jennifer cannot afford good health insurance and this is another worry that is never far from her mind. "Yeah. You're right about that. I certainly won't do it deliberately. I just wish I could find someone to tell me more about this horse before I piss him off."

"Why don't you call Eduardo?" Eduardo Muñoz had begun his career in horses at Beech Tree as one of Jennifer's Dad's grooms. He had slowly worked his way up through the ranks at the barn and was the assistant trainer when her Dad died. There hadn't been enough work to keep much of a staff after that and he hadn't stayed at Beech Tree. "I think he is an assistant trainer in Georgia somewhere. You know Jennifer, the assistants and grooms have a network of their own and he might be able to help."

"Mom, you're brilliant! I know he'll help me if he can. That's a great idea! I'll call him tomorrow."

Jennifer's microwave timer dings loudly and her mom wraps up the call. "Glad to help sweetie. I can hear that your dinner is ready. Now make yourself a green salad to go with whatever that is in your microwave and sleep well. And give Jelly a pat for me."

Jennifer opens the microwave door and wraps up the phone call "Thanks mom. I'm glad I called. I've been obsessing about this all day and I'm worried that I've been set up to fail. I needed a dose of your optimism."

"Quit being such a worry wart. You've been talking about taking Beech Tree to the next level and a horse like Toreador can do that for you. When you succeed with him, you'll have one of the top amateur gaited horses in the industry in your barn. As you know, that will bring more clients with plenty of money."

"True. And that will allow me to add on to the barn and get more help. And then I can start saving a little money and stop worrying quite so much about making ends meet every month. And then I can marry the Prince of England and go live in a castle."

Her mother laughs, "He's already married, I think. But we can find a suitable alternate, I'm sure."

19

Jennifer ends the call, "Calling Eduardo is a great idea. Thanks Mom. Love you."

CHAPTER 6

The grooms are just completing the feeding at Stuart Stables on Monday and they are all giving Johnnie's office a wide berth. It is easy to tell that he is in a foul mood and it is much safer to avoid him. No one has turned on the radio to the energetic Mexican station that is usually playing in the barn all day.

Johnnie is in his office talking to Dave Snell, his longtime friend. "She's an ungrateful bitch. She owes me everything. That horse would be nothing if I hadn't trained him." As Johnnie talks, his anger builds. By the end of his final sentence, his words are tight and short. He pauses and then says, "I don't know what that Hornig bitch did to steal that horse, but they'll both be sorry they screwed with me."

Dave is quick to fuel Johnnie's rant, "You're not the first trainer with a rich client that thinks they know more than they really do. She'll probably come crawling back to you after the horse is ruined by Hornig."

Johnnie curses loudly and says, "That bitch will have to get down on her knees and beg if she ever wants me to take him back."

Dave sips from his coffee cup. "You have a barn full of good colts. You can win again."

"Dammit Dave! It took me 35 years to win that class." Johnnie spits out his response and picks up the Copenhagen tobacco can setting on his desk and throws it as hard as he can against the wall, leaving a dent in the paneling and causing the tobacco to spill across the floor.

He gets up from his desk, strides out of his office, spies Jose' at the end of the aisle and yells, "God dammit, Jose'. Get to work! We leave for Indianapolis on Thursday. Get my three-year-old saddled and in the ring, NOW!" Jose' disappears into a stall, and Johnnie looks out the window to see his assistant, Bobby Acton, driving up to the barn. Johnnie walks toward the attached ring, knowing that the grooms will bring him his first horse to work within minutes. ON his way down the aisle, he passes Toreador's stall. It is conspicuously vacant, reigniting his anger. He rips Toreador's nameplate off the stall

21

door as he stalks by and throws it on the floor. Without turning he yells, "Get a horse in that God damned stall NOW!"

This is the first thing Bobby hears as he enters the barn and he realizes it will be a very tense day. The grooms are busily preparing horses for their work sessions. Bobby can see that Johnnie's favorite three-year-old, SS Night Train, is in cross ties and two grooms are hurrying to get him ready so they can get him out to Johnnie. Bobby steps into the stall to help bridle the colt and to double check the grooms' work. Jose' tightens the girth on Johnnie's saddle and when they are both done, Bobby leads Night Train from his stall. As he and Jose' walk the horse down the concrete corridor to the ring, Bobby points at Toreador's stall and then points at Night Train.

Jose' nods, confirming that Bobby has told him to move Night Train into Toreador's stall.

This is a symbolic promotion for Night Train. Although just three years old, he has already demonstrated his potential by winning both shows in which he was entered over the summer. Like Toreador, Johnnie bred and trained Night Train and expects to make a lot of money when he sells him. Johnnie has set a seven-figure price for the young stallion, believing he has an exceptional future in the show ring and the breeding shed.

The Three-Year-Old Futurity Championship is next weekend in Indianapolis and is the premier event for young horses in the breed. Breeders and owners enter the horses when they are born and pay installments on their entry fees for three years, betting on their horse's potential to claim a portion of the prize money. The owner of a horse can quit paying the entry installments at any time, removing the horse from the qualified entries and forfeiting the money they've already paid. This year, the winner of the three-year-old gaited sweepstakes is likely to win more than $50,000, one of the largest payouts in the industry.

While Night Train has been getting the most attention, Stuart Stables actually has two entries in the Futurity's Three-Year-Old Five-Gaited Class. The second horse is Vendome Copper, a tall chestnut gelding with a narrow white strip on his face, owned by Johnnie's long-time customer from Illinois, Mrs. Louise Clancy-Mellon. Vendome Copper, known as Vendome around the barn, will be shown by Bobby for the first time in Indianapolis on the upcoming Saturday. Bobby hopes that Vendome will show well, but he knows that almost anything can happen the first time a young horse enters the ring.

After delivering Night Train to Johnnie, Bobby goes to Vendome's stall where the big gelding is standing in cross ties. He is already saddled and his bridle is on a hook just outside the stall door. Bobby pats him and calmly bridles him. The colt is probably his favorite horse in the barn. He is calm and willing to work hard, even though he rarely shows the flash and fire that Night Train shows every day.

When Bobby leads Vendome into the ring, Johnnie has already finished warming Night Train up, and the young bay stallion is slow gaiting down the long side wall of the indoor ring. Bobby delays mounting Vendome as he admires the other three-year-old.

Night Train is a beautiful horse. His black mane and tail are full and flowing as he works around the corners of the ring, and Johnnie looks relaxed and confident as he works to keep Night Train's balanced. Night Train's neck is slightly shorter than ideal, a fact that is more noticeable as the young stallion's hormones cause him to bulk up in the neck and chest. In contrast, Vendome is much taller, finer boned, and elegant. The comparison extends to their personalities. Where Night Train's carriage and attitude is that of a barroom brawler, Vendome is poised and aristocratic and likes to stand with his head high and slightly tilted, as though he is begging to be noticed and admired.

Bobby tears his gaze away from Night Train, mounts Vendome, and cues him to step off quietly. It is time to get to work. After today, he'll only have one more practice ride before Vendome's debut in Indianapolis, so he'd better get moving.

CHAPTER 7

Jennifer spent a restless night, unable to stop thinking about her challenges with Toreador. She and Jelly were in the barn earlier than usual and by 8AM, she already has all the horses fed and the stalls cleaned. She pours herself a fresh cup of coffee from the pot in the tack room and goes to her office to call Eduardo, knowing that he will already be at work, too. As she dials the number, she wonders if Eduardo will be able to help her.

A man with a thick Hispanic accent answers the barn with a short "Abel Barn." Jennifer resurrects some of her high school Spanish, "Eduardo Muñoz, por favor."

"Un minuto." She hears the phone being set down on a hard surface and then someone in the background, "¡Eduardo, telefono!"

A few moments later Eduardo answers. Having been born to Spanish-speaking parents and raised in KY, Eduardo's drawl is overlaid with a strong Latin accent, "Hello?"

"Eduardo, this is Jennifer Hornig. Can you talk for a minute?"

He quickly responds, "Jennifer! It is good to hear from you. I am about to get on a colt. Can I call you back?"

"Absolutely. Call whenever you get a free minute." To kill time before Eduardo calls back, she takes a grooming box to Toreador's stall. The horse is standing with his head in the far corner and his butt towards the door. Before opening the door, she sweet talks him a bit and he finally stares at her, immobile except for an occasional blink of his eyes. She gently slides the door open and he immediately lays his ears back flat against his neck. Jennifer recognizes his clear signal of anger and unhappiness. She takes a peppermint in her pocket and crinkles the wrapping, hoping that he will soften his expression and turn towards her but he remains in exactly the same position. She removes his halter from the hook on the front of his stall door and starts to enter the stall, softly clucking with her tongue to get him to move his butt over so she can approach his head. After some resistance, she successfully halters him and attaches each side of the halter to light chains that are attached high on the sides of the stall. Once he is attached to the cross ties, he is forced to face the front door

24

and to stand relatively still while she grooms him. As she works, she talks to him and pats him but he doesn't seem to enjoy the process at all and she is careful to avoid giving him an opportunity to kick her.

Eduardo returns her call nearly an hour later. After making some small talk, she explains, "I'm not sure if you've heard, but I have SS Toreador here at Beech Tree now."

"Congratulations! He is a very nice horse. But I've heard that he is difficult to get along with."

Jennifer replies, "The transition happened suddenly, so I don't know anything about him. He is unhappy and anti-social and I was hoping that you might know how I can get some information about him. I can't ask Johnnie Stuart, that's for sure."

Eduardo pauses and then says, "My nephew's best friend is a groom at Stuart Stables. I'll call him and see what I can learn."

In a little more than an hour, Eduardo calls back and says, "I don't have good news. The grooms at Stuart Stables were happy to see Toreador go. He kicks and bites without warning. He is touchy about how you tighten his girth and hates having his tail done for a show." Eduardo tells her everything he has learned about the horse. He ends his call with a warning. "Jennifer, be very careful. Toreador is dangerous."

Jennifer thanks him and disconnects the call but almost immediately hits redial and calls him back. "Eduardo. Please come back to Beech Tree as an assistant trainer and help me with Toreador. It is time for you to come back to Kentucky and I really need your help."

Eduardo laughs as though he has just been waiting for her to ask. "I will be there in two days."

As she hangs up, Jennifer takes her first deep breath in 24 hours.

CHAPTER 8

By 11 AM it is already hot and muggy, but this doesn't seem to have slowed Emily and Jeremy down at all. They have already seen the lions and tigers and are now approaching the water park area in the zoo. They can hear other kids splashing, screaming and laughing, and Emily reaches up to grab Angela's hand. "Will the water be cold, Mom? Will the kids be big?"

"Relax Emily. It will be fun, you'll see." Jeremy answers before Angela can and Emily's attention switches to him immediately. She releases Angela's hand and runs to catch up with Jeremy, leaving Kenny and Angela on their own.

"This is fun," Angela says. "I know you had a lot to do today and you'd probably rather be with the horses, but I'm glad you made time for this."

Kenny looks at her, trying to determine her mood. There is no secret in the Rivers family that Jeremy has learned his talent for sarcasm from his Mom, but her expression is open and honest. "You're right, this is fun and we should do this kind of thing more often," he admits.

Kenny and Angela help Emily quickly strip off her shorts and t-shirt to reveal the pink ruffled bathing suit underneath and then watch as the little girl runs to join the other small kids that are cooling off in the wading pool. Jeremy wanders over to the area of the splash park for older kids, leaving his parents alone on a bench, watching Emily.

"Kenny, I've been thinking."

Kenny looks away from his giggling daughter to his wife. It is obvious that she has something serious on her mind and he feels his heart rate elevate as she continues.

"Aren't you a little tired of the struggle of the barn? I know you love the horses and being around them all day, but we can't make ends meet like this. Half of your clients don't pay their bills on time. It seems like the horses we own never turn into anything that sells for much. I hate to open the mail or answer the phone because of the bill collectors. I'm tired of driving a beat up old car. Jeremy and Emily

26

need new clothes for school and Jeremy wants to play sports. I don't know how to tell him we can't afford it."

This is an old argument. Kenny takes a deep breath and matches her lowered voice. "Angela, can't we just have fun today? Do you seriously want to sell the place and move to an apartment in town somewhere? If that's really what you want, then I could probably get a job working construction." He can hear the edge in his voice and he stops speaking.

She shakes her head. "That isn't what I want. But I've been reading about a stable out west that is solely about kids and kid events. You know, birthday parties, trail rides, kids' lessons, summer camps, that kind of thing. They say that they are doing really well and they are expanding."

"So you want us to move out west and for me to go to work saddling horses for six-year-old kids?" Kenny is looking directly at her and his jaw is tight.

"No! That isn't what I mean at all!" She sighs, looks away from him and says, "This conversation isn't going at all like I planned. I've been waiting until the horse show was over to talk to you about this. If we converted Riverside into a barn that focuses on kids, we could make a lot of money. We could sell lessons by the semester so that we get paid up front and I could help organize fun parties and camps in the summer. Parents are always looking for something for their kids to do in the summer." Her voice tails off as she looks back at his face and sees his tense expression.

"But we don't have enough stalls for that many lesson horses." Kenny can tell that Angela is excited about her idea and he tries to keep his tone calm and rational.

"But that's just it, Kenny. The lesson horses aren't show horses. They don't need to be in box stalls and get expensive feed. They don't even need to be Saddlebreds with their fancy shoes and their long tails. Just think how much easier it would be to work with a bunch of older, well-broke, solid citizen quarter horses. I think we'd make better money and you wouldn't have to work so hard, and you'd have much less chance of getting hurt than you do now."

Kenny doesn't know how to react. He knows that they are barely treading water with Riverside Stables. In fact, there are feed bills that

27

are past due that Angela doesn't even know about. But he can't envision himself in the kind of business that his wife is describing. He decides his best option is to try to put her off to give himself time to find an alternative.

"I understand what you're saying, but the show season isn't quite over yet, so we can't make this change right now, anyway. The Kentucky State Pleasure Horse Finals are in two weeks and all of the clients are going. We can't pull the plug until the end of the season."

"I know that, but at least tell me that you'll think about it." Angela glances over at Maddie, still splashing in the pool, and says, "I've put together a business plan and I'd like you to look at it."

"So you've had this idea for a while, then." Kenny knows it is irrational, but he is hurt that she has been working on this on her own.

"Like I said, it was about a month ago or so when I read that article. But I wanted to convince myself it could work before I suggested it. And I didn't want to distract you from the Louisville show. I know that you had high hopes for the show and I didn't want to get in the way of that."

"And now that the show is over and none of those hopes paid off you think it is a good idea to kick me while I'm down?" Despite his hurt, he keeps his voice low. They're in a public place and while Emily is still splashing with other kids her age, he notices Jeremy is watching them both from a bench. "Look. I promise I will think about it. Let's not spoil this day for Jeremy and Emily. Why don't you get lunch out while I round up the kids?"

He stands up from the bench and walks across the patio area to join Jeremy. "Hey pal, are you hungry?"

"Are you and Mom fighting?" Jeremy asks, looking directly at Kenny, worry showing in his dark eyes.

"No! We're just talking about business stuff. Nothing at all for you to worry about. Let's try to pry your sister free from all those new friends she's making and have some of the sandwiches your Mom made for us." Kenny tugs down on the brim of Jeremy's ball cap and smiles at him. He knows that Jeremy has noticed the mounting tension between Angela and him and resolves to do a better job of sheltering the kids.

28

In the car on the way home, Kenny checks to make sure the kids are dozing, then quietly says to Angela. "Look honey, I just never pictured myself being anything other than a Saddlebred trainer. It's why I went to school at William Woods. It is what I have wanted to do ever since I was Jeremy's age. It is not just about being around horses. For me, it is about being around Saddlebreds."

"Kenny…" Angela tries to interrupt him, but he cuts her off.

"No. Please let me finish. I know we have to change something. We can't go on like this. But maybe there is some middle ground between your idea and where we are now. Maybe we could start some sort of Junior Rider program without completely trashing the business we have. Can we try to meet in the middle somewhere on this thing?"

Angela sits back in her seat and is quiet for a moment. "Sure. Absolutely. Maybe this fall we can get our feet wet by doing some stuff to increase the social life of the people that come to the barn. Maybe potlucks and an open house or two to get some younger customers. Even if we just had a couple of lesson horses, it could increase our income every week. You are a great riding teacher. Let's keep talking about it and figure out a way forward. I think we agree that we must do something different, and that's good enough for me right now." She blows him a kiss from across the car and they share a smile.

CHAPTER 9

Eileen is just finishing her workout in her home gym when she hears the distinctive ring on her cell phone that tells her the call is from Holly McNair, Spy Master's trainer. She grabs a towel and hurries to pick up her phone. "Holly! Is he here?" She's been waiting for this call and hopes that Holly will tell her that the horse van from Kentucky has arrived in California with Spy Master safe and sound.

She hears a throaty laugh on the line. "Let me guess. You have been sitting there waiting for this phone to ring for the last two days."

"Well, that isn't ALL I've been doing but I admit that I have been doing a bit of that. I'm like an over-protective mother."

"Well, you'd better get over here then or you'll miss being here to celebrate the arrival of your champion. The truck driver just called. Everything went fine and he should be here in an hour."

"Yikes. I need to jump in the shower. I'll be right there." Eileen disconnects the call and runs upstairs to the main level of her beautiful home overlooking the Pacific Coast. Morning Star Barns, the California facility where Spy Master lives and trains is forty minutes from Eileen's home. As she turns on the shower and selects some clean jeans and a t-shirt, she looks in the mirror and smiles broadly. She is anxious to see her horse and welcome him back home.

Slightly less than an hour later, she pulls through the Spanish-style wrought iron gate that marks the entrance to Morning Star. As she pulls into her usual parking place next to the outside riding ring, she notices that there are more vehicles than usual for a weekday morning. She quickly gets out of her car and opens the main door, entering the lobby which is dominated by a large glass window overlooking the indoor ring.

The lobby is full of people and the antique black oak table in the center has been rearranged to showcase Spy Master's Championship Ribbon. Several people start congratulating her at once and before she has even closed the door, she is surrounded by her friends from the barn. Her best friend, Karen Shields, moves forward to give her a big hug. "We heard Spy Master was coming home today and we came to greet him and give him some peppermints."

"Wow. What a nice surprise! He'll love all the attention. I can't wait to see him."

"We all got together to watch him on the streaming video and we just knew he would win! He looked amazing." The others immediately chime in, agreeing with Karen.

Eileen smiles as she thanks her friends but is interrupted by the sound of a truck approaching. The boisterous group moves out of the lobby and into the parking lot as the 18-wheeled horse van rolls slowly up the driveway. She hangs back and lets Holly work with the driver to get Spy Master safely unloaded. Her young stallion comes out of the truck, puts his head and tail high in the air and snorts, causing everyone to laugh. "There's our boy," someone says.

Yes, Eileen thinks. There's our boy. Every time she sees him, she admires him. Even with a blanket and shipping boots on, it is obvious that he is a very beautiful and proud animal. "Well, he clearly thinks a lot of himself," she says aloud.

"Yeah! Those Kentucky horses don't hold a candle to our California boy. Just look at him strut his stuff." Karen is standing at her elbow, watching Holly and the grooms walk Spy Master into the barn. He continues to snort and blow as he dances at the end of his lead rope.

Eileen gives Holly a moment to get him into his stall and in the cross ties before she approaches. Holly is removing the heavy wraps from his legs as the truck driver watches.

"We didn't have any trouble at all," he says.

"Yes, I'm sure he's fine. I just want to check him thoroughly while you're still here." Holly is the cautious type which is one reason that Eileen trusts her to train and care for Spy Master. In Holly's barn, everything has a place and everything is in that place. After the wraps are off and neatly set aside, Holly goes over each leg carefully, feeling for any signs of heat or injury. Then she removes his blanket and runs her hands over the horse's body. She finally is satisfied that he is fine, so she signs the paperwork the truck driver is holding and thanks him. "Would you like some coffee for the road?"

"No, but thanks," he says as he walks quickly out of the barn. "I've just got one more horse to drop off before I can rest and then head back East."

31

Holly turns to Eileen and says, "I'm sure Spy Master has been snacking the entire way from Louisville, but we'll give him a little bit of hay and something to drink. Then we'll take his temperature and hand walk him a little just to make sure he's comfortable."

Eileen enters his stall and pulls three starlight peppermints from the pocket of her jeans. "Just a few treats and then I'll leave him alone to rest," she says. She's got his full attention as he leans forward for the candy. He loves peppermints and like most show horse owners, she always has a stash of them ready. He gently takes them as she lays them on her flat palm, one at a time. He tickles her hand with his lips and leaves plenty of slobber behind, which she wipes on the front of her jeans. She pats his neck and rubs his favorite spot just behind his ear before leaving his stall and turning back to her trainer. "I'll get out of your hair, Holly. Thanks for everything. What's his schedule like for the rest of the week?"

Holly pauses from checking the bedding in Spy Master's stall to make sure it is fresh and properly fluffed up. "Well, we'll give him a couple of days of really light work. We'll hand walk him today and maybe just jog him for a couple days after that. He should be ready for a workout on Saturday. He isn't going anywhere until Kansas City, so we have about eight and a half weeks before we ship out. I think we can give him a mini-vacation so that he can freshen up a little."

"That sounds great. I'll see you on Saturday." Although she would rather hang around the barn for a while, Eileen decides to leave so that the crowd around Spy Master's stall will thin out, giving him a chance to rest and Holly a chance to work in peace.

She and Karen walk toward the parking lot together. "Want to catch lunch?" Karen asks. "It will give you a chance to tell me all about Louisville. And not just the horse stuff. Did you meet anyone fun?"

Eileen laughs and says, "Everyone I know that is fun is right here. But yes, let's have lunch and catch up." They quickly agree to meet at their favorite café and get in their cars.

Later that evening, Eileen has just fallen asleep when she is awakened by her ringing cell phone. It takes a moment for her to recognize Holly's distinctive ring tone. She scrambles free of her sheets and reaches for her phone, knowing that this can't possibly be good news.

"Holly? What happened?" She asks breathlessly, pushing herself into a sitting position and swinging her legs over the side of the bed.

"Spy Master is colicking. The vet is here and is treating him. He says he will be okay, but he gave us a scare." Despite the reassuring words, her trainer's voice is tight and tense.

"Oh my God. What happened?" Eileen realizes she is repeating herself as she tries to understand Holly.

"When I did the 8 o'clock check of the horses, he just didn't look quite right. He was restless and kept nosing his water but not drinking it." Holly continues, "I checked his stall and it was still clean. There wasn't any fresh manure and his pulse was a little high. So I called Dr. Simon and he came over right away."

Dr. John Simon is a very skilled equine veterinarian who has treated all of Eileen's horses over the years. She is relieved to know that he is treating Spy Master and is already at the barn. She allows herself to relax a bit. "So then what happened? How is he now?" Eileen peppers Holly with questions, trying to understand Spy Master's condition.

"Dr. Simon thinks it was probably caused by stress and the change in feed since getting home. He tranquilized and tubed him first thing and didn't find any blockages or twisting." Holly is describing a procedure where the vet passes a tube through the horse's nostril into the stomach to see if there is any fluid build-up in the intestinal tract. "We've been walking him and Dr. Simon gave him some Banamine as a pain killer. He seems more comfortable but we're waiting to see if we should take some fluid from his belly to see what might be going on."

Eileen takes a deep breath. "I'll be right there."

"Well, you can come if you like, but there's not really anything you can do. Why don't you wait and come in the morning? We'll be with him all night and we'll make sure he's okay. If anything unexpected happens, I'll call you right away."

Eileen agrees with Holly's plan and hangs up the phone. She knows that colic is a painful gastrointestinal condition that often requires surgery and is sometimes fatal. She also knows that she will never be able to go back to sleep so she puts on a robe, goes into her office and googles 'Horse Colic' on her computer.

The more Eileen reads, the more her worry increases. Colic is the number one medical cause of death in horses and the primary symptom is abdominal pain that stems from a potentially long list of causes, the most common of which is dietary. As Eileen hastily pages through the information on the internet she learns that there are several types of colic. As she reads, she quickly rules out types that are caused by parasites, knowing that it is very unlikely that Spy Master has worms since he is on a very strict worming regimen. She also remembers that Holly said that Dr. Simon had ruled out an impaction, so she guesses that it might be spasmodic colic, in which excess fluid or gas has built up in Spy Master's digestive track. This would be relatively good news, in that it probably wouldn't require surgery. She forces herself to stop when she starts reading about types of colic that are caused by infection, viruses and bacteria. Since Spy Master was just in Kentucky sharing a facility with more than 1,000 horses from as far away as South Africa, she realizes it is possible he has picked up something serious. Without any more hesitation, she quickly returns to her bedroom and puts on the jeans she just took off, throws a sweatshirt on, and quickly runs a brush through her hair. She grabs her keys and her handbag from the table by the door and hurries to her car.

When she arrives at the barn, the lights are on and the vet's truck is backed up to the sliding door that leads to the stalls. She walks into the barn and sees Dr. Simon at the end of the corridor near the indoor ring. She joins him as he watches Holly slowly lead Spy Master around the ring. Her horse looks completely different from the proud animal she saw that afternoon. He looks sleepy, his ears are droopy and his head is low as he slowly follows Holly.

"How is he?" she asks the vet.

Dr. Simon looks at her and smiles. "I figured there'd be no way to keep you from coming down here. I think he'll be fine. He only looks like that from the tranquilizer and Banamine. I don't think he's in any pain at all. We'll let the drugs wear off a bit and make sure he's still okay before we leave him alone."

"What do you think caused it?"

"It's hard to tell. We'll probably end up labeling this as idiopathic, meaning that we don't really know what caused it. He's been through a lot of stress recently. Holly told me that he just got home this morning, so it could be a change of feed or exercise or just the stress of travel."

"I'm so thankful this didn't happen on the truck," Eileen says.

Dr. Simon nods. "Yes. That could have been serious."

Holly and Spy Master have finished their circuit of the ring, and she lets him stop next to the vet who uses his stethoscope to listen to the sounds in the horse's abdomen and counts the horse's pulse.

Dr. Simon finally stands back. "Yes, he seems fine now. I'm getting normal gut sounds. Let's put him back in his stall and see how he acts."

Eileen follows Spy Master and Holly down the corridor and watches as the horse calmly enters his stall. As soon as Holly releases him from his halter, he goes to his water and takes a long drink. The vet laughs softly, "My work here is done."

Holly smiles tiredly. "Thanks for coming so quickly Doc. I'll keep an eye on him for a bit."

Eileen walks the vet back to his truck. As he puts his equipment away the vet says, "I hear your boy in there had a good show in Louisville."

"Yes, he won the four-year-old gaited championship. It was such a thrill."

"Are you going to more shows this fall?"

"Holly and I thought we'd go to the Royal in Kansas City in November, but I am a little worried about that now."

The vet pauses from washing his hands using the tap on his truck. "Oh, I don't think you should let this incident stop you. This kind of thing is fairly common and it shouldn't cause any lasting problems. Don't cancel your plans because of this."

Relief floods Eileen as she realizes how much she trusts this man. "Thanks so much for saying that. Now please drive carefully and thanks so much for coming out. I really appreciate your help." She stands in the barn door and waves as his truck goes up the driveway.

Eileen returns to Spy Master's stall where Holly is standing. "Look at that." Holly is pointing to a pile of fresh manure in the stall and the women hug each other. "I never thought I'd be quite this happy to see manure in a fresh, clean stall."

CHAPTER 10

Johnnie enters his barn a full two hours before daybreak, automatically hitting the master light switch that turns on the long banks of fluorescent lights above the stalls and down the long center aisle. This is his favorite time of day, when he is alone in the barn with only the sound of 40 horses starting to ask for their breakfast. He has an hour to himself before the grooms arrive to feed and begin cleaning the stalls, and then another hour before he begins working the horses. Following his daily routine, he walks down the aisle of the barn, looking into each horse's stall to make sure everything is normal and then returns to his office and settles at his desk with a large cup of coffee to prepare the day's work assignments, using a large grid with his horses' names down the first column and the remaining columns for each day of the week. Each morning, Johnnie fills in that day's column to identify the equipment that he wants on each horse. The grooms use this sheet to make sure each horse is properly prepared for their session. Today will be the last full workout for Night Train and Vendome before the Three-Year-Old Sweepstakes in Indianapolis on Saturday Night.

Later, when Johnnie and Bobby meet in the tack room, Johnnie says, "Well, on Saturday we find out what kind of three-year-olds we've got."

"Will it bother Mrs. Clancy-Mellon that you aren't riding Vendome?" Bobby asks.

"Maybe I still will if he looks better than Night Train today." Johnnie smiles as he says it, but he has no intention of switching horses with Bobby this close to the show.

"Do you want to ride Night Train first, or do you want to see Vendome?" Bobby knows from experience that Johnnie will want to watch Vendome work so that he can assess the horse and suggest last minute changes. Johnnie will want Bobby and Vendome to place second, right behind Night Train.

"My horse is ready so let's not keep him waiting." Johnnie raises a hand and motions to Jose' who is waiting outside Night Train's stall. The groom quickly ducks into the stall and leads the young horse out a few moments later.

At three years old, the dark bay stallion already acts like a champion. He steps out of his stall, pauses, and looks around. Jose' softly urges him forward but Night Train ignores him, continuing to look haughtily at the other horses in the stalls that line the aisle between him and the ring. After a few seconds, he responds to Jose' and begins a careful, deliberate walk down the aisle, his shoes ringing loudly against the concrete. Johnnie is watching and laughs softly, saying to Bobby, "He just wants to make sure we all know that this is all his idea."

After entering the ring, Jose' continues to hold the horse while Johnnie walks around him, checking to make sure the tack is correct and that the bridle, bits, and girth fit perfectly. Finally satisfied, he moves back to the horse's left side, puts a foot in the stirrup and mounts. Jose' quickly steps back as Night Train lunges forward and Johnnie laughs.

Bobby laughs too. "He's ready to rock and roll," he says.

Johnnie warms Night Train up slowly, glancing at his wrist watch to mentally record how long it takes so that he will know how much time to allow on Saturday. As soon as he feels his horse start to relax, he pauses in the middle of the ring to recheck his watch and then moves into a brisk trot working counter-clockwise around the ring. Bobby and Jose' stand in the middle of the ring watching as Night Train raises his head and gains speed coming out of the first turn. Johnnie makes a clucking noise with his tongue and Night Train responds by squatting in his hind quarters just slightly and increasing his energy and momentum. Bobby and Jose' exchange smiles, knowing that Johnnie will be pleased with that trot.

After two complete circuits of the ring, Johnnie stops Night Train, widens his hands and clucks again. Night Train begins to slow gait and as he moves down the ring, Johnnie makes slight adjustments with his body and hands until he can feel and hear an even and separate four beats as Night Train's feet hit the ground. It takes several rounds before Johnnie is satisfied and Bobby notices that Night Train shows some frustration by laying his ears back on his head, rather than pricking them forward. Johnnie swiftly reverses direction and repeats the trot and slow gait. After 15 minutes, he pulls Night Train to a halt. The bay horse is covered in sweat and his neck and shoulders are lathered. Jose' quickly moves forward to take the horse back to his stall.

"How did he feel?" Bobby asks.

Johnnie pauses a minute. "I think he'll be okay. He doesn't have much tolerance for me trying to help him out."

Bobby laughs. "Ah. You mean that he's a little like a teenager. He already thinks he knows everything."

"Yeah. I hope he won't get in his own way on Saturday," Johnnie responds. "He'll have more to look at with the lights and the crowd and I think that'll help him. He has a tendency to get distracted. The judge will notice that right away because his ears will be flicking all over, rather than being up and forward. As long as I can keep him focused on what's in front of him and keep him looking through his bridle, I think he could win it."

As Night Train leaves the ring, one of the grooms enters, leading Vendome Copper. Bobby mimics Johnnie's earlier movements, double-checking the bridle, saddle and girth to make sure everything fits properly and is secure. Then he mounts Vendome and makes him stand before walking off. Vendome walks quietly down the ring and Bobby talks to him.

"Good boy. Nice and easy today, ok?" Vendome flicks an ear back briefly, but then returns both ears to a forward position. Bobby clucks, and Vendome begins an energetic trot. As Bobby rounds the end of the ring, Johnnie remains standing in the center, watching attentively. Vendome gains speed and confidence as he works and maintains his happy expression throughout the session. Once Bobby finishes, Johnnie leaves the ring without making any comments.

Before leaving the barn for the day, Bobby opens the door of Johnnie's office and waits for Johnnie to look up before speaking. "Hey boss. Just wanted to know what you thought of Vendome. Do you have any suggestions? Is there anything you want me to adjust before Saturday?"

Johnnie leans back in his chair and says. "He's a nice colt. It looks like he'll make a nice amateur's horse." The morning's workout has convinced him that Vendome lacks the fire and desire that define a five-gaited stake horse.

"He is a nice colt," Bobby agrees. "I'm really happy with him. He works hard every day and makes my job look easy. Will Mrs. M be at the show?" Bobby is using the nickname that Johnnie uses for his best client.

"Naw. I was just about to call her and tell her that he really seems to like you and that ya'll are getting along with him." Johnnie has been avoiding making this call. With so much prize money on the line, it could be a difficult conversation and there is no way to disguise the fact that Johnnie has chosen to ride his own horse in the Sweepstakes rather than hers. She is a savvy show horse owner, and he is worried that she will be unhappy with his decision.

Before leaving, Bobby asks, "Is there anything you want me to change on Saturday?"

"I think you should keep him off the rail if you can. It might be hard for him to catch the judge's eye, otherwise." Without saying it directly, Johnnie has just confirmed that he doesn't think that Vendome is showy enough to compete at the highest levels.

"Got it. See you tomorrow."

Johnnie uses the next hour to catch up on some paperwork before dialing his client. She answers on the first ring.

"Johnnie. I was just getting ready to call you. How does Vendome look?"

Johnnie puts a smile in his voice and begins his sales job. "He looked great today. He'd plateaued a little and I just felt like I needed to try something different, so I asked Bobby to ride him today so that I could watch him work. They got along like two peas in a pod." Johnnie draws out his Kentucky accent a bit and uses his most charming voice.

"I'm happy to hear that. There is a lot of money at stake on Saturday and I'd sure like to get a piece of it."

"Well, I think he has a chance." Johnnie goes on, "I'm thinking though, that he seems to like Bobby a lot better than he likes me. You should have seen him brighten up. I think we'd be better off to have Bobby ride him on Saturday."

He pauses and waits for his client to respond. There is silence on the line and he fights off a momentary panic that she will insist that he ride her horse. With the loss of Toreador, he is heavily invested in Night Train's success on Saturday as a way to save some face among the trainer community.

"Hm. That's interesting. I'm surprised that you would make that decision after one ride. Especially a three-year-old. And particularly during the last ride before the Sweepstakes."

"Well, I just want to make sure he has the best possible chance this weekend and I'm really pleased with what Bobby's doing with him."

Mrs. Clancy-Mellon confronts the issue head on. "Johnnie, I suspect this has something to do with that three-year-old- you own."

Johnnie attempts to interrupt her, but she continues, "I understand that your assistant will be showing Vendome on Saturday. I can accept that. But I have eight horses in training with you. I live several hundred miles away and I have to be able to trust you. I'm not going to second guess your training decisions. But I will second guess the results. If you are telling me that you are sincerely making the best decision for my horse, then we'll see how that works out on Saturday."

Johnnie hurries to assure her that her horses are his first priority. After ending the call, Johnnie sits at his desk and wonders if he has just risked losing his biggest client. Of the 40 horses currently in the training barn, 34 belong to clients. The vast majority of his customers only have one horse, a handful have two, but Mrs. M is the only client with more than two horses. If she decides to remove all of her horses, it will reduce his income by nearly 25% and will severely impact his ability to maintain his current living.

As he stands up from his desk and prepares to turn off the light he thinks to himself that Bobby better not let him down with Vendome.

CHAPTER 11

Kenny Rivers has finished feeding horses and cleaning stalls and is just getting ready to work them when his cell phone rings. He glances at the caller ID and sees it is Holly McNair. He and Holly first met as classmates in the Equestrian Science program at William Woods University in Fulton, Missouri. They eventually became close friends, and then lovers. The relationship ended just before graduation, and he can no longer even remember what triggered their breakup. They have remained friends and keep in touch through email and Facebook and the occasional telephone call, but he is surprised to see her name because he just saw her at the Horse Show.

He greets her, "Well, you're up awfully early for a California girl."

"The early bird gets the worm," she says, laughing.

"But the late worm doesn't get eaten by the early bird." They pick up their banter easily. "You never miss a chance to give me a hard time about being late for class occasionally."

"Occasionally?" She laughs again. "It was more like every day." She quickly takes a more serious tone. "Hey, do you have a minute to talk?"

Kenny catches the change in tone and leans against the door of his tack room. "Of course. What's up?"

"I need to talk through something with someone but you cannot tell a soul, ok?"

"Holly. If there's one thing I can do well, it is keep secrets." Kenny flinches at the irony of his statement since one of the secrets he has kept is from telling his wife Angela that he and Holly were more than platonic friends in college. And he doesn't need to be reminded that the Saddlebred community is a small group. Gossip travels fast and it has been helpful to have another trainer to talk to about troublesome horses and clients without worrying that their personal business will become public knowledge.

"If I remember correctly, there is a lot that you can do well. But never mind that." She hesitates briefly and then goes on, "Spy Master colicked." Holly rushes through the words.

42

"Oh my God. How is he?" Kenny is completely still, hoping that the four-year-old survived.

"He seems okay. It happened last night and I haven't left his stall since." Holly tells Kenny the entire story and he listens quietly, hearing the worry in her voice. She ends by saying, "The vet doesn't seem particularly concerned but he's my first big deal horse and I've waited a long time for one this good. I can't lose him."

"You won't lose him." Kenny knows that she needs him to say something comforting, but he completely understands her concern. "What do you think caused it?"

"Well, I'm afraid it was the long trailer ride."

"That makes sense. But that's not anything to panic about. You only do that once a year, and next year you'll know to be especially careful when you take him home. Or maybe you'll have to fly him both ways next time." Kenny is referring to the fact that Holly transported Spy Master to the Louisville show by air and only used ground transportation to take him home. While expensive, she and Eileen chose this so that Spy Master would avoid the stress and exhaustion of the long trailer ride to Louisville.

"True." Holly pauses and then says, "But what if this becomes chronic? Or if every time I put him in a trailer from now on, he colics? Unlike you spoiled people in Kentucky, I can't get to a show without a long trailer trip and several overnights."

Kenny knows that Holly is correct. From his barn, he can take a horse to a show on almost any weekend from May through October with less than a 90-minute trailer ride. The only horse show that requires an overnight stay is the big show in Louisville, and that's only because the schedule is too grueling to move horses home every night. "I think you're borrowing trouble." Kenny continues to calm his friend. "It isn't like this was his first trailer ride. Sure, it was his longest, but you've been showing him all year. Didn't you take him to Arizona a couple of times? And Vegas? He was fine then, right?"

"Yeah. We started in mid-March at Carousel Charity in Scottsdale. It is about six hours to get over there and he was fine."

"Fine?" Kenny laughs. "I saw it on live feed. He blew their doors off. That was his debut and he looked incredible."

43

Holly's voice is more relaxed when she says, "Yes, you're right. He was really good. Thanks Kenny. I knew that you would be the voice of reason that I needed to hear this morning."

"I'm happy to help. Are you going to take him to the Royal?" Kenny is asking her about the show in Kansas City in mid-November.

"I had hoped to. But after this, I'm not sure."

"Holly, if he is going to be a show horse, he has to show up in Kansas City. If you trailer him yourself, he'll be all right."

"Well, we don't have to decide now. Thanks so much Kenny. I really needed someone to talk me off the cliff this morning." She changes the topic abruptly, "How is everything with you?"

Kenny replies, "Well, the kids and the horses are healthy, so that's good. But Angela thinks we should give up on the training business and turn the barn into a kiddie barn."

"Oh? And what do you think?"

"I'd rather dig ditches than have a string of shaggy ponies and old lesson horses. I'm not a riding teacher. I'm a horse trainer. Or at least, I think I'm a horse trainer." Kenny tries to lighten his tone a bit.

Holly doesn't hesitate to reassure him, "You're a GREAT trainer, and I totally understand why you don't want to take that path. You just need a good horse, like I got."

"And clients that pay their bills on time. My clients know that I won't stop feeding their horse if they're late paying their board and training bill."

"True." She continues, "It helps that I'm the only Saddlebred trainer in 40 miles. You have at least 60 reputable barns within that distance."

He ends the call, saying "Hey, I better get back to work. Don't worry about Spy Master. It was probably a one-time thing." Kenny ends the call and picks up the training bridle he was adjusting before his phone rang. He is happy that his friend has a great horse and knows that she works hard and deserves to do well, but he can't help but be a little jealous. Maybe he and Angela should consider moving out of Kentucky. That would be a lot more palatable than becoming a barn that does birthday parties and trail rides for kids. He deliberately puts that thought aside and returns to his tasks.

CHAPTER 12

When Jennifer and Jelly arrive at her barn on Thursday morning, Eduardo is already there and is busily sorting through the contents of the tack room. She greets him with a huge hug. "When did you get here?"

"Very late." He smiles and hugs her back. "It is good to be back."

"I am so glad you're here! Have you met our big shot yet?" She motions towards Toreador's stall.

"Yes. He already tried to kick me." Eduardo shakes his head.

"Well, I've been waiting for you to show up before I ride him. Let's do that first thing, ok?"

Eduardo nods. "I have told the grooms to stay away from him until we get to know him better. We do not want them to get hurt. For now, I will groom him myself." He picks up a grooming box and a short whip and moves to Toreador's stall. Jennifer watches from the aisle as he slides the door open and softly says "Whoa boy," to the big chestnut.

Toreador looks up from eating his hay, makes eye contact with Eduardo, and lays his ears back. His hay manger is in the corner at the rear of his stall, so he is facing away from Eduardo.

"Don't forget that he kicks," Jennifer cautions.

Eduardo nods and clucks his tongue to get Toreador's attention but the horse stubbornly refuses to turn towards the door. Eduardo gently touches Toreador's butt with the end of the whip to get him to move while clucking. Instead of moving his butt away from the whip, Toreador leans into it and shakes his head in a clear sign of aggression. Eduardo stays clear of the horse's kick zone and increases the pressure on the whip until Toreador finally turns towards him.

Jennifer holds her breath while Eduardo cautiously enters the stall and continues to talk to the horse while slipping a halter over his nose. After getting the horse in the cross ties without incident, Jennifer breathes a small sigh of relief. "One small step for man," she jokes.

"Jose' told me none of the grooms at Stuart Stables were able to make friends with him, but I hope I'll have better luck." As Eduardo grooms the big chestnut horse, he gently talks to him and pats and pets him.

Once the horse is tacked up, Jennifer slides the stall door fully open while Eduardo releases Toreador from the cross ties, maintaining a strong grip on the rein next to the bit. He clucks to the horse and takes a small step toward the stall door.

Toreador leans back and raises his head to resist, but Eduardo maintains his hold and continues to coax the horse forward. Toreador suddenly lunges toward the stall door and explodes into the barn aisle, banging his body against the stall door opening and scraping the side of Jennifer's saddle. His steel shoes cause him to slip on the cement floor and ring loudly as he drags Eduardo several steps down the barn aisle. Jennifer and Eduardo both yell "Whoa!" several times and Eduardo finally manages to stop the horse. Eduardo pauses to catch his breath, and then coaxes Toreador down the aisle toward the indoor riding ring.

She motions at the small round pen surrounded by strong steel panels that occupies the center of the indoor ring and says "Let's start out in there. It will make him easier to control if he decides to buck and run."

Eduardo has summoned a groom to help and they both hold Toreador while Jennifer mounts. Toreador lays his ears back and doesn't move. The groom quietly leaves the round pen and Eduardo continues holding the big horse's bit himself. When Jennifer nods, he moves to Toreador's left side and attempts to lead the horse forward a step. The horse refuses to move. Jennifer and Eduardo both cluck softly and Jennifer applies gentle pressure with her legs, but Toreador still doesn't move. Jennifer reaches back with her left hand and gently touches the crop she is carrying to Toreador's hip and he suddenly lunges forward, dragging Eduardo toward the fence. Jennifer yells at Eduardo to let Toreador go so that he doesn't get trampled or crushed against the side of the ring. She pulls back on both reins to keep his head up and pushes her heels down in her stirrups to make her seat more secure, simultaneously yelling, "Whoa!" to get the big horse to slow. She anchors her seat deep in the saddle and uses her upper body's strength to pull her left hand up and back to force Toreador into a tight circle to the left, but the horse continues to push toward the side of the ring, throwing his right shoulder into it with a loud crash. As soon as he hits the steel panel, Jennifer releases him slightly so that he won't continue pushing his body into the outer fence and making it less likely that he will crush her right leg against the steel panels. Once she equalizes the backward pressure on the reins, he stiffens all four legs and crow hops around the round pen. Jennifer concentrates on using the martingale to keep his head up and rides through the hops knowing that if gets his head down, he will be able to buck hard and will probably launch her into the steel fence. After nearly three full circuits in the round pen, he finally breaks into a fast trot. Jennifer allows him to keep the trot as she works to collect him and to get him to start obeying her commands. After several minutes, he finally slows down and allows her to pull him to a stop. She reverses direction and trots several rounds to the right after which Toreador begins to relax and respond, putting his ears forward and stopping and starting on command. Jennifer continues working him until he will stop and stand quietly whenever she asks.

Cautiously, she rubs his neck and glances at Eduardo, who is still watching her from outside the ring. "Tomorrow, we'll lunge him first to wear him down a little." She tries to sound amused but he is an intimidating animal and she knows that she has barely escaped a serious injury. If he had mashed her knee into the steel panel, she might not have been able to stay on him. She decides to quit while she's ahead and cautiously dismounts.

"Good idea." Eduardo voice is concerned as he quietly enters the round pen and reaches for Toreador's bridle to lead the tired horse back to his stall.

Jennifer leans against the fence to catch her breath. Toreador appears to be a wicked and dangerous horse, and her initial concern that Blair won't be able to handle him escalates. After a few minutes, she walks back up the aisle to Toreador's stall and pauses at the door.

Eduardo has removed his tack and is rubbing the sweaty horse with a towel. He looks over his shoulder at Jennifer and asks, "Is the new owner a good rider?"

"She's okay. The big problem is that she is easily scared. As you know, a horse can always tell when the rider is scared. I think her fear and this horse's craziness will be a dangerous combination." Jennifer shakes her head. "Do you think he'll settle down?" Eduardo has had much broader experience with horses than she has, and she hopes he will be encouraging.

Eduardo hesitates, "Maybe. Lunging is a good idea. He was better once he got a little tired. I will call Jose' again. Now that I have seen him in action, I have more questions to ask him."

"As it is right now, I can't picture even a great amateur riding him. I hope that we can teach him to take it down a notch."

Eduardo shrugs. "The amateur classes are tough and it might take a horse as talented as Toreador to win. Maybe we just need to get a different amateur."

Jennifer laughs softly. "Fat chance. I suspect that we'll only get to keep him in the barn if Blair rides him. The way he was today, I wouldn't even be comfortable putting Missy Phillips on him."

Missy Phillips is an amateur rider who has been successfully showing Saddlebreds since she was five years old. The wealthy and beautiful 35-year-old daughter of the senior US Senator from Virginia, Missy is a skilled rider and has competed successfully in several divisions throughout her career. It is no secret that she wants to own a top five-gaited horse that can win in Louisville.

"Maybe today was the worst of it." Eduardo says it hopefully, but they both know that they have a lot of work ahead of them.

CHAPTER 13

After making sure the horses are comfortably settled in their stalls at the Indiana State Fairgrounds, Bobby has a few spare moments and decides to take the opportunity to get familiar with the layout of the facility. As Bobby walks toward the Coliseum, he sees tonight's class schedule posted on a stall. There are 17 classes tonight and they will start promptly at 6:30. Vendome and Night Train are in the ninth class. At a typical horse show, a class will take about 12-15 minutes, but tonight's show has several championship and sweepstakes classes. These will take quite a lot longer and may average over 20 minutes or more. He makes a mental note to listen carefully to the loud speaker in the barn area when the show is underway so that he can pace the grooms' work and get Vendome and Night Train ready to show at exactly the right time. If he is too early, the horses are likely to get fidgety and spend too much energy worrying about what is happening. If he is too late, he and Johnnie won't have enough time to get their horses properly warmed up. He remembers that Johnnie needs about 12 minutes and Vendome needs slightly less.

He shows the wrist band that identifies him as a trainer to the attendant and is allowed to walk through the dirt-covered entrance and into the Coliseum show ring. It is an impressive sight and he feels butterflies in his stomach as he looks at it. The ring is oval-shaped and is one of the largest rings Bobby has shown in, including the World Championship in Freedom Hall. As he looks around, he admires the sparkling lights, double-decked seating, and an immense overhead LED video screen that is currently showing highlights of past shows. The sound system is booming with the orchestral score of a highlight video, and Bobby tries to put himself in Vendome's place so that he can anticipate how his young and inexperienced horse will react to the huge ring, the crowd, the noise, and the lights. He makes a mental note to keep using cues from his body so that Vendome will stay focused on the job that Bobby needs him to do and not get distracted by all the new sights, smells and sounds of the ring.

Bobby spends some time thinking about his strategy and reminds himself of how the class will be judged. There will be three judges, all of whom will be standing in the center of the ring. All the horses in the class will be in the ring at the same time and will change gaits and directions when the announcer tells them to do so. At the end of the class, each horse will be stripped of its saddle so that the three judges can evaluate each horse's conformation. Each judge will independently assess each horse's performance, presence, quality, manners and conformation and will independently rank the top ten horses. At the end of the class, the horse with the best combination of rankings will win.

Bobby decides that he will begin his warm-up back in a quiet area of the barn so that Vendome will stay calm and relaxed. He will enter the warm-up ring with just enough time to do a short trot and slow gait each direction. When the winner of the previous class is being presented to the crowd, he will ask the grooms to remove Vendome's blinkers and put the final touches on his tail. Then, once the previous class' winner leaves the ring, he'll be ready to enter with a big, energetic trot. He thinks back to Johnnie's advice about making sure that Vendome is noticed by the judges and decides that he'd like to enter the ring very early in the class, maybe even first. Vendome is brave and shouldn't need to follow another horse into the ring in order to go strongly forward. Also, Vendome has plenty of stamina so the extra time or two that he'll go around the ring while all the others are entering won't cause him to tire later in the class. Bobby takes one last deep breath, works to convince himself that the butterflies he feels are caused by excitement rather than nervousness, and walks back to the stalls.

As he approaches, he notices that Mrs. Clancy-Mellon is standing outside of Vendome's stall talking to Johnnie. She is a large woman with short gray hair, bright lipstick and brightly rouged cheeks. She is wearing billowing black pants and a bright pink sequined jacket. He can tell by her body language that she is having a serious conversation with his boss. To avoid interrupting them, Bobby steps into the tack room and once again checks to be sure the bridles, saddles, girths and boots are all clean and ready to go on the horses. As usual, the grooms have everything organized and adjusted, and there is little for him to do. He leaves the tack room and notices that Mrs. M is just saying

50

goodbye to Johnnie and she gives Bobby an encouraging smile. "I hear that you're getting along pretty well with my horse."

"Yes ma'am." Bobby nods and smiles. "It is my privilege to ride Vendome. He's got a real willingness to do this job."

Mrs. M responds, "I'm glad to hear that. Go out and win me some of that purse now, won't you? Don't worry at all about beating your boss."

"Oh no ma'am. I'm not worried about that," he assures her. "I'd like nothing better than to hand you a pretty ribbon and a big check after the class."

She laughs heartily. "That would be the first time a trainer handed ME a check." Turning to go, she tosses one last "Good luck to you both!" over her shoulder.

Bobby and Johnnie stand together and as they hear the National Anthem being played over the loud speaker. Johnnie quietly says, "It's show time. We'd better get our suits on."

Johnnie and Bobby both don their dark formal riding suits complete with ties, vests, and homburgs, and then work with the grooms to put the finishing touches on each horse. The horses are perfectly groomed with shiny coats, flowing tails and manes, polished feet, and neatly clipped ears and noses. Their manes each have a traditional red ribbon braided into it near their ears. Bobby tries to stay busy to quell his nerves and is relieved when the class right before theirs is invited into the ring and it is time for them to mount.

Johnnie and Night Train immediately move off towards the warm-up ring at an animated pace. Bobby walks Vendome to a small, quiet aisle near the rear of the barn. His horse feels alert and a little tense but acts calm and level-headed as Bobby works at a slow relaxed trot, gradually asking Vendome to pick up the pace. Within 10 minutes, he finishes his warm-up and moves towards the Coliseum so that he can get in place to enter the ring early. He is in time to see Johnnie finish warming up Night Train, and he looks like he has his hands full. Night Train's head is high, his eyes are bright and his shiny coat is already dark with sweat. Bobby glances around the other competitors and estimates there are at least 20 horses getting ready to enter the ring. It is likely to be a wild class filled with nervous horses and

51

aggressive riders, and he edges closer to the entrance so that he can enter the ring at the front of the crowd.

In just a moment, he hears the bugle that announces the ring is ready for the new class and the gates swing open. He clucks his tongue and times it perfectly as Vendome hits the entrance at the head of a long line of three-year-olds. When they enter the ring, Vendome hesitates slightly as if to ask Bobby is he is certain that they should be entering this bright and loud place. Bobby urges him forward and Vendome raises his head and begins a fast, animated trot counter-clockwise around the show ring. As they reach the far end, Bobby hears horses behind him and edges Vendome off the rail and towards the center so that the judges will be able to see him easily and to avoid being cut off by another competitor. Vendome hesitates again and Bobby clucks to him to remind him to move on.

By the time Vendome completes a full round of the ring, horses are still entering and Bobby notices Night Train coming in the entrance. Night Train looks like his name. He charges into the ring with his mane and tail streaming and Johnnie quickly moves him towards the inside of the ring. Bobby attempts to follow him on Vendome, but Night Train is easily outpacing every other horse as he charges to the end of the ring. Bobby loses track of Johnnie as he focuses on keeping Vendome square and even and on looking ahead to avoid any traffic jams with his competitors. When he hears the announcer call for a walk, he has already picked out a place on the rail to stop Vendome's trot and to give him a very brief chance to catch his breath so he will be ready to start the slow gait when the announcer directs.

After the class works through all five gaits going counter-clockwise, the announcer tells the riders to "Reverse your horses and trot." Bobby waits for a gap in the traffic to turn Vendome and to give his horse enough room to develop a perfect trot before sweeping past the first judge. As he goes around the end, he is pleased that Vendome has stayed calm and hasn't been too distracted by the enthusiastic crowd or by all the other horses around him.

Near the end of the class, Bobby finds himself slightly behind and to the inside of Night Train. He can tell that Night Train is tiring and realizes that Vendome might be able to pass his bay stablemate on the next straightaway. Since speed is a significant element of the performance score, Bobby knows that if he can maintain Vendome's energy and strong four-beat cadence during this pass, it will evoke huge cheers from the large crowd and is likely to impress the judges. He cuts the corner short so that Vendome is on Night Train's right flank as they begin their pass down the side of the ring. Bobby works his fingers on the reins to remind Vendome to stay in his gait. He clucks and gently squeezes his thighs to drive Vendome forward and sees that they are gaining on Night Train. Half way down the ring, Vendome pulls even with the bay and Bobby hears Johnnie clucking to Night Train but Night Train is clearly exhausted. As Bobby and Vendome push past Johnnie, the crowd roars.

After completing all five gaits the second direction, the announcer tells them to line up. Bobby selects a place at the end of the line and pulls Vendome in. Johnnie pulls Night Train in next to him and both horses are breathing heavily. The announcer directs them to dismount and strip their horses. As the riders dismount, the grooms for all the horses in the class jog into the ring to remove the saddles and towel off the sweat so the riders can present their horse to the judges. The lights in the Coliseum are dimmed, and the announcer calls the first horse forward.

Each rider leads his horse forward at a trot and poses it in front of the judges with its body stretched long and its neck and head high. A spotlight hits the horse as the three-year-old's name, sire, dam and owner are announced. The judges slowly walk around the horse to assess its conformation as the crowd applauds. When the judges stand back, the announcer dismisses the horse to loud applause and the rider leads him back to the lineup where the grooms replace his saddle.

While they are waiting their turn, Johnnie moves over to stand next to Bobby and growls, "Nice move kid."

It takes Bobby several seconds to figure out that Johnnie is referring to Vendome passing Night Train during the rack and that he doesn't mean it as a compliment. Bobby glances at Johnnie's grim face and decides that it is safer to avoid responding, so he reaches up and arranges the ribbon in Vendome's mane.

The announcer calls Bobby's number and he coaxes Vendome forward to the spotlight. As Bobby stops Vendome to pose him, he hears a sharp whistle from the ring side seats and recognizes Mrs. M's voice cheering for her horse. Vendome's sides are still heaving from the exertion of the class, but he stands perfectly still with his ears forward.

When Night Train's turn comes, the young stallion is truly magnificent. He poses perfectly, cranes his neck and snorts loudly at the crowd. His sweaty coat is so dark that he looks black under the spotlight. The crowd clearly loves him as they applaud, whistle, and yell.

Once all the horses have been presented and their saddles have been replaced, the announcer tells the riders to mount and releases them to wait at the end of the ring until the awards are made.

Unlike most horse shows in which the winner is announced first, the sweepstakes announces the top eight places from the bottom up. As the announcer announces the 8th place horse and the rider trots the horse up to collect the ribbon, several of the other riders quietly leave the ring, knowing that their performances weren't good enough to earn a position in the top eight. Bobby waits nervously, knowing he had a good ride but unsure about how he compared to the others in the class. When the announcer names the third place winner, there are only a handful of hopeful horses left in the ring, including Night Train and Vendome.

"The Reserve Champion award goes to Night Train! Owned by Stuart Stables in Kentucky, trained and ridden by Johnnie Stuart."

Bobby hears Johnnie say, "Shit!" as he trots Night Train forward to get the second place ribbon. Bobby looks at the other two horses left in the ring with Vendome and realizes that one of them is just about to be named the winner of the Sweepstakes while the others will have to leave the ring with no award. He holds his breath for what seems an eternity.

"And now, the winner of the Three-Year-Old Five-Gaited Sweepstakes is Vendome Copper! Owned by Mrs. Clancy-Mellon of Chicago, Illinois. Trained by Johnnie Stuart and ridden by Bobby Acton."

Johnnie was changing clothes in the tack room when Bobby returns to the stalls after his victory pass with Vendome. Mrs. M, several of her friends, and a few of the other trainers quickly arrived to congratulate Johnnie and Bobby, and it was only after the horses were cool and dry and loaded in the trailer for the trip back to Kentucky that Johnnie finally spoke to Bobby.

"You had a nice ride but don't let it go to your head. Night Train just used too much energy before he went in the ring. He is twice the horse Vendome is and any decent judge would have recognized it. There is no way that Vendome could have passed him if we'd have had a good warm-up. And that damned trainer out of North Carolina cut me off in the first canter and screwed me up. We had some piss-poor luck."

Bobby decides his best choice is to agree with his boss. "You're absolutely right. I can't believe they gave Vendome the win. The few times I had a chance to see Night Train, he was dominating everyone else." He keeps his eyes straight ahead but can see Johnnie relax in his peripheral vision.

"Don't go getting too attached to that horse, Bobby. With any luck, Mrs. M. will sell him out from under you in a heartbeat. He'll make a nice horse for an amateur, and the 10% commission I'll get from the deal would make my pocket jingle." Johnnie laughs and his mood lightens perceptibly. In that moment, Bobby realizes the best part of his job is working Vendome. And even if Johnnie shared part of any sales commission, it wouldn't make up for the losing Vendome from his string. So Bobby finds himself in the unusual position of hoping that Vendome doesn't attract a buyer that is willing to meet whatever price is set.

CHAPTER 14

Missy Phillips pulls her Mercedes SUV to a stop outside a perfectly manicured paddock and turns to her dad. "We're finally here. Thank you so much for coming with me on this horse hunt."

Her father smiles. "It is exactly the break I needed from all the fighting with my colleagues in the Senate. A nice drive from Virginia to North Carolina to look at great horses with my favorite daughter is the best vacation I can imagine." Jim Phillips looks every bit the senior Senator from the Commonwealth of Virginia. At 65, he still stands over six feet tall with a thick head of gray hair that he combs straight back.

"Your ONLY daughter, too. Well, I hope this mare is as nice as I've heard. I've watched her on video and she might be the one." Missy is looking for a gaited horse that is capable of winning the amateur championship at Louisville. She has consistently been at the top of the amateur ranks in the other divisions for most of her life, but has never had a top horse capable of doing all five gaits.

As she extracts her saddle and closes the rear hatch, an older woman emerges from the door to the barn and walks toward them. "You must be Missy Phillips. Here, let me take that saddle. Welcome to Big View Farm. I'm Annie." She is a small woman with a throaty voice and a quick manner. The words come out in a rush and are accompanied by a warm, friendly smile.

Missy returns the smile and hands her saddle to Annie. "Yes, I'm Missy. It is great to meet you. And this is my father, Senator Phillips."

Missy's dad steps forward and laughs. "Please just call me Jim."

"Well it is great to meet you both. I hope your drive went smoothly and that you didn't have any trouble finding us. Come on in and grab a cup of coffee. I'll introduce you to Josie."

Annie leads them both to a stall near the middle of the barn. The door is open and a pretty mare stands in the cross ties. She is a dark chestnut with a big white blaze on her face, four white feet and a blond mane and tail. "This is Josie. Josephine's Dream, when we're being formal." Annie strokes the mare fondly on the neck as she speaks.

56

"Oh my gosh! She is beautiful!" Missy exclaims. "The videos and photos don't do her justice, do they?"

"I don't think so. But then, I'm biased." Annie laughs again as she starts to saddle the mare. "I think she is just coming into her own. She's only five and it seems like every day she gets more regal. I'm just crazy about this mare. She's been easy to work since the first moment I brought her in out of the field."

Missy steps forward to pet the mare and laughs when the mare leans forward. "She is checking to see if I have a peppermint."

"Yeah. She's a mooch. She loves peppermints. Do you want me to ride her first, or would you rather get on her cold?"

Missy pulls a cellophane-wrapped candy from her pocket and unwraps a bright red and white starlight mint. Josie nickers when she hears the cellophane and leans towards Missy as far as the cross ties allow. "I'm happy to have you warm her up so I can watch her from the ground first."

"Look! You're friends already. I'm amazed at how well bribes work with horses." Missy's dad laughs, stands back and watches the mare chew the candy as Missy pats her neck. They step away from the stall to let Annie finish getting Josie ready and Missy tells her father, "Now, your job is to be critical and take some videos that we can talk about later. And make sure that my checkbook stays in my purse!" They both know she has a tendency to fall in love with every horse she meets and she is depending on her dad to help her see any faults that she might overlook.

"Don't worry. I've seen enough horses in almost 30 years of watching you show that I know what a good one looks like." Jim Phillips has spent thousands of hours in barns and show rings since Missy discovered horses when she was five.

Once Josie is ready, Annie leads her to the indoor ring and mounts her. She stands quietly until Annie clucks softly and then begins an animated walk around the ring. Annie warms her up slowly, and the mare is energetic and bright. Missy smiles as the mare flashes by where she and her dad are standing.

Annie pulls her to a stop and dismounts. "Are you ready?"

"Absolutely!" Missy pulls on a tight pair of gloves and moves forward to mount.

Annie steps back. "She should be pretty tolerant. I know you're an experienced rider so I'll just give you a chance to figure her out."

After a brief walk, Missy works Josie through all the gaits and both directions while her dad records it on his smartphone. Annie stands back and proudly watches her young mare, occasionally making a suggestion to Missy about how to communicate with the horse.

Missy finally pulls the sweating horse to a stop in the middle of the ring and pats her on the neck. "She is lovely!" she exclaims. "What an engine! She just gets better and better as she goes."

"Yes," Annie agrees. "There is no quit in this mare. She has great focus and does everything I ask of her. She is really special."

Annie motions at a groom to take Josie back to her stall. "Let's go sit in my office while the grooms cool her out and wipe the sweat off your saddle."

Once they are sitting in the office Annie says, "I can tell by the smile on your face that you enjoyed your ride."

"Oh yes! She is amazing. I can see why you love her and why her price is so high."

Annie smiles. "There aren't many out there like her. As you know, she won the mare stake at Louisville two weeks ago and we ended up third in the Championship Stake. She's always been sound. She behaves in the stall. She ships well. I can't think of anything I'd like to change."

"Well, I think I'd make her about half a hand bigger." Jim is an experienced negotiator and remembers his daughter's instruction to keep her checkbook in her purse.

Annie nods. "That's true. She isn't going to be the biggest horse in the ring. But her white legs will make a judge look at her, and she's got a bigger engine than anything she'll go up against. And Missy, you're so petite that you fit her perfectly."

Missy says, "When you're on her, you forget that she isn't very big. She goes with a big step."

"I think this mare can take you to the winner's circle at any big show. You won your first World Championship when you were just 10, right?" Annie waits for Missy to nod, and then goes on, "Then you know it takes a special horse to pull that off. I really believe Josie has the most important parts. She's beautiful, she has a big engine, and she loves being a show horse." Annie finally asks the question she is most curious about. "Once you buy a horse, who will be your trainer?"

"I'm honestly not sure." Missy's long-time trainer is in Virginia but has limited experience with five-gaited horses. "I know that the place I'm at now is probably not a good match for a gaited horse. I'm willing to commute, so I'm considering Illinois and Kentucky. I want to make sure that I'm competing with the best."

"Well, if you buy Josie, I'd sure love to keep her here for you. We get stiff competition here in North Carolina and we travel to all the big shows. By the time you got to Louisville, you'd have competed against all the big horses at least once."

"Honestly, I never thought of that. You've given me something to think about." Missy knows that matching the personalities of horses and trainers is critically important and moving a successful horse to a new trainer doesn't always work out.

Missy and her dad spend a few moments back at Josie's stall before saying goodbye to Annie. As they pull away from the barn, Jim turns to his daughter and says, "It's hopeless. I can tell you're already in love."

"Oh Dad. I didn't want to give too much away in front of Annie, but she is unbelievable. I don't think I have ever ridden anything so exhilarating in my entire life. It makes you feel like you are sitting on a rocket when she is slow gaiting, and she is just waiting for you to light the afterburner."

"Yeah. She's quite a sight when she comes down the straight away. Maybe you should have a good vet check her out and make sure there aren't any issues anywhere before you go any further. You're going to be spending a lot of money on whichever horse you choose, so it won't hurt to proceed carefully." Jim knows that Missy makes decisions quickly and he hopes that he can slow her down a little. This horse will cost half a million dollars, and he wants it to be the right one. "Also, you might want to look around a little more. There are always a lot of nice horses for sale."

"Yes, but I also don't want anyone else to buy her while I ride every other horse in the country, either." Missy accelerates onto the highway back towards Virginia with a big smile on her face.

CHAPTER 15

Kenny Rivers is just returning a sweaty horse to its stall when he sees Angela entering the barn. "Hi honey," he greets her and listens to gauge her mood.

"Hey babe. I brought lunch for us." She has a smile in her voice and he immediately relaxes.

"Oh. That sounds great. Your timing is perfect. I just finished with this one." He removes the horse's bridle and quickly begins toweling the animal dry.

"It's a nice day. I'll take it outside to the picnic table. Meet me out there when you're ready."

In a few minutes, Kenny makes his way outside and joins Angela at the table where she is unwrapping sandwiches.

"How many horses are you taking to the show in Shelbyville on Saturday?" she asks.

"Well, right now it looks like four. Juan didn't show up to work today so I could use a hand grooming if you can help me. If he ever comes back, I'll fire him. I already changed the combination on the lock to the tack room." Kenny can only afford to hire the grooms that have already been rejected by all the bigger barns, so they are notoriously unreliable.

"Wow. That didn't take long. I'm not sure I even met Juan. Of course, I'm happy to help. I'll call my mom and see if she wants to spend the day with Jeremy and Emily. Are the classes all packed together? Or do we have more than one horse in the same class?" Angela is an experienced groom and knows that timing is everything at horse shows. "I can run the grooming if you can manage the warmups and the ring."

"They're all in different classes but they're pretty well spaced out. It won't be bad as long as we don't have any drama." Kenny's clients are typically a bit stressed at shows and a single incident can sometimes derail the whole group. "I hope they keep their wits about them and manage to get ribbons so that the show season begins to

61

wind down on a good note. Sometimes it seems like they must lay awake at night thinking of new ways to sabotage their rides."

Angela laughs and then says, "Have you said anything to them about the changes we've decided to make here at the barn?" She busies herself opening a bag of corn chips and doesn't make eye contact.

"No. We can't afford for anyone to leave us. I want to introduce the changes so gradually that there won't be any controversy. Of course, the first time someone comes out for a lesson and has to maneuver around a bunch of little kids in party hats..." His voice trails off as he realizes how he sounds.

"And we were having such a nice lunch, too." Angela abruptly stands up, wrapping the remains of her sandwich.

He apologizes quickly. "You're right. I'm sorry. I'm just still getting used to the idea. Please sit down and let's talk about something else."

But Angela is angry and wants him to know it. "Look. I know you aren't happy with this decision. But we can't continue as we are. We will end up in bankruptcy and lose everything. You act as though we have a choice but we really don't. I am trying to find a way to keep our home. And our barn. The clients we have are nice people but there aren't enough of them and they NEVER pay their bills on time." Now that Angela has started, she can't stop herself. "I love you but I am tired of struggling. I'm tired of telling the kids they can't have something that all their friends have. I'm tired of checking every price of every item at the grocery store and worrying about whether the card will be accepted at check out. I'm tired of not being able to afford health insurance for any of us. If you get hurt or our kids get sick, we could be ruined." By the time she takes a breath, her voice is cracking and there are tears in her eyes.

Kenny softens his voice and acknowledges the truth of what she says. "Yes. You're right. Let's get through this show and then put together a serious business plan for the new concept. I've been an ass. I'll get on board."

They finish their lunch quietly. When Angela stands to go, they are overly polite to each other, and he tells her he'll be home around

5. As he re-enters the barn, he admits to himself that it is time to accept the inevitable.

CHAPTER 16

Late on Monday afternoon, Jennifer and Eduardo are sitting in her office at the barn talking about how all the horses are doing when they finally get around to the topic that worries them both the most, Toreador.

"I'm not ashamed to admit it. He scares me." Jennifer sits behind her desk, with her chair leaning back against the wall.

Eduardo has been watching carefully, expecting to see her over-balance the chair and crash to the floor. "You are smart to be scared. I have been trying to make friends with him all week and have not made any progress. I do not know if he was abused or if he is just crazy. It does not really matter because the result is the same. He is dangerous."

"Well, dangerous or not, Marianne expects that Blair will show him next year. I have no idea how we'll pull that off."

Eduardo sighs. "Maybe Blair will do us a big favor and back out of it after she sees him work. If she is as timid as you say, he should scare her."

"True, but it is a big risk. It might convince Marianne that we aren't capable of handling Toreador and she might move him. I really want this to succeed. If we can get this horse in the ring, it will show everyone in the industry that we are for real. It could really change things for this barn. It could be our gateway to better clients and better horses." Jennifer pauses. "Maybe we should talk to Blair privately and see what she's thinking. Unfortunately, it will be hard to get her away from her mother."

Eduardo nods. "I have been thinking that we could give him a calm-down shot."

Jennifer looks at him sharply. "Really? We should tranquilize Toreador? You mean to train him?"

"Yes. I think that we could get something from the vet that just takes the edge off. If it works, we could work him on it for a couple of months to see if he gets more trainable. I know we cannot show him on drugs, but it might help us get him going. We used to do that once in a while at the barn in Arizona."

64

"That might be a good idea." Jennifer returns all four legs of her chair to the floor and turns towards the laptop computer on her desk. With a few keystrokes, she unearths a thesis from Auburn University that discusses whether a horse can learn under the effects of mild doses of Acepromazine, a commonly used tranquilizer. Quickly skimming the research report, she reads the conclusion out loud to Eduardo, ending with a summary. "It says here that if used effectively, Acepromazine doesn't impair learning and does help make a horse more tractable." After clicking and scrolling, a smile creeps across her face. "As usual, you are brilliant. Good idea Eduardo! I'll call the vet and talk to him about it." Newly energized, she picks up her cell phone and auto-dials her veterinarian.

CHAPTER 17

Johnnie is opening the small refrigerator in his office to get a soft drink when the telephone on his desk rings. He quickly glances at the caller ID, but the display shows 'Not Available.' He hesitates but answers it anyway. "Stuart Stables, Johnnie here."

"Hi Johnnie. This is Missy Phillips. You may not remember but we met a couple of years ago at the Rock Creek Show." The voice is friendly and happy.

"Of course I remember you! I never forget a pretty woman. How can I help ya'll, Miss Phillips?" The smile in his voice is genuine. Every Saddlebred horse trainer in the country knows who Missy Phillips is and it is no secret that she has been shopping for a five-gaited horse, so there can be only one reason that she is calling.

"Please just call me Missy. I'm calling because I'm looking for a gaited horse and I know that you have some great talent in your barn. Any chance you have anything for sale that could be ready for someone like me to show next season?" Despite her question, Missy knows that nearly every horse in every training barn is for sale. It is only a matter of price.

"Well, I've got some stuff that might interest ya'll. Why don't you tell me more about what you're looking for?" Johnnie is an experienced sales person and he knows that if she describes her ideal horse, it will give him a chance to recast his candidates into terms that will appeal to her.

"Well, I'll cut to the chase. How about Toreador?"

Johnnie is stunned. He had assumed that Jennifer Hornig would have told the entire industry that Toreador had moved to Beech Tree. "I'm sorry ma'am. His amateur owner has already started her transition of him and he might be the one horse in all of Kentucky that ain't for sale."

"Oh. I didn't realize that Blair was going to ride him. I thought my challenge would be to pry him away from the Open Stake Class." Missy's disappointment and surprise comes through in her voice. "How is that going?"

Johnnie realizes that Missy assumes that Toreador is still in his barn and takes the opportunity to spin the story. "Well, let's just say that she is going to have her hands full. I don't mind telling you that I was afraid for that girl's safety. My conscience got the better of my wallet, and that was something her mother didn't want to hear. So they've moved him to a different barn." He plows on before Missy can ask too many more questions about Toreador. "I've got another young gaited horse that you should come ride. He just had a great show at the Three-Year-Old Sweepstakes in Indy last Saturday night."

"Three is a little young for me. I really wanted something that I could show this next year." Missy can't hide the disappointment in her voice. "I was really looking forward to trying Toreador."

Johnnie leans forward in his chair. This might be exactly the opportunity he needs to move Vendome into the Amateur Class, decreasing Night Train's competition. "Well, this three-year-old is special. He's level-headed, big and elegant. You need to come give him a try. Trust me when I say that ya'll are going to love this horse. And he'd be good for you for another six or seven years, minimum." Johnnie intentionally doesn't use Vendome's name as he doesn't need Mrs. M to hear through the grapevine that her horse is for sale before he can discuss it with her.

"Well, that sounds interesting. I'm actually going to be in your neighborhood next week. Is Monday too soon?" Missy hadn't planned to drive to Kentucky tomorrow, but she has promised her dad that she will ride as many prospects as she can before settling on Josie and she is anxious to move forward.

"Monday's perfect. While you're here I'll see if I can dig up another couple of horses to give you a spin on, too. Give me a time and we'll be ready for ya'll."

Johnnie hangs up and grins, but it fades when he realizes that he only has a couple of days to talk to Mrs. M about selling Vendome. As he thinks through how he wants to approach her, he realizes that he doesn't need to borrow trouble. If Missy rides Vendome and doesn't want to buy him, then there will be no need to discuss anything with Mrs. M and he can avoid the conversation completely. It is only if Missy likes him that he'll need to determine whether Mrs. M will part with him. He knows that he'll be safe if he sets an absurdly high price as every buyer will attempt to negotiate and he can always say his owner has changed her mind if he can't get Mrs. M to be reasonable.

"She just has too damned much money." He says it to himself, acknowledging that wealthy clients are a blessing and a curse. Trainers make a large portion of their money on the commissions they receive when they sell horses, but wealthy owners aren't always motivated by money and don't always go along with a trainer's recommendation to sell, even when the price is fair.

Johnnie pulls out his work assignment grid and looks at the horses he wants to show Missy, carefully planning the order in which she rides horses so that she will fall in love with Vendome. He pauses when he reads Night Train's name. He decides that he will not show her Night Train, justifying it to himself with the expectation that Night Train's value will increase with additional training and it makes sense to maximize his own profit since the entire amount will go in his own pocket. He admits to himself though, that he wants to keep the horse that he believes will enable him to repeat his Stakes win in Louisville and make everyone forget that Toreador existed.

CHAPTER 18

The weather is perfect as the National Anthem is played to open the Kentucky State Pleasure Championship Show in Shelbyville on Saturday. Kenny has four horses showing and he divides his time between making sure they are all perfectly groomed, reminding his clients of the adjustments they need to make in the ring, and greeting the parents, relatives and friends that are buzzing around the stalls in the show barn. His clients are nervous and excited, helping each other put their hair back in perfect buns, admiring each other's riding suits, and chattering about their horses, the classes they are showing in and the competition.

Angela is an experienced groom and she and Kenny efficiently divide the tasks and the riders so they can keep everything organized. Their first rider is a twelve-year-old girl that has a nice ride in her class, getting and keeping the walk, trot and canter both directions despite the large number of horses in the ring. Although her horse is not particularly talented, he is solid and safe and she loves him dearly. Her parents don't ride themselves and they don't really understand what she is doing poorly or well in the ring, but they cheer loudly when she is announced as third place out of 16. This puts the entire barn in a good mood and the rest of the day goes well, with all of Kenny's riders getting good ribbons and being happy about how they've done. At the end of the day, each of his clients has fed her horse most of a bag of starlight peppermints and has left the show grounds smiling.

Before loading the horses in the trailer for the trip back to the barn, he and Angela help themselves to the cookies that one of their clients has brought and take a moment to relax. "That went well. I couldn't have done it without you." Things have been tense since their conversation on Monday, and Kenny makes a point of thanking his wife for all of her help.

Angela agrees, "It did go well. On days like today, I can see why you find this so rewarding."

"Well, as you know, it doesn't always go like this. We often have tears." They both know that their clients are often disappointed with the outcomes in the ring. He continues, "Why don't you head home? I can finish up here and bring the horses. You can stop by your Mom's and get the kids and maybe we can watch a movie tonight or something."

"I thought you'd never offer! Are you sure you've got it from here?" Angela is already moving to the tack room to find her purse and keys.

"Of course. I'll be home in about an hour and a half."

As Kenny is loading his last horse in the trailer to go home, he sees Clark Benton coming towards him. He is surprised to see the well-known horse trainer at this show. He is easily recognizable by his tall, thin frame, his completely bald head, and his obviously bowed legs. Clark is the head trainer for one of the biggest breeders in the industry, Mr. Kiplenan, and he doesn't typically come to pleasure horse shows because he focuses on young horses and doesn't have any seasoned show horses or amateur clients.

"Hello Clark. I'm surprised to see you here. Are you slumming it today?" Kenny laughs and extends his hand for a hearty shake.

"Naw. I was just wondering who might be around today. I'm going to need some more help breaking some youngsters this winter and I was seeing if I could hunt someone up. I've got a big crop of yearlings and two-year-olds that I need to get started."

Kenny doesn't hesitate. "Really? I'm your man. I would really appreciate the opportunity to work with some of Mr. Kiplenan's young stock and put some of my education to use. And I think that I could also learn a lot from you." Kenny figures that a little flattery can't hurt and this job would be a perfect opportunity for him.

Clark hesitates slightly, but then nods. "Well, why don't you come out to the barn on Monday morning and we'll see how it goes for a week? If it looks like a fit, I can pay you $800 per week but I'll need you six days and it'll take a solid 8 hours each day."

Kenny grins happily. "Perfect. I'll see you bright and early on Monday. Thank you so much for the opportunity."

When they are sitting in their living room later that evening, Angela doesn't even raise her eyes from the magazine she is leafing through when she surprises him with, "You've been acting weird since you got home. Maybe you'd feel better if you just spit it out."

70

Kenny stares at her in astonishment, clears his throat nervously and decides to dive in. "Well, I wasn't going to say anything until it was a sure thing because it seems a little too good to be true." He has rehearsed the story in his mind several times, working through strategies that will avoid negative reactions from his wife, but all his plans desert him as she stares at him intently. "Just after you left the fairgrounds, Clark Benton stopped by. He offered me a trial job working at Kiplenan's." He watches her eyes narrow and her lips thin as though she is physically holding the words inside her closed mouth. Kenny rushes on, "Honey, it's perfect. It will give us the extra money we need, I'll still have enough time to keep the clients we have, and it is an amazing opportunity. Clark is getting old and Mr. Kiplenan will eventually want a new trainer. I could be in line for the best training job in Kentucky." As he talks he can't keep the smile from creeping onto his face. He finally pauses and studies her, trying to get a read on her coming reaction.

"So I don't even get to vote?" She says it quietly.

"Of course you get to vote. But it is only a week-long trial. He might not even offer me a long term job, so there might not even be a decision to make."

"All he has is young horses. That is the best way in the world to get hurt. You know that. He can't offer enough money to make that a risk worth taking."

"He's offering enough for us to afford health insurance. I could get a policy in place right away. And I'll be back here by early afternoon every day so I can still keep our place running. It will provide money for us to get through the winter. In the spring we can still transition our barn like you want. There won't be any business for kid's lessons and parties in the winter anyway." Kenny hears the pleading tone in his voice and stops talking.

She keeps her voice low but is clearly angry. "When do you start?"

"Monday." He can't think of any way to avoid admitting he already agreed to the job.

"Ah. So you already accepted it. I thought we were making decisions together." Angela looks like she wants to say more, but instead she gets up from the couch and leaves the room.

71

He hears their bedroom door close loudly a few seconds later and realizes he will be sleeping on the couch. He knows her well enough to know that she will get over her anger eventually and he realizes that he should have handled it differently. He also admits to himself that she is right about the risk of getting hurt. He moves to the old computer that is stashed on an old desk in a corner of the family room and begins searching for the least expensive health insurance policy he can find.

CHAPTER 19

On Monday morning when Bobby arrives at the barn, he glances at the training ring to make sure Johnnie is busy working horses and then stops by Johnnie's office to review today's grid. He has avoided his boss as much as possible since Vendome's triumph over Night Train in Indianapolis. He senses that Johnnie is still angry that he and Vendome passed him on the last racking pass, so Bobby has been careful to keep his head down and stay out of Johnnie's way.

Bobby likes to work Vendome as his first horse every day so that he can start the day off well. He consults the schedule, expecting to see that Vendome is to be long-lined, but instead sees 'Show – ride' next to Vendome's name. He squints, thinking that he is misreading Johnnie's poor penmanship, and uses his finger to follow the grid across. It definitely says that Vendome is to be shown and ridden. Bobby's first reaction is that Mrs. M is coming to the barn to see her horses, so he quickly glances at the rest of her horses, but their assignments all look routine. He scans through the rest of the grid and notices that two other horses are also being shown. They are both older gaited horses, currently being shown by amateurs.

Bobby hears hoofs coming up the aisle and turns to see that Johnnie has finished working his horse and is leading it towards him. "Good morning boss. I see that you have Vendome scheduled to be shown today. What time do you want him ready?"

"An amateur is coming by to look at gaited horses this morning. I really want to sell her that 7-year-old mare that's in the end stall, but I need more for her to look at so I put Vendome on the list. Vendome is too much for this rider." Johnnie lies easily.

"Oh. That makes sense," Bobby is careful to hide his relief. "Do you want me to ride him or do you want to show him yourself?"

"I'd like you to warm all of them up and then we'll put her on. Let's make Vendome the last one of the three." Johnnie continues leading his horse down the barn aisle.

Bobby looks after him, sensing that something is awry. Typically, if a trainer was showing multiple prospects to a potential customer, he would save the horse he really wants to sell for last. Bobby is

73

surprised that Mrs. M would sell Vendome. After the show in Indy, she was talking about winning the Junior gaited stake in Louisville next year and how long she's been waiting for a horse as good as Vendome.

A short while later, Bobby sees a black SUV approaching the barn and quickly steps into Johnnie's office to start a new pot of coffee for the visitor. As the fresh coffee starts to drip into the pot, he hears Johnnie welcoming someone.

"I'm so glad ya'll could come down here and look at my horses today, ma'am." He hears Johnnie's lazy southern drawl.

A woman answers. "I'm happy to be here, and please call me Missy."

Bobby realizes in a flash that the visitor is Missy Phillips. His first reaction is that he can't imagine why she would be interested in the mare that Johnnie has said he intends to sell her. That mare is a nice enough horse, but Missy Phillips can afford to ride the very best. And then he realizes that Johnnie intends to sell Vendome to Missy Phillips. He emerges from the office to offer Missy a cup of coffee and to take her saddle. After confirming with Johnnie the order of horses he wants to show, he hurries to get the first one ready to ride and leaves Johnnie and Missy to talk.

It takes Missy about an hour and a half to try all three horses, and as she dismounts from Vendome, she hands the reins over to Bobby and turns to address Johnnie. "This last one is way better than the others. It's too bad he's only three. Like I said on the phone, I really want something I can show this next year."

"Yeah. He's only three, but ya'll rode him better than my assistant does and he won the Sweepstakes in Indy on him just a week and a half ago. This horse is the real deal. Let's go up to my office and talk about him a bit." Bobby can't hear the rest of his conversation as he leads Vendome back to his stall.

Late in the afternoon, Bobby and Johnnie are in the tack room together and Bobby casually comments, "Missy Phillips seemed to like Vendome."

Johnnie looks up from the bridle he is adjusting. "I don't see as how that is any of your business. And I'm sure that I don't need to remind you that what happens in this barn stays in this barn. Got it?"

74

Bobby is so surprised by this response that he takes a step backward. "Yes sir. Absolutely." He quickly leaves the tack room knowing that Johnnie's reaction confirms that Mrs. M hasn't been told that her horse was going to be shown to a buyer.

CHAPTER 20

10 AM September 18, Morning Star Barns

It is a beautiful Wednesday morning in California, and Eileen turns into the driveway of Morning Star. It has been two weeks since Spy Master's colic, and she still feels anxious as she approaches the barn. He is fully recovered and she is here to watch Holly ride him for the first time since Louisville. As she enters the barn, she notices that Spy Master's stall door is open and he is in cross ties with a saddle on. Holly is in the stall, adjusting the girth.

"I hope you didn't have to wait on me." Eileen pets Spy Master's nose as she talks to Holly.

"Not at all. I have to admit that I've been looking forward to this. It seems like forever since that last magical ride we had in Louisville and I can't wait to ride him. I'm getting as bored as he is with ground work."

Eileen laughs softly. "I'm sure that he'll be wonderful."

"Yes, me too. For being only four, he is steady and reliable." Holly finishes adjusting his tack and Eileen steps back into the barn aisle to give Holly room to lead him out of his stall.

In the ring, Holly mounts and moves through her warm-up routine. Spy Master is fresh and lively, and Holly has to repeatedly use her voice, hands and body to keep him from going too fast. Eileen watches from the middle of the ring, looking carefully for any sign of soreness or unhappiness in her chestnut stallion.

When Holly finally pulls him to a stop, she has a wide smile on her face. "Does he look as good as he feels?" As an experienced trainer, Holly knows that the answer is yes.

"Wow. He looks amazing. He looks great." Eileen knows she is gushing, but she still is in awe of Spy Master's athleticism. "I think he's back to as good as he was in Kentucky."

"Yeah, me too. He feels every bit as good as he did then." Holly decides there is no better time to ask the question she's been wanting to ask. "So what do you say? Do you want to take a run at the Royal?"

Holly is talking about the big horse show in Kansas City in November that is held in Kemper Arena during the American Royal Stock Show. The Saddlebreds compete for more than $200,000 in prize money, and it is known as the third show in the Saddlebred 'Triple Crown,' along with the Louisville World Championships and the Lexington Junior League Show that is held in July.

"How would we get Spy Master there and back?" The colic incident is fresh in Eileen's mind and she wonders what ideas Holly might have.

"I've been thinking about that. Let me put him away and then we can talk in my office."

In a few minutes Holly meets Eileen in the small office where every wall has several framed pictures of Saddlebreds. When Holly enters, Eileen turns from the admiring one of the pictures and says, "Where will you put the picture of Spy Master's victory pass from Louisville?"

Holly laughs. "Front and center of course! I want that picture to be the first thing everyone sees when they walk in here. I can't wait for the photographs we ordered to get here."

Eileen and Holly both help themselves to fresh coffee and settle themselves into comfortable chairs. Holly begins, "It won't surprise you to know I've been thinking about this a lot. Kansas City is about 1,600 miles. That makes it roughly a 24-hour drive. So we have three choices. First, I could drive him there myself. We'd stop the first night in Albuquerque. I have a cousin that lives there and she has a small property with a barn. I'm sure he'd be safe there and it would give him a rest."

Eileen nods. "Yes. That could work. I'd feel better knowing that you had your eye on him at all times."

Holly goes on. "I think you know that I have a camera in the trailer and I'll take his groom with me so we can be watching him the whole time."

Eileen says "What are the other options?"

"Well, we could hire a commercial transport van to get him there. They would drive straight through but he'd be in a box stall the whole time and his groom would ride with him."

"Like the one he was in when he came back from Louisville?"

Holly can tell that Eileen doesn't like this scenario, so she moves on. "Yes. Like that. The third option is flying him both ways. As you know, that will be very expensive since it is an unusual route for

77

equine air transport. It will be much more expensive than the San Diego to Kentucky route."

Eileen leans back slightly in her chair. "Yes. I'd say that about sums it up. Do you have any other horses going?" While Eileen isn't too concerned about having to bear the entire burden of the travel costs for the horse, groom and trainer, she has several other reasons for this question. The trip will take Holly away from the training barn for nearly two weeks. If Spy Master doesn't go with her, he will lose two weeks of training while she is gone.

"Well, I'd really like to take that young harness gelding we have. He'll definitely go by ground. I'll need the buggy too, so my preference would be to take him and all our equipment myself. If you decide you want Spy Master to go but you'd like to use some other way to get him there, I'll figure out how to be sure that someone is in Kansas City in time to receive him."

Eileen sighs heavily. "Well, then, it looks like the question really boils down to whether we go. I think that it's clear that the best way to do it is by having him go in the trailer you pull."

"I think so too. Honestly, I'd feel much better having my eyes on him the whole way there and back."

Eileen swirls the coffee in her cup. "What do you think about the weather?"

"It's a southern route. Basically, from here to Phoenix to Albuquerque the first day. Then on to Wichita and Kansas City the second day. We could get some early winter weather as we get near Kansas City I suppose, but it would be pretty unusual."

Eileen hesitates before answering, "Well, let's do it."

Holly has been hoping this would be Eileen's decision and flashes a big smile. "Great! I'll get going on our training schedule to make sure he is ready for a great performance there. I'm sure he will ship well. We'll take all his food and bedding from here so that everything is familiar and I'll watch him like a hawk."

"I know you will. He couldn't possibly be in better hands." Eileen stands and goes to the sink to rinse her coffee cup. "I also think we'd better find out now whether we have a chronic problem with shipping him by ground. If we do, then we're in big trouble as far as his show career is concerned."

"I know what you mean, but my Grandmother's favorite saying was 'never trouble trouble until trouble troubles you' so I've been trying to keep that in mind. I'm really happy you want to go to the Royal. I think Spy Master will blow their doors off like he did in Louisville. I believe your horse is going to be one of the most famous five-gaited horses ever."

Eileen laughs. "I hope you're right. And when he becomes a breeding stallion, I hope his foals are as good as he is." She pauses at the door and looks back at Holly. "I really hope I'm not letting my desire to show all those Kentucky and Midwest horses that we have some nice ones out here get in the way of what's right for Spy Master."

"I think you already showed them that in Louisville." Holly stands and follows Eileen out the door. "I need to get back to working horses."

CHAPTER 21

The phone rings at Stuart Stables just as work is winding down for the day. Johnnie is standing near the phone and picks it up on the first ring.

"Stuart Stables, Johnnie here."

"Hello Johnnie. Just calling to check on my herd." It is Mrs. M and although Johnnie has spent time over the last few days trying to decide whether to say anything to her about Missy Phillips riding Vendome, he needs a few minutes to organize his thoughts.

"I was just going to call ya'll," he lies. "I'm standing in the barn aisle. Let me go down to my office and talk to ya'll from there." He uses the time it takes to place the call on hold and walk to his office to collect his thoughts and decides to mention Missy's visit but to downplay it.

He picks up the phone in his office. "That's better. I've got the crew hosing down the aisle and was having trouble hearing you. All your horses are doing really great. That new two-year-old filly ya'll just sent down is a real rock star." He begins describing how each of her horses is doing in their training, leaving Vendome for last.

Mrs. M asks a few questions about each horse as he talks. As the conversation winds down she casually says, "So, tell me about Vendome. He sure had a nice show in Indy. Have you been resting him?"

Johnnie senses a trap and matches her casual tone. "Missy Phillips called me and begged me to let her see him so I worked him when she was here earlier in the week. He looked good but we've been letting him take it pretty easy." A split second later, he is happy he has mentioned Missy's visit.

"Well. I heard that she was out at your barn last Monday and rode him. Evidently she thinks he is for sale."

Johnnie feels the blood rush to his face and begins with "I don't know where she got that idea." But Mrs. M quickly cuts him off.

"Now Johnnie, don't lie to me. She got that idea because you gave her that idea. I've been waiting since Monday night for you to call

80

and tell me about this, and here it is Saturday. I'm tremendously disappointed that I had to call you."

"I'm not sure what you heard but it wasn't what you think." He tries to regain control of the conversation, but she interrupts him again.

"Johnnie. Let me be perfectly clear. Vendome is not for sale. I don't appreciate that word has gotten around that he is. I'm going to give you the benefit of the doubt. I'm going to assume that you know I'm a practical woman and that you know that everyone has a price. And maybe you are trying to make a good commission on him by getting someone to offer more money than I'm willing to turn down. But if I were the suspicious type, I'd think that you showed him to an amateur because you're trying to find a way to move him to a new class to clear the way for Night Train next year."

Johnnie, his heart pounding, hurries to speak when she pauses. "Ma'am. I think you've gotten the wrong idea." He tries again to learn where her information came from, "I don't know what you heard or who you heard it from but..."

Mrs. M interrupts him. "Johnnie. I do not want to talk about this anymore. I may never know the absolute truth of what happened on Monday. You are a good horse trainer and I like the work you do, but this is the second time in recent memory that your story doesn't ring entirely true." Then she abruptly closes the conversation. "I'm done with this conversation. Have a nice weekend."

Johnnie hears her phone click off before he even has a chance to respond and finds himself seated in the chair behind his desk with a silent phone in his hand wondering who told his client about Missy Phillips' visit. He knows that it probably came from Missy herself, perhaps through a conversation with a friend, another trainer, or anyone else in the tightly-knit Saddlebred community that passed the news on until it eventually got to his client. The only other person that could have leaked the information would be Bobby. Johnnie feels his anger build and vows to himself that if he finds out that Bobby said anything after being told to keep his mouth shut, Bobby won't ever find another job training Saddlebreds.

81

CHAPTER 22

As Jennifer stands in the ring quietly talking to Marianne Smithson and her daughter Blair, she watches Eduardo lead Toreador down the aisle towards her. She continues her conversation with Toreador's owners. "He's been a real tough nut to crack. As I've told you on the phone, the Acepromazine makes him less volatile and we've found that he can learn new behaviors more quickly when he is calm."

"He sounds like he has an attention deficit." Marianne is also watching the horse come toward them and goes on. "He looks perfectly calm, and Johnnie Stuart never complained about him." She says it as though she doubts that her horse is as difficult as Jennifer has described in her weekly telephone reports.

"He's making great progress. The transition to being a horse that is a good fit for Blair is a big change for him. We've spent a lot of time getting him to do basic stuff, like stand quietly and wait for me to get on and just be more tolerant about everything."

"Should we be worried that he'll lose the fire that makes him so great?" The question comes from Blair and are the first words she has uttered since their arrival. In fact, she has seemed far more interested in petting Jelly and playing tug-of-war with him than in her new horse.

Jennifer considers how to respond to her and decides to be as open as she can. "I think that when we wean him off the Acepromazine, we might have the opposite problem. He might shift back into the tense and impatient personality that he had." Jennifer specifically avoids labeling Toreador as angry, but it is the best adjective she can think of to describe him.

"Can Blair ride him today?" Marianne asks the question that Jennifer has been dreading, indicating that she still doesn't fully understand the gap between the horse's level and her daughter's capability.

Jennifer and Eduardo exchange a glance and Jennifer smoothly says. "Of course, if she wants to. I thought I'd show him to you first and then Blair can decide if he's ready enough for her to feel

82

comfortable. It's a cool day and he'll be frisky." Jennifer hopes that Blair recognizes the lifeline that she's been thrown.

It has been almost two months since Toreador has been receiving regular doses of Acepromazine and he has shown significant improvement. Jennifer approaches him carefully and slowly, patting him on the neck and checking her saddle's girth to be sure it is tight enough to mount, but not tight enough to cause him to buck. Over the last two months, she and Eduardo have focused on identifying the triggers that cause Toreador to react so dangerously and have implemented routines to get the big horse to trust them.

Satisfied that her tack is secure, Eduardo holds the horse and she mounts. Toreador flicks his ears back towards her but continues standing quietly as she gathers her reins. She clucks quietly and Toreador dances off, showing the energy that he brings to every training session. Jennifer allows him to trot, using her voice and body to keep him calm and steady. As she warms him up, she marvels at how exhilarating it is to ride him. She can feel his speed and power build as she continues around the ring. She and Eduardo have been working him in long sessions for two solid weeks so that he would come into today's session tired, but she can tell right away that they haven't blunted his energy at all.

Once she feels him start to even out his trot, she halts him and then gives him the signal to slow gait. He squats on his hind quarters, bringing both front legs off the ground and snorts loudly before lunging into the new gait. After three rounds of the ring, Jennifer changes direction. Toreador's speed continues to build and he flashes around the ring getting more agitated with each pass.

Jennifer focuses on keeping him steady and square. After three rounds going the second direction, she pulls him to a stop. He immediately starts to shake his head and dance sidewise. She softly repeats "whoa, whoa" until he is standing still and Eduardo smoothly moves forward to hold his bridle while she dismounts.

Jennifer peeks at Blair from the corner of her eye. The young woman has edged away from the horse and looks as though mounting him is the furthest thing from her mind. Jennifer's attention shifts to Blair's mother, who is smiling broadly.

"He is grand," Marianne exclaims and quickly starts to move toward the horse. Even though Eduardo is holding him, Toreador snorts and flinches away from her.

Jennifer tries to deflect Marianne's attention. "Yes. He is truly talented. He just gets in his own way. He's made great progress. As you can see, he stands to be mounted and he takes the gaits I want. But as his blood starts to boil he still is a big handful." Glancing at Blair she says, "I think I'd feel better if we gave him another 60 days before Blair gives him a spin. I have a lot more lessons to teach him before he's ready for a new rider." Jennifer hopes that another 60 days will allow her to deliver on her implicit promise to have him ready.

Marianne looks disappointed and replies, "I think you're underestimating Blair. She is a beautiful rider and the first show is in April. She'll need plenty of time to get used to him."

Blair interrupts quickly, "Now Mom, I'm not in a big hurry. Jennifer will give me plenty of time to be ready for next season. We don't want to get in the middle of her training plan. I'd rather keep working with one of the older horses until this one's ready for me."

Jennifer hopes that Marianne won't insist on Blair mounting Toreador today. She and Eduardo have already decided that they'd have to refuse in order to keep the girl safe. Fortunately, Marianne relents. "I guess you're right but we don't want to wait too long. I can't wait to see your first victory pass."

Jennifer quickly motions to Eduardo to return Toreador to his stall before Marianne can change her mind and he carefully leads the horse out of the ring.

"When will you wean him off the drugs?" Marianne asks.

"We need to do that pretty soon to find out whether he'll retain all the new stuff he has learned in the last 60 days. As I mentioned, we're asking a lot of him. As a stake horse, he was encouraged to run a little wild. The amateur classes require good behavior. That's not something that Johnnie Stuart cared about. I'll talk to the vet, but we might want to wean him in a month or so to see what he's like." Jennifer, Marianne and Blair are all walking back towards Toreador's stall. Their progress is slow as Blair stops at almost every stall to talk to each horse and feed them peppermints. Jennifer notices that she does not attempt to approach Toreador when they pass his stall.

Later, after Marianne and Blair have left, Eduardo and Jennifer compare notes.

"We were lucky" Eduardo begins.

"Yes. For a minute I thought I was going to have to fake a heart attack to keep Marianne from insisting that Blair ride him." Jennifer smiles weakly.

"I would not have been faking my heart attack." Eduardo laughs and Jennifer joins him. She realizes how lucky she is to have Eduardo as an assistant. Each small increment in Toreador's progress has been hard fought with her and Eduardo working together to find innovative ways to teach the horse to relax. They've even gone so far as to name their most recent approach 'Operation Peppermint'. They hope that by teaching him to like the candy, he'll begin looking forward to human contact and let down his guard a bit.

"Were you serious about stopping the drugs?" Eduardo returns to the topic that worries him.

"Yeah. I want to talk to the vet, but it is better that we find out sooner rather than later whether he reverts. If he does, I'll have to level with Marianne. I'm truly afraid that he would hurt Blair the first time she made a mistake and bumped him in the mouth by not having steady enough hands when she rides. At least he's physically healthy, even if he is mentally screwed up. The worst thing that can happen is that she sells him as a stake horse and we lose face. That's a lot better than seeing someone get hurt."

CHAPTER 23

Sunday afternoon in Kansas City is clear, cool and windy. Banners announcing the UPHA (United Professional Horseman's Association) National Championship snap in the wind, and Holly carefully maneuvers her truck and trailer through the entrance to the show grounds. She stops briefly at the registration booth to find out where her stalls are located and to present the health certificates for her two horses. As she parks her truck near the stalls, she glances at the camera in the cab that shows a clear view of the horses in the trailer. Spy Master and the harness horse both appear alert and calm. They spent the previous night in Albuquerque, but she doubts either horse rested. They were agitated and anxious when she loaded them in the trailer early this morning for the last half of the journey from California.

"Would you please go bed the stalls before we unload?" She looks over to her groom and he nods, opening the door to get out. "Oh. And be sure to check them for nails or anything sharp, ok?" He nods again and hurries away from the truck.

Holly takes her time with the horses so that their stalls will be ready by the time she gets to them. She unloads Spy Master first, talking to him as she backs him out of the trailer. "Whoa boy. Easy. How's your tummy feel?" She looks at him critically, and is satisfied that he appears healthy, although tense and nervous. He has his head high with his ears forward and the muscles in his neck are quivering. He whinnies shrilly, as though wondering if he knows any other horses in the barn. She leaves the harness horse in the trailer and leads Spy Master carefully to his stall.

It takes her about two hours to get her horses settled and fed, to unload the contents of her trailer into her tack room and to hang the Blue and Gold curtains with the Beech Tree logo. She has brought enough food for both horses from California to avoid disrupting Spy Master's diet, knowing that this is the best way to prevent colic. She decides to wait until late at night to hand walk him, knowing that several other horses will be out working and her young Stallion could be difficult to handle in a new environment. Before leaving to park her trailer and then check into her hotel, she studies him carefully. Although he isn't eating, he appears comfortable with no signs to indicate that he might be feeling any abdominal pain. "So far, so good," she says to herself.

As she is returning to her truck and trailer, she walks down the aisle towards the door and notices that Stuart Stables is just moving into the stalls next to hers. Although she doesn't know Johnnie well, she greets him.

"Hi. I see we're neighbors. I'm Holly McNair from Morning Star," she says as she extends her hand to him.

He takes it with a smile. "Well hello neighbor. I'm Johnnie Stuart. I'm happy to have such a good looking young lady next door. Please tell me ya'll don't have a husband stashed somewhere."

Holly laughs. She has heard that he is a flirt with a reputation for leaving a trail of one night stands behind him. "I've never needed any help protecting myself." She smiles and then says, "Who'd you bring?"

"Well, we brought some junk that was standing around the barn looking like they needed to go to a show." He smiles.

"Well, I sure hope you haven't discovered a Junior Gaited Horse since the Louisville show." Holly is using this as a way to remind him that she is Spy Master's trainer and she can see that he has made the connection when he leans back and looks over her shoulder to her stalls.

"Nope. Can't say that I have. I guess I'll leave that class to ya'll. But I've got a couple of fairly decent three-year-olds."

Ah, Holly thinks. Then it is true that Toreador isn't in his barn anymore. She is certain he would be sure to mention the reigning World Champion if he'd brought him along. She was paying close attention to the results of the Sweepstakes in Indianapolis and knows that horses Johnnie is training ended up placing first and second. "I can't wait to see them go," she says truthfully. "I saw the video feed from Indy, and they both looked good and we know that the video never does a horse justice. Congratulations on your big wins."

Johnnie gives her his most genuine smile, "Aw shucks. There were lots of good horses there. Mine just happened to catch the judges' eyes."

87

Oh man, she thinks. Did he really just say 'aw shucks?' She is going to have to remember this moment to laugh at later. She quickly makes her excuses and heads for her truck.

Johnnie watches her depart and thinks that this week might be fun after all. He walks down to Night Train's stall. Bobby is in the stall checking the bay stallion's legs for any signs of heat or injury. "How's he look?"

"He looks fine. No issues. It looks like everyone made the trip in fine shape." Bobby begins re-wrapping Night Train's legs in soft bandages.

"I want you to just hand walk every horse today and make sure they are all sound. The three-year-olds show Wednesday night so we'll ride them tomorrow and give them Tuesday off so they'll be fresh."

"Yes Sir." Bobby nearly asks when Mrs. M will arrive, but stops himself just in time. He wonders if Johnnie has considered the likelihood that Mrs. M. might run into Missy Phillips here and find out that Johnnie is trying to sell her Vendome.

Johnnie walks down toward the ring to see who else is at the show and almost immediately meets Annie Jessup. Annie is leading her gaited mare and carrying a long lunge whip. They know each other from many years of competition so he greets her with a friendly wave. "Hi Annie. I'm glad to see you made the trip."

Annie returns the greeting and stops to talk to him. "Yes, it is a long trip, but I wanted to give this mare a chance to win the Triple Crown in the Five-Gaited Mare Class so I figured we had to come."

"I'm surprised you haven't sold her," Johnnie says honestly. "That mare is a game little sister and seems to think real good." His compliments are genuine as he knows that horses that love to go forward like Josie does are often too hot-headed to handle.

"Thanks Johnnie. I appreciate your compliment. We've had a few lookers but she isn't cheap and it takes the right buyer."

Johnnie laughs knowingly. "Yep. I know what you mean. There ain't that many folks around with deep enough pockets to buy something like her."

"Hey, I heard that the folks that owned Toreador decided they were going to bump him down to the Amateur Class. Can that girl ride well enough to handle him? He's a big, strong, boy."

Johnnie appreciates that Annie has directly asked him about Toreador and sees this as an opportunity to spin the story to his advantage. "Yep. I tried to talk that woman out of it. But you know how crazy some owners are. I told her that I wasn't going to take responsibility for that girl of hers getting hurt. So she got pissed and moved him to a trainer that would go along with her crazy-ass plan. I'm real worried about that girl's safety. That horse sure won't take care of her."

Annie knows the story and the personalities well enough to know that Johnnie's story is probably not completely true, but she agrees with him that Toreador is not a likely mount for an amateur. "I certainly hope they don't regret that move. If that girl gets hurt, you certainly warned them." After a few more words, she moves on and returns Josie to her stall.

CHAPTER 24

Annie is in Josie's stall, where the beautifully groomed mare is standing in cross ties when she hears the announcer over the speakers in the barn area. "Welcome to the Opening Night of the Saddlebred Show of the Kansas City Royal!" She tunes out the remainder of his patter and checks her watch. Patting the mare's neck, she says "Hey pretty girl, we just have 17 classes to wait until your qualifying class. Just get me a nice ribbon tonight and then we'll concentrate on the Saturday night finals. It sure would be nice to win that big $50,000 prize." She smoothes Josie's mane and laughs softly, "You might even get an entire bag of peppermints if that happens."

She decides to go down to the ring to watch a few other classes while she is waiting. As she walks towards the ring she sees Missy Phillips coming towards her.

"I was hoping I'd see you before Josie's class. I wanted to be sure to wish you good luck." The younger woman greets her with a friendly smile.

Annie returns the smile and says, "I'm so glad you made it. You obviously brought your three-gaited horse to show tonight." The riding tuxedo Missy is wearing contributes to the elegant appearance of three-gaited horses, whose manes are trimmed short to show off their long, elegant necks.

"Yes. I'll have a chance to see Josie go before I have to warm-up," Missy replies. "I imagine tonight will be a cake-walk for Josie. You only need to get in the top eight"

"Yes, that's true. But Josie doesn't know how to go any other way than full out. She gives it everything she's got every time she hits the ring. A little local county fair might as well be the World Championship as far as she's concerned."

"Well, I'll be cheering you on." Missy gives Annie a little wave and moves on to greet another group of riders that is coming towards them.

As Annie proceeds to the ring, she sees Holly McNair leaning on the rail of the warm-up ring. They don't know each other well, but she catches Holly's eye and goes over to say hello. "I was wondering if you'd bring your junior gaited horse here. You're an awful long way from home."

Holly smiles at Annie. "Yes. We couldn't resist it. I've also got a harness horse that shows tomorrow. It will give me something to do while we wait for Spy Master's class on Friday."

"Well I'm awfully glad you brought him. I didn't get to see his class in Louisville, but I understand that he won it easily."

Holly rolls her eyes. "Maybe it looked like that, but I assure you that it didn't feel like that riding him. He was on fire, and I had to watch him every step."

Annie smiles and nods. "The young ones are fun, but they sure do keep you on your toes, don't they?" She hears the announcer announcing the Park Pleasure Open, so she turns toward the ring. "I'm going to watch these Park horses."

Holly smiles. "Every time I hear 'Park Horse' I think of something my dad said once when someone asked him what a Park Horse was. He said they were horses that wouldn't rack, weren't pretty enough to be a three-gaited horse, and wouldn't flat walk so couldn't be shown in a pleasure class."

Annie joins her in her laughter. "Your Dad had a point. But they are fun to watch."

After watching a couple of classes, Annie returns to her stall area to finish preparing. Her warm-up on Josie goes smoothly and as she waits for the announcer to call Josie's class to the ring, she looks around the warm-up area to review the competition and finds few surprises. Most of the top eight horses from the Louisville show are here, yet she knows that if she rides Josie well, she should be able to place highly. The real test will come in the Stake on Saturday Night when the mares, stallions and geldings compete head-to-head.

She hears the bugle play and the announcement that the gate is open for the Five-Gaited Mares Class blares over the speaker. She shortens her reins and asks Josie for a trot as she heads through the tunnel into Kemper Arena.

Josie's class passes in a blur with Annie focusing on making sure her horse is always on the inside of the ring so that she will be sure to catch the judge's attention. She goes deep into the end of the oval ring on every trip around, giving herself two or three steps to put Josie in a perfect frame before beginning each pass down the straight-away. Josie responds perfectly, keeping her ears up and her white legs flashing, never being distracted by the horses around her. When the announcer finally calls the class to line up, Annie and Josie are in the perfect position for their final pass. Annie knows this is her final opportunity to impress the judges and she settles deep in her saddle, spreads her hands, clucks to Josie, and applies pressure with her seat and thighs. Josie reacts instantaneously and in three steps she is racking at full speed. As she makes the last turn and passes in front of the judges, Annie feels Josie's four beat cadence as she races down the ring. The crowd is whistling and whooping as Annie and Josie sweep past three other horses, around the corner and then pull to a stop in the line-up. Annie pats Josie on the neck and smiles, knowing she had a great ride and that Josie will certainly place highly.

It is no surprise to anyone in attendance when the announcer calls Annie's number as the winner of the mares' five-gaited qualifier. As he is handing her the blue ribbon, the ringmaster poses with her for a picture and congratulates her. "It looks like you're more than ready for Saturday night," he says.

Annie smiles. "Yep. My mare is ready. Bring on the boys!" She knows that as good as Josie was, she will have her hands full on Saturday Night when she competes with the larger and stronger Stallions and Geldings.

CHAPTER 25

Holly arrives at her stalls early on Wednesday morning. She is worried about Spy Master. He hasn't seemed himself since arriving in Kansas City. When she left the barn area late last night, he still hadn't eaten much of his grain or hay. She had used a stethoscope to listen to his belly and she could hear gut sounds, so she was certain he wasn't colicking but he had seemed a little off. She had lain awake most of the night worrying about him.

She walks quickly up the barn aisle and goes directly to his stall. She can see that he still hasn't eaten his hay from last night, but he comes over to the stall door to greet her. She opens the stall and talks to him as she pets him. "Hey big guy. What's up with you? Do you feel ok?" As her hands rub his neck, she looks carefully around his bedding for fresh manure and is dismayed to see a very small amount. She knows that a vet is on call as part of the horse show staff and she quickly heads to the horse show office to see if he is there.

When Holly arrives at the office she is relieved to see that the veterinarian's truck is parked outside. As with many vets, it is easily recognized by the white aluminum insert in the bed of the extended cab pickup. These sophisticated inserts contain equipment, refrigerated sections for drugs, and many of them come with hot and cold water capabilities. The light is on in the registration office and she can see a small group of people gathered around a large coffee urn and a pink doughnut box.

Holly pushes the door open and the group inside pauses their conversation to look at her. "Good morning," she starts.

There are four people inside, and they all greet her at once. "Morning. You're up early. Looks like you need some coffee." The man closest to her starts to fill a fresh Styrofoam cup for her.

"Actually, I'm looking for the vet." She moves forward to take the coffee from him.

"Well, guess you found me. I'm Dr. James. How can I help?" A tall man wearing a Kansas City Royals baseball cap steps forward. He speaks in a relaxed tone and she hesitates before launching into her story.

93

"I have a four-year-old gaited stallion that just isn't quite himself. He seemed to trailer here from California okay, but he's not eating like he usually does. His manure output is decreased, and I'd really like you to take a look at him, if you would." As she talks about Spy Master's symptoms, she realizes that they sound typical for a young horse that is away from home and she feels a little embarrassed as she notices the other people in the office glance at each other.

Dr. James sets his coffee cup down immediately and moves toward the door. He opens the door for her and smiles. "Let's go over and look at him. Better safe than sorry."

As they walk back to Spy Master's stall, Holly tells him more. "It might not sound like much, but he had a bout of colic a couple of months ago after trailering home from the Louisville show. He's got some gut sounds this morning, but I just don't think he's right."

The vet looks over at her and quickens his pace. "If he's had a history of colic, you're right to err on the side of caution. Let's see what's up."

When they arrive at the stall, Spy Master looks much as he did when she left him. Holly puts his halter on him and connects it to the cross ties so that Dr. James can examine him.

The vet begins by looking at his eyes and gums, talking to the horse in a calm, reassuring tone. Then, he uses his stethoscope to listen to his stomach and takes his pulse and temperature. When he is finished, he kicks through the bedding of the stall.

Holly anticipates his question. "No, I haven't cleaned his stall since yesterday around 7PM."

Dr. James stands back but keeps his eye on Spy Master. "I can see why you're concerned. He's not really off but he's definitely showing some signs of distress. He's lethargic and his pulse is a little higher than I'd like. He's at about 50 beats per minute, which is borderline high. As you said, we can still hear some gassy sounds in his intestines but his left side is tympanic." Dr. James is describing the hollow drum-like sound he heard when he tapped on the left side of Spy Master's stomach. He goes on, "His manure is dry, which is cause for concern. Tell me about the last time he colicked."

"It started about four hours after he got off a trailer ride from Louisville to San Diego. We oiled him and my vet gave him a mild

94

tranquilizer and he essentially walked it off. My vet labeled it idiopathic."

Dr. James smiled. "In other words, he had no idea what caused it. You're from California, so I imagine he checked for sand."

Holly knows that horses that live in sandy areas can sometimes ingest the sand and have trouble passing it. "Yes. He did check for sand and didn't find anything. We're very careful to make sure their feed is clean. I trailered him here myself so that I could watch him and he seemed to tolerate the trip fine, but he starting getting a little dull yesterday afternoon."

"We can watch him, but I think I'd recommend that we do an ultrasound right away. I've got a portable machine in my truck, so we can do it right here at the stall. He's obviously a nice animal and I'd like to be sure he doesn't have a twist somewhere in his intestines."

Holly makes a quick decision. "Let's do it. His owner is in California and it's just after 3AM there so I don't want to call her and panic her, but I know she's good for it."

Dr. James nods at her. "Okay then. I'll go get the equipment and we'll see what's up with this beautiful horse of yours."

While the vet goes back to the office to retrieve his equipment, Holly begins to pace in front of Spy Master's stall.

By the time Dr. James returns to her stall area, Spy Master has broken a light sweat and is shifting his weight back and forth. The vet checks his pulse again, makes a note in the notebook he has opened, and turns to Holly. "I'm going to sedate him and have you start walking him while I get set up. I think we might be on the front end of an episode."

While Holly slowly walks Spy Master up and down the barn aisle, the veterinarian opens a machine that looks like a small laptop connected to a hand-held scanner. When he is ready, Holly puts the horse back into his stall.

As Dr. James moves the scanner over Spy Master's belly and towards his flank, he carefully watches the display and describes what he is seeing to Holly, eventually saying "I can see that his colon is lateral to his spleen. And I can see his left kidney. This might indicate left dorsal displacement of his large colon and would cause chronic bouts of colic."

95

Holly leans against the stall wall, unsure whether she is relieved to have a possible diagnosis, or whether she is even more worried. "Okay. Do you have to do surgery to fix it?"

Dr. James steps back from Spy Master and says quietly. "Possibly. But there are some things we can try first. I've had some success with rolling a horse. It doesn't always work, but we should probably try it first. I'd like to do it over at the clinic where we can fix a problem right away if we have one. I'll call my assistant and have him bring the trailer around so we can get your horse over to the clinic right away. You can ride with us if you want."

Holly nods and moves quickly to wrap Spy Master's legs to protect them during the trailer ride. She also hurries to alert her groom and to feed and water her harness horse in the stall next door, unsure how long it will be before she will be able to return.

Once they reach Dr. James' clinic, Holly and his assistant unload Spy Master and lead him into the indoor examination room. Holly hands the halter to the assistant and leaves the room to call Eileen, who answers on the first ring.

"Holly. What happened?" Eileen sounds fully awake despite it being 4AM on the west coast.

"Hi Eileen." As Holly carefully recites the facts, beginning with her feeling that Spy Master just wasn't quite right last night, Eileen listens in silence. Holly finally wraps up with, "So we're at the vet clinic now. They have sedated him and they're going to try the rolling procedure. If it works, then that will be all there is to it. If it doesn't, then he'll probably need surgery."

"I wasn't planning to come out until tomorrow morning but I can get there today."

"Let's wait to see how this goes." Holly replies. "I'll have the vet call you with the details as soon as we know more."

"Okay. I'm going to call the airline to see how quickly I can get there but I won't confirm anything until you call me back. Good luck." Eileen sounds calm but worried.

Holly returns to the examination room to see that the vets have inserted a long hollow tube into Spy Master's nose. Dr. James notices she is watching and says quietly, "Before we go any further, we're just confirming there isn't too much fluid in his stomach. Our next

96

step will be to give him some medicine to temporarily reduce the size of his spleen. If his colon is still trapped, we'll anesthetize him and physically roll him back and forth until we free his colon. With any luck at all, that will do the trick. If it doesn't we'll have to consider surgery." He asks Holly to go to the waiting room and assures her that he'll be out with news as soon as he knows more.

Holly spends nearly an hour fidgeting in a chair in the waiting room and keeping a close eye on the door to the examination area. She is watching the door when it opens, and Dr. James emerges. He has a small smile on his face and she immediately leaps to her feet. "How is he, Doc?"

"He's fine. We did have to roll him and we were able to free the colon, so his belly is now in good shape. He's starting to wake up so you can come back and see him. I'd like to keep him here for a day or two so that we can give him some extra fluids and make sure he's not going to relapse on us, but I don't really expect any problems." Holly feels tears of relief come to her eyes as she thanks the vet and follows him to the examination area where Spy Master is standing, looking sleepy. She dials Eileen and hands her phone to the vet so that Eileen can get the news directly.

CHAPTER 26

Holly is watching the horse show from the rail on Wednesday evening when Johnnie Stuart approaches. "I see that your four-year-old isn't in his stall."

"Hi Johnnie. He tried to colic on me this morning. Scared the crap out of me. He's over at the vet clinic so they can keep an eye on him." Holly says it lightly, downplaying the incident so that she can quell any rumors about Spy Master's health.

Johnnie looks concerned. "It must've been pretty serious for ya'll to send him over there to stay. Are you going to be able to show him?"

"I don't think I will. I haven't scratched him from the class yet, but I'm not sure either of us will be up to it." Holly smiles weakly.

"That's too damn bad," Johnnie says. "I was looking forward to seeing him and I think that the Four-Year-Old Class would have been easy pickins' for him. I think the other Stallions and Geldings that are here are nothing special." Johnnie pauses to see whether Holly agrees.

She does. "Yes. The four-year-old classes don't have any surprises in them. I saw the Open Mare Class and Annie Jessup won that easily. The Stallion Class last night didn't have anything decent in it. I was hoping to see Toreador in the Gelding Class." She provides an opening to hear what Johnnie has to say about Toreador.

He looks away from her as though something in the ring has caught his eye and then he says, "I don't know if we'll see Toreador in the ring again. He's a stake horse, not an amateur horse. I don't care who the horseman is, I don't believe they'll ever get him to dial it down and I believe they'll ruin him trying. And that girl that's got him isn't a good enough horseman to handle him." Johnnie speaks with passion and Holly can tell that he still has raw feelings about losing Toreador.

"Well it's a shame," she looks back to the ring herself and changes the subject. "The gelding qualifier is tonight. Is there going to be anyone worth watching?"

Johnnie is relieved to no longer be talking about Toreador. "There are a couple of geldings here that might give that mare a run for her money in the stake on Saturday night. I've got a couple of three-year-olds that might beat everything in the gelding qualifier, though."

"They show on Saturday afternoon, don't they?" After Johnnie nods, she continues. "I was really looking forward to seeing them in person, but I'll probably take my horses back to California as soon as I show my harness horse. When I expected to show Spy Master on Friday, staying through Saturday wasn't a big deal but there's no point in me sticking around until Saturday night now."

"Are ya'll worried about trailering him home?" Johnnie asks.

"The vet here says I shouldn't worry about it. He had a left dorsal displacement and they fixed it by rolling him. They think that he's going to be fine to travel and we shouldn't see a relapse. But I won't lie. I have a camera in the trailer and I'll be watching him like a hawk all the way back to California and for two solid days after we get home. He's a valuable animal and he means a lot to me." Tears come to her eyes and Johnnie puts his arm around her shoulders and squeezes.

"I'd trust the vets. I'm sure they know what they're doing. If they say ya'll are good to go, I'd get on down the road." He says it kindly, and Holly wonders whether his reputation as a self-centered and ruthless jerk might be undeserved.

She goes on. "His owner is flying in tonight and she'll drive back with me and our groom."

Johnnie smiles. "Well, the next time I see ya'll, I hope it'll be under happier circumstances. After looking over the crop of stake horses out there, I think the good gaited horses are mostly three- and four-year-olds. If my three-year-old keeps coming along like he is, I might just graduate him to the Open Class next year."

Holly's eyes open wide. "Really? Wow. It would be a very big deal for a four-year-old gaited horse to move up to that class. Are you talking about Vendome Copper?"

"No. Vendome is a nice enough horse but I don't think he's got the killer instinct that a stake horse needs. But please don't tell his owner that." Johnnie gives her an exaggerated wink and waits for Holly to confirm that she won't spread the information around before he goes on. "I think Night Train is going to be a kick-ass stake horse."

"Well, you certainly know what a kick-ass stake horse looks like, so I'll take your word for it and keep an eye on him." Holly relaxes as she talks about something other than Spy Master's colic. They move on to talk about other topics until Holly looks at her watch. "I need to run to the airport to pick up my client. I'll be watching out for you in the Stake at Louisville next year."

Johnnie extends his hand. "Well, good luck to ya'll. I want you to get your horse back safe and sound because you have a lot of work to do this winter. I want him to be in top shape so that my horse can kick his ass next year."

Holly shakes his hand and gives him a genuine smile. "Thanks for the early warning. And you're going to wish you'd left your horse in the Junior Class next year if you come after Spy Master."

CHAPTER 27

Holly is finishing unloading the trailer from the long trip back from Kansas City when her cell phone rings. She glances at the caller ID and sees that it is Kenny Rivers. She wonders why he is calling so late and quickly answers. "Hey Kenny. What's up?"

"I'm calling to figure out what's up with you. I kept expecting to see you on the video feed from Kansas City tonight. What happened? Aren't you at the show?"

"Oh. It's such a long story. But I'm glad you called. I need someone to talk to." Holly tells her friend the story of Spy Master's trip to Kansas City, ending with, "And we just got back to California tonight."

Kenny is quiet for a moment. "So how is he?"

"He looks fine. He acts like his old self. He's in his stall munching hay and pestering the horse next to him. He looks happy as a clam. As soon as we got home we had his regular vet come out and he said that everything looks normal." As Holly talks, she looks into Spy Master's stall and verifies that he is a perfect picture of health. "You'd never guess that he caused me and his owner several nights of lost sleep this week."

"What are you going to do?" Kenny gets right to the point.

"I don't know. If I'm to believe the vet in Kansas City, I don't have anything to worry about. His intestines are now sitting in his belly like they should. I have to admit though, that I'm not confident. It doesn't make sense to me that this is the same problem that caused the colic when he got back from Kentucky. And if it isn't the same thing, then I wonder if I will ever be able to trailer him anywhere without worrying that he's going to try to die on me."

"Gosh. I know what you mean. At least he's a stallion. If you can't show him, then he has just earned himself an early trip to the breeding shed." Kenny goes on, "I think that you just have to watch him carefully and hope that the vet is right on this one."

"Well I certainly don't have enough nerves left to test him again very soon. I'm going to watch him pretty carefully over the next two days just to make sure he doesn't pull this stunt again. If I get through

101

the next two days, then maybe I can relax. His owner rode all the way back from Kansas City with me and his groom and she's pretty tense, too. She says that she knows there is nothing I could have done to prevent what happened, but I'm not so sure that she doesn't blame me a little. I really encouraged her to go to that show."

Kenny pauses before replying. "I think that when things go wrong, people just naturally need something to blame. I'm sure she trusts you completely but her nerves have to be shot. Do you think she is considering moving him to someone else? She has to know that he wouldn't get better care anywhere else."

"I don't think she's seriously considering that," Holly replies. "I just think she is worried that she has a very expensive horse that she loves and she realizes that as big and strong as he looks, he can get seriously ill quickly. We both are hoping that the colic stuff is behind him, but if we can't travel this horse without putting his health at risk, we've got a big problem. The vet said that recurrence happens less than 10% of the time, but that is small comfort. "

Kenny says "Well, I know how much you have riding on him, no pun intended. I'll keep my fingers crossed for you."

They go on to talk about the Kansas City show, with Holly asking Kenny for his opinions on the gaited classes. "What did you think of the qualifying classes?"

"Honestly, I was under-whelmed," her friend says. "Other than that mare from North Carolina, I haven't seen much. The class that Spy Master should have been in was won by a horse from Illinois that looked great for the first half, but he ran out of steam going the second direction. The three-year-olds go tomorrow afternoon, so I probably won't be able to see that. I don't think I'll be home from work in time."

Holly seizes the opportunity to ask him about his job. "How's the job going at Kiplenan? You've been there about two months, right?"

Kenny replies enthusiastically, "It's great. It's perfect for me. I'm working 15 two- and three-year-olds and I make most of the decisions about how to train them. Clark is a quiet guy and once in a while he'll give me a pointer but otherwise he waits for me to ask for help. He's a really good trainer, especially with the young ones, so I'm learning a lot. And the place is huge and beautiful. It is clean and organized and everything is in great repair. It's a trainer's dream and probably the nicest breeding facility in our industry."

"I'm happy that it's going so well for you. Have you been able to keep up with everything at your barn, too?" Holly wonders if Kenny has been able to keep his clients and their pleasure horses while working at Kiplenan as an assistant trainer.

"Luckily for me, everyone decided to give their horses a vacation after the Pleasure Horse Finals. So I pulled all the horses' shoes off and all I'm doing is turnouts, cleaning stalls, and feeding. Angela has been a big help. Around the first of February I'll have to figure something out though, because I come home exhausted. Riding colts is hard work."

"Yeah," Holly agrees. "Luckily I don't do much of that. You have to watch them every step. Sometimes it seems like they're just looking for an excuse to try to dump you in the dirt."

Kenny laughs softly. "Actually, we do so much ground work before we get on that there isn't much excitement. And we don't have any criminals that are trying to hurt you. Clark won't keep that type of horse around."

Holly suspects that Angela is probably within earshot because she knows that Kenny is downplaying the risk of working with young horses. They are easily spooked and their reactions can be hard to predict. After a few more questions about how his family is doing, she says goodbye. Before turning off the lights for the night, she takes one last look at Spy Master. When he hears her approach his stall, he looks up from munching his hay. She can tell from how he looks that he feels fine. "Well boy, let's just hope that was the last of this colic thing. I don't think my nerves can take any more of that, ok?"

103

CHAPTER 28

The Saturday matinee performance has been underway for two hours before Bobby and Johnnie begin making their final preparations to show Vendome and Night Train. All afternoon, Johnnie has been friendly and appeared relaxed, laughing and joking with Bobby and the grooms. But he now has his game face on and tersely gives orders for saddling and bridling the horses.

Bobby hears the announcer calling the class before theirs to the ring and he nods at the grooms to lead Night Train and Vendome out of their stalls. He helps Johnnie mount and then turns to Vendome as Night Train jogs off.

"Just like last time, eh boy?" He pats Vendome on the neck and talks softly, then walks him to the quiet back aisle to begin his warm-up.

After making sure Vendome is ready to go, he moves to the warm-up ring that serves as the staging area and sees that there are about a dozen three-year-olds waiting to enter the ring. Night Train is agitated and all the others have moved away from him as he prances, switches his tail and shakes his head. Bobby can tell that Johnnie is trying to keep him quiet and conserve his energy for the ring but Night Train is not cooperating. Bobby hears the bugle blow and turns his attention back to his own horse, shortening his reins and clucking softly. Vendome is the third horse into the ring and is moving freely and with confidence as he makes his first trotting pass in front of the judges. Bobby maneuvers Vendome off the rail and towards the inside of the ring, working to make sure his horse makes a strong impression on the judges. As he finishes his first full circuit, he can see Night Train coming into the ring and he is a beautiful sight. His head is high and his front knees are pumping up to his chest as he flies down the side of the ring. Bobby tears his eyes from Johnnie and his horse to focus on his own mount.

As the ride proceeds, Bobby finds himself actively trying to avoid Night Train. Johnnie seems to have his horse barely under control as they work through the gaits. Bobby witnesses two near-collisions and notices other riders are also leaving Johnnie a clear path. As a result, the group of young gaited horses is forming into clumps and Bobby starts to struggle to stay clear of the traffic jams.

When the announcer calls for all the horses to reverse and trot, signaling the class is half over, Bobby knows that he and Vendome are going to need to step up their game and take a more aggressive path around the ring. He gathers his horse and cuts to the inside of the ring.

"We have a time-out. Time-out is charged to number 1127. Please work at your leisure." The announcer then goes on. "Will the farrier please report to center ring?" The announcer repeats the call.

Bobby knows that horse number 1127 has thrown a shoe and he pulls Vendome to a halt next to the rail, watching as the class becomes completely disorganized. The rider wearing #1127 on her back has dismounted and is standing next to her horse in the center of the ring. After nearly a full minute, the farrier enters the ring through a side gate and walks toward the horse. He has five minutes after he first touches the horse to replace the shoe and Bobby knows that it could take nearly twice that long before the class is called back to order. He begins thinking about what strategy he should take to benefit Vendome. Since the announcer has instructed them to work at their leisure, riders can either stand to let their horses rest and relax, or they can continue working them. Horses aren't supposed to be judged during a time-out, but Bobby knows that the crowd and the judges are still watching all the horses in the ring, and good and poor passes will be remembered.

He decides to let Vendome stand quietly until the last two minutes or so of the timeout and glances around to see where Johnnie is. Johnnie and Night Train are standing at the end of the ring near the gate. Night Train's sides are heaving, and Bobby sees one of the Stuart Stables grooms enter the ring and notices Johnnie motioning to the groom to adjust the bridle. Bobby knows that any rider that didn't cause the time-out can take the opportunity to make adjustments to their gear without being penalized. If the horse that has caused the time-out causes another delay, it is disqualified from the class. Bobby watches the groom quickly towel off Night Train and realizes that the time-out is probably exactly what Johnnie needs to give Night Train a chance to get his breath back. He contrasts it to his situation and

105

begins to worry that Vendome will lose energy if allowed to stand and relax. He decides to get Vendome moving and glances around to make sure that none of the other three-year-olds are beginning a pass.

Bobby begins a slow gait and focuses on making a perfect pass down the ring. Vendome picks his head up and sustains a perfect four-beat cadence down the ring. At the end near the entrance gate, Bobby turns him and clucks to him. Vendome picks up speed and executes a perfect rack up the other side of the ring. By the time he gets half way up the ring, the crowd notices him and begins whistling and yelling. Bobby pulls Vendome to a halt, having achieved his goal of keeping Vendome on edge and reminding the judges and the crowd that he is riding a great three-year-old.

As Bobby pats Vendome, he hears the crowd roar and looks up to see Johnnie and Night Train racking at full speed toward his end of the ring. Night Train looks like a barely controlled explosion as he barrels around the end of the ring and back towards the gate. Bobby can't tear his eyes from Vendome's stablemate as Johnnie tries to halt him after he completes a full revolution of the ring. Night Train doesn't fully halt and prances down the ring fence, causing other riders to quickly move their horses to get out of his way.

"This class is called back to order. Please take the rail going the second direction at the trot." Bobby hears the announcement that signals the time-out is over and he refocuses on Vendome. In less than 10 minutes, the horses have completed all their gaits going the second direction and the class finishes without further incident.

The Kansas City Horse Show announces awards in the traditional order, beginning with first place and progressing through eighth. As all the riders wait in the lineup for the winner to be announced, Bobby is pleased with Vendome's performance and knows that his horse did well. He glances down the row of horses and knows that there are at least seven or eight really nice horses in the class and begins to worry that Vendome's effort wasn't flashy enough to win.

The announcer finally opens the microphone and begins. "We had a great group of three-year-old gaited horses this afternoon. Tonight's winner comes to us from the State of Kentucky. Please join me in welcoming SS Night Train to the winner's circle!"

The crowd erupts and the rest of the announcement is drowned out as Johnnie pulls Night Train forward, removes his hat and waves to the crowd as he holds the reins in one hand and racks Night Train to the end of the ring where the photographer and the trophy are waiting. Although Bobby is disappointed, he joins everyone else in Kemper Arena as they admire the bay stallion charging down the ring. They will put the ribbon on Night Train's bridle and take photos. After all the other three-year-olds have left the ring, Johnnie will make the traditional victory pass, giving the crowd another opportunity to applaud him and for the photographer to get a picture of Night Train in motion with the ribbon streaming.

The announcer then awards second place to a chestnut from Illinois and Bobby starts to worry that Vendome has been overlooked. His anxiety quickly changes to relief, as the announcer goes on. "Third place winner is Vendome Copper, owned by Mrs. Louise Clancy-Mellon of Illinois and trained by Stuart Stables of Kentucky." Bobby walks Vendome from the line-up and slow gaits to get his ribbon, tips his hat to the crowd, and leaves the ring.

Bobby returns to the stall area, dismounts and pats Vendome and then hands the reins to a groom while he ducks into the tack room to remove his suit. He and the grooms have nearly finished toweling off the sweaty horse when Bobby hears Johnnie and Night Train approaching.

"My horse dominated. He was on the money the whole class. And we got judges that recognized a good horse when they saw one." Johnnie is elated and Bobby congratulates, holding Night Train as Johnnie dismounts. Johnnie suddenly seems to remember that Bobby was in the class. "Did ya'll get a ribbon?"

For a split second, Bobby doesn't know how to react. Johnnie was in the ring waiting to make his victory pass when the announcer announced all the awards. He responds, "We got third" when Johnnie laughs and slaps him on the back. "Just kidding kid. I know you got beat. Wasn't my horse a sight?"

"I only got to see a couple of his passes, but they were really good."

"He was great." Johnnie ducks into the tack room, still talking about how great Night Train was.

By the time the matinee' performance is over, both horses are dry and have been fed and watered. Bobby and the grooms are cleaning tack and Johnnie is accepting congratulations from a steady stream of people coming by the stalls when Bobby notices Mrs. M approaching.

"Congratulations Johnnie. You had a nice ride." She adds her congratulations to those in the crowd surrounding the trainer but continues walking past Johnnie until she gets to Bobby.

Bobby straightens from his task to greet her and wonders how she will react to getting third place. He is relieved when she smiles. "You had a nice ride too," she says. "These judges didn't seem to notice him much until you made that racking pass during the time-out. That was a good decision."

"I really like your horse. I think I could have put a little more pressure on him early in the class. He was steady as a rock and maybe I should have been more aggressive with him."

Mrs. M looks at him carefully and smiles. "You might be right, but he has a long career ahead of him and I'm satisfied with that performance. I'd rather you take him along a bit slowly and let him tell us when he's ready to step up. I'm happy with how you're doing with him." She then lowers her voice and leans closer to him. "Frankly, if it hadn't been for that time-out, Johnnie wouldn't have won. Night Train was running out of gas. That break gave him the chance he needed to stay in the game."

"Oh?" Bobby knows that Mrs. M is a discerning owner and he doesn't doubt her judgment but he can think of no other way to respond to her statement.

"Yes. He was lucky. He won't always be lucky. That horse is breathtaking when he's on, but he's going to have to get better control in order to be more consistent." Mrs. M notices Johnnie approaching and raises her voice again. "Well Johnnie, you have ended the season in style. Well done."

"Thank ya'll. That was a great class. Any of the top three could have won." Johnnie is gracious to his customer and Bobby marvels at how quickly he transitions from bragging about how Night Train dominated the class. Johnnie continues, "Next year's crop of four-year-olds is going to be exceptional. We'll have to see what shows up in the Stake tonight, but if the qualifying classes were any clue, all the gaited talent is in the three- and four-year-olds."

Mrs. M cocks her head and looks at Johnnie carefully. "After what happened a few weeks ago, I thought you were of the opinion that Vendome could be ridden by an amateur. Are you saying now that you think he has a future as a stake horse?"

Bobby immediately recognizes that the conversation is veering into sensitive topics and quietly returns to the tack room. When he emerges several minutes later, Mrs. M is departing. She catches his eye and then she turns to Johnnie and says "We may not have the same vision for Vendome's future, but I want you to know how happy I am with the work Bobby is doing with him. Congratulations to you both." Bobby looks to Johnnie for more explanation but Johnnie just shakes his head and returns to his friends.

CHAPTER 29

Missy Phillips sits next to her father near the middle of the second row at Kemper Arena on the final night of the show. She has been watching all of the gaited classes carefully this week, with the eye of an experienced shopper. As the National Anthem ends, she leans over to her father and quietly says, "I'm glad you got here tonight so you can see the Stake Class but I'm sorry you missed the three-year-olds this afternoon. It would have given you a better chance to compare the two horses that I'm trying to decide between."

"Yes. I'm sorry I couldn't get here earlier. I guess I'd forgotten that the other horse is only three." Senator Phillips keeps his voice low by habit, as he has learned from experience that his private comments often make it into print.

"His name is Vendome Copper."

Her dad looks at her and smiles. "That's a great name. He's obviously named after the company that makes the stills that produce that great Kentucky bourbon. I'm guessing that he's brown."

"Funny Dad. He's chestnut."

"Eskimos have a 100 words for snow and horsemen have a 100 words for brown." They laugh together at the old joke.

Missy continues, "He looked pretty good today but he's not very flashy. He ended up third and it was a really tough class. There was a lot of demolition derby action going on and he never lost his cool."

"Well, that's saying something. It sounds like he's level-headed for being that young. You went to Kentucky to ride him, didn't you? Remind me how that went." He remembers the description of Vendome from Missy's call to him shortly after she left Stuart Stables last month, but he is enjoying their conversation and he likes to watch his daughter light up when she talks about horses.

She begins telling him about her recent trip to Kentucky. "Vendome is much bigger than Josie. I really liked him, but I have to say that there is just something about Josie. I can't quit thinking about her."

"Well let's see how she does tonight. It'll be good to see her in the ring against other Stake horses."

110

"Yes, that's true." Missy settles back and tries to watch the show, but as is usually the case when she is out in public with her dad, they keep getting interrupted by people who are anxious to meet Senator Phillips and complain about the present administration, the immigration bill or their taxes.

After two hours of championship classes, it is finally time for the Stake Class. The announcer asks the crowd to stand as each horse is individually introduced.

"Introducing Josephine's Dream. Owned by Big View Stables of North Carolina. Trained and ridden by Anne Jessup." Josie is the first horse to be introduced and the crowd applauds as the chestnut mare trots through the gate and to the end of the ring, her white legs flashing. Annie pulls her to a stop at the end of the ring as the announcer introduces the remaining eight horses that have entered the class. Once the last horse is introduced, all the others begin to trot counter-clockwise around the ring as the announcer continues, "Please take to the rail and pick up your trot. The Five-Gaited Championship Stake is now underway."

The crowd settles into their seats as the horses begin to battle. Missy only has eyes for Josie, and she likes what she sees. Her dad watches her in his peripheral vision as her body twitches as though she is riding Josie herself. After the horses finish all the gaits going the first direction and the announcer tells them to reverse at the trot, Missy leans over to her dad, "I can't stand it anymore. I'm going to go down to the rail. Can you meet me later at the Big View stalls?"

Her dad smiles. "Are you sure that you don't want me to come along and make sure that your checkbook stays in your purse?"

"Too late for that, I'm a goner."

By the time the horses have finished their last rack, it is clear to the entire audience that Josie is easily winning the class. When she makes her last pass before the lineup, the crowd is on their feet, cheering for the energetic and flashy mare. Shortly after, the announcer exclaims what everyone expects. "With a unanimous decision from all three judges, the winner of this year's Five-Gaited Stake is Josephine's Dream!"

When Annie returns to her stalls with Josie, Missy is already standing there with a signed check in her hand. "Is your previous price still good?"

"On one condition. You have to leave her in training with me at Big View for at least one year."

Missy grins and hands Annie the check. "I thought you'd never ask."

CHAPTER 30

Johnnie and Bobby are nearly finished working horses when one of the grooms brings in the day's mail and hands it to Johnnie. Johnnie removes his gloves and thumbs through it, pausing at the *Saddle Horse Report*, a weekly publication filled with news and advertisements from the Saddlebred industry. He glances at the cover and notices it is a photo of a pleasure horse, so he shuffles it to the bottom of the pile to read later. He also notices a manila envelope addressed to him with a return address from Mrs. M. He walks towards his office as he opens it. Mrs. M always sends a Christmas bonus for Johnnie and often includes some cash for the grooms. Johnnie tosses the rest of the mail on his desk and sits down to see what Mrs. M has sent. Her horses had a good year and he expects her to be generous. He thinks to himself that if it is large enough, he might even give something small to Bobby.

He extracts three smaller envelopes from the larger one. There is one for him, one for the grooms and a sealed white envelope with Bobby's name on it. This catches Johnnie off guard, as he immediately suspects that Mrs. M has decided to provide a bonus directly to Bobby. As Bobby's employer, he believes he should have total discretion in deciding whether an employee should be rewarded and he holds the envelope up to the light to see if he can tell what is in it. It is a heavy white envelope, similar to the one with his name on it, and it appears to contain a card. Johnnie sets it aside and opens the one addressed to him. It contains a Christmas card and there is also a bonus check, but it is much smaller than he expects. He looks closely at it to see if he is misreading the number of zeroes and then tosses it back on the desk in disgust. He then picks up the unsealed envelope for the grooms and sees that there are several hundred-dollar bills in the envelope. He quickly verifies that there is one for each groom, and then pulls out his wallet and stuffs them inside. "For safekeeping," he thinks to himself.

He picks up Bobby's envelope again and examines the seal to see whether he might be able to open it and reseal it, but it is secure. He then decides to open it and tell Bobby that it was loose in the manila

113

envelope. Barely hesitating, he tears open the white envelope and pulls out a card. He quickly tosses the envelope in the trash can and looks down to make sure that Bobby's name on the front of the torn envelope isn't showing.

Johnnie opens the card. He doesn't read the lengthy hand-written message on the inside, but focuses on the check, immediately noticing it is written for twice the amount of his own. He furiously considers destroying it but realizes that his client will know because the check won't be cashed. As he thinks more carefully, he realizes that he will have to give it to Bobby.

He stands up with the card in his hand and leaves his office. Bobby is in the tack room, changing the bit on a bridle and Johnnie walks up to him and hands him the card. "Mrs. M asked me to give this to you. I hope she was generous with ya'll. I sang your praises when I talked to her last weekend. It wasn't your fault that my horse beat hers in Kansas City."

Bobby takes the card and opens it, reading the hand-written note. He then looks at the check and a full grin creases his face. "Wow. That's amazing! I can't believe she did this."

Johnnie feigns innocence. "It must be big. I'm glad she listened to me."

"It's huge." Bobby laughs. "I really needed this. Maybe I'll get the clutch replaced in my truck." He then looks at Johnnie. "Thanks for the good words, Johnnie. I really appreciate it." Bobby carefully inserts the check in his wallet and puts the card in the pocket of his coat. "She sure is a nice lady."

Johnnie replies. "Yep, she's a nice lady alright." He turns on his heel and leaves the tack room.

A couple of hours later, Bobby is sitting in his office, thumbing through the new *Saddle Horse Report* when the phone rings. "Stuart Stables, Johnnie here."

"Hey man, what's up?"

Johnnie recognizes his friend Dave's voice and relaxes. Dave often calls late in the work day to trade gossip. "Not much. What's up with you?"

After making a couple of comments about the miserably cold weather and discussing holiday plans, Dave casually says, "I heard that they've been sedating Toreador so that they can ride him."

"No shit? Where'd you hear that?" Johnnie pauses from flipping pages in the *Report*. He has been wondering how Jennifer Hornig is getting along with Toreador.

"My sister-in-law's best friend is an assistant in her vet's office."

"I knew they wouldn't be able to handle him. How long has that been going on, do you know?"

Dave doesn't have details but decides to embellish the story anyway. "Months. Maybe ever since he left you. You were right, as usual. She's in way over her head."

"I wonder if Marianne knows." Johnnie is thinking about whether he can use this information to his advantage and maybe get Toreador back.

"Hard to tell. Even if she does know, they can't show him on that drug. Eventually, they'll have to take him off it and then all hell will break loose. You're the only trainer around that can handle him." Dave feeds Johnnie's ego as he continues. "If she asks you to take him back, would you?"

"That bitch would have to beg." Johnnie says it quickly, although he would be thrilled to have Toreador back. "In fact, she'd have to get on her knees. I imagine he's ruined already, anyway. There's no telling what they've done to him." He pauses and then continues. "Besides, Night Train might just be better than Toreador."

"Are you going to show Night Train in the open classes next year?" Dave hopes to pick up some gossip that he can use elsewhere.

"Well, if the Royal was any clue of what's out there, Night Train can kick ass in the open classes next year. The mare that won KC got bought by Missy Phillips, so she'll be showing with the amateurs next year. She should have bought this horse I showed her. Even though he's outta his league with Night Train, Vendome Copper is a much better horse than that mare."

After trading a little more news, they hang up and Johnnie leans back in his chair to think about what he has just learned and how he might take advantage of it.

CHAPTER 31

"Bobby. Come here!" It is the end of the work day on Christmas Eve, and Johnnie is standing in the door of his office.

"Sure, boss." Bobby quickly puts the saddle he is holding on the saddle rack in the tack room and follows Johnnie into his office.

"Close the door and sit down."

Bobby gets the immediate sensation that something is wrong. Johnnie has been quiet the last few days, and is not making eye contact now. "Is something wrong?"

"Things have slowed down a little around here and I'm not going to need you anymore. I think this check is everything I owe you." Johnnie extends his hand, holding a check.

Bobby is stunned. "Are you serious? Did I screw up?"

"No. Nothing's wrong. I just don't need ya'll around here anymore." Johnnie repeats himself and moves toward the door to end the conversation.

"Are you serious?" Bobby asks again in disbelief, finding himself taking the check that Johnnie is still holding out to him. "It's the day before Christmas. I'll never get another job in the winter."

"Ah, son. You never know. I'll put in a good word for ya'll if anyone asks. And you can probably live off that check from Mrs. M for a couple of months." Johnnie's hand is on the door knob and he pulls open the door. "Don't forget to take all your tack. And you'll need to be out of the apartment by January 1st."

Bobby tries to remain calm, but his voices rises an octave and he says, "But you know that training barns don't hire during the winter. And I have to find someplace to live in less than a week?"

"Here's a piece of advice. Don't ever get between a trainer and an owner." Johnnie walks out of the office leaving Bobby sitting there, staring after him in disbelief.

Bobby slowly stands and then walks to the tack room in a daze. As he gathers his saddle, chaps, spurs and other belongings, and loads his things in his pickup, he mentally runs through his bills and realizes that he needs to focus on finding a job and a place to live quickly. As

116

he drives away from the barn, he tries to calm himself and murmurs, "Thank God I haven't spent Mrs. M's check yet."

CHAPTER 32

It is a cold, windy, gray Wednesday morning when Missy pulls into the gates at Big View Farm. She has been looking forward to this morning since buying Josie two months ago. She parks her Mercedes and reaches into the bag on the passenger's seat to grab her gloves and pull them on before quickly opening the door and stepping out into the cold morning. She removes her saddle from the rear of the SUV, holding it with one arm as she struggles against the wind to close the rear hatch and then to open the barn door. By the time she finally gets into the barn and out of the wind, she is breathless.

The barn is cold and dimly lit but is full of activity. There is a radio playing and several of the stall doors are open. While the barn is neat and orderly, it is clearly a working barn. There are wisps of hay scattered in the aisle and several of the stalls have grooming boxes outside them or equipment hanging on the doors. As Missy proceeds down the aisle, she glances at each of the stall doors, unsure which one belongs to Josie. She sees several young horses in cross ties, obviously waiting to be worked, and passes a couple of busy grooms that barely look up at her as they go about their tasks. About half way down the barn, she sees Josie. Her mare is quietly standing in the cross ties, watching the activity in the aisle through her open stall door. Missy looks around for somewhere to put her saddle, and places it on a collapsible saddle rack attached to the barn wall.

"Hey girl. How have you been?" Missy talks to her mare, and approaches her quietly. The mare leans towards her and Missy pulls off her gloves and pats her neck. She notices that Josie is perfectly clean and that her white legs are sparkling. She decides to go look for Annie so that the trainer will know she has arrived. She heads down the aisle toward the indoor ring. Every minute or so, she sees a horse being ridden past the door between the barn and the connected ring. As she gets closer, she sees it is Annie, bundled up in a sweatshirt and down vest.

"Good morning! Welcome!" Annie doesn't pause from trotting her horse and doesn't even look at Missy as she goes by. There is a huge kerosene heater in the middle of the ring and it is roaring, making it difficult for Missy to hear Annie.

Missy moves into the ring and toward the heater to get warm as the trainer continues to work the young horse. After another ten minutes, Annie finally stops the horse and dismounts. A groom quickly appears and leads the horse back towards the stalls.

"Welcome back to Big View. You picked a cold day to come."

"Thanks. I'm happy to be here." They are both talking loudly to be heard above the heater, and Missy follows Annie as she walks back towards the stalls.

"How has she been?" Missy is anxious to hear how her horse is doing.

"Well, as you know, we gave her about six weeks off after Kansas City. I'd rather have given her more, but we need to make sure that you have plenty of time to get to know her before show season. We've only started her back in training for about two weeks, but she is doing great. She's a little heavier than I'd like, but she's coming along fine."

As Annie stops speaking, they are in front of Josie's stall. The mare now has Missy's saddle on and has light chains around all four feet. Annie removes a training bridle from the hook near the door and begins to bridle the mare. "We've just been working her in a snaffle and giving her pretty gentle rides. I'll start today and point out a few things before we put you on."

"Great." Missy mimics Annie's business-like tone and within minutes, they are back in the ring. Annie mounts Josie and the mare continues to stand as Annie gathers up her reins.

"We've been reminding her of her manners. We need to make sure that she waits for you and behaves herself." Annie clucks at Josie and the mare walks forward quietly. "I always warm her up by walking first. As I do that, I move the bit back and forth in her mouth to let her know that we've come to work and to give her a chance to chew on it a little. I think that the quality of your ride is established in the first 30 seconds, especially with a mare. You really need to start a conversation with her through her bit that sets her up for the ride." Annie is talking loudly, but Missy finds herself following them as

119

Josie walks away so that she can hear Annie over the roar of the heater and the rattle of the chains on Josie's feet.

"Once we are communicating, I always move on to a slow park trot until I feel her start to get loose. Only after we get a solid, square, even trot, will we slow gait." Annie keeps talking as the mare starts a slow, animated trot and Missy focuses on watching the mare move. After three times around the practice area, Annie stops the mare in the center of the ring, and a waiting groom quickly removes the chains.

Annie continues talking. "I never rack her except at a show. She'll never have any problem going fast and if I let her go fast here at home, it is all that she'll want to do. So we concentrate on doing everything correctly." Annie spreads her hands and Josie immediately begins the strong four-beat cadence of the slow gait. After two times around each direction, Annie pulls her to a stop in the middle of the ring and looks at Missy. "Ready?"

"Absolutely!" Missy moves to Josie's left side.

"Now when you get on she's going to be ready to go, so gather up your reins quickly. I'm going to keep a hold of her and we'll just walk in a small circle until you're comfortable."

Missy nods and mounts carefully, settling herself gently into the saddle as Annie continues talking. "Now make sure you have a strong hold on that snaffle rein." As Missy gathers it up, Annie is still leading Josie in a small circle while watching Missy. "Shorter. Shorter still. You need them really short! When I let this mare go, her head is going to come up and you need to have a short rein!" Annie's formerly friendly tone has disappeared, and she is barking directions to Missy. Missy keeps tightening the rein until Annie finally nods. "Now, I just want you to park trot up the side of the ring going the first direction. Make sure you don't go too fast and keep that rein short!" Annie finally releases the bridle and steps back.

Josie quickly begins to jog forward and Missy sits a few steps before beginning to post. Annie is already barking directions to her. "Straighten her head. Straighten it. Missy! Straighten her out! And raise that snaffle."

Missy is immediately overwhelmed by the constant barrage of sharply worded instructions from Annie and controlling Josie as she energetically trots down the ring. Annie continues to yell, and Missy struggles to hear her over the roar of the heater and the pounding of Josie's hooves. As she rounds the corner, she hears Annie again. "Inside leg! More inside leg! Inside snaffle! Help her in the corners!" Missy concentrates on reacting to Annie's instructions but quickly realizes that she is applying all the corrections too late. By the time she hears Annie and figures out what she means, Josie is already around the corner and charging down the long side of the ring.

Annie continues yelling, "You're going too fast! Take a hold of her! Now! Now Missy!"

Missy shortens the reins and slows her post, but Josie doesn't noticeably slow and before Missy knows it, Annie is yelling again. "Inside leg! You MUST use your inside leg in the turns! Your hands are too high!"

Missy feels herself getting agitated and begins to ask Annie, "How do I..."

Before she gets any further Annie yells, "No questions! Just ride her!"

Missy feels a flash of anger, thinking to herself, "She just told me to raise the snaffle, and now my hands are too high." She feels like she is riding a freight train as the mare pounds around the ring and reminds herself to breathe as she struggles to hear Annie's instructions, which continue to come in a stream of short and sharply worded commands.

"Stop her in the middle!"

Missy is relieved to finally hear an instruction that she understands and she yells, "Whoa!" The mare obediently stops in the middle and stands quietly. Missy's mind is reeling and she tries to catch her breath as Annie steps forward.

"Now look. You must ride with a shorter rein. This mare has a huge engine and she was ahead of you from the first step of that ride. You need to think faster than she does. You were her victim out there. You were along for the ride. We're going to slow gait next and you need to start riding this mare. Now shorten your reins! When I tell you, I want you to raise your hands, separate them, and cluck once. Don't let her go too fast. Just slow gait!" Annie steps back again. "Now, go!"

121

Missy separates her hands and clucks. Josie leaps forward and Annie immediately yells "Lower your hands! Shorten that rein! Don't go any faster than that! Get your left leg into her!" After twice around the ring, Missy finally hears, "That's better," but has no understanding of what she did to get the positive feedback.

After three times around the ring each direction, Annie tells Missy to stop. "That's enough for today."

Annie steps forward and reaches for Josie's bridle as Missy dismounts. "To win, you're going to have to learn to take charge of this mare. She'll take advantage of you if you let her. You need to set the speed and when I tell you to adjust something, you need to do it right away."

"I wasn't ignoring you. I was having trouble hearing you and understanding what you wanted." Missy hears the defensive tone in her reply and wonders for the first time if she has made a mistake by selecting Annie as her trainer.

Annie looks at her and immediately softens her tone. "Okay. Let's talk through your ride step-by-step." She hands Josie to a groom who takes her back to her stall. During the next 20 minutes, Annie and Missy talk through the entire session with Annie providing detailed responses to each of Missy's questions. By the end of the session, Missy thinks she is beginning to understand Annie's lexicon.

As their conversation starts to wind down, one of the grooms brings another saddled horse into the ring. Before mounting, Annie pats Missy on the back and earnestly says, "You'll be back tomorrow, right? We'll try it again. You can ride this mare. You just need to start acting like you're in charge. Riding a gaited horse like Josie is not about looking pretty. It is about being effective. You can't get in her way but you can't let her have her way."

Missy mumbles a thank you and leaves the ring, pausing at Josie's stall on her way back to her SUV. The mare is already groomed and has her legs wrapped and a flannel cooler draped over her body. "Holy smokes, girl. That was rough." Annie digs a couple of peppermints out of her pocket and feeds them to her horse.

Later, as she sits in a nearby café and picks through her salad, she calls her dad.

Before even greeting her, he asks, "How did it go?"

"Oh Dad," Missy sighs. "It was rough. Annie was yelling at me with every step and I couldn't understand what she wanted me to do. When I tried to ask a question, she yelled at me to not ask questions! It was frustrating and humbling."

Jim Phillips immediately reassures Missy. "Honey. You're an excellent rider. You know how to ride. It seems unreasonable of Annie to not even answer your questions."

"Yeah. I hope tomorrow goes better. The experience I just had was definitely not fun."

"Maybe you need to find another barn for Josie. You're paying the bills and I don't know what makes this trainer think she can treat you like that."

"Well, I'd like to give it another try and see how it goes. My goal is to win Louisville this year. I believe that Josie can get me there. And Annie definitely knows how to ride Josie. I don't want my ego to get in the way of my goal."

"Well, I just know that I wouldn't take any abuse from a trainer. It is up to you, of course, but you're a good rider. And you can easily find a trainer that will treat you with respect."

"Thanks Dad. I needed a dose of confidence. I'm not ready to throw in the towel yet." With that, she hangs up.

The next morning, Missy returns to Big View Farm determined to show Annie that she is a competent rider who can accept criticism and learn from it. Before getting out of her vehicle, she takes a deep breath and silently reminds herself of the lessons she learned yesterday.

As she walks by Josie's stall, she can see that the mare is already saddled and ready to go. She pulls on her gloves, and glances towards the ring to see that Annie is just dismounting from another horse. Annie waves at her to let her know that she sees her and begins walking toward her. As she gets near, she says "I've been thinking about yesterday and I'm going to change things up a little. I'm going to let you get on first today. I think that it will be easier for you two to get in synch if you start together. And I'll turn off the heater so you can hear me better."

Missy smiles at Annie, happy to learn that Annie has been thinking about how to help her. "That sounds great. Let's do it."

While they are leading Josie to the ring, Annie makes small talk about nearby restaurants and shopping, setting a much more relaxed tone than the previous day. Once Josie is in the ring, Annie gently says. "We'll start slow, much like I did yesterday. Just keep your snaffle rein short and stay ahead of her."

Missy mounts carefully and then Annie releases Josie and begins her instruction. "Just walk her in a circle and keep her quiet. Start moving the bit gently back and forth in her mouth so that she knows you want to communicate with her." As Missy works with Josie, Annie starts providing positive feedback. "There, that's it. That's right. Now change directions and do the same thing the other way. Can you feel her starting to relax? Can you tell that she's listening to you?"

As Missy works and listens to Annie, she can feel her body start to settle into the saddle. Annie continues, "Now when we trot, we're going to make her warm up gently. We want a slow, controlled and totally square gait. Don't let her rush you. Don't hang on her mouth, just use your fingers to remind her that you're in control. If she gets going too fast, just slow your own body and she'll come back to you. Are you ready?"

Missy nods immediately and Annie says, "Shorten your reins a bit and then go ahead and start."

Missy moves her hands another inch down on the reins, quietly clucks at Josie and gently squeezes her legs. Josie immediately steps off into a trot and Missy steadies her hands and works to keep the mare moving squarely and slowly.

"That's it. Keep her slow and relaxed. When you get to the corner, use inside leg and inside rein to keep her from cutting the corner and leaning." As Missy goes around the corner, Annie continues to encourage her. "Good Missy! That's it. Let's do an entire round at that speed and then we'll step it up a little."

After they've finished trotting and have paused at the end of the ring, Missy is smiling and enjoying her ride. Annie says, "Okay, let's slow gait. Her favorite thing is to go fast and then faster, so don't let her take charge. Stay deep in your seat and keep your reins short. When you're ready to go, spread your hands and cluck once to her."

Missy takes a deep breath and shortens her reins, spreads her hands and clucks. She leans very slightly forward with her upper body to take control of the mare and slow gaits down the ring. Unlike the day before, the mare feels light and airy. Missy can hear each foot hit the ground and she can tell that her horse's legs are flying, but the forward speed of the gait is about half of what it was the day before. Missy feels like she is in complete control as Josie goes into the first corner, and when she hears Annie yell "Inside leg! Inside hand!" she quickly responds. Annie continues yelling "That's great! Good! Do it again but be a little earlier! Inside leg, inside hand! Don't hang on her mouth. Keep talking to her!"

Soon, they've worked both directions and Annie tells Missy "That's good. Let's stop there."

Missy pulls Josie to a stop and pats her before getting off. "Thanks Annie. That was a lot better."

Annie hands the horse to a groom and responds, "Yes. You were a lot better today."

Missy smiles and avoids mentioning that she wasn't the only one in the ring that had improved since yesterday. As with the day before, they spend several minutes replaying the ride and Annie patiently answers all of Missy's questions. As they walk together up the barn aisle, Annie asks "So, when will you be back?"

"I'd like to come every two weeks and ride two days in a row. Will that work for you?"

"That will be perfect. That will give me time to work on some changes between your visits. We'll probably canter the next time you're here so that I can figure out where we're at with that final gait. It will probably take more work than the others."

Missy can see that Annie is already thinking through the training steps she will be taking with Josie in the upcoming months. "Well, I'll let you get back to work and I'll feed her a couple of peppermints and hit the road. Thanks for everything." Missy hesitates and then pointedly adds, "I really enjoyed today," softening the message with a smile.

Annie smiles back. "We have a lot of work to do. I know you can win on this mare and sometimes I get a little over-enthusiastic but we'll get it figured out."

With that, Annie returns to the ring to work another horse.

On her drive back to Virginia, Missy thinks back through the last two days. She wonders about the difference in Annie's tone between the riding sessions and wonders which version of the trainer will greet her on her next trip.

CHAPTER 33

Kenny carefully checks the bridle and girth of the next two-year-old that he is getting ready to mount and tries to remember her name. All of the young horses at Kiplenan Stables are home-bred stock, and they share many traits. They are mostly chestnuts, and most of them have a narrow strip of white in their face and two white socks. Kenny smiles to himself and remembers that this filly's name is Marigold. Clark has told him that Mr. Kiplenan has a theme every year when he is trying to name his foals. The two-year-olds are mostly named after flowers and plants. The three-year-olds are named after famous places. The yearlings are named after composers and authors.

Kenny focuses on the young horse in front of him, and carefully mounts. The filly stands quietly. He has ridden this one for about eight weeks now and is really pleased with her progress. As he begins to trot up the side of the ring, he notices that Clark is standing in the ring waiting for the grooms to bring him another horse and he is watching Marigold carefully. Kenny keeps the horse straight and quiet, making sure that the trot is square and consistent for the entire length of the ring. He halts her and turns her around to trot back.

"Looks like that one is going to rack. I like how she moves her rear end. You've been doing a real nice job with her." Clark doesn't often make too many comments about the horses that Kenny is assigned to work, so the compliment is gratifying.

"Yeah. I like this one a lot. She learns fast and keeps a level head. She really tries to figure out what I want." It doesn't take long for each young horse to make their personality apparent.

Clark smiles ruefully. "She might not have a big enough engine to be a top horse, but if she'll rack, that'll help."

Kenny knows that finding a horse with the necessary combination of conformation, talent and willingness is difficult. And even when you think you've found a horse with all the necessary traits, it can be hard to maintain them as they grow and learn. He asks the filly to trot back down the ring as the grooms bring another young chestnut for Clark to mount. Just as Kenny and his trotting filly near the door that leads to the stalls, a flash of black fur darts through the entrance, with

127

a barking dog in close pursuit. Kenny just has enough time to recognize one of the groom's dogs and realize it is chasing a cat before his filly erupts. She quickly spins to her right, towards the ring wall and away from the dog. Kenny immediately yells, "WHOA!" and works to contain her. But she is already panicked and she rears up on her hind feet. Kenny immediately realizes that he needs to get off her and away before she falls on him, and he bails off her left side. As he pushes away from her, she lunges, driving him into the ring wall as he falls.

As he goes down, his left shoulder slams into the wall and he feels a sharp, searing pain. He can hear Clark and the grooms yelling, "Whoa, Whoa!" and realizes that he is lying in the dirt next to the wall. His first thought is to be thankful that his head didn't hit the wall. He quickly struggles to get up, embarrassed that he has been dumped in front of his boss and the grooms. As he struggles to his feet, he realizes that his shoulder is really painful and his left arm is tingling.

"Are you okay?" The grooms are still trying to catch his filly, who is racing around the ring with the reins and stirrups flying, but Clark is striding towards him with a concerned look on his face.

"I don't know. I think I hurt my shoulder." Kenny is dazed and groans when he experimentally moves his left arm.

"You'd better sit down. Can you get up to the office? I'll help the boys catch this filly and then we'll have someone run you to the hospital." Clark is clearly concerned about Kenny and looks over his shoulder as the frightened filly races away from the grooms.

"Yeah. I can make it up there. Damn it. And just when things were going so well, too." Kenny tries a half-smile but he can tell that his shoulder is injured as he clamps his arm next to his torso. His next thought is about what he will tell his wife Angela.

Two hours later, the emergency room doctor re-enters the curtained examination area and says, "It is what I thought. You've broken your collar bone. The good news is that it is a simple break and won't require surgery. There doesn't appear to be any damage to the nerves or blood vessels. There isn't any displacement, so that is also good news. We're going to put you in a sling, but it is very important that you don't use your arm and that you give the break time to heal."

Kenny isn't surprised at the diagnosis and is relieved to hear he won't need surgery, but quickly asks the question foremost in his mind. "How long before I can go back to work?"

The doctor looks up from the paperwork she is filling out. "You're going to need to keep your shoulder immobilized for four to six weeks. You might be able to remove the sling after that, depending on whether it still hurts. You won't get full use of your arm back for at least eight weeks and maybe twelve. It just kind of depends on how quickly you heal. But since you're a horse trainer, I'm guessing that you won't feel like you're back to normal for twelve weeks."

The doctor goes on to say something about physical therapy but Kenny is no longer listening. The next thing he knows, she is standing at the curtain and is handing paperwork to a nurse. "Since this is a worker's comp claim, we need a few extra minutes to fill out all the forms, but we'll get you a prescription for pain medication to take with you. Someone will be back right away with a sling. Do you have any questions?"

Kenny hasn't really processed anything the doctor has said, but he shakes his head slowly and then winces as the movement causes a sharp stab of pain.

The nurse moves toward him. "Maybe you should call your wife. The man who brought you in gave me your cell phone before he left." She tries to hand him his phone and when he doesn't move to take it, she sets it down next to his right hand. She looks at him sympathetically and then says, "You know, it could have been a lot worse. Maybe you should start by telling her that."

Kenny slowly picks up the cell phone with his right hand and uses his thumb to speed dial Angela.

She answers quickly. "Hi honey. I was just going to call you and ask you to stop and get some burger buns for dinner."

"Babe, I'm sorry. I'm going to need you to come get me. I hurt my collarbone and am at St. Luke's. One of the grooms brought me over here, but I'm not going to be able to drive home."

"Oh my God. Are you okay?" She barely pauses and then says, "Of course you aren't okay. You're at the hospital. Oh, Kenny. What happened?"

"I'll tell you about it later. Don't worry. I'll be fine. And no need to rush over here. I'm not going anywhere." He keeps his voice upbeat and downplays his injury, but he knows that he will lose his job at Kiplenan's and is extremely worried about the impact this will have on his own business as well.

CHAPTER 34

Johnnie is leading a steaming and sweaty horse to its stall when he sees the door at the end of the barn open and Mrs. Clancy-Mellon enters. He is very surprised to see her, especially since she has never before visited the barn without calling ahead. He mutters "Shit!" under his breath, but quickly pastes a smile on his face.

"Mrs. M! I didn't know ya'll were going to visit us today! How are ya'll?" He hands his horse off to a groom and strides forward to meet her.

"Hi Johnnie. I was in the neighborhood and thought I'd drop by. I haven't seen any of my horses work since last fall and I need a horse fix!" She returns his smile and then raises her eyebrows. "I hope it isn't an inconvenience."

Johnnie suspects that she has intentionally timed her visit to surprise him, and hurries to mask his discomfort. "Absolutely not! You're always welcome here. I was just going to long-line Vendome next."

"Oh. Since it is Saturday, I was hoping to see you ride him today. Could I get you to change your plan?"

He hesitates. He knows that he will have to agree to ride her four-year-old today, but he hasn't been giving Vendome much attention since firing Bobby. He's been having the grooms lunge him every day and he occasionally does some ground work with him, but he hasn't ridden him in several weeks. Despite telling Bobby that the workload was slowing down, he has too many horses to work through each day so the training on several of them has begun to slide while he has focused on the ones with local owners or that he expects to sell in the spring. He regrets having told her that Vendome hadn't been worked yet today. If he had known she would want to see him, he would have told her that he'd already been ridden.

"Yes ma'am. Why don't ya'll help yourself to some coffee while I tell the boys to get him ready?" He works to keep his voice relaxed as he heads to Vendome's stall.

"Oh? Isn't Bobby still working him?"

131

Johnnie suddenly remembers that he hasn't ever told his client that he fired Bobby. He briefly considers telling her that Bobby quit, but then he decides there is too much risk that she has heard something different. "I thought I'd told you that I had to let Bobby go. He just wasn't working hard enough. He'd started to cut corners and I couldn't live with it. It wasn't fair to the horses."

Mrs. M is clearly surprised. "No. You never told me that. I'm surprised and sorry to hear that. I thought you really liked him."

"Yeah. He fooled me for a while, but I think he might have started drinking or something. He started showing up late for work and was always looking to get outta here in the afternoon." Johnnie watches her face carefully to see if he can detect any mistrust, but she looks sincere.

"Really? When did that happen?"

"'Bout Christmas time. I think the holidays get to some people and maybe that's what happened to him." Johnnie lies smoothly and tries to change the subject. "Let me get going on your horse. Do you want to see Vendome first? Or maybe that little two-year-old?"

But Mrs. M isn't ready to let the subject go and ignores his question. "Have you replaced him? Do you know where he is?"

"I've been looking for a replacement but haven't found the right horseman yet. I don't know where Bobby ended up. He has a brother here in town and he might have moved in with him. I'm not really sure." Johnnie walks away from her as he talks, leaving her standing in the aisle looking after him.

It is nearly 30 minutes before Vendome is groomed, saddled and bridled. As Johnnie leads him down to the ring he glances back at the horse, trying to predict how the young gelding will react to the long period since last being saddled. He is relieved to see that Vendome's expression is alert and calm, and it puts Johnnie's mind at ease.

He carefully mounts the horse and Vendome stands quietly, waiting for a signal to walk off. Johnnie gathers up his reins and touches him with a spur to move him forward. Vendome flinches sideways away from the spur and starts to trot up the ring with his ears laid back against his head. Johnnie can tell from his ears and his short steps that the horse is agitated and pushes him harder to get him to lengthen his stride. Vendome speeds up but keeps his ears back and

Johnnie can feel a tightness in the horse's back. As Johnnie works the bit, Vendome braces against it.

Johnnie continues to work the horse and while Vendome doesn't overtly resist and eventually starts to relax, it is clear that he's not happy. When Johnnie asks him to slow gait, Vendome's gait is uneven and he has particular trouble in the corners. Mrs. M is standing in the center of the ring, and when Johnnie finally stops the horse, he can see from her expression that she is upset.

She has always been direct with him, and she doesn't hesitate to confront him. "What in the hell happened to my horse? He looks like shit."

"He's just going through a little adjustment. I changed his bit and his shoes last week and he's still getting used to it." Johnnie dismounts and attempts to smooth over the poor performance but knows that she may not accept his explanation.

"Johnnie. He looks like shit." She slowly repeats herself, clearly enunciating each word.

The trainer tries again to smooth it over. "I gave everyone shots yesterday and I think he probably isn't feeling well. That's why I didn't plan to ride him today."

Mrs. M just stares at him, slowly shaking her head. "I don't know what to say. I'm shocked." She pauses and presses her lips tightly together as though she is physically trying to stop more words from coming out. Finally, she just repeats herself. "I don't know what to say."

While he takes Vendome back to his stall, she slowly follows him up the aisle. She pauses for a moment at Vendome's stall, and then decides to leave the barn before she says something she'll regret and goes out the door without another word. She zips up her coat and pulls on her gloves while standing outside the barn, trying to decide what she should do. She would like to see her other horses work to see if they perform better than Vendome but she decides that she just can't be nice to Johnnie and she gets in her car and drives away.

Within a mile of the barn, her disappointment with Vendome's performance is already transitioning to anger with Johnnie. When she thinks back over the last few telephone calls with him, he has always assured her that Vendome was doing well. She knows that today's

133

ride was probably not an isolated incident and is convinced that she certainly needs to move Vendome, and probably all of her horses, to another trainer immediately.

She pulls her car over into the parking lot of a church and puts the transmission in Park as she tries to think through her options. She then pulls her cell phone out of her bag and looks through her contacts, finally pausing when she sees Lee Kiplenan's name. They have known each other for decades and she has purchased many top horses from him. She dials his number without hesitating.

His gruff voice comes on the line after two rings. "Hello?"

She puts a smile in her own voice and works to disguise her anxiety. "Hello Lee. This is Louise Mellon. How are you?"

It only takes a second for him to reply in a warm tone. "Louise? It is great to hear from you. I'm sick and tired of winter and I'm ready for warm weather. How are you?"

She laughs lightly. "I totally agree that warmer weather will be welcome." She decides to get right to the point. "I need a big favor."

"And here I thought you were calling because you have some money burning a hole in your pocket and you want to buy one of my horses." He laughs and she joins him.

"I do love your horses, but that's not what I need today." She proceeds to tell him about her morning's experience at Stuart Stables, ending with, "So I need to get my horses out of there sooner rather than later. I might have caught him on a bad day, but I don't trust that man. I was really pleased with the way his assistant was getting along with Vendome, but now I think Johnnie has been taking advantage of me and I won't be treated like a fool."

Lee responds quickly. "Yes. I understand what you mean. He's a good horseman, but he has always struck me as a bit of a crook." He goes on, "I'm not sure how many empty stalls we have, but I'll call Clark and ask him. As you know, we've got more young ones than we have room for, but I'll see what we can do. I know Clark is pretty busy because he just lost his assistant."

This statement piques Louise's interest. "Really? Are you looking for a new assistant? Bobby Acton was Johnnie's assistant and I can try to find out if he's still available. Do you think Clark would be interested in talking to him?"

134

"Well, I can't speak for Clark. I let him make all the decisions associated with the training barn, but I'll mention it when I call him. I'll call you back later today."

After thanking him, Louise leans back in her seat and rests her head against the headrest. She hopes that she might be able to place one or two of her horses at Kiplenan's, but she has a total of eight that need places in good training barns, so she goes back to her cell phone and continues making calls. Ten minutes later, her phone rings.

"Mrs. Clancy-Mellon, this is Clark Benton. Mr. Kiplenan told me that you're looking for a training stall or two."

After she thanks him for calling her back so promptly, she repeats the story that she has told his boss. She ends with "I understand you might be a little short-handed and I'd be happy to see if I can locate Bobby Acton if you're interested in talking to him."

"Actually, I'm very interested. That young man knows how to work a horse and he might be of some help to me. If you can find him, I'd much appreciate hearing from him." Clark's slow, drawling voice continues. "I can definitely fit two horses in here if I can get some good help."

Louise relaxes. "It's a deal. I'll find Bobby and have him call you right away. I'll wait to order a trailer until I hear back from you, but I'd really like to take care of this quickly."

After disconnecting the call, she puzzles about how she will find Bobby. She decides to try the most obvious route first. She guesses at his full name and then types "Robert Acton, KY" into the white pages directory search engine on her phone. Within a few seconds, she receives a list of more than twenty people in KY named Robert Acton, along with their cities and estimated ages. She doesn't recognize most of the city names and notices that most of the people in the list don't have phone numbers listed. She then realizes that he is certainly a member of the American Saddlebred Association. She recently received a booklet in the mail that contains the Association's membership directory and Bobby is almost certainly included in that directory. It just takes one more call to the Association's Executive Director to get Bobby's published cell phone number and email address. She quickly dials the number, hoping that he will answer.

A man answers, "Hello?"

"Hello. I'm trying to reach Bobby Acton. Is this him?" She waits in suspense.

He replies cautiously. "Yes. This is Bobby. Who's calling, please?"

She responds quickly. "Bobby. I'm so glad to get in touch with you. This is Louise Clancy-Mellon. Vendome's owner."

The young man's voice instantly brightens, "Mrs. M? Wow. What a surprise. How are you?"

"Bobby, I just found out today that you aren't at Stuart Stables anymore. What happened? Where are you?"

Bobby hesitates but decides to take the high road. "Oh, Mrs. M… it's a long story and I don't really even know that I understand what happened myself. I do know that I sure miss Vendome though. How is he?"

"He's awful. There isn't any other word for it. Just awful." She then goes on, "But where are you? What are you doing?"

"You might not believe this, but I'm selling used cars out here in Shelbyville. I don't really like it and I'm just barely good enough at it to keep from starving." He laughs weakly.

"Well. This might be your lucky day." She goes on to tell him about her decision to move her horses and that Kiplenan Saddlebreds is in need of an Assistant Trainer.

When she finally pauses, he says. "I'll call Mr. Benton right now. I'll call you back as soon as I can." He thanks her profusely and hangs up.

Within a few minutes her phone rings and the caller ID shows that it is Bobby. She barely has time to greet him before he says. "Mrs. M! You are my guardian angel! Mr. Benton told me to show up for work in the morning. He told me to tell you that you can send two horses to him anytime tomorrow. He also said that if you don't mind putting them in the breeding barn, you can send another six to him as well. He doesn't start foaling until April 1, so that will give us six weeks to figure out what to do next."

"Oh, Bobby! That's great news. I'll take you up on that and send all eight horses over tomorrow. I'm so glad that you'll be reunited with Vendome. Please give me a call when they've all arrived safe and sound. Also, once you've spent a little time with Vendome, I need to know what you think." She ends the call and dials an equine transporter to order transport for eight horses from Stuart Stables to Kiplenan early the next morning.

Finally, she takes a deep breath and dials Johnnie Stuart's number. She is only mildly surprised when the call goes to voice mail. She leaves a brief message. "Johnnie. This is Louise Mellon. I've got a truck picking up my horses in the morning. Please make sure that everything I own that is at your barn is on the truck when it leaves. Don't forget all the tack. Once it arrives, I will check it against my inventory. I'm sorry that we had to end our association this way. Call me if you have any questions." As she hangs up, she closes her eyes and hopes that Johnnie will follow her instructions. She is afraid that he will 'forget' to include a harness or two, but she hopes he will realize he has very little to gain if he tests her.

CHAPTER 35

"Do you think she will do it today?"

Eduardo's question startles Jennifer and she looks up as she finishes brushing Toreador. "I don't know. We've been through this routine five or six times, haven't we? She's had the flu twice, a cold three times, and a sore arm once. It is nearly the end of February. Maybe she doesn't intend to ride him this season."

"I am not sure that her mother will allow that." Eduardo answers cautiously, looking over his shoulder to make sure they are alone.

Jennifer goes on. "The thing is that I actually think that she might be able to ride him. As you know, I wasn't at all sure that was possible, but he has come a long way since last fall. He listens and waits, and as long as you move slowly on him, he's a good boy. Look at him now! Who would have thought that you'd be able to brush him without worrying that he was going to kick or bite?" She stands back and proudly looks at the chestnut horse.

Eduardo shakes his head, unconvinced that Toreador has turned over a new leaf. "Well, we will see. He might be a very different horse at a show. If Blair does decide to show him, the first show will be the real test."

"You're right about that."

As he talks, Eduardo has been watching the door to the barn and notices Blair enter, carrying her saddle. He looks back at Jennifer and says quietly, "She is here."

"Really?" Jennifer feels her stomach lurch and realizes that she is very nervous about how this ride will go. "Is her mother with her?"

Eduardo raises a hand to wave at their client and quietly says, "I do not see her."

Jennifer responds under her breath. "Hm. That's interesting." She exits the stall to greet their client.

"Good morning Blair. I'm happy to see you. You look ready to ride." Despite her words, Jennifer notices that Blair is clearly nervous as she approaches hesitantly.

"Hi Jennifer. I guess I'm as ready as I'll ever be." Blair hands her saddle to Eduardo, bends down to pet Jelly, and laughs weakly as though she is joking, but her tense and unhappy expression is evidence that she would rather not be there.

Although she has never experienced the fear of horses that she suspects plagues Blair, Jennifer sympathizes and offers her client another opportunity to avoid the ride. "You know, Blair. You don't have to do this. If you'd rather we put this off for a while or even forever, we can do that."

Blair's eyes well and she shakes her head. She drops her eyes and begins fidgeting with her gloves. "My mother isn't going to let that happen. I have to do this."

Jennifer again glances toward the door. "Is Marianne coming today?"

"No. That's why I've been canceling. I finally found a Saturday that she couldn't make it. She doesn't know that I'm here."

Jennifer feels herself relax, realizing that Marianne's absence improves the likelihood of a good ride. She also decides to be completely up front with Blair. "Well then, let's talk about how we want this to go. I think we'll make this ride very short, and just walk, trot and maybe slow gait, if all is going well. I don't want to warm him up for you because he gets stronger and stronger the longer he goes, and I don't think we want that to be your first experience on him. Also, we gave him some Quietex about 2 hours ago. This is just a gel that takes a little bit of the edge off.

Blair has been listening carefully and now she quickly says. "I'm fine with that. I'm not going to second guess you with any of your decisions, although I admit I'm worried about getting on him cold. Is he still on that other drug you were using?"

"You mean the Acepromazine. No, he's been off that for almost 60 days. It did a nice job for us. It helped him transition to our training program. Turning him into a good horse for you requires a much different approach than his previous role as a Stake Horse."

While the women are talking, Eduardo has put Blair's saddle on Toreador and carefully and slowly tightened his girth. Jennifer notices the horse is ready and she gives Blair a reassuring smile. "Well? Shall we do this?"

"I guess we should." Blair stands back so that Eduardo can lead Toreador from the stall. The horse hesitates slightly before rushing

139

into the alley. Once in the alley, Eduardo quietly halts him and makes him stand.

Jennifer calmly says. "We can't seem to make him understand that he doesn't have to be worried about going through a stall door. He rushes like that going in and coming out. But at least now he will relax when he gets through it. For as big and strong as he looks, this boy sure has some fears."

For the first time that morning, Blair laughs. "Well then, maybe we have more in common than I thought."

Once Toreador is in the ring, he stands quietly but looks around alertly. The muscles in his neck twitch slightly as Jennifer brings a mounting block over to the horse's left side. As she and Eduardo lower the stirrup irons and prepare the horse for Blair to mount, Jennifer keeps talking quietly. "Now, mount fairly quickly because he still isn't the most patient horse in the world. Don't worry, Eduardo and I will have a strong hold of him. Work quickly to gather up your reins while I lead him off. Just keep your legs off him and sit quietly. I won't let him go until you're ready."

Blair nods nervously and adjusts the mounting block with her foot. She hesitantly steps on to it and reaches for the rein. Her hesitation gives Toreador time to sidle away from her, putting her stirrup out of range. Jennifer and Eduardo make eye contact and Jennifer says to Blair. "Let's try that again. You need to be a little quicker."

Blair takes a deep breath and readjusts the mounting block. This time, she succeeds in mounting the horse. As she settles in the saddle and shortens her reins, Jennifer and Eduardo maintain their grips on the horse's bridle and talk quietly to him as they lead him off. Jennifer keeps her voice quiet and low as she talks to Blair. "Well done. Gently gather your reins but try to relax your seat. Keep your legs off him and make sure your heels are down."

Blair quickly makes the adjustments as Jennifer coaches her, and Jennifer continues. "Good job. Eduardo is going to let go now, but I'm going to have him. We're going to just walk around in a big circle. You're doing great. Just shorten your reins a little." Jennifer provides Blair a steady stream of gentle guidance and positive feedback. Once she detects that the horse and rider are both relaxing a bit, she decides it is time to move to the next step.

"Now when you're ready, I'll let go of the bridle. I want you to continue walking him in this same circle." She immediately notices a flash of fear cross Blair's face and Toreador flinches. "Now don't tense up. See how he reacted to that? Just stay relaxed and quiet in the saddle. Keep your hands steady." As Blair deliberately relaxes, she goes on. "There. That's it. That's good. Now I'm going to let go, but he might not even notice. Stay relaxed."

Jennifer steps slightly away from the horse and he moves forward a few steps before breaking into a jig. Jennifer continues encouraging her client. "That's okay, Blair. You're doing fine. Shorten your reins and let him trot down the side of the ring. Try to keep him as slow as you can."

Blair begins posting in time to Toreador's trot as he moves down the ring. Despite Jennifer's instructions to stay slow, the horse picks up speed with every step. Jennifer raises her voice. "Shorten your reins, Blair. When you get to the corner, sit back in your saddle and keep your heels down!" Her instructions start coming with greater urgency as she tries to help Blair remain in control of the big horse. "Slow your post, Blair. Use your body to slow him down. That's right. That's good."

Jennifer notices that the positive feedback helps Blair relax and the ride starts to improve. Jennifer sees Eduardo standing on the far end of the ring and knows that he is giving Blair similar advice. She lets Toreador go around three times and notices that he is starting to pick up speed and power as he warms up so she decides to interrupt the cycle. "When you get back to me, ask him to walk and then bring him into the center of the ring and halt."

Jennifer has spent countless hours teaching Toreador to stand quietly when he is halted in the center of the ring, and that training pays off when Blair is able to stop him without incident. Blair is out of breath and Jennifer suspects that her nerves have kept her from breathing properly as she rides. She moves forward to gently grasp Toreador's bridle and asks. "How are you?"

Blair continues looking straight ahead and takes a deep breath. "I'm okay, but he is a handful."

"Yes. But he's being really good for you. Do you want to trot the other direction?" When Blair nods, Jennifer goes on. "Just like last time. Keep your heels down and keep your legs off him. If he gets going too fast, just slow your post. He'll want to stay in synch with you and that will help you slow him down a bit. Keep your reins short but try to communicate with him through his mouth. Don't just hang on him." She pauses for a minute to give Blair a chance to ask questions and then she steps back from the horse. "Just give him a slight squeeze to move him forward and say 'Whup Trot'."

Blair obediently follows Jennifer's directions and they begin trotting clockwise around the ring, with Jennifer and Eduardo giving guidance similar to the previous direction. But now that Toreador is warmed up, it is clear that he has his own opinions about how fast to go and he begins to take control of the session. Jennifer quickly detects this and after two circuits of the ring, she instructs Blair to bring him back to the center and halt him. When Blair has him stopped, Jennifer asks her if she wants to try slow gaiting him and is relieved when Blair smiles faintly and says "Actually, I think I've had enough."

"Okay. Why don't I finish the workout with him?" Jennifer doesn't want him to finish his session with some of the bad behaviors that he has displayed with Blair, like cutting corners and going at his speed rather than the rider's. As she takes Blair's place in the saddle, she focuses on reminding him that she is in control. The workout ends without incident but by the end of her ride, Toreador is agitated and tense. She makes him stand quietly in the center of the ring before she finally dismounts and pats him on the neck.

As Eduardo leads the sweaty horse back to his stall, Jennifer and Blair talk about the ride.

"So what did you think?"

Blair smiles at Jennifer. "It wasn't as scary as I thought it would be, but I can see that he gained steam as he worked. I'm not sure I could have handled him by the end of the ride. And I'm a little concerned that you'd even given him some Quietex."

"Yes. He has huge energy. Honestly, I'm not sure that the Quietex had any impact on him at all after he got warmed up. I think he probably metabolizes that stuff at warp speed once his blood starts to boil." Jennifer adds encouragingly, "You did really well, though. Do you want to try this again next week?"

Blair hesitantly responds, "I think so, but I don't really want to do this in front of my mother. Is it okay if we keep this between ourselves? I can sneak out here during the week next week if that's okay with you."

"Absolutely! I think that is wise. It will let us proceed at a pace that you're comfortable with. I'll just avoid the issue if she asks me about it." Jennifer is encouraged that Blair wants to continue trying to ride Toreador and she is also happy that they will continue to work together without the added pressure of Marianne's attendance. As Blair leaves, carrying her saddle, she turns back to thank Jennifer. "I appreciate your patience with me. I'm still not convinced that I can do this, but I'm going to give it a try."

After she's gone, Eduardo and Jennifer work together to cool down the bay horse. Eduardo laughs and says, "She does not seem hopeful."

Jennifer laughs too. "Yes. Not exactly a ringing endorsement. But look at the bright side. She walked out of here. We didn't have to call an ambulance. And, to top it off... she's coming back voluntarily! I call that a win!"

CHAPTER 36

2 PM April 4, Del Mar Fairgrounds

Holly is sitting outside Spy Master's stall at the Del Mar Fairgrounds just over an hour north of Morning Star Barn when Eileen arrives. She quickly stands to greet Spy Master's owner. "Hi there. I'm glad you made it. I hope you didn't have any problem finding us."

"Not at all. It was easy. I'm glad they moved the show here this year. It is so much closer than San Juan Capistrano and this facility is beautiful!" As usual, Eileen is carefully dressed with matching accessories and perfect makeup.

"I like it too," Holly says, suddenly aware of the dust on her jodhpurs and the grease stain on the cuff of her sweatshirt. "I only wish they hadn't moved it to early April. It is chilly out here. The woman on the weather channel said it would only get to the low sixties today."

Eileen moves to the door of Spy Master's stall and looks in. "How's our boy?"

Holly joins Eileen and watches the stallion calmly munching hay. "He's good. He trailered fine and he acts like he feels fine. I'm going to leave him alone as long as I can. He is in the last class of the day so it won't happen until nearly six."

"I hope he stays healthy." Eileen is clearly nervous about her horse and his previous bouts with colic.

"Me too. I feel good about it, though." Since coming home from the disastrous trip to Kansas City, Spy Master hasn't left the barn. "He has been working really well and today's show is a good opportunity to find out if we can take him somewhere without him getting a belly ache. Today's a big day for him. He's debuting as an Open Horse."

"Five years old, and finally in the big leagues." Eileen pulls a peppermint from her bag and Spy Master looks up and his ears prick forward when he hears the rustle of cellophane. "You still agree that we're taking him home tonight even if he wins, right?"

"Absolutely. We decided that we'd only show him in this one class and skip Sunday's Championship, regardless of how he does in

144

this afternoon's qualifier. I don't see any reason to change our plan, and we'll all feel better if he's sleeping in his own stall. I can watch him more carefully there. Dr. Simon assures me that he's fine and we can quit treating him with kid gloves, but my heart can't take another scare like the one he gave us last fall." After a moment, Holly continues, "That's the big reason that I didn't bring more horses today. I didn't want to be distracted from focusing on your boy."

Eileen opens the door of his stall and offers her horse the peppermint. As he gently takes it from her palm, she pats his neck with her other hand. "I appreciate that. I don't think my heart could take it either. If this goes well, we can talk about the next step. Maybe I'll be brave enough to try an overnight show." She pauses as the loud speaker hisses and then the ring announcer calls the next class to the ring. "I think I'll go watch a bit of the show. I know someone that is showing her Friesian horse here and I just love seeing those big, black horses move. I can't believe how graceful they are. That's what I love about our shows out here in the West. You get to see different breeds and styles of riding. Kentucky shows seem to be just full of Saddlebreds with a few ponies here and there."

Holly agrees, "True enough. Go enjoy yourself and we'll see you later. I think I'm just going to stay close to our boy."

Holly watches Eileen leave, marveling at how graceful and elegant her client looks. She glances down at her dusty jods and tries to brush them off before shrugging and returning to her chair. She has at least three hours to kill so she picks up the most recent copy of *Saddle & Bridle* and starts paging through the advertisements to try to get an early assessment of who the top Five-Gaited Stake Horses are likely to be this season.

Two hours later, Holly has seen every advertisement in the magazine at least twice although she hasn't retained anything she has seen. She finally gets up and makes eye contact with Spy Master's groom. "Let's get him in the cross ties and start getting him ready." She knows she is a little early, but she is anxious to get going. She won't know for sure how he feels until she is mounted, and she is anxious to reassure herself that the colic episodes of last fall are behind them. The show ring is large, the weather is cool, the ground is in perfect condition and there will only be four horses in her class. All these elements are perfect for Spy Master.

Holly, picks up a trot and guides her horse into the ring when the ring announcer calls Spy Master's class. She knows in the middle of the first pass that her horse is on his game. His head is up, he is focused on the end of the ring, and he feels soft in her hands. As they both settle into the ride and she guides him around the ring, he is responsive and athletic and he gets stronger as the class proceeds. When he makes his final pass, he shifts his body into a completely new gear. He strides out confidently, with his head up and his four white feet flashing.

It doesn't surprise anyone watching when Spy Master is announced as the winner. As Holly accepts the ribbon, she breathes a big sigh of relief, and smiles broadly as the photographer records her and Spy Master posing with the ribbon.

By the time Eileen has made her way back to Spy Master's stall, Holly has changed back into her work clothes and is toweling the horse off. "He was stunning. He had that won from the very first pass. I don't think I've ever seen him that good. Not even in Louisville last year." Eileen's typically composed exterior has been replaced with a giddy happiness and she comes over to hug Holly. "Well done!"

Holly returns the hug and then steps back. "Watch out! I'm covered in sweat."

Eileen hugs her again. "I don't care. You were amazing out there!"

Holly goes back to toweling Spy Master as the groom combs and braids his tail. "He was incredible. I'm so pleased. Every time I asked him for more, he was right there for me. Your horse was a superstar out there."

Eileen begins to speak but is interrupted by friends and acquaintances stopping by the stall to offer their congratulations and Holly takes advantage of the opportunity to make sure Spy Master is clean and comfortable.

By the time the well-wishers have all moved on, the horse is completely cool and dry. Holly leaves the stall as the groom begins to wrap the horse's legs in protective bandages for the ride home. "I think Spy Master just erased all my doubts about whether he wants to be a Show Horse."

"Mine too. I know he's young, but he put on a clinic in there today. I would like to get back to Louisville at the end of August and show those people in Kentucky that Spy Master is all grown up and is ready to be a top notch Open horse." Eileen's eyes narrow slightly. "I'd like nothing more than to kick some butt back there."

Holly makes eye contact with her client. "A lot can happen between now and late August, but today was a good start. Why don't you come by the barn sometime this week and we'll talk about what you want to do for the rest of the season?

"Yes. It is hard not be euphoric right now, but let's make sure he gets through the next couple of days without any signs of colic before I get too far ahead of myself."

They make plans to meet later in the week and Eileen joins the groups of people heading to the parking lot. As Holly and her groom begin packing their tack, her cell phone rings and the display shows that it is Kenny Rivers. She answers happily. "Hey there!"

Kenny begins talking immediately. "Wow. You dominated that class! Everyone else was riding for second place from your first pass on!"

Holly laughs. "I won't lie. It was fun!"

"Well, it certainly was fun to watch, even though the live feed wasn't great. You're going to be the talk of the industry with that ride."

As she talks, Holly keeps an anxious eye on the young stallion but he seems completely oblivious to her anxiety. He nibbles on hay and takes a deep drink of water as he patiently stands in his stall, waiting to be loaded on the trailer for the short ride back to the barn. "Thanks, Kenny. I couldn't be happier with him. But as you know, I won't relax until we get through tonight and maybe tomorrow without colicking."

"Yes, I know you're nervous about that, but I imagine that's all behind you. When they rolled him at the clinic in Kansas City, they probably fixed that problem for good."

"I hope you're right." Abruptly switching topics, she asks, "How are you? How's the collar bone?"

147

"Everything's good. I have to run, but I'll call you later to catch up."

After quick goodbyes, Holly resolves to get her friend to tell her more about how he's doing the next time they talk.

CHAPTER 37

Missy Phillips leans on the rail at the JD Massey Classic Horse Show in Pendleton, SC, trying to keep her nerves under control. Tonight, she debuts Josie in the highly competitive Amateur Class. Their last few practice rides have gone really well and even Annie, her perfectionist trainer, has seem pleased. After working with her for the past few months, Missy now takes Annie's incessant criticism less personally and especially values the rare compliments. She takes a deep breath and glances at her watch one more time before deciding she'd rather be down near Josie's stall than up here pretending to watch the show.

The stall area for Annie's Big View Farm is buzzing with activity. Annie has brought 12 horses to the show, and several are showing in this evening's performance. Missy's class is the last one of the night, so she sits in one of the chairs to stay out of the way of Annie's other riders and makes small talk with the parents of the 14-year-old who is showing next.

After complimenting them on how calm and confident their daughter appears, Missy asks, "Have you been with Annie long?"

"Oh yes." They both say at once. The woman continues, "We've been with Annie since Emily started riding. It's been about nine years now."

"Well, no wonder she looks so calm." Missy watches as Annie gives Emily last minute instructions on ring management strategies while the young girl listens attentively and nods.

"She may look calm, but it's a façade," Emily's dad says. "She has learned to disguise her nerves pretty well. A lot of that is due to Annie's training. You probably know yourself that Annie expects perfection and professionalism."

"Yes, it has taken some adjustment for me. I've never ridden with anyone that was so demanding. But I believe it will pay off." Missy smiles slightly, "At least I hope it will. We'll find out tonight."

Emily is now mounted and heads towards the warm-up ring with Annie and two grooms. Her parents stand up to trail after them while everyone remaining in the barn area shouts their good wishes at the departing rider.

Missy goes into the dressing room to finish putting on her suit and hat and to put the final touches on her makeup. By the time she is finished, Emily, Annie and a large celebratory group is returning from the ring. Emily's horse has a first place ribbon attached to its bridle and the girl is wearing a huge smile. She dismounts and Missy hears Annie say "While the ride is fresh in your mind, let's talk about that second canter transition." Missy smiles to herself, amused to see that Annie's intense coaching style continues even when the ride has obviously gone well.

As soon as Annie has finished coaching Emily, she motions at Missy and walks towards Josie's stall. "Okay. Let's talk about your ride and what you need to accomplish."

Missy adopts the posture that she observed with Emily, standing quietly and nodding as Annie talks through the class.

"Going the first direction, your goal is to get every gait and get a feel for how Josie is in the ring. She's going to be a much different horse from the one that you've been riding at the barn. She has gears you haven't seen before and she's going to show them all to you tonight. By the time you turn around and start the second direction, you need to be 'in it to win it'. That's when you need to step it up and show the judge that you want to beat somebody. I want you off the rail with nothing between you and the judge on every pass. On the final pass, you need to be smart. Make sure you are by yourself and I want you to rack that mare as fast as she'll go. Go right past the judge. I want you to make his eyes water. Don't get distracted by anything. Don't lose your focus for a single step, or she'll break a gait. Stay thinking about what's in front of you no matter what happens. You can outride anyone in the ring. Just keep your brain turned on through the entire ride." By the time Annie is done, Missy is focused and determined.

Within minutes, Missy is mounted and Annie is holding Josie by the bridle, leading them to the warm-up area and talking through what she needs to accomplish in the warm-up. "We're going to do a park trot until I can see her loosen up. Then I'll have you come into the center of the warm-up ring and we'll talk about it. After that, we'll

150

slow gait one time around the ring each direction. Keep watching out for traffic."

Missy nods, happy that her trainer is so explicit about how she expects the warm-up to progress. Once they enter the practice ring, Annie releases her gentle hold on Josie and tells Missy, "Now just a nice park trot. Not too fast. Give her a minute to adjust."

Missy nods, says "Whup. Trot" to Josie and begins posting as the mare steps off. Josie is steady, with her ears up as she starts to gain speed.

Missy hears Annie yell "No faster. Keep your hands steady but play with the bit a little to soften her mouth. Get a conversation going." Annie keeps up a steady stream of instructions, and Missy starts to relax, recognizing the terms Annie is using from her sessions at the barn. By the time the warm-up session is over, Missy's nerves are gone. Annie gives her a few final instructions, ending with "Go kick some ass."

The gate is now open and the other riders are streaming into the ring. Missy takes one last deep breath, deliberately relaxing her shoulders and hands, and enters the ring. As she makes her first pass, she can hear Josie's hoofs pounding the dirt and the sounds of the organ and announcer fade into the background as she focuses on Josie. Her mare is animated and is quickly gaining speed on the horses around her. As Missy finishes her first circuit of the ring, she can hear Annie on the rail yelling, "Slow your post. You're going too fast. Use your snaffle and slow her down."

Missy grits her teeth as she tries to slow Josie, feeling like she is riding a freight train accelerating on a downhill track. She intentionally slows her posting to lag Josie's strides by a fraction of a second, and Josie responds by coming back into her hands just slightly. The next time Missy sweeps by Annie, she hears "Good. Keep your snaffle short. Shorter!"

Missy hurries to shorten her snaffle rein and hears the announcer call for the horses to walk. In the Amateur Class of the Five-Gaited Division, horses aren't required to flat walk, but they are expected to behave well during transitions. Missy lets Josie finish her pass and then tells her, "Whoa." As Josie jogs around the rail at the end of the ring, Missy thinks about the next gait. When the announcer tells the horse to slow gait, Missy separates her hands, subtly rocks them back and forth, and clucks once to signal Josie that she needs to slow gait. Josie responds immediately and begins a true four-beat gait without hesitation. Missy leans her upper body slightly forward to stay with her horse and keeps rocking her hands back and forth focusing on keeping her horse as slow as possible.

As she sweeps by Annie again, she hears her trainer coaching from the rail. "Keep working at it. Stay with her. Stay slow."

That's all Missy can hear before she is past Annie and out of range. By the time the announcer asks for the rack, Missy just has to loosen her reins slightly for Josie to pick up speed. Missy has to maneuver the mare off the rail and towards the center of the ring, as Josie is moving much faster than most of the horses in the class and gaining speed with every stride. When they go by Annie on this pass, Missy can't hear a word and she isn't sure if it is because Annie ran out of words or if it is because her breathing and the sound of Josie's feet is drowning out all other sounds. The announcer finally calls for a walk, and Missy carefully aims to an empty spot on the rail so that she can collect herself and her horse for the first canter. This gait is causing her the most anxiety, as she knows that she'll need to be very deliberate about how she cues Josie in order to get it right. When the announcer tells the class to canter, it takes two tries for Missy, but Josie eventually takes the gait and gallops around the ring with her head low. Missy definitely hears Annie on this round as her trainer yells, "Top rein! Top rein! Shorten your snaffle. Lower your hands." Missy desperately tries to react as her horse continues to gain speed. She is relieved when the announcer finally tells the class to walk, and then to reverse and trot.

Going the second direction in the ring passes much like the first direction, just faster. Missy feels as though she is on the verge of losing control, as her horse gets more headstrong with each gait. By the time the announcer calls for the horses to line up, Missy is out of breath and exhausted. Despite her struggles, Missy grins and pats her sweat-soaked horse, knowing she has had a good ride. It only takes a moment for them to be announced as the winner. When Missy meets Annie in the winner's circle to receive her ribbon, Annie shares her smile and congratulates her.

"Good job. That's a good ride to build on."

Missy laughs, "Oh my gosh. That was the most amazing experience. She was twice the horse she is at the barn. What a thrill!"

True to form, Annie responds. "We have a lot to work on but it's a good start."

CHAPTER 38

Kenny is cleaning stalls when his phone rings on Monday morning. When the caller ID show it is Holly, he hesitates before answering. He's not really in the mood to talk about her success with Spy Master.

"Hey there! I thought you were going to call me back. How are you?" Holly's voice is bright and cheerful.

Kenny finds himself making excuses that are only partially true. "I'm great. Just real busy. You know what this time of the year is like."

"Are you all healed up? How's your collar bone?"

"It's good. I'm back to full speed. Got rid of the sling a couple of weeks ago. I still take a handful of Advil every day, but it's almost as good as new." While Kenny's statement is mostly true, he has been surprised at how painful it still is to raise his left arm. It is taking more time than he expected to get full use of it.

"Well, that's good to hear. How's your family?"

Kenny begins to relax as he tells her about Emily and Jeremy. He continues to avoid talking about his barn for several minutes, until she finally addresses it directly. "Are you going back to Kiplenan now that you've healed up?"

He takes a big breath and says, "No. They replaced me and Clark seems really happy with the new guy. I'm actually at a crossroads. I do have a job offer on the table but I'm not sure it's right for me."

"Really? What is it?"

"Johnnie Stuart called me last night. He's looking for an assistant. I told him I'd have to think about it. In fact, it's really ironic, but his previous assistant is the guy that has my job at Kiplenan."

When Kenny doesn't go on, Holly asks, "What's your hesitation?"

Kenny attempts to keep the annoyance from his voice. "It's obvious, isn't it? He has a reputation as an asshole. His ethics are questionable. Some say that he even drugs his horses. He treats his people like crap. Other than that..." He lets his voice trail off.

"Well. I don't know the guy at all, but let's say all that is true. You didn't tell him no right away so you must be considering it."

154

Kenny runs his hand through his hair. "I have to consider it. It would put bread on the table and he does have some good horses. I'd probably learn something. Even if it is what NOT to be like."

Holly laughs softly. "All true. What's the alternative?"

"I finally convinced Angela that I don't want to be a birthday party and summer camp barn, but she's right that there is a large market for beginner riders. I'm considering focusing on Academy riders."

The Academy Classes are where many riders begin their show career and is specifically designed for new riders of all ages to develop their skills before committing to the expense of owning their own horse. Many of these riders go on to purchase horses and transition to the Juvenile and Adult Amateur Classes.

"That's really interesting. I think Academy instructors have a unique opportunity to shape our industry. Heaven knows, we need new riders all the time. Who else is going to buy all these fancy horses we breed and train?" Holly goes on, "I think you'd be really good at that. You're patient with people. You're positive and optimistic. You get a lot of joy from helping young kids learn new stuff."

Kenny is happy that Holly is reacting positively to his idea. "Thanks. Yeah, being a dad has taught me a lot about how to make everyday stuff fun. And I really do like working with kids."

"Well it sounds to me like you've made up your mind."

"I guess maybe I have. I just don't want people to think I've sold out and that I'm not a real trainer." Kenny finally confesses to the real source of his hesitation and unhappiness.

"Are you kidding? It takes a great trainer to prepare and maintain a horse for a beginner. Most trainers will shy away from that."

Kenny quickly shifts the topic. "So how are you?"

"I was going to ask you a favor, but now I realize that it might not fit into your plan at all, so feel free to say no."

"What do you need?"

"Well, I've convinced Spy Master's owner that it would be good for him to get acclimated to Kentucky before Louisville. So she's agreed to let me take him back there for the Shelbyville show. I plan to drive him back there myself about July 15th. But I still have other

155

horses here, so I'd need to leave him there and fly back and forth from California to show him. I need someone I trust to keep him in condition and to keep him healthy when I'm not there. Obviously, I thought of you." She goes on, "You don't have to answer now, but we'd obviously pay for board and training. As you know, he's a stud, so I don't want to send him to anyone that I don't know really well. But he's well-behaved, so he'd be happy in a barn that had lots of kids to feed him treats."

Before she goes on, Kenny jumps in. "Are you kidding? I'd love to have him and I'm happy you asked. I think it's a great idea to bring him out a little early and I'll make sure he's happy here. Can you bring plenty of hay so we don't have to switch his feed?

For the remainder of the conversation they talk excitedly about Spy Master's needs. When they finally hang up, Kenny quickly dials Angela to give her the great news that they might have a new paying customer.

CHAPTER 39

4 PM May 11, Woodside CA

It is a cool, windy Sunday afternoon on the final day of the UPHA Chapter 1 Horse Show in Woodside CA. Holly's clients from Morning Star Barns have had a successful show, and Spy Master's Championship is the only class remaining for them. Holly and her grooms are repacking a harness into one of the tack trunks when Eileen arrives at the stalls.

"How's our boy?" As she asks about Spy Master, Eileen moves to his stall door and looks in. The chestnut horse is already groomed and in the cross ties. His ears are in perpetual motion and he is shifting his weight back and forth.

"He's been acting a little squirrely today," Holly answers. "I imagine that part of it is the weather. Wind always gets on a horse's nerves. I think he feels fine, though. He's eating and his manure is fine."

"Well, I'm looking forward to the championship, but I'll be glad when he's back home safe and sound." This is the first overnight show for the young stallion since the Royal and Eileen has been concerned all week that he will have a recurrence of colic.

Holly joins Eileen at Spy Master's stall door. "Me too. By the time we get out of here tonight, it will probably be almost six, though. So we won't be home until 1AM or so. I still haven't gotten used to the schedule on this show. If they had a lighted facility, we could have evening performances. I think that would make it possible to have the show in fewer days and make it a bit easier on everyone."

"True. At least it has been cool this year. Remember a couple of years ago when it was 90 degrees and windy? We were out here baking in the sun and dealing with clouds of dust. I don't think any horse put on a good show."

"I do remember that. We had some young horses that we didn't even put in the ring because they were so over-stressed by the heat and wind. That was really disappointing." Holly smiles at her client. "We don't have to worry about that this year. I think Spy Master is going to have plenty of energy today."

157

Eileen turns her attention back to today's performance. "How many horses are in his class?"

"Six. It's just the right number. Too many more than that and it gets a little like a demolition derby. But I'm glad there aren't fewer because he will benefit from learning to deal with traffic. This competition is exactly what we were hoping for."

There are about three months left before the Louisville Show and Holly and Eileen have spent many hours strategizing about which shows to attend. Since deciding to move Spy Master to a Kentucky-based barn about a month before Louisville, they've carefully selected locations and classes to give him the experience he needs. As the summer progresses, the classes will get larger and more competitive. If all goes according to plan, by the time they are at Louisville, Spy Master will be used to large classes and a variety of environments so that he will be less distracted in the ring. Holly glances at the schedule that is taped to the tack room door as the loud speaker crackles and another class is announced. She then makes eye contact with her lead groom and motions at Spy Master's stall. "That's our cue. Time to get him saddled up."

"Well, I'm going to wander down to the ring. Have a great ride." Eileen gives a little wave as she turns to walk towards the ring.

Holly doesn't respond, as she is already busy inspecting each piece of equipment that the groom is bringing out of the tack room.

Holly's warm-up is tense, as Spy Master is distracted and skittish. She sits deep in the saddle, applies a stronger leg, and uses her hands to work the bit in his mouth so that he stays focused on her. She hangs back and intentionally enters the ring last so that he will have another horse to follow. As she enters, she can feel him tense up and he breaks into a canter. She firmly says "Whup, trot" but it still takes three full strides before she has him back into a trot. She continues her first pass, talking to him softly. "Whup, whup, easy, whup," and she manages to keep him trotting down the rail. He continues to be skittish, trying to move sideways as he passes a sign that is flapping in the wind. By the time the announcer has asked the horses to walk, he has already worked up a nervous sweat. She lets him jog down the rail before gathering him up for the slow gait. She decides to move him off the rail to avoid the flapping signs and jackets and almost

158

immediately feels him relax and focus. Her slow gait is much faster than she'd like, and when the announcer tells the riders to rack, she waits until she is approaching the judge before she asks him for more speed. He responds by stepping up, but she feels him lose some of the evenness of his stride. She quietly says "Easy boy," and squeezes him with her thighs and seat to get him refocused.

As the ride continues, Spy Master relaxes and improves. By the time the horses are finishing the gaits the second direction, Holly can tell that he is out-performing the other horses in the ring and hopes that her strong finish will convince the judge to overlook some of her early mistakes.

As they wait in the lineup, she looks at the horses around her. All of them are seasoned campaigners and she knows that Spy Master is by far the youngest and least experienced. She notices Eileen sitting near the rail and makes eye contact. She raises her eye brows and Eileen shrugs to show that she is uncertain how the judge will place her horse.

Finally, the announcer begins. "Ladies and gentlemen. First, please provide a round of applause for our Five-Gaited Stake Class." As the crowd claps, Spy Master dances toward the horse on his left, showing that he has plenty of energy left and causing Holly to nudge him ahead and make a small circle before returning to his place in line. Just as she says "whoa," she hears the announcer call her number. With an immense smile of relief, she slow gaits Spy Master up to receive her winning ribbon.

Holly tells Eileen later at the stalls, "We might have gotten away with one this time. I should have warmed him up more. I was worried that he wouldn't have enough energy but he came into the ring a little too hot."

Eileen laughs. "Well, I certainly won't complain about the result. He is still undefeated! I think his slow gait and rack the second direction was so much better than everyone else's that the judge had to give it to you. Of the six horses out there, three of them were pacing. I imagine it was rough enough to loosen a couple of the riders' teeth."

Holly smiles. "I could tell that because of the way the riders were bouncing when I passed them. But not every judge recognizes it when

159

a gaited horse paces instead of racks. And if they recognize it, they don't always penalize it. I'm glad we got a judge that cared about seeing a true rack."

Holly and Eileen continue discussing the difference between a pace and a rack. While they are both lateral gaits, a pace is a two-beat gait, in which the front and rear feet on the same side hit the ground at the same time. This gait is the correct gait for many harness racing Standardbreds, but it is a very rough gait to ride because the rider's body bounces in the saddle as the horse moves from side-to-side while going at top speed. But Saddlebreds are racking horses, in which the lateral gait is a four-beat gait, and each foot should hit the ground at separate times and in a rapid, regular rhythm. Properly done, it is an extremely smooth and comfortable gait to ride, as your body barely moves in the saddle.

"I agree. I'm glad this judge knew the difference and thought it was important that a horse in a racking class could actually do the gait properly." Eileen takes the winning ribbon from Holly and tucks it carefully in her bag while they briefly discuss Spy Master's training schedule for the upcoming week. Before departing, Eileen hugs Holly, "Please drive carefully with our precious cargo and let me know when you get back to the barn. Don't worry about how late it is. I won't be sleeping anyway and I probably won't be that far ahead of you."

"I'll do that, but I don't think you need to worry. I'll watch him in the camera and will stop and check on him every couple of hours but I don't think we're going to have any problems."

CHAPTER 40

It is Friday night at the Asheville Lions Club Horse Show, and Missy Phillips notices Johnnie Stuart watching the horses in the warm-up ring. She steps into the open spot next to him on the rail and says, "Why didn't you show me that bay horse when I was at your barn a few months ago?"

Johnnie has been focused on watching the horses and hadn't noticed her approach. "Well hello there! You like that one, do ya'll? Aw, he's just something I found in a back stall one day and decided to try."

Missy laughs. "Now you've just confirmed for me that you can tell a big fib without even blinking. Seriously, though. He looked great. You deserved the unanimous win. He dominated the other four-year-olds last night."

Johnnie thanks her and drops the false humility. "Night Train is a nice colt and he's had some big wins this year. I haven't seen another four-year-old in the country that can beat him."

"You own him, don't you?" Missy knows that Johnnie does, but she wants to give him a chance to keep talking about his horse.

"Yep. I do. Bred him myself." Johnnie goes on to describe Night Train's bloodlines and it is evident that he is very proud of his breeding program at Stuart Stables.

"Is he for sale?"

"Well, every horse is for sale I guess. It's just a matter of price. I think he's going to earn a pretty ribbon in Louisville in August so the price is going to have a lot of zeroes in it." He watches her reaction closely.

She fails to take his bait. "Well, good luck with the rest of the show. I'd better get ready for my class." Missy leaves the warm-up ring and heads back to where Big View Farm is stabled, faintly curious about Night Train's price.

When she arrives at Josie's stall, Annie is removing tack from one of the trunks in the aisle and Missy decides to ask her opinion of Night Train. "Hey Annie. Did you see the Junior Gaited Class last night?"

161

Annie pauses from her task and looks up. "I did. Johnnie Stuart won it easily."

"Yeah. What do you think of his horse?"

The horse is talented, no doubt. I don't think anyone has beaten him yet this year. I bet that horse can be a bit of an asshole, though. And it always looks to me like he's going to run out of gas before the end of the class. He looked good last night, but the ring was cool and the class was short. I don't think he'll look like that when he's outdoors on a hot afternoon."

"There are rumors that Johnnie is using drugs on him." Missy hesitates to say it but is curious about Annie's reaction.

"I wouldn't know about that, but if he is, he'll get caught. The tests they use get better all the time."

"So why does he run out of gas? Is it a conditioning problem?"

"It might be partly conditioning but it could be just how the horse is built. Do you notice how heavily he breathes going the second direction? He might not be getting enough air." Annie goes back to arranging the contents of the trunk as they talk.

"I've heard of some horses having surgery for that."

"Yes. It doesn't always work though, even if that is the problem. A vet would have to run a camera down the horse's throat to see if his airway has any obstructions. That might not even be a factor with that horse, though. It's hard to tell." Annie then changes the topic. "Are you ready for your ride?"

"Yes, but let's talk through the game plan. I don't want to get beat again." Missy and Josie placed a disappointing third in the qualifier earlier in the week.

"Right. It's an amateur class and the judges want a well-behaved horse. You need to clean up your transitions and she was going too fast on the trot. It looked like she was in control. Remember to slow your post down just slightly. When you ask for the canter, sit deep and be crystal clear about your cues. Keep your shoulders back over your hips. In the qualifier, you leaned forward and she didn't take the canter like she should have. With three judges in the ring, you can't make a single mistake. Somebody will always be watching you."

In another hour, Annie is standing next to Josie and Missy in the warm-up ring and the grooms are toweling the mare off to make sure

162

her coat is spotless. When they hear the bugle, Annie pats Missy's leg and says "Now, take control of this mare and take control of the ring. Have a good solid ride and make sure you keep thinking a few steps ahead of your horse. Now go win this thing!"

A little more than fifteen minutes later, Missy is collecting her second place ribbon and leaving the ring. Annie meets her at the out gate and says "Much better ride this time."

Missy tries to hide her disappointment and quietly says, "Yes. But I was hoping for a better result."

On the way back to the stalls several people congratulate her and she graciously accepts, barely wincing when Johnnie Stuart says, "That mare looked like a stake horse. I thought you had it won."

Missy smiles and thanks him, thinking to herself that he hit the nail on the head. After dismounting and patting her horse, Missy turns to Annie. "I wasn't ignoring you in the ring when you kept telling me to slow her down. Every time I took a stronger hold she resisted me. I couldn't figure out how to slow her and still keep her ears forward and her head up."

Annie can see that Missy is frustrated, so she softens her voice. "First of all, I thought you had a great ride. I'll be interested to see the judge's cards, but you were definitely in it. I think that at this show we happen to have judges that want a pretty, well-behaved, calm and collected amateur gaited horse. That isn't what we've got. We've got a gutsy, game, scrappy mare who out-racked every horse in that ring. I thought you had it won. You shouldn't get down on yourself or on Josie for that performance. I was really proud of your ride."

Missy hesitates and then brings up the issue that has been bothering her. "I love Josie and I believe in Josie. I just wonder if we're in the wrong class."

Annie looks at her sharply and replies, "She'll have a tougher time in the Ladies Class. Most top-tier ladies' horses are elegant and fine-boned. And your transitions would have to be very controlled."

"That's not what I mean. What would you think about moving her up to the Open Class?"

Missy's question takes Annie by surprise. The Open Class is the cream of the crop and very few amateur riders are skilled enough to contend. "Well, we know she got a ribbon in that class at Louisville last year, but she didn't win it. Are you looking for a win in Louisville? If so, I think you have a better chance in the Amateur Class. You won't always get judges like the ones we had this week."

Missy says, "Yes, true. But I can't help but feel that we're trying to jam a square peg in a round hole. Maybe we should consider it." She then quickly adds, "At least let's think about it."

Annie agrees to give the matter careful thought as she hangs the red ribbon on the tack room wall.

CHAPTER 41

Kenny is just finishing cleaning the final stall and Jeremy is helping by sweeping the aisle when Kenny hears Emily's excited voice. "Daddy! Jermy! Breakfas'!"

Jeremy makes eye contact with his dad and says, "How old do you think she'll be before she learns to say my name right?"

Kenny laughs. "Maybe never. She'll probably call you Jermy for your entire life."

By now Emily is at the door of the stall, jumping up and down. "Come eat! Come eat!"

Angela is standing behind her. "I made breakfast burritos. Come out to the picnic table." She catches Kenny's expression and says, "I know you're busy and it's a big day but you can take a ten-minute break."

The family eats hungrily and Angela says, "Two new customers today, right?"

"Yeah. One at 10:30 and one at 11:30" Kenny answers. "Plus, we have four regular customers and the two new ones from last week are coming back. So we have eight lessons today. It will be busy. Jeremy is going to groom for me. We're going to need another lesson horse or two, though, or I'll have to start turning people away. Everyone wants Saturday lessons, but school will be out soon and I'm hoping we can spread it out a bit. Maybe get people to go for two lessons a week instead of one."

"I bet we can do that. Especially if we make one of them a group lesson so that we can teach them how to maneuver around other horses in the ring." Angela goes on, "I got an email the other day from the Saddlebred Rescue place. They have some horses that look like they could be decent lesson horses. Do you want to call them?"

Jeremy looks up from his burrito and says, "That would be cool. We could get a horse that really needs a home."

Kenny says, "I'll call them. We'll have to be careful. It is hard to know what kinds of bad habits a horse might have if we don't really know its history." As he talks, he sees Angela's mouth tighten as he

165

criticizes her idea and he quickly adds, "But it is worth a call for sure. We're pretty much out of stalls. We need to save one for Spy Master."

"He doesn't show up until July, right?" When Kenny nods, Angela goes on. "By then, maybe we can fence in an outside paddock for lesson horses. They don't really need to be in box stalls, do they?"

"True, but they need a lot of shade and good water so they can get out of the weather."

Jeremy interrupts Kenny. "I can help build it. I think we should put it over by the big tree."

"That might work. I've been thinking that when you get out of school for the summer, we'll need to put you on the payroll. I'll need your help grooming and keeping this place looking good for our customers. Are you up for that? It will be hard work, and you'll have to do it every day." Kenny looks at his son and when Jeremy earnestly nods, he continues. "Mom and I will talk about what a fair wage will be, okay?"

Jeremy maintains his serious expression. "Will it be enough to buy a new bike?"

Angela smiles at her son. "I imagine it will. But you won't be able to sleep in all summer."

Jeremy quickly replies, "I don't like to sleep in anyway."

As they all continue to talk about where they might put the new corral and what kind of materials they will need, Kenny realizes that his enthusiasm is growing. It is fun to have new customers and for the whole family to work together. He had been worried that it wouldn't be challenging enough to work with older horses and while he is often frustrated by the short attention span of most of his young riders, he is enjoying the sense of accomplishment that is coming from growing the business. "We'd better hustle, Jeremy. Meghan will be here in 15 minutes. We need to have her horse ready to go."

CHAPTER 42

"Would you mind watching me work Vendome this morning? I want to make sure he's ready for Rock Creek and could sure use another set of eyes on him." It is the Saturday before the Rock Creek Horse Show and Bobby and Clark are using it as a dress rehearsal for the horses that are entered. Rock Creek is a significant show for Kiplenan as it has classes for young horses, and it is the first opportunity of the season to show the two- and three-year-olds.

Clark finishes adjusting the harness he is holding and replies. "Yeah. Let's do him next if you're ready."

Since becoming Clark's assistant in February when Mrs. M abruptly moved her horses from Johnnie Stuart's barn, they have developed a solid working relationship. Although Clark is clearly in charge, they often ask for each other's input on training issues. This week has been unusually tense, though. The Rock Creek Horse Show is in an affluent Louisville neighborhood and marks the beginning of the Kentucky Horse Show social season. Mr. Kiplenan invites his family and friends to attend and they usually occupy two boxes of seats at ringside. Bobby knows that he and Clark are under immense pressure to do well so that Mr. Kiplenan will be proud of his entries.

By the time Bobby has warmed up Vendome, Clark is standing in the center of the practice ring. As Bobby trots Vendome by him, Clark watches critically. "I'd step him up just a little."

Bobby hears Clark's suggestion and gently squeezes Vendome into a slightly faster trot.

On his next pass, Clark says, "That's it. That's good. That's where you want him."

Bobby concentrates on remembering the cadence Vendome has so that he can repeat it in the ring, and then moves on to the slow gait. While he can't put his finger on the issue, Bobby has had a vague uneasiness over Vendome's slow gait and rack for the past few weeks. Vendome does the gait as willingly as ever, but he occasionally slips out of the steady four-beat rhythm Bobby wants. He makes two or three passes, and Clark whistles sharply to get

167

Vendome's attention as he comes out of the turn and begins his next pass. Clark watches Vendome carefully as he goes by.

When Bobby reaches the end of the ring he halts Vendome, looks at Clark and says, "I can't put my finger on it, but he's not quite right."

Clark doesn't hesitate. "I agree. It's his right hind. He's not setting that foot down as flat as he should. It mostly shows up on the turns."

While Bobby is grateful for Clark's diagnosis, he is dismayed that the imperfection has appeared so close to the horse show. "Do you think it is too close to Rock Creek to change his hind shoes?"

"Well, the corners in that ring aren't as tight as the ones here so it might not show up too much, but I think I'd try to fix it. The farrier is coming out on Monday anyway. He's got a great eye. If I were you, I'd let him watch Vendome slow gait. He'll know how to fix it." Clark says reassuringly.

"Did you see anything else I need to fix?"

Clark smiles slightly. "Nope. He looks good at the trot. I'd just keep his speed up. The competition will be stiff and he'll need to be bright to catch the judge's eye."

"Yeah. I agree." Bobby dismounts as he talks and hands Vendome's reins to a waiting groom. "I'm sure Johnnie Stuart will have Night Train there. Did you see that he won Asheville?"

"I did see that. But you beat him in Indy last fall."

"And he beat me in Kansas City." Bobby pauses and then continues. "I admit that I'd get a lot of satisfaction from kicking his butt."

Clark smiles. "You'll have to get in line. I think almost everyone I know would like to kick that jerk's butt. From what I hear, you might get a little help from the weather. Next week is supposed to be hot and that horse just might run out of gas."

"He's a lucky man, though. When that happened in Kansas City, a horse in our class threw a shoe. Night Train got the time he needed to catch his breath and went on to win." Bobby shakes his head and says, "My luck always tends to run the other direction."

As one of the grooms leads a harness horse into the ring, Clark moves forward to attach the horse's harness to the jog cart. As he works, Clark continues talking about Johnnie. "Well, I'd like to think that what goes around comes around."

Bobby smiles. "I hope you're right. I admit that winning next Wednesday is less important to me than beating Johnnie. I'd rather be next to last and have Johnnie end up last than be second place and have him win it."

"I understand, but Mrs. M probably wouldn't agree." Clark goes on to ask, "When is she coming to town, do you know?"

"Yes. She called last night. She'll be at the show on Wednesday. Mr. Kiplenan invited her to sit in his box."

Clark gets in the cart and clucks at his harness horse to get him to walk off. "Well, let's do our best to give them plenty to cheer about."

CHAPTER 43

"Make sure you stay close to the gate. If I call a time-out, I want you to come in on the run. If I tell you to adjust the curb, just act like you're adjusting it. Leave it where it is, no matter what I say. Understand?" When his groom nods, Johnnie Stuart mounts Night Train and jogs toward the warm-up area for the Junior Five-Gaited Class at the Rock Creek Horse Show. It is a warm and humid Kentucky night, and the heat has been a factor all week. He knows this will be a competitive class and he doesn't want Night Train to run out of energy, so he keeps his warm-up short and tries to keep his horse calm and quiet. Despite his efforts, his horse is soon agitated and sweating.

Over the past few days, Johnnie Stuart has walked through the stall areas several times to find out how many four-year-old five-gaited horses will be competing. As he expected, there are eight horses entered in Night Train's class, including Vendome Copper. Several of the others are unfamiliar to Johnnie, but he has made a point to watch them while they were being worked by their trainers throughout the week and he is confident that Night Train is the best horse in the class. His primary concern is with the judge, an equitation instructor from the West coast. The previous night was the opening night of the show, and it quickly became obvious that she was being extremely strict about behavior, even in the performance classes for young horses where behavior should be a smaller element of the total score than in equitation or pleasure classes. She also was slow to make up her mind and the classes ran very long. This gives Johnnie ample reason for concern. In addition to worrying that she will penalize Night Train for his aggressive attitude and his rough transitions, he is also worried that Night Train might tire before the end of the ride, so he has developed several strategies to mask these issues.

When the announcer calls for the horses to enter, Johnnie loiters and waits until the last possible moment to enter, noticing that Bobby Acton and Vendome are already in the ring. He hasn't seen Bobby since late December when he dismissed him from Stuart Stables, but

170

he knows that Bobby is now the assistant at Kiplenan and that several of Mrs. M's horses are there now as well. He blames Bobby for Mrs. M's removal of her horses from his barn and suspects Bobby of bad-mouthing him to her and others. This makes him even more determined to win.

As he enters the ring, he quickly focuses on putting the strategies he has planned into action. As he expects, Night Train builds up speed and power with every step. As he works his young bay stallion around the ring, he stays on the rail and away from the other horses as much as he can, making sure he keeps his horse deep in the corners so that the judge will be less likely to notice how much faster he is going than the others. He has noticed that this judge tends to make the horses trot at least three full rounds of the ring before she calls for the walk. He has also noticed that she won't call for the slow gait until she has seen that every horse in the ring has attempted to walk, and she appears to penalize any horse that just stops on the rail and waits for the next gait. Johnnie knows that Night Train won't walk and is likely to get more agitated and jumpy the longer he has to wait to begin slow gaiting. So, when he hears the announcer tell the class to walk, he begins another trotting pass with Night Train so that there will be less time for his horse to get agitated between the trot and slow gait. When he finally pulls Night Train to a stop, he glances over his shoulder at the judge. She has her back to him, so he halts Night Train, keeping his eye on the judge. When she turns her head towards him, he releases Night Train slightly, and his horse jogs down the rail a few feet before Johnnie halts him again, making sure he stays behind the judge so that she is less likely to see his next transition.

Once the announcer calls for the slow gait, Johnnie takes another glance to make sure her back is turned, spreads his hands wide and clucks at Night Train. Night Train leaps into the slow gait. As the class continues through the rack and then the canter, Night Train performs well and but he feels his horse beginning to tire. When the announcer calls for the reverse, Johnnie trots Night Train to the center of the ring and pulls him to a stop, waiting for the judge to acknowledge him.

As soon as the steward starts to approach, Johnnie says "My curb chain needs adjustment." The steward motions to the announcer that a time-out has been called. His groom jogs into the ring with a towel in his hand. Johnnie stays mounted, and his groom goes through the motions of adjusting the bridle. Johnnie knows that he is allotted a full five minutes for the time-out so he motions the groom to towel off Night Train's neck, taking maximum advantage of the break.

Once the class is complete and the four-year-olds have lined up to wait for the awards, Johnnie takes a moment to look at his competitors. Several horses away, Bobby is smiling, apparently happy with Vendome's performance. Johnnie experiences a momentary flicker of doubt, but it is quickly replaced by satisfaction when he is announced as the winner. As he accepts the first place ribbon, he hears the announcement that Vendome Copper has received second place.

His friend Dave Snell is one of the first people to arrive at his stalls to congratulate him. "You have that horse firing on all cylinders! That's the best gaited horse I've seen at the show, so far. I bet he could win the Stake Class on Saturday night!"

Johnnie smiles at his friend. "Thanks, man. He's working real good for me."

Dave continues "So how about it? Are you going to bring him back for the Championship on Saturday Night to show everyone how it's done?"

Johnnie acts as though he hadn't considered it, despite the fact that it is already his intent. "Well, I don't know. It's only a couple of days away and that's a darn big ask of a four-year-old. I'm awful glad ya'll like my horse and I just might have to think about giving him a chance on Saturday."

At the next barn over, the grooms are busy cooling Vendome when Mrs. M and Mr. Kiplenan arrive at the stalls. As they approach, Clark and Bobby are discussing the ride. Clark says, "I thought you had a good chance to win that, but that horse of Johnnie Stuart's came on strong after that time-out. That short break saved him."

"Damn, I'm disappointed," Bobby replies. "Vendome had a good go. We had a small problem with that first canter because we got trapped behind that one that couldn't get his lead right, but other than that I thought Vendome was good."

Mrs. M chimes in, "He was good. I am pretty surprised the judge didn't give him the win. I'm satisfied, though. It was a very tough class."

Mr. Kiplenan nods in agreement. "I thought any of the top four could have won. This year's crop of four-year-olds is exceptional. I also think that Vendome was the most mature of them out there. His trot and slow gait were exceptional."

Bobby smiles. "Thank you, sir. I actually have Clark to thank for that. We adjusted Vendome's shoes a little on Monday and it made a world of difference. He felt as even as a metronome."

Mrs. M then acknowledges their disappointment with a small laugh. "Usually I don't mind getting beat by a good horse, but I just wish it wasn't Johnnie Stuart's. That time-out was a little too obvious, don't you think?"

Clark shrugs and says, "He'll use every weapon at his disposal. If that horse doesn't gain some stamina though, he'll never make it through a workout." Clark is referring to the extra gaits that judges can request of the top few horses when they are having difficulty making up their mind. All horses the judge selects to participate in the workout must be worked both ways of the ring at whatever gaits the judge chooses. Workouts are common at larger shows and at the World Championship.

"Well, he's only four. Maybe his stamina will improve as he matures." Mr. Kiplenan then goes on, "Most of the traffic should have cleared on by now, so I'm going home. I'll see you all tomorrow."

"Don't worry, Bobby. We'll get Johnnie the next time." Mrs. M turns to follow her host.

CHAPTER 44

2:30 PM June 5, Rock Creek Horse Show, Louisville, KY

"I still don't understand why you aren't showing him this week." Jennifer can hear Marianne's voice, even though she and Blair are still several yards away. Blair's reply is inaudible, but Jennifer has heard various versions of this conversation a dozen times over the past few months and she can easily anticipate Blair's response. She expects it will include a subtle eye roll, a long sigh, and then a plea for her mother to be patient.

Blair has been riding Toreador weekly for more than three months at Beech Tree under the watchful eyes of Jennifer and Eduardo. The trainers have been careful to let Blair determine the pace at which she progresses, encouraging her during each session without pressuring her. As a result, Blair's progress has been slow.

Once Marianne learned Blair was riding the horse, she insisted that Rock Creek would be the perfect venue to debut him. Although she has been careful not to disagree with Marianne directly, Jennifer assured Blair they wouldn't enter a show until Blair felt completely prepared, and the two of them had spent most of the spring deflecting Marianne's suggestions.

As the Rock Creek show approached, Blair and Jennifer agreed that they were not yet ready to enter but had reached a compromise with Marianne when Blair agreed to ride Toreador in the ring during the afternoon practice sessions, when few people would be around to watch. This would give Blair an opportunity to experience how Toreador might perform in a show ring environment and to measure how close they might be to competing. They have chosen today for their ride and Jennifer and Eduardo are in Toreador's stall, preparing him. Jennifer steps out to greet their clients. "Hi there. Your timing is perfect. He's ready to go."

Marianne turns her attention to Jennifer. "I still don't understand why Blair isn't showing him here. I think you are all underestimating her. I watched the Amateur Class last night and Toreador would have wiped them out. It isn't at all clear to me why we're doing this today."

Jennifer glances at Blair who is busily adjusting her gloves and doesn't meet her eyes. "I think it will pay off to be a little patient. We want every show ring experience to be a good one for Blair and Toreador. Our goal today is to give Blair a chance to get used to how he will behave when he's away from home."

At thirty years old, it amazes Jennifer that Blair is still intimidated by her overbearing mother. Blair's posture is that of a small, timid child and Jennifer immediately wonders whether this ride is a good idea. Blair needs to sit up and take charge of Toreador or he is likely to take advantage of her. While she and Eduardo had previously decided that Blair should get on him at the stalls and they would all walk up to the ring together, Jennifer is now wondering whether she should ride him herself first so that she can remind him that he needs to respect his rider.

"We've just got a few adjustments to make so I'm going to help Eduardo. We'll be ready in a minute or two." Jennifer ducks back into Toreador's stall, where Eduardo is making sure the horse's snaffle training bridle and martingale are adjusted properly.

She notices that he looks tired and disheveled today and that he is moving slower than usual, but she pushes her concern to the back of her mind. "Blair looks like a scared puppy out there. Toreador will take about a millisecond to figure out that she isn't going to take charge and this could be a very bad idea."

Eduardo shrugs. "Yeah, but we have to find out sooner or later."

"I'm thinking that maybe I should ride him first. That will give her a chance to chicken out if he turns on his Stake Horse attitude out there."

Eduardo shakes his head. "If you get on him first, he will be warm before she starts. He gets faster and stronger the longer he goes. We should put her on when he is cold and pull her off before he gets going too fast."

Jennifer considers a moment and then steps back into the aisle. "Well Blair, let's talk about our game plan." Jennifer maneuvers so that Blair has to turn away from her mother to make eye contact with her trainer. "We're going to put you on him here in the aisle. Remember to be quick about getting up. He only has a snaffle on, so get a good, tight grip on the reins as soon as you can. Eduardo and I will have a hold of him, so don't worry about anything. Sit up straight, and get your heels down. Sit deep." She waits for Blair to

175

nod before going on. "We're going to walk you up to the show ring. He's likely to be excited about this. He hasn't been near a show since last year's Championship, so he's going to be a lot of horse. But just act like you do back at the barn. Sit up tall and take control." Blair looks nervous but Jennifer has her full attention so she keeps talking. "Once we get to the ring, he'll probably be very edgy, so we'll just have you trot around the ring once or twice. Stay on the rail and don't get going too fast. Once you go around once or twice, we'll have you come to the middle and stop. Eduardo and I will both be in the middle. Do you have any questions?"

Blair is very tense. "Are there many people around?"

"We just trailered him in a couple of hours ago and I don't think anyone even knows that he's here. We've deliberately picked a quiet time. It is really hot out, so no one else is working horses, and there isn't really anyone around. The heat will also keep Toreador's energy tamped down a bit." She then changes her tone, trying to impart a confidence that she doesn't really have. "Your rides at the barn have been going well. Just ride here like you do there."

Marianne says, "I think you are too concerned about Blair's ability. She is a beautiful rider and I still don't understand why you're so hesitant to show everyone what we have."

Jennifer politely but firmly interrupts. "We just want to do this right. Blair and Toreador are going to be a pair for many years. It will pay off to be patient and get started on the right foot." She glances at Blair. "Are you ready to do this?"

Blair meets her eyes and says tentatively, "I think so."

This is not the confident response that Jennifer wants, but she nods at Eduardo and says, "Let's do this."

Eduardo carefully leads Toreador from the stall. The instant the spectacular chestnut gelding gets out of his stall and into the aisle, his head comes up and he poses as if to say, "Hey everyone. I've arrived."

With the help of Eduardo and two grooms, Blair mounts without incident. Jennifer continues talking to her as she grips the left side of Toreador's bridle and Eduardo takes the right side. They both remain very close to the horse as they lead him up the aisle. Eduardo focuses on talking to Toreador in a low, calm voice while Jennifer focuses on her rider.

"See? No big deal." Jennifer looks up at Blair who is looking down at her reins, as she shortens them and laces them through her fingers. "That's it. Good job." Jennifer keeps up a running commentary. "Just relax a little but keep a good hold on him. Make sure he doesn't get those reins away from you. We're going to do this just like at the barn."

As she talks, Jennifer is encouraged as Blair's shoulders relax slightly. She keeps talking. "Now, we're going to walk out the back door of the barn, walk up the back side of the ring where it is nice and quiet, and head towards the gate." She pauses again and looks at Blair's face, "Ready?"

Blair nods again, still not saying anything.

They all move towards the back door of the barn, making a small parade with Jennifer and Eduardo leading Toreador, followed by two grooms carrying towels, and then by Marianne. As soon as Toreador steps out of the barn, Jennifer and Eduardo allow him to pause. He again lifts his head and looks at the scene in front of him. The horse exhales loudly, with a "poof" of air announcing his excitement.

It is quiet in the ring, just as Jennifer hoped. There are a few individuals working in the barn area they just left and there are a few more under the large tent housing more than 100 temporary stalls that is adjacent to the show ring, but the ring is empty.

They slowly lead Toreador into the center of the ring and Jennifer scrutinizes Blair as Eduardo checks the horse's equipment once more. "Okay. When I tell you to trot, just steer him out to the rail and do a nice, slow, park trot. Keep a real good hold on him." For the final time, she asks her rider, "Ready?"

Blair nods and Jennifer motions at Eduardo to step back. Jennifer retains her hold on the horse and leads him a step towards the rail before releasing him. "Okay. Now just go slow."

Despite all their preparation, Blair immediately flinches when she realizes that Jennifer no longer holds Toreador. Toreador feels the sudden tightening in her legs and seat and leaps forward toward the rail. Jennifer yells, "Whup, TROT!" at the horse and he begins a very fast, animated trot and barrels down the rail. Blair tries to post, but the energy in his hind legs and hocks throw her up towards the front of her saddle. She stays in the saddle but is obviously unbalanced as her heels come up and she struggles to get control.

Jennifer tries to keep the urgency and worry from her voice as she yells commands to help Blair get control. "Shorten the snaffle. Talk to him. Take a hold of him, Blair!" She and Eduardo move out towards the rail so that they will be in a position to intercept the horse as he comes around, if necessary.

As the horse and rider continue around the ring, the situation doesn't improve. Blair's hands bounce and the rein remains loose. The big show horse takes advantage of this freedom and his speed and energy increase with each step. Before he has completed an entire circuit of the ring, Eduardo and Jennifer both yell, "WHOA!" and move closer towards the rail to help Blair slow the horse.

"Blair! Stop him. Tell him 'whoa' and sit down. Use your reins." Although Jennifer is focusing on the horse, she glances at Blair's face. The young woman's eyes are wide and her mouth is frozen open. She looks terrified. Jennifer immediately realizes that this ride is a terrible idea and that it is unsafe for Blair to continue. Fortunately, Toreador is listening better than his rider and he halts on the rail. Jennifer and Eduardo quickly move forward and grasp his bit so that he is under control.

Jennifer looks up at her rider. "Are you okay?"

"I want to get off." Blair is still looking straight ahead, but Jennifer can see tears forming in the woman's large eyes.

"Absolutely. Let's just walk him to the center of the ring. You can get off and I'll get on." She pauses. "Okay?"

Blair nods, so she and Eduardo lead Toreador to the center of the ring. Jennifer helps Blair dismount and Eduardo continues talking softly and calmly to the horse. Blair steps back and Jennifer moves into position to mount. As she picks up the reins, movement outside of the ring catches her eye and she sees Johnnie Stuart and Dave Snell standing near the fence, watching intently.

Jennifer collects her reins and begins working Toreador at the trot, but he is agitated and fretful. He has had a small taste of freedom and it takes her several rounds of the ring to get him into a good frame and to get his respect. By that time, he is sweaty and clearly feeling the effects of the heat and humidity, so she ends the workout. Eduardo opens the gate and she rides the horse back to his stall, trying to quell her irritation with Blair at this significant setback.

Everyone is quiet back at the stabling area as Jennifer dismounts and Eduardo leads Toreador back into his stall. Jennifer takes a deep breath and turns to Blair.

Before she can speak, Blair begins to apologize. "I'm sorry. I know that was all my fault. I don't know what happened. I froze. I couldn't get control and I didn't know what to do." Blair's voice chokes up and she starts to cry.

Jennifer moves forward to hug her. "I know. He sensed it and it took him a fraction of a second to take advantage of it." She tries to comfort her rider and her anger and frustration melt away as she realizes how frightened Blair is.

Before she can go on, Marianne attacks. "This is all your fault, Jennifer. You clearly are not the trainer I thought you were. This horse is out of control and it is not at all clear to me what I've been paying you for."

Blair pulls away from Jennifer and turns angrily towards her mother. "Mother, stop it right now. This is not Jennifer's fault. It was my fault." As the tears roll down her face, she takes a deep breath and says, "This wasn't any fun at all. He scares me."

This admission is so sudden and stunning that Marianne and Jennifer both step backward. While Jennifer has always known that the horse intimidates Blair, it is shocking to hear a rider admit her fear.

Marianne recovers her voice first. "Don't be silly," she says brusquely. "This was NOT your fault. You are a beautiful rider." She points at Jennifer, "It is HER job to have the horse ready."

"I don't want to do this." Blair addresses this comment to her mother, but it is not immediately clear whether she means that she doesn't want to argue or that she doesn't want to ride Toreador. Jennifer retreats into Toreador's stall to give Blair and Marianne some privacy. She can hear their conversation clearly, though, as she helps the grooms towel off the gelding.

"He's a great horse. He's just not for me." Blair's voice is pleading as she tries to get her mother to understand. "He scares me."

179

She inhales a long, shaky breath. "I appreciate that you have big dreams for him and me, I really do. And I think you're right that he can win everything for an amateur. But he's not for me."

Marianne attempts to convince Blair to give it more time, but Blair is steadfast. After nearly five minutes of back and forth, Jennifer hears the conversation winding down and rejoins them. "Blair, I admire your courage. It is hard to say that something scares us. We're taught to just suck it up and pretend we aren't afraid. I really appreciate what you said and how difficult this is for you." Jennifer gives Blair another hug and then addresses Marianne. "I think we ought to take a little time to figure out our next move. Why don't we take him back to Beech Tree when he cools out? Then we can meet tomorrow to talk about what you want to do next. I'll have some specific suggestions ready."

Marianne quickly reacts and it is clear that she is still angry. "I don't know what there is to talk about. He needs to be sold."

"Okay. I can do that." Jennifer keeps her voice calm. "I'll put the word out right away."

Marianne abruptly turns on her heel and stalks away. Blair looks at Jennifer and shrugs. "I'll calm her down. Don't worry. And I'm sorry. I shouldn't have let it get this far." She turns to follow her mother.

Eduardo emerges from the stall and Jennifer attempts a joke. "Well, that went well."

"I think we just lost our client."

Jennifer nods. "We did. And I'm really disappointed. Toreador has come a really long way and I'm proud of what we accomplished. And all isn't lost. He's sound and he's talented. At least we'll make a commission when he sells."

"Yes, unless she takes him away before he sells."

Jennifer immediately realizes that Eduardo is right. Marianne certainly didn't hesitate to move him from Johnnie Stuart and she suddenly wonders if another trainer will show up before they load him in the trailer for his return to Beech Tree. At that moment, she sees Johnnie Stuart approaching.

He begins speaking when he is still 50 feet away. "If you beg me, I'll take him back." His voice is amused.

Jennifer's immediate thought is of relief as it is clear that Marianne has not told Johnnie to reclaim the horse. "Johnnie, you know that where Toreador goes isn't my decision. It wasn't my decision when he left your place and it isn't my decision now. Marianne will do whatever she wants. It's her horse." Jennifer masks her irritation by adopting a patient tone.

"I knew you couldn't handle him. Moving him was a big mistake." Johnnie pauses and then can't resist getting ugly. "Ya'll probably ruined him. I might not take him even if that bitch that owns him begs me."

Eduardo steps towards Johnnie and Jennifer moves quickly to grab her assistant's arm before the confrontation escalates into a fist fight and says, "Johnnie. You've said enough. Please go away. We're busy here."

Johnnie smirks and turns away, saying. "All I've got to say is that ya'll must be a helluva trainer to take a horse from being a World Champion Stakes winner to what I saw today in just a few months. Bravo."

"He is an asshole." Eduardo is shaking his head.

"Yes, but what he says is true. This plan was doomed from the start."

Eduardo's face is serious as he realizes what losing Toreador could mean for Jennifer's reputation and the future of Beech Tree. "I think you should convince Marianne to let you show him. He needs to get in the ring or his price will be low."

"True. But he won the stake last year. Lots of people will be willing to take a chance on him now. It isn't as though he is totally unproven." Jennifer feels a spark of hope at Eduardo's idea, though. He is right that it will be important to demonstrate that Toreador is still a winner because it won't take long for stories of today's incident to get around. And the stories are likely to be exaggerated with each telling.

Eduardo says, "I think we should make Toreador beautiful, just like at a show. And then invite Marianne to the barn. You should ride him and show her what he can do. She has not ever seen you ride him, has she?" After Jennifer shakes her head, he goes on, "When she sees

181

him, you can suggest that you show him before everyone knows he is for sale. She will get more money for him after you win."

"Yes. But it all rests on her giving me the chance to show her that we can do that." Jennifer speaks slowly but feels herself getting more optimistic.

"Blair is on your side. You should call Blair and convince her this is a good plan." Eduardo is clearly getting excited about his suggestion.

"You're right. I'll call Blair. We really need that commission and I'll do my best to keep Toreador at Beech Tree until he sells."

Early the next morning, Jennifer dials Blair's cell phone number.

Blair answers after several rings, "Hi Jennifer."

"Can you talk about Toreador?"

"Yes. I'm glad you called. I am on my way to meet Mother for coffee but I have a few minutes."

"I've been giving yesterday's events a lot of thought and I have some ideas, but I want to be sure that they make sense to you before we propose them to your mother."

"I've been giving it a lot of thought too. I know I disappointed you…" Blair's voice trails off.

"Absolutely not. I meant what I said about admiring your ability to say that Toreador is not for you. I know how hard it was to say that." Before the entire scene from yesterday can be rehashed, Jennifer works to move the conversation on to her first reason for calling. "We need to start thinking about our next step and I have an idea." Jennifer pauses to take a deep breath and then asks, "Did you watch the Junior Gaited Class on Wednesday night?"

It takes a few seconds for Blair to respond and she says, "The four-year-olds?"

"Yes, it was the last one."

"I did watch it. Didn't Johnnie Stuart win it on that big bay stallion of his?"

"Yes. Did you notice the horse that got second?" Jennifer goes on to remind Blair of the horse she means, "Bobby Acton was riding him. His name is Vendome Copper. He's a big, good looking chestnut?"

182

"Yes. He was lined up right in front of us when they were waiting for the ribbons. I actually thought he might win."

"That's him. I think he might be perfect for you." Jennifer goes on to talk about Vendome. "He won the three-year-old stake in Indy last fall so he clearly has talent. And for as young as he is, he seems completely solid and sane. I don't know Bobby very well, but I really like how he works a horse. I've been watching this one and he looks like a real solid citizen."

"He was at Johnnie Stuart's when we had Toreador there, but I didn't hang out over there and never saw him work. Is he for sale?"

Jennifer smiles, because most clients would ask how much a horse would cost. This is clearly not Blair's first concern.

"I can find out. A real nice lady from Illinois actually owns him. She breeds a lot of horses but doesn't ride herself. I don't know why she wouldn't want to sell a gelding."

"How soon can we sell Toreador, do you think?"

"Well, that was the second reason for my call. Honestly, he'll be easy to sell. But I know your Mother is disappointed and I'd like to maximize what we can get for him. The Shelby County Fair is in two weeks. I'd like to show him in the Open Class and let people see that he's sound and in great shape. No one has seen him show since last August, and I think we need to remind everyone that he is fabulous before we put a price on him." Jennifer waits for Blair's reaction.

"Last night, Mother was talking about what to do and it won't surprise you that she is thinking about sending him to a different trainer," Blair says hesitantly. "I tried to convince her that's a bad idea."

"I appreciate your support." Jennifer is glad that the issue is in the open, "I know that Marianne is unhappy and I understand that. But horses and riders need to mesh and your personality is just not a good fit for Toreador, regardless of where he goes."

"I know. It is just hard for Mother to accept. And I think she's a little embarrassed because she was bragging so much about him. I think she's accepting that I won't ride him, but she wants to blame someone…" Blair's voice trails off.

"I get that. But I really like Toreador and it was hard to get him to trust me. I think that transferring him to another trainer might cause him to miss the whole season. That's unnecessary. Letting me show him at the Shelby County Fair is a low risk approach. And a nice show there would go a long way towards removing any embarrassment your mother might be feeling." Jennifer waits for Blair's response.

Blair takes her time, obviously mulling over the proposition. Then she slowly says, "I think you're right. I'll talk to her and try to convince her to let you take him to the County Fair." She then adds, "But you know how important it will be to do well."

"Yes, I know."

"I'll talk to her and call you back. I'll have to pick the right time, so don't worry if you don't hear from me for a couple of hours. I'm going to need to present this as my idea."

"Thanks Blair. As I said, I really appreciate your support. And please think some more about Vendome Copper, ok?"

CHAPTER 45

As soon as her mother answers the phone with her perpetually cheerful voice, Jennifer greets her. "Hi Mom."

"Hi Honey. You're calling earlier than usual. What's up?"

Jennifer can hear water running in the background and she pictures her mom standing in the sunny kitchen of her condominium. "I need advice."

Her mom chuckles. "And you called me?" She emphasizes the last word. "You know I always have lots of advice. What wisdom can I impart today?"

"Eduardo is late again today."

Her mom pauses, and Jennifer hears the water turn off. "What do you mean, 'again'? Is he late often?"

"It is getting to be a problem. Originally, it was just a day or so every couple of weeks. But now it is more often than not." Jennifer is standing in her office. She can see the front door of the trailer that Eduardo lives in on the barn property, but her assistant still hasn't emerged.

"Have you talked to him about it? What's causing it?"

"Well, I think he's drinking."

Her mom pauses. "That's bad news. Why do you think that?"

"The way he smells and looks when he gets here. Most days, the 'good Eduardo' shows up. But occasionally he looks like he slept in his clothes." After a brief moment she goes on. "I wasn't sure what the problem was until I found a vodka bottle stashed under some blankets in the tack room. Do you know whether he had problems with alcohol when he worked for Dad?"

"Your Dad didn't mention it if he did, but I know quite a few trainers that struggle with it." She pauses. "What are you going to do?"

"I'm not sure." Jennifer runs her hand through her hair, and then sighs.

"As awkward as it is, you have to confront him. It isn't safe to have him around horses if he isn't stone cold sober."

185

"I know. Especially with Toreador." She then tells her mother about the experience at Rock Creek, ending with, "Blair called me back last night and told me that Marianne agreed to let me show Toreador until he sells. I don't think she's happy about it, but I think she realizes that it is the best way to maximize what we can get for him."

"Oh honey. You must be disappointed. But you always thought he was too much horse for that girl."

Jennifer smiles weakly, realizing that her mom always knows the right thing to say. "I am disappointed, but I'm also a little excited. I plan to show him at the Shelby County Fair. It gives me a couple of weeks to get ready." She smiles at the thought of showing the horse. "But we have some big changes to make before then. Now that I'm not worried about getting him tuned for Blair, I need to change his bit and maybe even his shoes. I also want to change his feed and start shoving some powerful vitamins at him." She glances again at Eduardo's trailer. "That's why I really need Eduardo to be on his game. We're only going to get one chance with Marianne. If the show doesn't go well, she'll pull him out of here without any hesitation."

"Well, then, you're just going to have to put on your big girl panties and talk to him. He works for you, Jennifer. You need to start acting like a boss." Her mother puts a touch of steel in her voice. "Seriously, Jennifer. What are you afraid of? That he'll quit? That you'll hurt his feelings? That he won't like you? There is far too much at stake for any of that nonsense. Go over to that trailer, bang on the door, invite yourself in, and tell him that he has to straighten up."

"You're absolutely right. Thanks for the pep talk. I'm on it." She thanks her mom and hangs up.

Before she loses her courage, Jennifer leaves the barn and heads to Eduardo's trailer with confident strides. She knows that the grooms in the barn have seen her go and are likely to be watching her so she straightens her back, determined to remove any doubt about who is in charge at Beech Tree.

She knocks firmly on the cheap wooden door. She has to repeat her knock three times before she hears movement from inside. When the door opens, she is momentarily speechless. Her assistant is in a dirty t-shirt and sweat pants. His hair is standing on end and his eyes

186

are blood shot. She can see over his shoulder that the inside of the trailer is cluttered and filthy, and she can smell old food. He doesn't speak, looks down at the floor and mumbles "I overslept."

"What's up with you? Can I come in?"

"I am sick. I have the flu." Eduardo mumbles the words, squinting his eyes against the bright Kentucky sunshine.

"Can I come in? We need to talk."

Eduardo glances over his left shoulder at the room behind him and she takes advantage of the movement to step forward into the living room of the small space. A round table and three chairs are directly on her right, with a small kitchen beyond them. Every flat space she can see is covered with clutter. Old pizza boxes, papers, magazines, and fast food wrappers are everywhere. She can also see an overflowing garbage can filled with clear, empty bottles that once held cheap vodka. As she looks around the smelly space, she is dismayed that she has hesitated to intervene. It has been almost two months since she first suspected something was awry with Eduardo. All she can say is "Oh, Eduardo. I think we both know that you don't have the flu."

Eduardo shuffles to the countertop in the kitchen and starts to pile dirty dishes, as Jennifer stands in the door shaking her head. "Eduardo. Stop. Let's talk about this. I think you're drinking too much."

He doesn't make eye contact but says defensively, "I have the flu. I will come to the barn in ten minutes. Please go away."

She detects he is embarrassed and turns to leave. "I'll go away now, but we are going to talk about this. Take today off and clean this place up. Come over to my office this afternoon after the grooms are gone and we'll talk."

As she turns to leave, he asks "Am I fired?"

"No. I am not going to fire you today. You have to fix this, though. I need your help at the barn, but you're no help to me when you're in this shape." She tries to make eye contact, but he won't meet her gaze. "I'm serious. Take the day to clean this crap up and get yourself straight. We'll go from there." She firmly closes the door behind her and returns to the barn.

CHAPTER 46

1:00 PM June 14, La Jolla, CA

"Gosh, I'm glad we did this." Eileen Miller and her best friend Karen Shields are sitting in the back patio of a French restaurant, a short walk from the pricey boutiques in La Jolla's shopping district. They are both wearing dresses and sandals, and large-framed designer sunglasses. The waiter quickly arrives with glasses of water and dainty slices of lemon. They both order a glass of California Chardonnay.

While they wait for it to arrive, Karen takes a careful look at her stemmed water glass. She picks it up and looks at it critically. "When did restaurants decide to quit putting ice in water glasses?"

Eileen laughs, "I know! I just can't figure out why some trends get started."

"Well, this trend needs to end. It's almost like they don't trust us to keep from bumping our nose on an ice cube or something."

"Well, you must admit that you've done that." They both laugh heartily.

Eileen and Karen have been best friends since they were teenagers. They were both raised in southern California, the daughters of wealthy parents. They both married young to successful men, and both divorced after more than twenty years of marriage. While Eileen never had children, Karen has two daughters, the youngest of which is getting married in the upcoming fall. Their shopping trip today is aimed at finding Karen a suitable 'mother of the bride' dress.

"So tell me about the wedding. How is the planning going?" Eileen knows that Karen is likely to have several hilarious stories and she looks forward to hearing them.

"Oh my god. How would I know? That daughter of mine doesn't tell me anything. But if she really doesn't want me to know anything, she really should change the passwords on her bank account. She's forcing me to be Inspector Clouseau and resurrect all those skills I acquired nosing around when she was a teenager. I figured out what florist she was using by looking at her credit card statement. I had to call them and pretend to be her to find out what kind of flowers she had selected. Can you believe she chose roses? Such a cliché."

"Oh! Please don't tell me that you changed them."

Karen laughs. "No. I was tempted to do that just to show her how clever I am. But I'm not sure that she'd get the joke. She has completely lost her sense of humor." Karen launches into a stream of funny stories about how she has discovered the wedding details.

By the time their salads are finished, Karen turns the conversation back to one of their favorite subjects, horses. They both ride at Morning Star Barns. Karen no longer shows, but she never misses her weekly riding lesson with Holly. "So how is Spy Master doing? I never get to see him work anymore. I get to the barn too late on Wednesdays."

"He's doing really well." Eileen takes another sip of her wine and smiles at her friend. "I admit that I was really afraid we were going to lose him last fall when he colicked." She pauses and then says, "Twice."

Karen interrupts "As if once wasn't enough."

"Right. As if once wasn't enough. But we've shown him three times this year so far and he is undefeated. I feel so lucky to have a horse as talented as he is."

"What are your plans for him? Are you going to sell him or will you keep him once he retires to a breeding farm? Do you want to keep showing him?" Karen knows that Eileen has changed her mind several times about Spy Master's future.

"Well, we're going to go for it this year and try to win the Stake at Louisville. If we can get that done, I might retire him to a stud farm in Kentucky. It would be fun to go out on top."

"Why Kentucky? Wouldn't you miss him?"

"Absolutely, but I want him to have the best chance at being famous and he'll have more opportunity to breed the best mares if he is out there in the middle of it all. As you know, Kentucky dominates the Saddlebred breeding business."

The waiter arrives with their grilled fish entrees, causing a momentary pause in the conversation. As he moves away, Eileen continues. "Holly convinced me to move him to Kentucky early this year, rather than flying him into Louisville a couple of days before the show."

189

Karen looks at her friend and raises a perfectly plucked eyebrow. "Really?"

"Yes. She believes that the extra time to acclimate will give him an advantage. I imagine she's right, but I'm still not sure about it."

"I can see why. Is she going with him?"

"No. She has a friend out there with a training barn and he'll move there around the middle of July. We'll take him to the big Shelbyville Show at the end of July."

Karen can tell from her friend's tone that she is not enthusiastic about Spy Master's move. "How do you feel about that plan?"

"As you can probably tell, I'm conflicted. I suspect she's right that if I want to win the Stake, I need to give him every advantage."

"He won last year and wasn't acclimated." Karen has used her fingers to make air quotes around the final word of her sentence.

"That's what I said. But Holly pointed out that he was just competing against four-year-olds last year. This year he'll be up against older and more experienced horses. And I think she is also worried that the trip could trigger colic so she wants to have plenty of time for it to resolve before the show."

"Do you know anything about this trainer that he's going to?"

"That's kind of worrying me as well. Evidently it is Holly's college boyfriend, so I'm not sure that she is being completely objective about him. He doesn't seem to be that successful as a trainer. I've been googling him and his clients have a few nice ribbons at local pleasure shows, but he doesn't seem to have anything very good."

"Is he still single?" Karen has spent a fair amount of effort trying to find a man that Holly is interested in and has been unsuccessful.

"No, I understand that he's married."

"Do you think she is using Spy Master to reconnect with him?"

"I don't know for sure what's going on there. She has logical reasons for choosing him. She says that he's agreed to put up barn cams so that we can watch Spy Master's stall and all his workouts on line whenever we want. And she didn't want a big name trainer because she didn't want to have arguments about training methods or have to compete with another Stake Horse in the same barn." She picks at her fish. "The whole idea makes a lot of sense when we talk about it. I'm not sure why I'm not completely sold."

"Well I know why!" Karen looks intently at her friend. "Spy Master is your baby and it probably feels like you're sending him off to college. And he won't call and he won't write. He'll make friends you've never met. You won't know what grades he's getting or if he's even going to class. Before you know it, he'll decide he wants to marry someone you don't even really know." Karen sniffs.

"We're talking about you again, aren't we?" Eileen appreciates her friend's attempt to lighten the conversation with humor.

Karen laughs. "Oh. That's right. Sorry. Seriously, though, you do need to give him the best chance to win. I'd go out to Kentucky to meet this new trainer, though, and inspect his place. If you get a good vibe, then go for it. If you don't like what you see or feel, then keep Spy Master at home."

Eileen is completely still as she looks at Karen. "Now why didn't I think of that? That is a great idea." She pauses for a few seconds and then repeats, "That is a great idea. That's why you're my best friend. You always come up with the perfect solution."

"Well, maybe you should tell my daughters that!" Karen scoots her chair back on the stone patio. "Let's get going! Shopping awaits!"

CHAPTER 47

Johnnie Stuart is sitting in his office, leafing through the most recent *Saddle Horse Report* when Dave Snell enters. "Hey buddy. What's going on?"

Johnnie looks up, but maintains his relaxed position, with his feet on his desk. "Not much, man. What's happening?"

Dave chooses the chair nearest the standing fan that is whirring and removes his cap. His hair is wet with sweat and he rakes his empty hand through it. "Geezus Christ. It's a hot, humid sonofabitch out there. I keep thinking I should move to Montana or something."

It is an old refrain between the two friends and one of them mentions it in nearly every conversation during each long, hot, humid Kentucky summer. And the response is the same as always, "Yeah, but then you'd have to watch Quarter Horses instead of Saddlebreds. Wouldn't that be the shits?"

They exchange news about the weather and talk about how Johnnie's horses are working, and then Dave says, "Have you been watching the Midwest Horse Show on the video feed?"

"A little of it. The picture on my computer starts out good but goes to shit after about a minute and I can't see what the hell is going on. My niece says my connection is too slow. I keep thinking I should get a nerd out here to fix it, but I've got better stuff to spend money on, I guess. Like good booze and bad women." Johnnie laughs and takes a drink from the Gatorade bottle sitting on his desk. The condensation on the outside of the plastic bottle drips onto the front of his shirt when he tips it up. He gestures at the small refrigerator sitting in the corner of his office. "Help yourself."

Dave doesn't speak again until he is back in his chair, popping the top on a can of light beer. "That mare of Annie Jessup's got beat last night at Midwest in the Amateur Class."

"I saw that. She got screwed. That mare is a game bitch and she was the only one in that ring that was racking her ass off." Johnnie shakes his head. "That chick that rides her can really ride, too."

"She had some screw-ups and her canter was about twice as fast as everyone else in the class. I think she lapped a couple of them."

Dave relaxes back in his chair and extends his long legs in front of him.

"Well, the judges seem to think that the Amateur Five-Gaited Class ought to be a pleasure class. If you ask me, it's just going to make it damn near impossible to sell a horse that's got any starch to it." Johnnie continues leafing through the newspaper that contains the latest show results, pausing when he sees an advertisement for a five-gaited horse.

"I heard that stud that won the Junior Gaited Class at Louisville last year is undefeated so far this year."

Johnnie snorts. "Well, shit. That don't mean much. As far as I can tell, there ain't any competition out there in California. My cousin lives in San Diego and saw him win the qualifier for the Charity Fair out there in Del Mar this week. He said that Spy Master was the only sound horse in the ring."

Dave takes another deep drink of beer and says, "Maybe so, but that sonofabitch is the real deal."

"I wouldn't count on it. He colicked in Kansas City. And that trainer is a babe in the woods." Johnnie smirks, "And I do mean a babe. I wouldn't mind getting to know her a little better."

"Maybe you should call her and give her some helpful advice."

"Maybe I will." Johnnie goes back to the newspaper, turning a page as he talks. "I'm trying to figure out who's going to show up in the Stake Class at Louisville this year. It looks to me like my horse might have a chance."

Dave sits a little straighter in his chair. "No shit? Night Train is only four."

"Yeah. He's still got some growing to do. He wouldn't be the biggest or strongest one in there, but I'm not seeing anything around that can out rack him."

Dave settles back in his chair again. "Maybe so. But he's going to have to make it through at least one, and maybe two workouts. I'm thinking about all the horses that were shown in that class last year. We both saw that Toreador's a disaster." He rushes on before Johnnie can rant about Toreador. "The horse that was second is lame. That mare of Jessup's was third and she's moved to the Amateur Class." He pauses, thinking through the competition. "You might be right.

193

This might be a pretty light year for stake horses." As he talks, Dave is already thinking about who he will call to spread the news that Johnnie Stuart is thinking about showing his four-year-old in the big class at Louisville this year.

"Toreador has gone to shit, all right. My farrier works over there at Beech Tree, too. He said that they've changed his shoes and that girl is going to show him at the Shelby County Fair." Johnnie is trolling for more information about the horse he won the stake on last year, but Dave appears to know less than he does.

"I figured his owner would have sent him back to you by now." Dave takes another drink of beer.

"Nah. That ain't going to happen. That bitch has let her ego get in the way of her brain. I told her she was making a big mistake when she pulled him out of here. I don't imagine she'd have the nerve to come crawling back. She'd have to pucker up and kiss my ass before I took him." Johnnie snorts and finishes the Gatorade that is now room temperature. "I feel like a steak tonight. Ya'll want to meet down at the steak house in Simpsonville later?"

Dave takes the cue, quickly finishes his beer and replaces his still damp cap on his head. "Damn straight, I do. How about 7 o'clock?"

CHAPTER 48

"Make sure you sweep the aisle after you finish the stalls, okay Jeremy?" When Holly called him to tell him that Eileen wanted to go to Kentucky to see where Spy Master might be spending July and August, he had asked her if she would be looking for anything specific. Holly had said that she was unsure, but that maybe Eileen needed reassurance that Spy Master would be well cared for. Kenny was looking forward to having the horse in his barn and he and Jeremy had been working hard in the last two days to finish the new turn-out pen and shelter and to make the barn entrance attractive. Angela had even pitched in, planting colorful flowers in old bourbon barrels and placing them by the main door.

Kenny is finally satisfied that the barn looks ready for her inspection and decides to begin working a horse, reasoning that it will be a good way for Ms. Miller to observe his training style. He is well aware that today's meeting is actually a job interview.

Kenny has just mounted the horse when he glances through the windows in the ring and notices a late model sedan pulling off the main road into the driveway leading to the barn. He quells his nervousness, knowing that Jeremy will meet their guest and escort her down to the ring. It is nearly ten minutes and he is well into his ride before Jeremy and their guest enter the ring, quickly moving to the center so they don't interfere with Kenny's ride. Kenny can see that Jeremy has given Ms. Miller a mug of coffee and they are chatting brightly. He pulls his horse up immediately but doesn't dismount.

"Good Morning! Welcome to Riverside. I'm Kenny Rivers and I can see that you've already met my assistant Jeremy." She is exactly as Holly described. She is a very attractive woman, slim and tall, and is neatly and expensively dressed.

"Hi Kenny. I'm Eileen Miller. Yes, Jeremy was kind enough to get me coffee. I got in from California last night, so it is pretty early for me to be up and about."

"If you don't mind, then, I'll give you a minute to enjoy your coffee while I work this horse, and then I'll give you a tour." Kenny knows that part of today's audition is to make Holly's client

195

comfortable with Kenny's ability to work a horse. Although Holly will be making all the training decisions, Kenny will be working Spy Master every day.

As he moves his horse back into his work, Jeremy positions a canvas-backed camp chair in the center of the ring for Eileen before returning to the stall area. Eileen seats herself comfortably and sips her coffee as she watches him work the horse. The horse is clearly a pleasure horse and Kenny spends time halting, flat walking, and pays particular attention to achieving a slow, relaxed and balanced canter. When the training session is finished, Kenny halts the horse in the middle of the ring, pats him on the neck, and dismounts.

"Nice horse." Eileen rises from her chair and takes a few steps towards Kenny, offering her hand for a hand shake.

"Yes. This gelding is a trooper. His owner is a novice rider and he really takes good care of her. He never loses his cool and I've seen him get the correct lead even when she does absolutely everything wrong." Kenny laughs lightly and reaches forward to meet her hand shake. Her eyes are intelligent and while she appears to be friendly, there is a serious edge to her smile that worries him a little. "Let me put him away and then I'll give you a tour and answer any questions you have about our operation."

Eileen and Kenny walk together out of the ring toward the stalls. Jeremy sees his dad coming and quickly comes over to take the gelding's reins. "Jeremy, untack him and cool him out please. Then wash his tail for me and get started on the tack, ok?" Jeremy nods and leads the horse off.

"He seems like he's great help."

"He is. I'm really proud of him. This summer is his first helping me, and he's the best groom I've ever had." Kenny quickly goes on to say, "Of course, if you decide to send Spy Master out here next month, I'll take care of him myself. Holly tells me that he's great in the stall, but he is a stallion and it is better to be safe than sorry."

"Do you have other grooms?" Eileen is looking around at the barn and sees a small, but neatly kept and apparently well-organized barn. She mentally compares it to Morning Star and can't help but be a little disappointed by the difference in size and grandeur.

"We typically put on one around show season but this year I haven't needed to do that. Jeremy cleans stalls and gets the horses cleaned up. I tack them myself. My wife Angela is a huge help at shows and helps me get everyone in and out of the ring." He pauses for a moment. "Of course, if Spy Master comes, I imagine it will change the pace of things around here a bit."

Eileen changes the subject to avoid committing herself to a decision about Spy Master. With a small smile she says, "Well, why don't you give me a tour and we'll go from there?"

"Sure. Let's start with the stalls. This stall would be Spy Master's." Kenny pulls open the door of the stall nearest his office. He kicks back the immaculate bedding to reveal a thick rubber mat. "As you can see, the horses all stand on the best quality mats we can buy. We completely change the bedding every Thursday. When we do that, we check each stall for any new signs of cribbing, loose nails, or any edges that might injure a horse."

As he goes on to describe the daily routine of the barn, Eileen is impressed. The stalls are large and filled with natural light. Every horse looks well cared for and they are obviously used to a lot of attention, looking up from their feed and nickering at the sound of Kenny's voice. She begins asking questions and the edge starts to leave her voice. "So tell me about the feed and how you store it."

"Sure. As you can see from information on the blackboard attached to each stall door, every horse gets a custom feed mix every day. He opens an exterior side door and points out a large metal container that is set up off the ground on metal legs. "I store oats in this granary. It is off the ground to keep the grain dry and to keep rodents out of it."

Eileen interrupts him to ask a question. "I have a friend that moved a horse to Kentucky and it ended up with EPM. Is this one of the ways you avoid that?"

"Ah. Good question. It sounds like you've really done your homework and as you probably know, EPM stands for Equine Protozoal Myeloencephalitis and is essentially a nervous system infection. You probably know that EPM is a protozoa that is spread through possum feces. I've never had a horse diagnosed with it but we definitely work to prevent it. Since we have so many possums here in

197

Kentucky, we work hard to keep them off the property. We have a number of live traps set out and we make sure our feed bins are sealed. All of the waterers are automatic and are off the ground. Although they are good climbers and it is hard to keep them out of a structure like this one, we don't keep anything in the barn overnight that would attract them, like sweet feed, cat food or candy wrappers. Also, none of our show horses are let out to graze, where they would pick it up in the pasture. Finally, we pick through all of the hay before we feed it." As he talks, Kenny points out the live trap next to the hay and he breaks open a bale to show her the quality of the feed.

"How often do you catch one?"

"We catch one or two every summer. Enough so that I keep the traps baited all the time."

"Have they found a vaccine for EPM?"

"Every couple of years we'll hear about one, but I don't believe they've found one that has been proven effective yet. I've read that most horses that are exposed to the organism don't develop the disease, but it is notoriously difficult to diagnose and to treat. The vets all say that the best way to prevent it is to keep possums out of feed and bedding."

Everything that Kenny is saying is consistent with what Eileen has read and she is impressed with his ability to articulate his knowledge and with the obvious pride he takes in his property. She changes the subject. "Tell me a little more about your daily routine."

"Jeremy and I get to the barn at about 5:30 every morning. We feed together and then I start working horses while Jeremy cleans stalls. Every horse gets worked six days a week. In most cases, horses get ridden on Wednesdays and Saturdays. The other days we do long-lining or driving, depending on what each horse needs. We have four show horses and those clients come out to ride on Saturdays, although they often drop in during the week just to see how their horses are doing. We also have a bunch of academy riders and they come in the afternoons on Tuesdays, Thursdays and Saturdays if there isn't a show. A couple of show horses get fed at noon, just depending on what they need. Everything gets fed again at 4:30. I always check on them before bed, at around 10PM just to be sure they're all ok."

Kenny stops a moment to see if Eileen has questions, and then goes on. "The farrier comes every fourth week as part of our routine, although I sometimes need him to stop by and adjust something between regular visits. We have an exterminator come by every two weeks for fly and rodent control." Kenny can see from Eileen's face that she has a question.

"Let's talk about showing. Can you tell me about how a typical show goes?"

"Well, we trailer our own horses and we don't stable them overnight anywhere other than the big show at Louisville. We always get box stalls at the show grounds during the day so they are comfortable unless it is a small county fair that doesn't have them available. I can't imagine that Spy Master would go to one of those." He smiles a little and then goes on. "We tend to arrive about 2 ½ hours before the show starts so that all the horses get settled. I admit that I'm a worry wart. I have lists and lists of lists for shows. My wife teases me about it, but I just call it careful preparation!"

"It sounds like you and Holly have a lot in common."

"Well, we both learned much of what we know from the same place. William Woods is a great school for our industry." He wonders how much she knows about his previous relationship with Holly and he quickly changes the subject. "Tell me more about your goals for Spy Master."

If Eileen notices his discomfort she shows no signs. "Well, I'm not sure how much Holly has told you about the colic incident in Kansas City."

Kenny notices that she hasn't mentioned the first time that Spy Master colicked when he arrived home from last year's World Championship, so he doesn't mention it either and encourages her to go on.

"In Kansas City, the vet diagnosed a left dorsal displacement and they presumably fixed it, but I'm still a little gun shy about giving him the stress of a new environment. I'm probably being an over-anxious owner." Eileen smiles weakly.

"I don't think so. He's a very valuable animal. He's undefeated so far this year, right?"

"Yes. Thanks to Holly. She's wonderful."

"Then it is wise to do everything possible to minimize any risk with him." He opens the door to his office and steps back for her to enter ahead of him. He refills her coffee cup and they both settle into the chairs in his office. "My understanding is that Holly wants to maximize his chance to win the Stake this year and she believes that bringing him out early will make it easier for him to do well at Louisville. I think she's right. First, it allows him plenty of time to recover from the trip. Second, he gets a chance to adjust to our weather and humidity. Third, if he shows in Shelbyville it will give him a chance to win over some local fans. It won't hurt to have some more voices screaming for him in Louisville. Finally, if he wins Shelbyville he has instant credibility as a big deal stake horse." He has enumerated the reasons for Spy Master's early move on his fingers as he talks. "I know that it's a big decision and you need to take your time, but I want you to know that we will take excellent care of him. We'll install cameras in his stall and in the ring so that you can tune in on the internet and check on him 24/7. Holly will be able to watch him work and she'll remain in charge of all training decisions."

As Eileen has listened, she is impressed by Kenny's demeanor. He is convincing, yet respectful of her anxiety. "It is a big decision. I just keep thinking that he did well last year without coming to Kentucky early."

"He certainly did. But the Stake horse competition is a huge step up from the Four-Year-Old Class. I've watched your horse on streaming video at every opportunity this year. I think he could win it. I really do. But he's young and less experienced than the other horses that will be in the ring. He needs every advantage we can give him." Kenny hesitates when he realizes that he has referred to himself as part of Spy Master's team. But he quickly goes on. "There is one thing that I'd suggest though. Whether you decide to bring him early or just wait until a couple of days before the Louisville show, I'd recommend that you fly him out. I think Holly was considering trailering him, but I'd want to avoid the stress of three days on the road during the summer. She can ride on the plane with him and bring his tack, too. I could pick them up in either Lexington or Louisville, whichever is the most cost effective for you."

200

Eileen sighs. "Yes. I agree. I think that makes the most sense. You've certainly made me more comfortable that this situation could work for Spy Master." She stands and sets her empty cup next to the coffee maker.

Kenny stands as well and they shake hands as she moves towards the door. "Please call me if you have any more questions. I would be honored to have your horse in this barn for a while. I assure you that we will take good care of him."

Kenny escorts Eileen to her car and watches her drive away. Just as he is turning back into the barn, he notices Angela and Emily walking towards him from their small home, just across the driveway from the barn. Emily notices him standing at the barn door and she runs towards him, holding her favorite doll and screaming "Daddy! Tomorrow's my birthday!"

Kenny reaches down and lifts her up, putting a surprised look on his face. "It is? Are you sure?"

"Yes! I'm sure! I'm going to be five!" She is looking directly at him with a worried look, as though she is afraid that he will deny that her fifth birthday is the next day.

"Well. That's a pretty big deal isn't it?" He laughs and tickles her before setting her on her feet and greeting his wife. "Hi there. She's pretty excited, huh?"

"Yes. She's pretty excited. I think we should decide what the agenda is for the big celebration." Angela glances at her daughter to see whether she is paying attention, but Emily is standing at the fence of the new paddock, trying to coax the lesson horses into coming towards her by holding out stems of grass that she has picked. "How did your visit with the woman from California go?"

"It went well. I think she is still on the fence but I hope she'll send her horse out here." Kenny has detected a lack of enthusiasm from Angela every time the topic of having Spy Master in their barn comes up, but he has avoided confronting it.

Angela keeps her eyes on Emily and responds carefully. "Well, it wouldn't be the end of the world if she didn't send him."

"I'd be pretty disappointed." Kenny decides to appeal to Angela on terms that he thinks will matter most to her. "The money will certainly help us."

201

"Be honest. It isn't just about the money for you. We can fill that stall without him." Angela has let an edge creep into her voice.

"True. We can. But she will definitely pay her bill on time. I already checked with Holly about that. And it is a great opportunity for us to increase our profile. I'd like to be able to say that I worked a World Champion Stake Horse." Kenny is matching Angela's tone and he feels himself tense.

"I just thought that we'd decided to commit to a different path for the barn. I thought we had agreed about that. But it just seems that one request from your friend Holly derailed decisions that we'd made together."

Kenny tries to defuse the escalating argument before it gets out of hand. "Angela. I really want this chance. And it is only for a few weeks. It doesn't change any of our decisions long term, but I need you to understand that this is a chance for me to gain some respect in the trainer community. Anyway, it is out of our hands now. She may decide to leave the horse in California so let's not fight about it." He quickly changes the subject. "So what are we going to do for Emily's birthday?"

CHAPTER 49

10:00 AM June 18, Big View Farm

When Missy enters the barn for her practice session on the Wednesday after the Midwest Charity Horse Show, Annie is in the ring working another horse. Missy stops at Josie's stall. Her pretty mare is already saddled and ready to work. Missy enters the stall and pats her horse on the neck. "Hey girlie. How are you this morning? Are you tired?"

Josie looks well-rested and eager to work. Josie and the other horses from Big View left the show in Springfield Illinois at about midnight on Saturday night and they arrived back at the training barn just after noon on Sunday. Annie's horse trailer is a luxury model featuring air ride suspension and heavy rubber mats. The horses each have a small box stall so they can move around during the trip, making the ride significantly more comfortable than a standard trailer, but it was a long trip. As Missy leaves Josie's stall, Annie is walking down the barn aisle to meet her.

"Good morning, Missy."

"Hi Annie. How are you?"

"I'm good. Everything is good. When did you get in?"

"I drove down last night. It's an easy drive but I wanted to be here early and get our ride in before it got too hot." Missy knows the temperature is expected to reach 92 degrees today and the humidity is over 75%.

"Yeah. It is summer in North Carolina, that's for sure." Annie steps into Josie's stall and checks the mare's saddle and bridle.

"So, I've been watching the video and thinking about my last ride at Midwest." Actually, Missy has been thinking of little else for the past four days. "I am really disappointed that we didn't win. I know we had a couple of small baubles, but Josie out-racked everything in the ring."

Annie looks up from adjusting the girth. "She did slow gait and rack better than anything in the class. Possibly better than anything I saw at the whole show. But your transitions need improvement. With three judges in the ring, someone is going to see every mistake you make, however small. Mistakes that may be forgiven in a Open Class

203

won't be forgiven in a Ladies or Amateur Class. That's how the rules are written. Behavior matters more in those classes."

Missy sighs. "I know that. And I know that we'll eventually get those transitions smoothed out. I just don't know if we'll get it done before Louisville. Everything seems so dependent on the judges and what they like."

"Yes, judging is subjective. But let's not forget that a lot of that will work in your favor. They know Josie's record and many judges will cut her some slack. You're a well-matched pair, too. You are petite and a really pretty rider. While that isn't a judging criteria, it adds up to a nicer overall picture so you're going to get extra points there. When you go to a show, you pay your money for someone else's opinion of your horse. And that's what you get. Someone else's opinion. You need to have thick skin or else you really should spend your money on a sail boat." Annie softens her words with a kind voice and a smile.

Missy is listening intently. "True. I guess I just want to win every time we go in the ring. I want Josie to get the respect that is due her."

"She will. She's only six. And I'm happy that you want to win. That competitive spirit will help you get better and better."

"I'm still tempted to try the Open Class in Louisville this year."

"I know you are. It is like jumping into the deep end of a swimming pool, though."

"Yes, but the Amateur Class isn't exactly a walk in the park. There are a lot more horses competing at the amateur level. It's easy to get stuck in traffic in the ring. Also, as you said, the judges are less forgiving." Missy rushes on before Annie can speak. "Entries to the Championships are due the first of July. We need to decide soon."

"Well, we actually don't have to decide soon. As long as she's entered in the Five-Gaited Division, we can change our minds up until the last minute about what class to put her in. We'll do whatever you want to do, but let's not decide now. Lexington Junior League is our next show. It's the second week of July. The Lexington Show is where all of the horses really start to sort themselves into the classes they'll show in at Louisville. We'll pay attention to who goes where and make a decision after that. Let's enter you in the Louisville show as an Amateur and decide after Lexington what to do. Fair enough?"

"Yeah. Fair enough." Missy pulls her gloves on. "So you wouldn't change anything in her training if you knew she was going in the Open Stake?"

"No. I wouldn't change anything. You're still the rider and my job is to make this horse the best I can for you to ride. I'm happy with how you're handling the bit, for the most part. We might still want to adjust her shoes a little and give her a little more toe on the front, but we have time to sort that out."

Missy shakes her head. "I can't believe Louisville is only two months away. We just have Lexington and the Shelbyville Show left before the big one."

"Yes. The summer sure goes fast, doesn't it?" Annie makes that final adjustments to Josie's bridle and releases the mare from the cross ties. "Let's go work on those transitions."

CHAPTER 50

7:00 PM June 19, Shelby County Fairgrounds

"Those clouds sure look ominous." Clark's voice startles Bobby, who is putting the finishing touches on the tail of a three-year-old that they will show tonight under the Kiplenan banner.

Bobby looks over his right shoulder at his boss, "I don't suppose the rain will wait until we get all these young horses shown, will it?"

It is the second night of the Shelby County Fair and Kiplenan Saddlebreds is showing a total of six horses over a three-hour period. Three of them are just three years old, and the others are four. It will be a very busy night as this is the debut show for three of the horses and they are likely to be skittish and anxious. They have brought four of their most experienced grooms with them and Clark has choreographed their night by posting a list of tasks that must be done for each horse in order to make sure they are prepared in time to enter the gate when their class is called.

"We might get lucky, but I doubt it. Hopefully it will be a quick shower and then be over." Clark steps into the stall to help Bobby put the tail brace on a three-year-old fine harness filly. She is nervous and fidgeting and the groom standing at her head talks to her in soothing tones while Clark and Bobby make sure the brace is comfortable and stable. Bobby reaches across her hip to take a can of hair spray from a second groom and sprays the tail in place. He looks at Clark who nods his approval, and they both leave the stall. One of the grooms remains with her to keep her calm and make sure that she doesn't lean against the stall wall and mess up the work that they have just completed.

As they step back into the aisle of the barn, Bobby says, "We're lucky that the horses we brought are in classes that are pretty well spaced out tonight. We'll be busy, but we won't be frantic."

"Yep. They do a good job at this show of mixing amateur, kid, pony and young horse classes so that a barn like ours can bring quite a few horses and get them in the ring. They do about 20 classes in three hours, so it will move right along. I'm just glad we don't have multiple horses in the same class. I don't know how some of those big barns full of amateur pleasure horses do it. They sometimes have three or four horses in the ring at once."

206

Kiplenan Saddlebreds specializes in starting their home-bred young horses on their show horse careers. There aren't any amateur or juvenile riders in the barn, and the show string consists of two-, three- and four-year-olds that have been bred and raised on the farm. The only horses currently in training that weren't raised at Kiplenan belong to Mrs. Clancy-Mellon, a long-time friend of Lee Kiplenan and the owner of Vendome Copper, who Bobby will show later tonight.

"Is Mr. Kiplenan coming tonight?" As the heir to a furniture making empire with retail outlets in more than half the states in the union, Mr. Kiplenan is often away from Kentucky and is unable to attend many shows.

"He won't be here tonight, but he said he'd probably be here tomorrow. We're showing his favorite two-year-old for the first time tomorrow and he's anxious to see her go."

Bobby laughs. "It might be his only chance to see her under the Kiplenan banner. If she looks as special in the ring tomorrow night as she does at home, there will be plenty of folks trying to buy her."

"That's what it's all about." Clark pauses, "I noticed that Mrs. M is here. I saw her when I went up to check the footing in the ring. It is a long way for her to come for just a County Fair."

"It is, but she loves her horse and I think she'd love to see him beat Night Train. I thought she might show up." Bobby takes a small piece of paper that lists tonight's classes from his pocket and glances at it as he hears the announcement over the loud speakers that the first class of the evening has entered the ring.

Although Bobby has shown horses at more than 200 shows over the last 15 years, he still gets excited about it. This is particularly true when he has the opportunity to show nice horses that will be competitive, which is one of the reasons he is really enjoying his position at Kiplenan. The other reason is that he is working for one of the most experienced and knowledgeable trainers of young horses in the business. Finally, after his stint at Stuart Stables working with Johnnie Stuart, Bobby has enjoyed the peaceful atmosphere that surrounds the Kiplenan team.

Johnnie Stuart's Night Train will be showing against Vendome tonight. This will be the fourth time the two have shown against each other. Vendome won their first time-out last September in Indianapolis, but Night Train evened the score in Kansas City and also beat Vendome last month at the Rock Creek Horse Show. Bobby sincerely believes that Vendome is the better horse and is hopeful that tonight's judge will agree.

The next two and a half hours pass in a blur as Clark, Bobby and the team of grooms efficiently move from one horse to the next, preparing them for the ring, showing them and then cooling them out. There has been just a brief interruption to let a rain squall move through the area, and the shower has cooled things down and settled the dust.

"Any last minute advice for me?" Bobby has another few minutes before he will begin his warm-up and is standing next to Clark outside of Vendome's stall.

"Nope. You know how to ride this horse. There will be a lot of horses in the ring, but you know how to handle the traffic. I think your slow gait should stand out, so I'd keep it slow and steady. Johnnie Stuart will race his horse around the ring and you'll never be faster than him so you need to avoid playing his game. Just concentrate on keeping Vendome in a good frame so that every time the judge looks at him his head is up and his body is square."

"Got it." Bobby squares his shoulders, takes a deep breath, and gestures at Vendome's groom to bring the four-year-old out of his stall. He mounts carefully, gathers his reins and adjusts his suit coat before nudging Vendome and moving off towards the warm-up ring.

Even though it is near the end of the night, the warm-up ring is congested. Bobby counts seven other gaited horses warming up and sees that there are also several three-year-old Park Pleasure horses in the ring preparing for the class that follows Vendome's. As he trots and then slow gaits Vendome, he must carefully maneuver around the small ring. Despite the distractions, Vendome warms up well and is calm and prepared when the bugle summons them into the ring.

Bobby trots Vendome up the slight hill and into the ring. Near the center of the straightaway, he hears Vendome's owner urging him on. "Ride hard. Go get 'em!"

Vendome's head is high and he is trotting strongly down the rail when Bobby hears hoof beats close behind him. Johnnie Stuart passes him very closely on the inside and then cuts quickly back to the rail, causing Vendome to flinch backwards to avoid colliding with Night Train. Bobby doesn't react, knowing that he needs to stay focused on his horse. When he gets to the opposite side of the ring, Clark is standing by the rail and says "Step it up a little" as Bobby trots by.

In response, Bobby clucks his tongue at Vendome, who accelerates so that he is maintaining pace with every horse in the ring except Night Train, who is now staying to the inside of the other horses and is passing everyone. The remainder of the ride passes in a blur of activity, with Vendome performing consistently well in every gait. Once the class is complete and the horses are lined up, Bobby looks out at the crowd and smiles when he sees Mrs. M giving him a thumb up. He knows that he had a great ride with Vendome but is unsure how well he compares to the others.

After a long pause, the announcer begins. "Ladies and Gentlemen, please give this class another round of applause. This is a very fine set of four-year-olds in our Junior Five-Gaited Stake Class. Tonight's winner is…"

Bobby holds his breath as the announcer drags out the pause, and then finally finishes. "Night Train!" Johnnie whoops and racks Night Train up the side of the ring towards where the County Fair Queen is posing with a trophy and ribbon. Bobby watches Night Train, trying to hide his disappointment.

When the announcement comes that Vendome is second, the crowd erupts. It is clear that Vendome is the crowd favorite. Bobby smiles, collects his ribbon and leaves the ring. As he proceeds back to the barn, several people congratulate him on his ride and within minutes, Mrs. M. has arrived, all smiles. "Fantastic ride! Vendome looked fabulous."

"I'm glad you think so. I won't lie, though. I'm disappointed that he didn't get the blue ribbon." Bobby is relieved that Mrs. M is pleased, despite the second place finish.

"Well, as long as I've been in this business, I've learned to be satisfied with a good ride. It was clear to me that the crowd liked him and the people in this crowd know good horses. He was the only horse in the ring that did a true slow gait, and I'm really proud of him. You did well, so don't be too disappointed." Mrs. M pats him on the shoulder and then looks at Clark, who also followed the horse down from the ring. "He was good, wasn't he, Clark?"

"Yep. He was very good. I think there are a couple of things we can work on, but he did real well." Clark is also smiling and Bobby feels his spirits lift as he ducks into the dressing room to remove his suit coat and hat. From inside the dressing room, he hears others congratulating Mrs. M. on Vendome's performance. He overhears one of them remarking that Vendome looks like he will eventually be a great horse for an amateur rider and then asking whether Vendome is for sale. Bobby hears her say noncommittally, "He still has a lot to learn but I'm really proud of how he's coming along."

CHAPTER 51

Jennifer and Eduardo are standing together in the door of the barn in which Toreador is stalled. They are looking out at the drizzling rain, which has drenched the facility. The evening performance is just starting, and they can hear the organist playing the National Anthem over the loud speakers in the barn. Jennifer turns to Eduardo. "I'm going to go up and see how the ground is in the ring. If it is too soupy, I think we're going to want to scratch our horse tonight."

Eduardo nods. "Yes. Riding Toreador in a slick ring would be risky."

Since abandoning the goal of converting Toreador to a horse that Blair can ride, Jennifer and Eduardo have been allowing Toreador's aggressive personality to re-emerge. While they still make him stand quietly to be mounted, they no longer focus on keeping him quiet during his workouts and Toreador has welcomed the change. Jennifer is pleased with how happy he has become. His appetite has increased and he attacks each training session with an eagerness that keeps his trainers working hard to maintain control, even when he is just pulling a jog cart around the practice ring.

Jennifer pulls the hood of her slicker up over her hair bun and thinks to herself that she is grateful that she applied extra hair spray so that it will still look neat under her derby if they do decide to show Toreador. As she walks up the slight hill that leads to the show ring, she does her best to avoid all the mud puddles. The first class is the Amateur Three-Gaited Championship Class and will be very competitive. It will give her a good opportunity to see how well the performance horses handle the wet footing.

She reaches the ring just as the final horse enters the gate, and she can hear the splattering mud as the horse trots carefully into the ring. The class is much smaller than usual, with only four horses and the riders are all wearing rain gear over their suits. Jennifer knows that nine horses were originally entered, so several have decided not to compete because of the weather. She ducks under the covered grandstands and stays well back from the rail to avoid being covered with the mud that is flying up as the horses make their way around the ring.

She hears someone call her name and looks over her left shoulder. Marianne and Blair are huddled together in the mostly empty grandstand and Blair waves at her. Jennifer smiles and mounts the stairs of the wooden seating area to join them.

"What a mess." Marianne speaks first and Jennifer is happy that she is acknowledging the bad conditions.

"Yeah." Jennifer keeps her eyes on the horses in the ring as the announcer calls for the canter. "It definitely is not what we wanted for Toreador's first Open Class."

Blair looks away from the horses going around the ring. "How is he?"

"He's great. He has been training really well and he was great coming over here in the trailer." Jennifer smiles at Blair. "Since getting here, he's been tense. He obviously knows that he has come to play."

Blair laughs. Since they have all agreed that she won't show Toreador, she has been much more relaxed around Jennifer. The announcer calls for the horses to reverse direction in the ring, and the rider on the horse nearest them turns her horse sharply while maintaining a trot. His legs slip out from under him as he makes the turn and the bystanders all gasp. Fortunately, the rider recovers and sits back in her saddle so that her horse can regain his balance and avoid falling.

"Ooh. That was lucky." Blair's eyes are glued on the ring as she exhales, "That was scary." All three women are leaning forward and are now perched on the front edge of the wooden bench they share.

Jennifer decides that the risk of a horse falling in the ring is significant and looks at Marianne. "Marianne. It is your decision and we'll do whatever you want to do, but it looks awfully slick out there. I think the risk of Toreador getting injured by slipping or even by stepping on a shoe and jerking it off is pretty high. Do you want to show or do you want to pull out?"

Marianne keeps her eyes on the ring. "I'd really like him to show. It is a couple of hours before his class. Maybe it will quit raining by then."

Jennifer is grateful when Blair speaks up. "Mom, be serious. Even if it quits raining, it is a soupy mess out there. It isn't going to dry out before the last class."

Marianne looks at Jennifer. "We really need to figure out how he is, though. He hasn't been shown since last August and entries for this year's championship are due in about a week. We were going to decide tonight whether he is ready to defend his title at Louisville. I'm not very interested in getting embarrassed."

Jennifer looks at her client. "He is doing so well at home that I don't think there is really any doubt that he should be entered at Louisville. I admit that I'd like to get him in a ring so that I could get a good handle on how he is at a show, but we can either take him to another show later this month or wait for the big Shelbyville show in late July. We're lucky here in Kentucky. We can definitely find somewhere else to show him next week or the week after."

Marianne hesitates and finally takes a deep breath. "Ok. Let's scratch him from today's show. It's better to not risk it."

Jennifer tries not to look too pleased. "You're doing the right thing. I'll go tell Eduardo and we'll get him back to his nice, warm stall at home."

Marianne reaches towards the umbrella that is sitting on the bench next to her. "I guess there's no point in us sitting here in the rain since Toreador isn't showing."

She is obviously disappointed and unhappy and Jennifer consoles her. "I'll look at the show schedule tonight and pick out a couple other shows that you might want to go to. I'll call you tomorrow and let you know what I find." Jennifer looks around carefully to make sure that no one can overhear them, but the stands are essentially empty. "Also, remember that Missy Phillips is coming to ride him next Wednesday. I'll need you to let me know what price you want to set."

Marianne says, "I was hoping to use today's performance to help me decide on a price and also to decide whether he should go to Louisville at all, assuming we still own him in August. Honestly, I still can't figure out why she is shopping. Everyone is saying that her mare was on fire at the Midwest show and could have won the gaited stake. Do you think she's serious?"

213

Jennifer responds, "I do think she is serious. It is no secret that she wants a shot at winning the Open Stake in Louisville. Her mare is talented, but she's small. Annie Jessup got third on her last year, and although Missy is a great rider, I don't know that anyone can ride that mare better than Annie can. She's been showing as an amateur horse and doing pretty well. I imagine she'll stick there. As for the price, I think you should set it high. Toreador really does look good at home and I imagine he'll show well. I don't know if Missy can handle him and that might scare her off, but she has plenty of money so you might as well set a high price. I don't think a big price tag will bother her."

Marianne nods and they agree to discuss it on the phone the next day.

"By the way, did you get to see that four-year-old gaited horse named Vendome Copper show last night?"

Blair stays quiet as her mother answers, "Yes. We saw him. I actually thought he should have won, but Johnnie Stuart's horse beat him."

"I think he's going to make an exceptional horse for an amateur rider. He is level-headed, he's big enough to stand out in the ring, and his slow gait and rack are totally solid and square. If you're interested, I could call and make an appointment for Blair to go try him." Jennifer pauses to gauge Marianne's reaction.

But Marianne doesn't comment any further and she and Blair stand up to leave, pulling hoods over their heads. Jennifer follows them down the stairs and they hurry toward the parking lot as she returns to the barn where Toreador is stabled. Johnnie Stuart is leaning against the barn wall, just inside the door and she attempts to move by him without catching his attention.

"Are you finally going to let everyone see if ya'll can ride Toreador tonight? The last time I saw him, it looked like he was riding ya'll instead." He smirks at her in an attempt to pass the statement off as a joke, but his eyes are unamused.

Jennifer hesitates, debating how to respond. "My client has decided to put her horse's well-being ahead of our desire to show him off."

214

Johnnie maintains his relaxed pose, but she can tell from his expression that he is surprised. "A little mud never stopped any horse of mine. Are you sure ya'll aren't going home because you can't handle him?"

Jennifer stops just inside the barn entrance and tilts her head to the side. She furrows her brow and says, "Hm. Let me think." After pausing for a few seconds to look up towards the ceiling of the barn, she makes eye contact with Johnnie and shakes her head. "Nope. That's definitely not it." She turns on her heel and resumes her path to Toreador's stall where Eduardo is waiting.

She gives her assistant a small smile. "Let's pack it up and get him home."

Eduardo nods and starts collecting leg wraps from the nearest tack trunk. "It is a good decision."

"It's the right decision for the horse. But I have to say that Johnnie Stuart brings out the worst in me. I would give a lot to show him that Toreador is back, better and stronger than ever."

"We will do that. We will pick a time that is better for Toreador."

Jennifer sighs and then smiles at Eduardo as she pulls Toreador's blanket out of the trunk. "You're right. I really, really, really want to wipe that smirk off his face, though."

CHAPTER 52

This is the first time Missy Phillips has visited Jennifer Hornig's Beech Tree Farm and she is impressed by its neat appearance. There are window boxes filled with red and yellow flowers in the front windows and the facility is shaded by large pecan trees. A brick walkway leads to an office and lobby area. As she gets out of her vehicle, a large brown dog gallops around the corner of the barn to greet her. He stops directly in front of her, wiggling his entire body and happily wagging his stumpy tail.

"Hey boy. What's your name?" She reaches down to pet the happy boxer and he leans against her, still wiggling. She can't help but smile at this display of happiness and it lessens some of her anxiety. She has come to ride Toreador. She is well aware of the horse's reputation for being a bit of an outlaw but she also knows that he is extremely talented. She pushes the dog aside with her leg and opens the rear hatch, reaching in for her saddle and gloves.

"Jelly? Come boy!" The dog leaps happily in the air and races off towards the voice. Missy watches him go and sees a young woman come around the barn. She is wearing dark jodhpurs and a sleeveless blouse and her hair is tied back into a neat ponytail. She approaches with long strides.

"You must be Missy. I'm Jennifer Hornig. I didn't hear you drive up, but I guess Jelly did as he was obviously quicker than I was about coming out to greet you."

"Yes. I'm Missy. What a great name for a dog."

"It came from one of the kids here at the barn because he wiggles like a bowl full of jelly, and it just stuck. He's our version of a rescue dog. He just wandered in here one day and never left." Jennifer pats the dog and reaches for Missy's saddle, "Here, let me take that from you. Welcome to Beech Tree. I don't think you've been here before, have you?"

"No, I haven't. Although I know some of the history. Your dad started this barn, didn't he?"

"Yes, he did. Almost 40 years ago, now. I didn't take over until about ten years ago. I always knew that I wanted to be a trainer but he

216

did his best to convince me to go get a 'real job.' It didn't take him long to realize that I wouldn't be happy doing anything other than working with Saddlebreds Shortly after I joined him here, he died."

"I'm so sorry to hear that. I imagine that you think of him every day. It must be really fulfilling to be carrying on his legacy."

"It is. But it hasn't been easy. I would definitely benefit from his experience and knowledge, particularly on tough horses." She laughs, "Which brings me to the reason for your visit. Toreador is waiting to meet you."

"I've heard about his reputation. What can you tell me about him?"

As they walk into the barn together, Jennifer replays the events that brought Toreador to Beech Tree. "Ms. Smithson's daughter was taking some lessons from me and I think that it made sense to her that she'd move Toreador here so that they could learn together. But Toreador is way too much horse for Blair. I think we knew that right away, but it took a while for everyone to accept it and realize it was time to move on."

"The rumor is that he's dangerous."

Jennifer shakes her head. "He's not intentionally dangerous, in my opinion. In fact, I've gotten really attached to him. I would say that he is a little distrustful and was used to going at full speed every time someone stepped into the stirrup." She stops to hold the door open for Missy to precede her into the barn. "He's dramatically better now than he was. We've been working on making him stop and wait and stand since he arrived here last August, and most of those lessons have taken hold. But he is a lot of horse. I do think that there are only a handful of amateurs capable of tackling him and you are definitely a member of that small group."

"Thank you. I've been blessed with great teachers and horses. And I've been riding such a long time that I'm free from the fear that lots of amateurs struggle with. I think that it must be miserable to be afraid of your horse."

"Yes. It's a real problem for lots of riders. And it's one of the primary factors I consider when I'm trying to match a horse to a rider. If it's okay with you, I'll just warm him up for you in your saddle so we won't have to change saddles." She waits for Missy to nod and then goes on. "I also thought we'd have you try him in his training bridle with just the snaffle. We can put his show bridle on if you prefer, but I think this will make him a little more tolerant and will give you time to get used to him."

"That sounds perfect." Missy's tone is distracted. She is standing at the stall door staring in at Toreador. "Wow. He's much bigger than I expected."

Jennifer agrees. "Yes, he's a big, strong boy. And he was used to getting his own way. A terrible combination. He's come to respect us and now understands that he won't always get his way."

"He sounds a lot different from the mare I'm riding now. She is so easy to like. She's talented, and beautiful and flashy. But she's a little on the small side."

"You bought Josephine's Dream this winter, didn't you? I think I saw an ad in Saddle Horse Report early in the year."

Missy nods. "Yes. And I love Josie. She has a huge motor. But her size works against her when she goes up against the big boys."

"Yes. I imagine you have to stay off the rail to keep from getting covered up at the big shows. Although that mare has a big reputation and I imagine the judges keep an eye out for her." By now, Eduardo has finished saddling Toreador. He rechecks the bridle and signals that he is ready. Jennifer warns Missy to stand back and pushes the stall door wide open, making sure that the door latch is fully retracted so that Toreador won't scrape against it on his way out of the stall.

Toreador rushes from his stall, his shoes making scrambling sounds as everyone automatically yells "Whoa!" He stops and stands when he is in the concrete aisle. Jennifer says, "You may not believe it, but that stall exit is dramatically better than what he used to do when he first arrived here. We can't seem to convince him that the door isn't going to reach out and grab him. I like to think that he rushes out because he's so happy to be going to work."

Missy laughs. "A lot of horses do that. I've learned to stay out of their way."

Missy stands quietly in the center of the ring while Jennifer warms Toreador up, taking video on her cell phone of the horse to review later.

218

When Jennifer is finished, Missy quickly pulls her gloves on, mounts, and competently collects her reins.

"You'll notice that he'll get stronger and stronger as he goes. He doesn't need much leg, other than just some very light and steady pressure to keep him going straight and to give him some security." Missy nods as she listens to Jennifer's instructions and she allows him to jog over to the rail before beginning to post.

Jennifer yells encouraging words as Missy trots by. "Nice. Very nice. Try to keep that speed. Good Missy!" She glances at Eduardo and he is grinning, watching Toreador as he maintains an aggressive but manageable pace.

Missy pulls him to a stop, widens her hands, and signals Toreador that she wants him to slow gait. He rears up slightly in front, transferring weight to his rear legs, and dances sideways before she gets him to use his momentum to go forward. Within a few steps, he is slow gaiting down the ring, although it is clear she is having trouble keeping his body square and his gait even, particularly on the corners. Jennifer gives her encouragement "Good, Missy. Don't let him bully you. Take a stronger hold and give him some leg."

Missy again follows her instructions and the horse begins to even out but he also speeds up. After a few passes, she reverses direction. As with the first direction, the trot is much better than the slow gait, but the horse gains speed and momentum with every pass. Before long, Missy pulls him to a stop in the middle of the ring and Eduardo and Jennifer move forward together to grab the horse's bridle.

After he has been halted for a few moments, Missy quietly dismounts and then stands back. "Wow." Missy takes a few deep breaths and then repeats, "Wow." She pauses again. "So that is what a stake horse feels like."

"Yes, it is an amazing feeling, isn't it?"

"Wow." Missy looks at Jennifer and says, "I know I keep repeating myself but it is because I'm nearly speechless. What a rush."

"He's a handful but you rode him really well."

"Actually, he's two hands full. I can see why the Smithsons are selling him. He's not very suitable for an amateur."

Jennifer very briefly considers trying to defend Toreador's potential as an amateur horse and then abandons the strategy. "Right, although I will say that he has come a long way in the last ten months. But he is nine years old, so he's pretty set in his ways." She pats the horse and Eduardo begins to lead him back to his stall. "I'm really proud of what we've accomplished with him, but I do agree that he is best suited as a stake horse. Of course, rumor has it that you might be looking for a stake horse."

"Yes, I haven't made it any secret that my goal is to win the big class in Louisville. I actually think that Josie might be able to do it, but everyone knows that Toreador can do it so that's why I'm considering him."

Once they are standing outside Toreador's stall watching Eduardo towel the horse off, Missy continues, "Honestly, we have less than two months to go before the show. I'm not sure that I could learn to ride him well enough in that time to be competitive. I can imagine that I only saw a fraction of the energy he hands out when he's at a show."

"I understand what you're saying, but he's sound and healthy. He's nine, so it is likely that he'll be able to show for a few more years. We take good care of him. So even if you don't think you can show him in the stake this year, that doesn't mean that you lose the opportunity forever."

"Is anyone else looking at him?"

Again, Jennifer briefly considers stretching the truth to apply pressure to Missy and discards it. "I've had lots of calls. I think folks are waiting to see him show since they haven't seen him since last August. That's understandable. And he has a reputation as a wild child. So it is going to take a very special buyer. But he's a very special horse. There aren't any other proven stake winners currently for sale."

"Good point." After one long last look at the chestnut, Missy retrieves her saddle from the tack room. "I need to think about this a bit. Would you be willing to call me if someone else looks serious? I really am interested but I need to react with my head rather than my ego."

"I will call you, but as you know, someone could drive up here at any time with a check in their hand and I owe it to my clients to take the check if it's big enough. So I can't promise you anything."

"I understand. I'll think it over and call you in a couple of days." Jennifer walks Missy out to her SUV and they shake hands before Missy drives away.

After leaving Beech Tree, Missy stops at the first coffee shop she sees, orders a large latte at the drive-through window, and then parks in the parking lot to call her dad. He answers on the first ring.

"How was it?"

"The ride was amazing. He has gears that I've never felt before. He goes with a huge step and it keeps getting bigger." She pauses as she tries to find the words to describe her ride on Toreador.

"Hm. I hear a 'but' coming."

"You know me too well. I haven't really sorted out what I think. He definitely is talented. But he's really hard to ride. I can tell that it would be easy to piss him off. I don't know whether I could get it together in the two months that are left before Louisville. And I have to say that he's kind of a hard horse to like."

Her dad asks, "What do you mean?"

"It's hard to describe. When you stand at his stall door, he doesn't look at you or lean toward you like Josie does. He avoids eye contact and looks completely disinterested in the people around him." She hesitates and goes on. "Maybe I expect too much."

"Maybe. But I know that the relationships you have with your horses have always been really important to you. I'm sure you could learn to ride him. You're the best rider out there. Not that I'm biased or anything."

Missy smiles, "Thanks dad. You are biased, and I'm okay with that! I need to think about this a while, though. I did learn from that ride what it will take to have Josie be competitive against a horse like that. I need to make a decision pretty soon and get off the fence about whether she stays in the Amateur Class or we try for the stake win this year with her. I'm not riding her nearly aggressively enough if she's going to the Open Class."

"Sounds like you need to mull things over and maybe talk to Annie about it. I need to go off to a committee meeting, but drive back safely and call me tonight, okay?"

"Yes. Go be senatorial. I'll call you later." She disconnects the call, puts her Mercedes in gear, and heads towards North Carolina for another practice session on Josie before returning to Virginia.

CHAPTER 53

"I think there's a good chance that you'll get an offer for Toreador from Missy Phillips. She struggled a little to ride him and I think that put her off a little, but I could tell that she was tempted anyway. He behaved well for her." Jennifer is describing Missy's ride on Toreador that occurred the previous day to Marianne and Blair. They are all riding in Marianne's Lexus sedan on their way to Kiplenan Saddlebreds.

Blair is in the front seat on the passenger side and she twists her body so that she can see Jennifer. "I'm glad she struggled a little. It makes me feel a little better."

"Blair! For the last time, you need to quit putting yourself down." Marianne's tone is frustrated and she repeats her usual refrain, "You're a beautiful rider."

Blair rolls her eyes at Jennifer, but Jennifer says. "I agree. It really is just a matter of finding a horse that you mesh with. I'm really excited that you're going to try this horse out today. I've been really impressed by him."

After withdrawing Toreador from the show at the Shelby County Fair, Jennifer convinced Marianne to allow her to contact Clark Benton to see whether Vendome Copper's owner would consider selling him. It had taken a full 24 hours before he returned her call to invite them over to ride the young gelding.

Marianne asks Jennifer, "We saw this horse at the Shelby County Fair, but what can you tell us about him?"

"His name is Vendome Copper. He was bred in Illinois by Mrs. Louise Clancy-Mellon." As Jennifer sketches out Vendome's bloodlines and describes the characteristics of his dam and sire, Marianne peppers her with questions that indicate she has done her homework.

They discuss the show records of Vendome's siblings and half-siblings, until Blair gently interrupts them. "Why do you think he might be a good fit for me?"

"Clark said that his assistant, Bobby Acton, has been training Vendome since he was two years old. You'll remember Bobby from when he was Johnnie Stuart's assistant. I think you had Toreador there during that time."

Marianne quickly interrupts Jennifer. "He seemed quiet and competent, but Johnnie totally ran the show over there so I don't think I ever even had a conversation with him. Do you know him?"

Jennifer continues, "I don't know him well, just enough to say hello. I think he moved here from out West a few years ago. But Clark said he's a really good horseman and that he has done a great job with this horse. Clark said that the horse has a great brain. He never gets upset or frustrated. He has a great attitude in the barn and doesn't have any vices, like kicking or biting. He said that he works hard every day and is a happy horse that also happens to be blessed with a lot of talent."

Marianne adds, "I looked it up last night and saw that he beat 23 horses to win the Three-Year-Old gaited sweepstakes in Indy last fall." She is turning her car through the gates marked with the logo for Kiplenan Saddlebreds and mentions, "I've never been here before, but I've always been curious about this place."

"I was here with my Dad when I was really young, so I don't really remember it very well. It's an old place with a lot of history. There was an article on it in the *Saddle Horse Report* a few years ago." They are driving down a tree-lined lane and can see white-painted fences behind the trees on each side of the narrow road. As they slowly roll down the drive, they can see that the pastures behind the trees are filled with mares and foals.

Blair asks, "How many horses are here, do you know?"

"I'm not sure, but we should ask Clark. I think they breed around thirty mares a year." Jennifer tries to resurrect what she knows about the Kiplenan breeding operation. "I know that he has at least three studs here."

Blair shakes her head in disbelief. "Geez. If they have 30 foals every year, then there are 30 yearlings, 30 two-year-olds, and etcetera. That's a lot of horses!"

By now, the car is entering a large brick courtyard, anchored by a large central fountain and a central barn, fronted by a large white porch. It is bordered by several smaller white barns and buildings, all painted a bright white with red trim. Marianne says quietly, "Wow. Who knew there was this much money in the furniture business?"

As they park in front of the porch and get out of the car, they all pause to admire the property. "What a beautiful place," Blair breathes.

"Does he have a single son?" Marianne asks under her breath while she opens the trunk for Jennifer to extract Blair's saddle.

The barn porch is decorated with rocking chairs with horse-themed cushions and the rug in front of the door contains the same logo they saw on the front gate. Marianne opens the door and they enter a large lobby, lined with framed photographs of horses and containing beautiful antique cabinets filled with trophies and silver trays. The floor is oak and is covered with colorful, woven rugs. There are several comfortable looking, upholstered chairs with side tables, also containing a variety of silver cups and trophies. Directly across the room is a large plate glass window that looks into an empty training ring. Jennifer closes the door softly behind them. The room smells of furniture polish and they begin to admire the awards that are displayed.

In a few moments, the door behind them reopens and Clark Benton enters. He removes a baseball cap with the Kiplenan logo from his bald head and steps into the room to greet them, quickly focusing on Marianne. "Good morning. Ya'll must be Ms. Smithson."

"Please call me Marianne." She introduces Blair and then Jennifer. "You have a gorgeous place here."

Clark replies warmly as he reaches to take Blair's saddle from Jennifer, "I can't take credit for it, of course. My wife supervises the housekeeping and decorating for the farm. But I sure do agree with you. Mr. Kiplenan loves beautiful things."

"And beautiful horses, obviously," Marianne replies. "How long has this facility been here?"

"The Kiplenan family has owned this property for generations and a family member has always lived here on the farm, breeding Saddlebreds. This particular barn is relatively new and was just being finished when I got here, 21 years ago."

"You've been here a long time," Marianne confirms. "Do you see much of Mr. Kiplenan?"

"We don't see nearly enough of him. He's still running the furniture business, although his eldest son is about ready to step in."

"Oh! So he DOES have a son." She glances at Blair as she says this.

"Mother!" Blair rolls her eyes as she admonishes her mom.

"I'm just kidding!" Marianne says it quickly, and it is apparent that she didn't mean to be so obvious.

Clark laughs. "He's a widower. His wife died of cancer many years ago and he has two sons. The oldest is married and has two young children. They live in Chicago. The youngest son is still single and lives in Alabama. They both work for the furniture business and the youngest one runs a large manufacturing plant near Birmingham."

"Ah. Well that explains why we don't know them." Marianne continues, "If they were in Louisville, we'd probably run into them at charity events."

"Maybe, but they're a quiet family. I don't know how much they socialize." Clark then changes the subject, "I think you came to see horses today, right?" He invites them to follow him back to the barn area to meet Vendome. As he walks, he explains, "Vendome is one of the few horses in the barn that aren't owned by Mr. Kiplenan. As I think you know, he's owned by a lady from Chicago."

Marianne quickly inserts a comment, "Yes. Her horses were at Stuart Stables when our horse Toreador was there."

"Oh, right. I'd forgotten that you were there at the same time. She's a really nice lady and several of the horses she brought over were actually bred here at the farm so it was good to have them back."

They have entered the stall area and it is immaculate. The long center aisle is lined by polished wooden walls, with a leather halter and brass nameplate engraved with each horse's name and breeding on their stall door. A few doors are open and the aisle contains several red and white tack trunks, emblazoned with the Kiplenan logo.

Jennifer can't help herself from exclaiming, "Beautiful! Your place is just beautiful."

Clark replies with pride, "Thank you. We take good care of it."

By now, they have arrived at one of the open doors and Clark says, "This is Vendome Copper. Just like I can't take credit for the decorating in the lobby, I can't take credit for Vendome. His trainer

226

here, Bobby Acton, is fully responsible for turning him into the nice horse you'll ride today."

Vendome is standing in cross ties with his head near the open stall door. The chestnut gelding has a pleasant expression and looks at them with bright, interested eyes. Bobby is working with a groom to put Vendome's tail in a brace and he looks over his shoulder toward the visitors. "We're almost ready here. I'm glad you could make it today."

The women all greet Bobby and then stand back from the door, as Clark takes a girth from the tack trunk near the door and enters the stall with Blair's saddle.

"Oh. He looks so friendly!" Blair says as she reaches a tentative hand towards the big horse. He leans towards her, moving his lips to see if she has a candy in her hand.

Bobby smiles and says, "He thinks you might have a treat for him. But you're right. He's happy and very easy-going."

Blair gently pets his nose and the horse continues to stand quietly while the trainers and grooms finish getting him ready to ride. Once he is nearly ready, Clark invites Marianne and Blair down to the practice ring while Jennifer hangs back to talk to Bobby.

"I put the show bridle on, if that's okay with you," Bobby says as he looks to Jennifer for her reaction. "I figured we'd give you the full experience."

"That's great. I thought I'd ride him first and if he seems steady enough we can put Blair on after that. Does that sound workable?" Jennifer stands back as Bobby leads the horse from his stall. She admires how quietly he stands in the aisle. "Is there anything I need to know about him?"

"Nope. He's pretty solid." Bobby checks the girth one final time before leading the gelding to the practice ring.

Once in the ring, Jennifer mounts without incident and Vendome stands while she gathers her reins. His head is high and he looks hyper-alert, as though it is taking every ounce of self-control to remain still.

"I usually make him walk around the ring a time or two to get started." Bobby steps back from the horse, and Jennifer gently squeezes him forward. Vendome moves off at a walk, and Jennifer

227

rides him around the ring, walking him through serpentines and occasionally halting him. After a full circuit she begins trotting.

Vendome's ears remain pricked forward and he begins pumping his knees high as he moves around the ring. Clark positions himself near the center of the ring and whistles at the horse as he enters the straightaway and comes towards them. Vendome elevates even higher and trots forward eagerly. After only two circuits, Jennifer halts the horse near Bobby and asks, "Is there anything special I should do to slow gait him?"

Bobby shakes his head, "Nope. He knows how to do a proper slow gait. Just go ahead anytime you're ready."

Jennifer widens her hands, sits straight in the saddle, and clucks softly. After a single circuit, Jennifer changes direction and slow gaits clockwise around the ring. She then halts him in the center and looks at Blair. "Are you ready to get on?"

Blair shows a slight hesitation and asks, "Do you think I should?" It is clear to Jennifer that she is asking whether her trainer believes she is capable of riding the horse.

"Absolutely. He's totally ready for you."

After Blair has mounted, Jennifer looks up at her, "He's very nice. We'll just start with a slow trot. Remember to be soft with your hands and to use your body to keep him going slow." Jennifer glances at Bobby and says, "Do you want to call the gaits, since you know your horse?"

"Sure. And you can coach Blair through the ride." Before releasing Vendome, Jennifer reminds her client. "You're a good rider, just stay calm and quiet. He's got plenty of energy, but he's very respectful. He's going to do exactly what you tell him to do, so just be aware of the signals you're giving him."

Bobby's blue eyes meet Jennifer's and she nods, so he addresses Blair, "When you're ready, just walk him out to the wall and turn left. Just see if you can make him flat walk all the way around just once."

Blair looks very nervous, but nods and clucks softly to the horse. He steps forward and starts to jog as Jennifer says, "Just use your snaffle to remind him to walk and talk to him."

Blair obediently says, "Walk," and Vendome settles into a flat-footed walk. By the time they have gone completely around the ring, Blair looks relaxed and has a small smile.

Bobby tells her, "That is excellent. He's ready to trot any time you are."

Blair doesn't wait for instructions from Jennifer as she shortens her reins slightly, squeezes her legs, and says, "Whup, trot." Vendome immediately begins trotting and Blair posts along with his stride, looking more comfortable and secure with each step.

After two rounds, Bobby says, "Cut through the middle and go the other direction."

As Blair follows Bobby's instructions, Jennifer encourages her client. "Good, Blair. Keep sitting back. Nice!"

As Blair completes her second circuit going this direction, Bobby looks over at Jennifer and says softly, "He looks ready to slow gait. Okay by you?"

Jennifer smiles, satisfied with how the ride is going and says, "Absolutely. Let's do it."

Bobby raises his voice and says to Blair. "Go ahead and stop him when you're ready and we'll slow gait."

Blair halts the chestnut horse and Jennifer says, "He's really easy. Just separate your hands and cluck."

Blair follows her instructions and Vendome quickly steps off into the gait. Bobby says, "That's good, but he'll go slower than that. Take a stronger hold. Use your little fingers to tell him you want him to come back to you a little." Blair follows Bobby's instructions and the horse slows, maintaining a steady cadence.

After two rounds, Blair is smiling broadly and everyone in the ring can tell that she is enjoying her ride. After nearly ten minutes, Blair pulls Vendome to a stop in the middle of the ring, where he stands quietly. She reaches down to pat him on the neck and looks at Marianne, who has been uncharacteristically silent throughout the session.

"He is really fun!" Blair dismounts and steps back after patting the horse again, clearly happy with her ride.

"You look good on him," Marianne's first words are positive and warm. "It's easy to forget that he's only four."

229

Her last comment isn't addressed to anyone in particular but Bobby answers proudly, "It is. He's not quite finished, but he's pretty close."

Jennifer asks, "What do you think his weak spots are?"

Bobby smiles down at her. He is nearly six feet tall, and she is suddenly aware that he is a handsome man. "It's tough to criticize your children. I can see his faults because I'm with him every day, but I'm so proud of him." Bobby pats Vendome and continues. "He has a tendency to lean in the corners. I have to constantly remind him not to drop his shoulder. And I'm always working to make sure he is as soft and pliable on the right side as the left."

"I noticed that he's a little stiffer on the right but every horse has a favorite side. It's like being right- or left-handed." Jennifer stops talking, suddenly aware that she should be highlighting his faults, to bring the horse's price down in case Marianne and Blair want to make an offer.

As they leave the practice ring, Clark leads Marianne and Blair back to the lobby and Jennifer follows Bobby to Vendome's stall to retrieve Blair's saddle. "Thanks so much for showing us Vendome. I'd be very surprised if they didn't ask for a vet check."

"I admit that I'd be sad to see him go. I'm really attached to him. And I'm really looking forward to showing him in Louisville this year." Bobby is wiping down Blair's saddle as he talks.

"There's no reason he can't stay here until after Louisville even if they do buy him, is there? I have my hands full at Beech Tree and you get along with him so well that it would be to everyone's advantage to leave him here through August. After that, he can begin his career in the Amateur Class."

Bobby looks relieved. "That would be great, if it works out. I know that Mrs. M was really looking forward to having him through Louisville, too. Maybe Ms. Smithson would wait to complete the purchase after that show?"

"We're probably getting ahead of ourselves, but I can certainly suggest that." Jennifer takes the clean and dry saddle from Bobby.

As she turns to go, he abruptly asks, "Would you like to go get a burger with me sometime?"

She is so surprised that she hesitates to respond and he goes on, "Unless you're already seeing someone."

"Uh, No. I mean, I'm not seeing anyone and I'd love to go get a burger." She finds herself stammering as she accepts his invitation.

"Cool. How about Saturday night?"

They quickly make plans and he gives her a smile and watches her walk away to meet Marianne and Blair.

On their way back to Beech Tree, Blair chatters happily about Vendome and how much she enjoyed riding him. Jennifer listens but her thoughts keep wandering to her upcoming dinner with Bobby and how surprised her mom will be to learn she has a date. Her thoughts are interrupted when she hears Marianne say, "Let's get a vet check."

Jennifer leans forward and says, "I'll take care of it right away. If all the x-rays and tests come back clean, when would you like to take possession?" She tells them that he is already entered in the Junior Class at Louisville and that Bobby told her that his current owner is looking forward to that show. She ends with, "You might be able to negotiate a lower price if you're willing to wait to take ownership until after Louisville."

"That might work. Let's see what the vet says before we go any further." Marianne's reply makes Blair smile happily and she blows her mother a kiss from across the car.

Before saying goodbye to her clients that day, Jennifer asks Marianne whether she has made any decision about entering Toreador in the World Championships.

"I really haven't given it enough thought. Like I mentioned before, I'm hesitating because I'm afraid that he'll embarrass me," Marianne admits.

"Entry forms are due on Tuesday, so please let me know what you decide. If I enter him, you can always decide to scratch him later."

"Yes, but I won't get a refund on those huge fees unless a veterinarian provides a note, right?"

"That's right," Jennifer affirms. "I'll prepare an entry form but I won't send it unless you give me the green light."

CHAPTER 54

3:00 PM July 1, Stuart Stables

Johnnie Stuart has just finished filling out the entry forms for the World Championship Horse Show and has entered Night Train in the Junior Gaited Class, knowing that horses can move between classes as long as they stay within their division (five-gaited, three-gaited and fine harness). This means that he can still show in the Open Stake Class once he arrives at the show.

He hesitates before electronically submitting the forms and then picks up the phone before he can change his mind.

It rings several times and then Marianne answers, "Hello?"

He is quiet for a few seconds. Although he has rehearsed this conversation in his mind many times, he is unsure of the best way to begin. "Marianne, this is Johnnie Stuart."

Her voice is tight, "Hello Johnnie. What can I do for you?"

"I'm about ready to send in my entries for Louisville and wondered if ya'll would want to bring your horse back here so he'd have a chance to repeat last year's win." Marianne stays silent, so Johnnie continues, "I'd be willing to let bygones be bygones for his sake."

She is still silent. He interprets this as a willingness to consider the idea and is encouraged. "Now that girl that's got him might have ruined him, so I can't make any promises..."

She interrupts, "I bet all I'd have to do is tell everyone that I never should have moved him, right?"

"That'd sure be nice of ya'll, seeing as I'm willing to help you out."

She says sweetly, "Well Johnnie, it's really an interesting offer. And I have every confidence that Toreador will successfully defend his title."

Johnnie smiles, assuming that he will get Toreador back as she continues in the same sweet tone, "But I would rather walk barefoot over hot coals than give you the chance to show my horse ever again. Good day."

Marianne dials Jennifer at Beech Tree. As soon as Jennifer answers she begins, "In case I've been at all unclear, I want Toreador

232

entered in Louisville. You'll be riding, so you'd better be good. And I have every expectation of winning. Don't embarrass me."

All Jennifer can say is, "Yes ma'am."

CHAPTER 55

Mrs. M is sitting next to Mr. Kiplenan in his box seats at the Lexington Junior League Horse Show. This is probably the last year that it will be held at the historic Red Mile facility and they have been sharing memories of the famous horses that have shown there.

"The only problem with this place is that some gaited horses show well here and some don't," Mr. Kiplenan says. "The long straightaways are great, but it's a narrow track and it takes a pretty maneuverable horse to get around the tight corners. Lots of trainers believe that it's more likely to cause injuries than a traditional ring, so they leave their gaited horses at home."

"That's true. Johnnie Stuart never brings his gaited horses here for that reason. But my gaited horse really loved it." Mrs. M is very satisfied with Vendome's win in the Junior Gaited Class earlier in the week.

"Yes. You should be really pleased. That was a good class and he deserved the win." Her host lowers his voice and leans closer to her. "It's a shame that Night Train didn't show in that class. Your Vendome would have taken him to the cleaners."

Mrs. M agrees for several reasons. Vendome's tractable nature is well-suited to the ring and two members of the three-judge panel were equitation instructors. On the first night of the show, the judges had wasted no time making it apparent that they would reward horses that demonstrated good behavior and nice transitions, regardless of the class. While many trainers were grumbling about the way they were placing the classes, Vendome had benefited from their priorities and had received the blue ribbon. Mrs. M glances down at the program she is holding and notices that the next class is the Amateur Five-Gaited Mares. This is one of her favorite classes and she leans forward in her chair in anticipation.

As the previous class' winner completes her victory pass, Annie gives Missy some last minute instructions. "Now, you're going to have to work hard to keep her speed down in the straightaway so that you can get around the corners in good shape. Start slowing her down about three quarters of the way down the ring. These judges care

234

about behavior so you need to make every transition look easy. Be very deliberate about how you ask for the canter."

Just then, the bugle blows. Missy adjusts her reins and trots into the ring. She realizes on her first pass that she has vastly underestimated how much the proportions of the ring will play into her ride. Josie clearly loves the long sides and uses them to build up speed. Missy struggles to slow her down in time to make a balanced turn in the narrow ring. While Missy manages these adjustments fairly easily at the trot, she begins to struggle during the slow gait. It is very difficult to keep Josie slow along the entire side and the judges prolong the agony by waiting for two full circuits of the ring before calling for the rack.

Missy's challenges get even bigger at the rack. When Missy tries to slow Josie before the corner, her horse resists. Missy knows that the judges will notice that Josie's ears are not forward around the turns and that her cadence isn't as steady as it should be, even though she is using her inside rein and leg to keep her horse balanced. However, the real trouble comes in the canter. The announcer tells the class to canter when Missy is at the end of the ring. Josie's mounting frustration combined with the congestion at the end of the ring where several horses are bunched up, cause Missy to miscue her horse. Josie fails to execute a smooth canter takeoff. While it is a small mistake, Missy knows the judges will penalize her. The remainder of the ride passes in a blur and Missy is unsurprised when she receives a third place ribbon.

As Missy rides Josie back to the stalls, Annie walks beside her. Annie pats Missy on the leg and consoles her, saying, "Opinions are like assholes. Everyone's got one and they're all different."

Despite her disappointment with her ride, Missy acknowledges the truth in Annie's statement. They knew when they went into the ring that Josie would be at a disadvantage. The mare's fiery style was not a good match to the judges' obvious preferences. But Missy knows that she can learn from this ride and that the experience in the ring will ultimately help her improve.

CHAPTER 56

"Hi Mom!" When her phone rings, Jennifer answers it using the speakerphone feature. She is in her kitchen chopping celery, wearing pressed khaki shorts and a sleeveless top. Her long brown hair, still wet from her shower, is wrapped in a towel.

"Hi Honey. Are you busy?" Her mom's voice comes through the speaker, sounding very far away.

"Actually, I'm making your famous potato salad and you called at the perfect time. How much vinegar do I put in the dressing?"

Her mother reacts with stunned silence. After several seconds she says, "What? I thought you said you were making potato salad but that can't be true." Her mother teases, "Who are you and what have you done with my daughter?"

"Ha ha, Mom. Very funny." But her mother has a point. She hasn't cooked anything that hasn't involved the microwave in several months. "I'm having someone over for dinner."

"Then I guess we'll trade information. You tell me who's coming for dinner and I'll tell you how to make the dressing for the salad." Her mother waits expectantly.

"His name is Bobby." Jennifer quickly goes on, "Now don't make a big deal of it, but we went out last week and it was really fun." She smiles at the memory. They had burgers and beers on an outdoor patio at a local pub and had talked for hours. And not just about horses. He had traveled extensively and had spent several years in Sweden and then in South Africa as an assistant horse trainer. He had entertained her with stories of his experiences and they both had laughed over her stories of backpacking through Europe with her girlfriends after her college graduation.

Her mother demands more information, "That's not enough. Where did you meet him? Tell me about him."

"He's an assistant trainer at Kiplenan. I knew who he was but didn't really know him very well. He asked me out when I took Blair over to ride a four-year-old that he's training."

Her mother quickly interrupts, "Whoa, missy! Tell me about Blair! What's going on with Toreador?"

236

Jennifer smiles that she has succeeded in distracting her mom from grilling her about Bobby. "First, the vinegar. How much?"

Her mother gives her the proportions for the sweet and tangy dressing for the salad. When she is certain that Jennifer has mixed the dressing properly, she resumes, "Now, tell me about Blair and Toreador."

"Marianne finally accepted that Toreador and Blair weren't going to be successful together. I'd had my eye on a horse named Vendome Copper and finally convinced them to go look at him. Blair rode him and fell in love. He's a four-year-old gaited horse with a sweet personality. You should have seen her riding him. She looked so happy! She completely shed the tense and timid persona that she has with Toreador." She continues, "It was even obvious to her mother. We did a vet check and Marianne committed to buying him. The sale will complete after the Louisville show."

"So tell me about Toreador. What's happening with him?"

"He's for sale, but we've entered him in the Open Class at Louisville. I'll be riding him if he hasn't sold by then."

"Wow, honey! That's a big deal! What fabulous news! Congratulations! It's your first time showing in that class! And you'll be showing the reigning World Champion! Wow!"

"I'm pretty excited." Jennifer continues, "There's a lot of road to cover between now and the show, though. I'm showing him at Shelbyville in two weeks. It's the first time he'll have been in a ring since winning the stake last year." As she says it, she feels a nervous twinge.

"How's he doing?"

"He's doing absolutely great here at home. I think he's relieved to be able to get some of his 'go for it' attitude back. We were really trying to force a square peg into a round hole." Jennifer folds the dressing into the chopped vegetables as she talks. "And I've gotten really fond of him. I actually look forward to working him every day, although I have to do it early while I still have plenty of energy. The craziest part is that I think he's starting to like me as well. He actually came to the door of his stall to greet me this morning, rather than turning away. He even will take a peppermint from me, although he

237

bites it with his front teeth instead of chewing it like a normal horse."
She laughs lightly. "He has a very weird personality."

"How is Eduardo?"

This is the one cloud in Jennifer's currently sunny life, and she
covers the completed salad with cellophane wrap and places it in the
refrigerator before answering. "Most days are good. Some days are
not so good. I can tell that he's really trying."

"Jennifer, you know that you can't have him around horses if he's
drunk. He'll get hurt."

Jennifer sighs, "I know you're right but on most days he's fine. I
really need him, too. Business has really picked up this summer. All
the stalls are full and I especially need his help with Toreador.
Although he has improved a lot, I still don't ride him without Eduardo
being around to help." Jennifer turns to the sink to wash her hands
and keeps talking, "I feel bad because I talked him into coming back
to Kentucky. I can't just cut him loose. He doesn't have anywhere to
go. And I really need him through Louisville, at least."

He mom puts steel in her voice when she answers, "I know you
have a soft heart and you think you owe him, but you're not doing
him any favors. Do yourself a favor and make absolutely sure that
he's sober when he's with the horses."

"It's not that easy to tell if he's been drinking," Jennifer says
defensively. "But you're right. I know that I have to deal with it." She
glances at the digital clock that's on the microwave. "Holy smokes! I
have to go dry my hair. Gotta go, Mom."

238

CHAPTER 57

Kenny knows that he has found the right place at the Blue Grass Airport in Lexington because there are several other horse trailers in the parking lot. He looks across the pickup cab to Jeremy, "If they're on time, the plane should land in about 15 minutes, so keep your eyes peeled, ok?"

"Can I get out and watch from over by the gate?"

"Yes, absolutely. I'll check us in and then I'll meet you over there." Kenny steps out of the truck to hand his credentials to the approaching security guard. This is the first time that he has received a horse at the airport, and he is as excited and curious as his son.

Holly and Spy Master boarded a Boeing 727 in Ontario, CA a few hours ago along with two large tack trunks. And from the trailers parked in the lot, it is apparent that several other horses are also aboard. Holly told Kenny that this is a regular route for moving Thoroughbred race horses back and forth between Kentucky's Keeneland and Churchill Downs racetracks and the tracks on the west coast.

After checking in, Kenny joins Jeremy at the tall woven-wire gate that leads to the area where the plane will park once it has landed. Jeremy says excitedly, "I think it just landed. I saw a big white plane without any windows landing!"

"That's probably it, then. We'd better get back to the truck so we're ready to go when they open this gate."

A few moments later, a large white plane has taxied toward them and parked. As the pilot shuts down the engines, a pickup towing a wide ramp approaches it. The gate to the taxi area swings open, and Kenny follows the other trucks and trailers to the plane, parking a short distance from the ramp.

Jeremy and Kenny join the rest of the drivers and grooms that are waiting for the horses to come down the ramp, and one of the drivers asks Jeremy, "Is this your first time seeing the horses come off an airplane?"

"Yes, sir," Jeremy says, proudly. "We're here to pick up a World's Champion Saddlebred Stallion named Spy Master."

239

"Well, I bet you can get a tour of the plane if you ask 'em real nice."

Jeremy looks at his dad in surprise, "Dad! Do you think I could see inside?"

Jeremy has never been on board an aircraft of any kind before, and Kenny knows what a treat this would be for his son. "Well, as long as you make it quick so that Spy Master doesn't have to stand in the hot trailer waiting."

"I'll be fast!" His typically calm son is nearly jumping with excitement.

The man who has suggested the possibility of a tour tells Kenny, "I work for the transport company. I'll take him up the ramp and show him around while you take care of your horse."

Kenny thanks him and watches as the door to the aircraft slides open. A handler is holding the halter of a bay thoroughbred at the top of the ramp. He gives the horse several moments to adjust to the sunlight and to look at the wide ramp before him before carefully and slowly leading him down the ramp and handing his halter rope to a waiting driver.

Spy Master is the last horse to deplane and all the other trailers have departed when Kenny sees Holly at the top of the ramp, holding the halter of a large chestnut. The horse is wearing a light blanket and Holly is wearing a heavy coat and gloves, which look out of place in the hot afternoon. Spy Master stands at the top of the ramp and whinnies. Holly gives him time to look around and then begins to lead him down the ramp. After a brief hesitation at the top, he follows her without incident.

Kenny meets her at the bottom of the ramp and says, "Welcome to Kentucky! Did everything go okay?" Without waiting for her to answer, he says teasingly. "I know it probably seemed like a long flight, but it is still summer."

Holly laughs, "I need to peel these layers off. They keep the plane at 40 degrees during the flight. The last time I did this, I thought I was going to freeze to death, so this time I came prepared." As they lead Spy Master to the waiting trailer, Holly says, "I met your son. He was getting the grand tour. I left him in charge of getting the trunks unloaded. He seems like a really nice kid."

240

"He is and he's really excited about having Spy Master stay with us. I bet he didn't sleep a wink last night." Kenny and Holly load Spy Master in Kenny's trailer and then he steps back to look at his friend. Although he sees her at the Louisville show every August, he marvels at how little she has changed since they attended college together at William Woods. At 5'7", she is only a couple of inches shorter than him and as she peels off her heavy jacket, he can tell that she has maintained her thin, wiry frame. Her long, curly dark hair is in a ponytail and she still looks like a college student. She gives him a quick hug, and then starts back toward the plane, where Jeremy is struggling to carry one end of a tack trunk down the long ramp. Kenny and Holly take the trunk from Jeremy and the crew member from the plane and before long, they are headed back to Riverside Stables.

On the way, Jeremy talks about the airplane. "Dad, it was so cool! There are 21 stalls in the plane and there is one handler for every three horses. The stalls are about half the size of the ones in the barn at home. It kind of looks like a huge horse trailer, but bigger and taller. The horses can all see each other. The handler told me that it helps them stay calm."

Kenny smiles at his normally reserved son's enthusiasm and asks, "Did you get to see the cockpit?"

"Yeah! There is a pilot, a co-pilot and a navigator. The cockpit is really crowded and it is full of switches. There are so many switches that they cover the roof! I got to sit in the pilot's seat! I think I want to be a pilot."

Jeremy is sitting in the rear seat of the pickup cab and Kenny glances at him in the rear-view mirror. "I thought you wanted to be a horse trainer."

This momentarily silences his son, and Holly quickly interrupts. "Maybe he could be both."

Jeremy nods in agreement. "Yes. I think I could be both."

The rest of the hour-long ride passes with the three of them talking about Spy Master's training regimen. There are only five weeks to go before the Louisville show and Holly has planned each day's work.

"You still want to show him at Shelbyville, right?" Kenny asks.

"Definitely. That's two and a half weeks away and I'll come back a day or so early."

"Then you're still going back to California tomorrow morning?"

"Yes, I have an early flight. I was hoping that I could get you to run me over to the Holiday Inn by the airport after we get Spy Master settled. I can catch their shuttle in the morning. I've got to keep all the plates spinning back there. I don't have a good assistant like you do with Jeremy."

Jeremy smiles at her compliment and says, "I've got Spy Master's stall ready and we went to get all of his feed yesterday. I checked to make sure his stall is perfect."

"Thank you. I really appreciate that." She directs her attention to Kenny, "Did you have any trouble finding the same brands?" Holly had given Kenny a detailed list of the feeds in Spy Master's diet.

"No problem. They're higher quality feeds than what I give our horses, though, so I'm glad that you were specific."

"Yeah. Nothing but the best for our boy. Even though we haven't had any colic incidents since Kansas City, I'm still really careful," she says. "I really appreciate the trouble you've gone to. I hope that the money we agreed to is worth it."

"It is. And it is a privilege to have him." He slows the truck and turns into the driveway of Riverside.

Holly looks around at the small farm. "What a pretty place."

Kenny thanks her and acknowledges, "We've spruced it up this summer. Jeremy is pretty tired of painting fences, aren't you son?"

"I don't mind." Jeremy points the new fenced area next to the barn out to Holly. "We just built that new paddock this summer. And we have three new horses."

As Kenny brings the truck and trailer to a stop, Spy Master whinnies sharply from the back of the trailer. The horses in the paddock look up curiously.

Kenny begins to open the trailer door and says, "Jeremy, would you please make sure his stall door is open and put some fresh hay in it for him?" As soon as Jeremy steps away, he makes eye contact with Holly. "I thought Spy Master might come out a little feisty and I don't want Jeremy to get trampled.

"Good thinking, but he's usually pretty good. Especially for a stud." She steps into the trailer to untie her horse and slowly backs him out onto the grass in front of the barn. "Welcome to your home away from home, big boy."

The chestnut stallion snorts and looks alertly around, raising his head and smelling the air. She gives him a moment to survey his surroundings before leading him to his stall.

"Okay. The first task is to feed and water him, and then maybe I can get a tour. Then, we can go through the tack trunks and discuss the training schedule one more time. Will that work for you guys?" Holly addresses her question to Kenny and Jeremy.

Kenny replies, "Sounds great. Jeremy, why don't you grab a notepad from my office and take notes so that we don't forget anything, ok?"

Holly and Kenny walk to the hay stack that is stored in a covered area next to the barn. Kenny opens a bale and fans out the hay so that Holly can inspect it. "Wow. That looks like great hay." She picks through it carefully, looking for weeds and signs of rot or mold. Finding none, she straightens. "That is better hay than we get in California. I'm glad I didn't bother sending some of mine out to you. He gets two flakes in the morning and two at night."

They then move to the grain storage area and Holly continues, "Eileen told me that you had possum-proofed the feed. I'm glad you had that conversation."

"Your client seems like a nice lady. I think she's nervous about letting Spy Master out of her sight."

After Holly describes the grains and supplements in Spy Master's diet, Jeremy writes it down carefully and then asks, "Tell us how he eats. Does he normally just eat it all as fast as he can, or does he pick at it all day long?"

Holly looks at Jeremy with surprise. "That's a great question, Jeremy. He always eats his grain in a rush and then looks around for more. He eats about half his hay right away and saves the rest to nibble on all day. If you notice something different than this, pay close attention. It might be the first sign that he doesn't feel right. When he colicked, he quit eating and then quit drinking. Also, keep a close watch on his manure. I used to call him 'Sir Poops-A-Lot'

243

because his stall was always a mess. If it's too clean, pay close attention."

They return to the stall area, carrying feed for Spy Master. As soon as he is fed, Kenny asks Jeremy to feed the rest of the horses while he and Holly move Spy Master's tack trunks into the tack room. They open the large varnished wooden boxes with the Morning Star Barns logo on the front and top. As Holly removes each item, she and Kenny talk about it and quickly find themselves reliving events from their school years at William Woods when they learned many of the training techniques that they now use. Before long, they are laughing together about the time when Holly attached a martingale to a curb bit.

Kenny laughs loudly, "Do you remember Mr. Wilson's face when he saw it?"

Holly gasps with laughter and mimes their instructor by lowering her voice and drawling, "Miss McNair, I do believe you are trying to give me a stroke."

"It sounds like you're having a lot of fun."

Angela is standing in the doorway of the tack room. Holly wipes the tears of laughter from her eyes. Kenny can see from the stiff smile on his wife's face that she is not pleased, and he quickly introduces Holly. "Honey, this is Holly McNair. Holly, this is my wife, Angela."

Holly wipes a dusty hand on her jeans and offers it to Angela, "Hi Angela. I've heard a lot about you. It's great to finally meet you."

Angela shakes Holly's hand and then steps back to the door and makes eye contact with Kenny. "I thought I'd ask what time you wanted dinner tonight."

Kenny reads Angela's irritated expression and quickly invites Holly to have dinner with the family to smooth over the awkward interaction. But Holly has also picked up on Angela's mood so she says to Kenny, "That's so nice of you and I appreciate it, but we're almost done here and I was actually hoping for an early evening. It's been a long day and I have an early flight. I hope it won't be too much trouble to get you to just run me down to the Holiday Inn near the airport. I have a reservation there."

"Of course, that's no problem." Kenny then looks at Angela, "Honey, why don't you feed the kids and I'll figure something out when I get home, okay?"

His wife responds tightly, "Okay. I'll let you two get back to work then." She turns away quickly.

After she's gone, Holly looks at Kenny and raises her eyebrows, saying quietly, "Is it something I said?"

"No, don't worry about it." The formerly fun and happy mood between them has deflated though, and they return to their work more seriously.

It takes another hour for Kenny, Jeremy and Holly to finish reviewing the contents of the tack trunks. They then discuss Spy Master's daily training regimen and test the cameras in the stall and in the barn to be sure that Holly can link to them using an app on her smartphone.

"Jeremy, why don't you go over to the house and have dinner. Tell your mom that I'll be home in a couple of hours."

Holly quickly offers her hand to the boy. "Jeremy, thanks so much for your help with Spy Master. I feel a lot better now that I know what good hands I've left him in."

Jeremy lights up at Holly's compliment and gravely returns her hand shake.

When Kenny returns from taking Holly to her hotel near the Lexington airport, almost two hours later, he enters the house quietly. Jeremy and Emily are already in bed. Angela is sitting on the couch, watching TV, with the sound turned down low. Without greeting her he says, "Are you going to tell me what's wrong or are you going to make me guess?"

She continues staring at the TV. "What would your guess be?"

He can tell that she is angry, but they are both keeping their voices quiet to avoid waking the kids in the small mobile home. "That you are jealous."

She snaps back, "I'm not..." but then she stops. "Okay. Maybe you're right. Maybe I am jealous. Why wouldn't I be jealous? You never laugh like that with me."

"So what are you saying? I'm not allowed to laugh unless it is with you? Listen to yourself. What you did was awkward and

245

embarrassing. She's an old friend of mine and you embarrassed me in front of her." Kenny is letting his anger show, now. His fists are clenched at his sides and his posture is rigid.

"Well you two were acting awfully cozy. It kind of makes me wonder how good of friends you are."

"Angela. Stop it. Don't go another step further. I'm going to try to forget you said that." He takes a deep shaky breath, "But if you ever again come close to accusing me of cheating, I will not let it go. I bust my ass every day for you and for our kids. All I can think about is how to be successful enough to make you happy. For you to…" His voice trails off and he shakes his head. "I'm going to spend the night in my office. I need some time alone." He walks into their bedroom and removes his pillow from their bed. Without another word he quietly leaves the trailer house.

CHAPTER 58

It is the opening night of the Shelbyville Horse Show and it has been raining off and on all week. When Missy Phillips arrives at the barn where Annie Jessup's Big View Farm stalls are located, Annie greets her, "I'm glad you're here. You're in the first class tonight. You've never shown here before, have you?" When Missy shakes her head, Annie goes on, "Then let's walk up to the ring and talk about your strategy. There are some things you need to know about this ring. Also, this show is a little different from the others we've done, so it's important to approach it correctly."

Missy pulls the hood of her raincoat up over her bun as she follows Annie out into the drizzle. "Do you think they'll postpone?"

"I don't think so. This show typically goes off like clockwork, and I overheard someone saying that the Doppler maps show the rain will stop soon. Everyone says that the ring drains quickly. I imagine it'll be muddy but they'll run the show on time." Annie looks at the sky to the west as she talks, and the heavy gray clouds do appear to be lightening.

As they reach the ring, Annie continues, "There are a few things you need to know. First, notice the entrance to the ring. You come up a little hill, go under the crow's nest where the horse show office is, and then you make a hard right and trot slightly downhill down the rail in front of the judge." As Annie is talking, Missy steps forward to make sure that she sees the path that her trainer is pointing out. Annie goes on, "You must have a lot of control on the entrance or she will canter down the rail. Talk to her through the gate, keep telling her 'Whup, Trot' and you should be okay. Just be aware that you need to think your way through this to get it right."

When Missy indicates that she understands, Annie then says, "The second thing is that there is only one judge at this show and he's under a lot of pressure to finish the show in two hours, so you won't get many passes. We'll make sure that you get into the ring early, but you need to be sure that the judge can see you. Don't let anyone else get between you and him."

"Got it."

Annie then asks, "What do you notice about how the ring is positioned?"

Missy is momentarily confused by Annie's question and looks around and then it dawns on her. "The judge will be looking into the sun if he watches the side by the entrance gate."

Her trainer smiles, pleased that Missy has noticed this despite the overcast skies. "Exactly. So if the sun comes out, what does that tell you?"

"That he'll probably watch the horses come in, but he'll most likely be watching the other side of the ring for most of the class."

"Good girl. Now, since you're the very first class of the show, we won't know that for sure because we won't have had a chance to study what he does, but just keep in mind that he's more likely to watch the backside passes if the sun comes out, and it looks like it will."

"Got it."

"Now for the final thing." Annie goes on, "The rain might put a damper on it and its empty now, but that big pavilion on the end of the ring will be crowded with people, drinking and eating."

"Wow. Really?"

"Yes. This is the social event of the season. The second floor will even be filled. These people are not here to watch the show. They're here to see and be seen. The noise of clinking glasses will be louder than the organ when you're on that end of the ring. It can distract your horse, so try to time it so that your transitions are on this end, away from the pavilion."

"If the class is as short as you say, it will be difficult to control that."

"You're right, it will. Just be aware that she'll have a lot to look at on that end. It'll make transitions difficult."

"All right." Missy is all business as she and Annie return to the barn. "I'm going to do my best to kick some butt tonight."

A little more than an hour later, Missy is dressed in her suit and derby and is standing outside Josie's stall ready to mount. It has stopped raining and the sun is shining. As Annie makes final adjustments to Josie's bridle, she says, "I don't think it will be slick, but the ground will be heavy. So you might have to work harder than

248

usual to keep her racking. The mud is going to be hitting her belly, so she might be a little jumpier than usual, too. Just keep pushing through it and use your voice and body to keep her attention on you."

Missy feels the familiar twinge of nervousness in her belly, but nods confidently. "Yep. Got it."

The warm-up ring is indoors at Shelbyville, and Josie warms up well. She is as animated and alert as usual. When it is time to approach the ring, Missy is confident and ready. As they wait for the gate to open, Annie reminds her. "Now take the entrance a little cautiously, but as soon as you get in the gate and turned down the rail, ride hard. Be smart."

Missy is one of the first riders into the ring when the gates open. The first thing she notices is the sucking sound that the wet ground makes. She can tell that the mud is distracting her horse, as Josie is flinching a bit with every step. As they make their way towards the pavilion at the end of the ring, Josie's shies away from the colorful, animated crowd in the two-story structure. Missy immediately applies left leg to keep her towards that rail and starts talking, "Whup. Whup. Whup! Trot." Despite this, Josie breaks into a canter and it takes several strides before Missy can bring her mare back to a trot. Josie starts to relax on the far side of the ring, and as she passes Annie, her trainer says, "Cut that end short. Try to get away from it before you slow gait."

As she rounds the end, the announcer calls for the horses to walk. Missy is in the most awkward place possible. She knows that if she stops her trot now, her horse will be at the beginning of a long straightaway, and she is going to be frustrated. If she trots to the end of the straightaway, which is what she would do in every other ring, then she will be asking for the slow gait right in front of the pavilion. This is something that Annie clearly told her to avoid. She has a split second to make up her mind and decides to let Josie continue the trot to the end of the ring.

When she is about two thirds of the way to the end, she tells Josie, "Whoa." Josie is focusing on the pavilion, so she keeps talking to her and applies pressure with her legs and hands to keep her horse on the rail. The announcer hesitates before he calls for the slow gait, and Josie continues jogging up towards the boisterous crowd at the end of

249

the ring. Missy guides her off the rail and prepares to cut the end short when the announcer finally says, "Slow gait your horses. Rock your horses back and slow gait, please."

Again, Missy is in an awkward place in the ring. She is off the rail and has very little space to establish a straight and even slow gait before she goes by the judge. Missy works hard to slow her horse down, but Josie is going much too fast when she passes the judge.

As Missy rounds the corner, she hears her trainer. "She's ahead of you. You've got to be quicker and take more control. Talk to her." As Missy sweeps by Annie, she works hard to slow Josie down, but her horse is now racking towards the pavilion, and is picking up speed with every step. Missy hopes that the announcer will call for the rack before she passes in front of the judge on the opposite side, but her bad luck holds and he doesn't tell the class to rack until she has already passed by the judge, going much too fast.

The rest of the class goes much the same, with Josie moving much faster than the other horses in the ring. When they canter, she gallops. When they trot, she trots faster. Every transition is awkward and messy. Missy struggles to control her at every step and by the time the horses are lined up, Missy is exhausted. She is unsurprised when she receives a sixth place ribbon.

On the way back to the barn, Annie says very little. Once Missy has dismounted and is peeling off her mud-covered suit coat, Annie approaches. "While it's still fresh in your mind," she begins.

Missy grimaces and Annie hesitates and then starts again. "I know you're disappointed. I actually thought you'd get a better ribbon than you did. Josie was going too fast and you had some rough transitions, but she out-racked everything in that class. That judge obviously doesn't care that most of the horses in there were pacing rather than racking."

Missy is astonished that Annie isn't berating her for her poor ride, but Annie goes on. "I know the ride wasn't perfect, but the conditions weren't perfect. Your horse is six years old. You've shown her a handful of times. I thought you handled her pretty well. It is her first time ever in the mud. She was clearly looking hard at the pavilion. But you worked it out."

Annie's positive feedback is so unexpected that Missy's tears up and Annie hugs her. "I know you wanted to win this. I wanted you to win it. But every time out you're getting better at riding Josie. You were much better the second direction than the first. By the end of the class, she was paying attention to you."

"I'm so disappointed. I haven't been below third all season and it seems like I'm going backwards. We won the first time we showed at JD Massey. But since then, we've struggled. We got second in the championships in Asheville and Rock Creek. We were third in Lexington. We were sixth tonight." She takes a deep breath. "Louisville is only two and a half weeks away."

"I know that is how it feels, but you're actually getting much better. Your reactions tonight were on the money. She's young and she's a lot of horse. Learning how to work with each other is a process and it will come."

"I just want it to happen faster."

"I know you do." Annie gives her another small hug. "Don't worry. It'll happen. Just hang in there."

As Missy changes out of her muddy suit, she thinks more about buying Toreador. He will be showing on Saturday night here in Shelbyville, so she will watch him carefully.

CHAPTER 59

Kenny and Jeremy are just finishing re-bedding all the stalls when a car pulls up to Riverside. "Dad, they're here." Jeremy's excited voice alerts Kenny and he quickly wheels the unused clean shavings back into the storage shed. Spy Master has been at Riverside for a little more than two weeks and although he and Holly talk nearly every day and she has watched all of the stallion's workouts, he is anxious for her to see the horse and ride him for herself.

"Hi Kenny. Hi Jeremy." Spy Master's owner, Eileen, is entering the barn. "Holly's getting her saddle."

"Jeremy, would you please get Ms. Miller a cup of coffee?" Kenny walks out to the car to help Holly and greets her, "Hey there. Let me take that saddle."

"How's Spy Master this morning?" Holly hands him her saddle and reaches back into the trunk to retrieve her gloves and chaps.

"He's good. I knew you'd want to use your saddle, so I haven't tacked him up, but he's had his breakfast." Kenny smiles at Holly, "I'll admit that I'm a little nervous. I hope you have a good ride today."

"I'm sure it will go well. The important ride is on Saturday." Holly is referring to their plan to show Spy Master at Shelbyville on Saturday night in the gaited stake. It will be his first Open Class in Kentucky and he needs to do well to earn respect going into the Louisville show.

When they enter the barn, Jeremy and Eileen are standing in front of Spy Master's stall and Jeremy is telling Eileen about the care her horse has received every day. "Dad doesn't let me groom him alone, but he lets me help. He's such a nice horse and he seems really happy."

"He looks marvelous." Eileen is smiling and offering a peppermint to her horse.

"Hey big guy." Holly moves into the stall to pat the horse and then walks around him. "He does look marvelous," she agrees. "I don't think his coat was this shiny at home."

252

Jeremy quickly pipes up. "We put a special conditioner on it when we gave him a bath a couple of days ago. Wait until you see him in the sunshine!"

Kenny laughs, and enters the stall to brush the horse. "We've loved having him around." His attention shifts to Holly. "I assume you want a full bridle today, right?"

"Yep. That's right. Let's make sure I still know how to work with it."

They work together to get the horse prepared for his ride and everyone walks to the ring together, with Kenny leading the big horse.

Before Holly mounts, she says, "I've been watching you work him and noticed that you do a lot more walking than I did."

"Yes. I thought he needed extra time to look around and get comfortable. I used the time to work his mouth a little. He especially likes to look out the windows. I think the smells are different and he likes to check them out." Kenny pats Spy Master, holding him while Holly mounts.

After walking a few gentle serpentines, she begins trotting and then works through all his gaits each direction. She pats him and dismounts. "He feels great. I think he's a little softer on his right side than he used to be. That must be a result of the work you've been doing. He also feels a little more balanced in the canter."

"I'm glad you noticed a difference." Kenny is obviously pleased with her reaction. "I've been trying to slow his canter down just a fraction because I think it will show his motion off a little better." He reaches over to take the reins from Holly and pats Spy Master. "He's such a pleasure to work with. He doesn't get frustrated or upset. He's always happy."

Eileen chimes in, "He looks as good as ever. He looks ready to go to a show."

Holly asks Kenny, "Have you heard anything about who else might show up in his class on Saturday night?"

"Let's put him away and talk about the rest of this week." As they all walk back up to Spy Master's stall, they meet Angela and Emily coming towards them.

Emily shouts, "Daddy! Jermy! We brought bre'fas burritos." Angela quickly shushes her daughter and holds her back until Spy

Master is safely in his stall, reminding the little girl to be quiet and calm around the horses. In response, Emily tiptoes forward and repeats in a loud whisper, "We brought bre'fas burritos!"

Everyone laughs and Kenny looks at Angela with surprise. The atmosphere between them has been tense during the last two weeks since Holly's previous visit. He is pleased to see that she appears happy and relaxed and is introducing herself to Eileen.

"Come on out to the picnic table and help yourself to something to eat. I have fresh juice and coffee." Angela leads Eileen outside and Emily and Jeremy follow.

"We'll be there as soon as we take care of Spy Master. Save some for us!" Kenny starts removing tack from the horse.

Holly enters Spy Master's stall and makes eye contact with Kenny, raising her eyebrows at him. He gives her a small shrug and they work together to get the horse toweled off before joining the cheerful group outside.

Once they are seated, Angela asks Holly, "So what did you think? Is he ready for Saturday?"

"He looks and feels great. Kenny and Jeremy have done terrific work and I'm excited for the show." She then directs her attention to Kenny, "So who else do you think will show in the Open Stake?"

He finishes a bite and then says, "I expect that we'll see seven or eight good horses. The rumor is that Jennifer Hornig is going to show up with Toreador."

"Really? Has she shown him before? How's she getting along with him, do you know?" Like all other trainers in the industry, Holly is intensely curious about the defending World Champion.

"This will be the first time anyone's seen him show in nearly a year. I heard that they worked him at Rock Creek but it didn't go well. I haven't heard anything else." Kenny takes another bite and then goes on, "I don't think you could find two trainers more different than Johnnie Stuart and Jennifer Hornig. I imagine that it has taken a while for Toreador to get used to the change."

"Well, I hope she's successful with him. Just not more successful than us." Eileen laughs and everyone joins her.

Holly asks, "What's Johnnie Stuart showing? Does he have a stake horse?"

"He's a big fan of his four-year-old and there are rumors that he might show him in the Stake. I don't know if that's legit."

"What's his name?" This question comes from Angela.

"Night Train. He's talented, for sure, but he's only four. Everyone says that he runs out of gas so he'll have a tough time making it through a workout at Louisville."

Holly then asks, "Do they usually have a workout at Shelbyville? I've never shown there."

"You're going to the show tonight, right?" Kenny waits for her to nod before continuing, "Then you'll notice right away that this show is different. It moves really fast. I'd be very surprised if there was a workout."

Eileen says, "I've been watching the weather report. There's a pretty high likelihood of rain every night through Saturday." Everyone looks at the sky, which is currently bright blue with fluffy white clouds.

"It's been drizzling a little every afternoon," Angela answers. "The ring in Shelbyville can take a lot of water though. Unless it pours for more than an hour, the footing will be fine."

Kenny agrees, "Yes, and it dries out quickly. We showed a horse last night in Country Pleasure and the footing was fine even though it rained most of the day yesterday."

The group finishes the meal with conversation about the other horses that are likely to show in Spy Master's class, and they all agree that Toreador is likely to be the toughest competition.

CHAPTER 60

"That went pretty well." Jennifer has just dismounted from Toreador and addresses her comment to Eduardo.

"It did. I wonder if that is a good thing or a bad thing."

Eduardo smiles and Jennifer agrees. Toreador's workouts have been inconsistent, with good rides followed by disastrous rides. Although they have tried to discover the triggers that turn the horse into a wild and hard-to-control animal, it often seems to occur without apparent reason. She looks carefully at her assistant as she hands Toreador's reins to him. He is clear-eyed this morning and he even beat her to the barn. She hasn't detected alcohol for nearly two weeks and she suddenly recognizes the parallels between Toreador and Eduardo, as she also doesn't know what triggers Eduardo's drinking, nor does she know whether this long stretch of sobriety is a good thing or a bad thing. "Let's get him cooled out and then let's plan exactly how we're going to warm him up on Saturday, okay?

It is noon before they take a moment to sit down in Jennifer's office and she begins. "I want you to know how much I appreciate that you've been sober for the last couple of weeks. I really rely on you to help me."

Eduardo looks at the floor and Jennifer worries that she might have embarrassed him, so she hurries to prove her point by asking his opinion of Toreador. "How do you think we should manage him over the next two days?"

"His class is the last one of the night, so the crowd will be loud and the lights will be shining, so I do not think we have to worry about him running out of energy."

"Right," Jennifer agrees. "He hasn't been shown for almost a year, so he's probably going to be wild."

"I think we should long-line him tomorrow to remind him of his lessons. We can make sure he is respecting the bit and responding well to voice commands." When Jennifer nods, Eduardo goes on. "Then I think we should give him a short warm-up so that he doesn't have time to get his temper up before you go in the ring."

"I was thinking that we'd try to wear him out, but I see your point. He does get more hot-headed the longer he goes. We learned that we have better rides here if we shorten them." She thinks through it and then says, "I agree. Let's just trot and maybe slow gait a short distance each direction. Do you think we should get him out of his stall Saturday morning and work him?"

Eduardo takes a deep breath and takes a few moments to answer. "No. I think we should treat him like any other show horse on the day of a show and give him a bath, wash his tail, polish his feet and put a braid in his mane."

"Okay. That sounds good. If he starts getting agitated, we can always take him out and lunge him to let him burn off a little energy." Jennifer relaxes, content to have a plan for the difficult horse. Jennifer has been checking the weather forecast every day but uses her smartphone to check again in the hope that the forecast has improved. Unfortunately, it has not. "Chance of rain is 60%, so yes, it is supposed to rain."

"Maybe that is good. More horses will stay home in their dry barns." Eduardo says, hopefully.

"Look at you. Always looking on the bright side!" Jennifer laughs. "We can't control the weather and we need to show this horse, so it doesn't matter whether it's raining. We're going to be in that ring!"

CHAPTER 61

6:15 PM August 1, Shelbyville Horse Show

With only 45 minutes to go before the show begins on Friday night, a thunderstorm is moving through the area and it is raining heavily. Several trainers are standing in the covered warm-up ring discussing whether to scratch their horses or let them show in the mud.

"Well, I don't know about ya'll but my horse is no sissy. He's going to show up in the Junior Class and kick some ass." Johnnie Stuart is at the center of the group and hasn't hesitated to voice his opinion that everyone should show the horses they have brought.

Clark Benton is standing near the back of the group and has been listening to the discussion for several minutes. He shuffles his feet as though to get a more comfortable stance and then says quietly, "Well, I don't see much point in putting a young horse through this. It's important to me that every show ring experience they have is a good one. I'm sure Mr. Kiplenan won't want to show his youngsters tonight. I don't know what our client from Illinois will do with her four-year-old gaited horse." Bobby has been trying to get in touch with Mrs. M to find out whether she wants them to show Vendome.

The group starts to break up as the trainers return to their stalls and Clark hears Johnnie, still talking to a much smaller group. "If you ask me, we're coddling these horses. They aren't made of china." Johnnie's voice is drowned out by a sudden boom of thunder and Clark trots through the rain to the Kiplenan stalls.

When he arrives, Bobby is talking on his cell phone and motions him to come closer so he can hear Bobby's side of the conversation. "Yes ma'am. Yes, that was thunder you just heard." Bobby pauses, and then turns so that he can see into Vendome's stall. "He's okay. He's a little tense, but he's fine." After more nodding, Bobby says. "That's fine. That's a good decision. Have a nice dinner." After saying goodbye, he disconnects the call.

"She wants to scratch him, I hope," Clark says.

"Yes. She's not even going to come out here tonight. She's going to meet Mr. Kiplenan for a nice dinner."

"I'm glad. Vendome is already sold. There's no need to risk him slipping in the mud and pulling a shoe off or something."

"Yep. Do you want to pack everything up and go home now?"

"Let's wait 'til it quits raining. I wouldn't mind seeing Johnnie Stuart's four-year-old go. He seems determined to show him, although I'm not sure why."

"I'll let the grooms know that we're not showing and get them started on packing things up." As Bobby heads to the tack room, he sees Jennifer Hornig coming down the aisle towards them. He waves a greeting and smiles at her, realizing that he now has an unexpected opportunity to spend some time with her.

"Hi!" She returns his smile and greeting. "Marianne and Blair just called. They want to know if Vendome is going to show. They're in Simpsonville but are going to turn around and go back home if he's not going into the ring."

"Mrs. M just decided to scratch. I was just going to give you a call and let you know."

"I'll let them know. I think it's a wise decision. There's no point in risking an injury in this slop." Once Blair answers, it only takes a few moments for her to communicate that Vendome won't be showing. Before disconnecting from the brief conversation, Blair asks her whether she thinks they should show Toreador tomorrow if it is still wet.

"I think so. We need to get him in the ring before Louisville to work out any last minute kinks. Obviously, it's up to you, but I think we should go for it." She hears Blair relaying her comments to Marianne.

"Mother agrees. So we'll see you tomorrow night. I hope the weather is better."

"Me too!"

Bobby notices that her telephone call has ended. "Want to go up and see which brave souls are saddled up? I'd like to see Vendome's class and we're not going to show anything tonight. So I have some time on my hands and would like to spend it with a pretty girl."

"I'll see if I can find a pretty girl, then," Jennifer teases. As they walk toward the ring, she asks, "Are you disappointed that you're not showing Vendome tonight?"

"I know it sounds strange because the weather is so miserable, but I am. I just realized that I probably just have one more show on him. He's my favorite and I'm really going to miss him."

"I totally get it. The good news is that you sold a horse. The bad news is that you sold your favorite horse. It's a bittersweet feeling."

"It is, so I'd rather not think about it too much. Do you know if the Smithsons are going to put him in training with you?"

"They haven't committed to it, but I'm hopeful." She deliberately tries to lighten his mood, "If he does end up with me, I might even allow you visitation."

He laughs, "Oh yeah? What will it cost me?"

"I'll have to give that some thought and get back to you." On this happier note, they purchase hot chocolate and hurry to the covered grandstands where they sit close together on the damp bench. They are watching the horse show and commenting about the horses and riders when Missy Phillips and Annie Jessup enter the stands. Jennifer calls out a greeting to Missy, "Aren't you glad that you came all the way from North Carolina to show in the rain?"

"Boy, it is nasty weather."

After everyone has been introduced, Jennifer makes room for them next to her on the bench and asks Missy, "Are you going to show your mare in the Amateur Championship tonight?"

Missy and Annie exchange a looks and Missy says, "We've just been talking about that. I need all the practice I can get with her, but we've decided to show against in the Open Class tomorrow night instead. I'm hoping the weather will be better."

Jennifer widens her eyes in surprise and says, "Ah. Then she'll be in the same class as Toreador."

Missy nods and then downplays the decision. "Yes. I didn't want to miss the chance to get another practice ride and this seems like the best alternative. But I was looking forward to watching Toreador. I'm going to get the videographer to record him for me so that I can watch it later."

Jennifer is glad to hear that Missy is still interested in Toreador. "Sounds great. Good luck tomorrow. I hope you come in second, right behind me!"

CHAPTER 62

"At least the weather finally improved." Bobby and Clark are walking from the barns to the Shelbyville show ring, where the gate is about to open for the final class of the show, the Five-Gaited Open Stake.

"Yeah. Tonight is the first night it hasn't rained in the whole show." Clark is distracted as a large chestnut stallion trots by. "That's Spy Master, isn't it?"

Bobby glances at the horse, "Yep. He's filled out a little since Louisville, last year, hasn't he?"

"He has." Clark watches as the horse makes his first pass and then asks, "Did those people from California move him out here permanently?"

"Nah. They just brought him out early for Louisville. He's staying over at Kenny Rivers' place. That gal that's riding him is a friend of Kenny's from college." He goes on, "He's unbeaten so far this year."

"Well, it looks like he'll get a run for his money tonight." Clark's comment is triggered as Toreador charges by. The gelding looks like a barely-controlled explosion. "That gal of yours better hang on tight."

They both tear their eyes from Toreador as another horse trots in the ring. Clark says, "That's Annie Jessup's mare."

"Yeah. I met them last night. They've been showing her in the Amateur Class all year but didn't want to show in the rain last night. Since they'd come this far, they wanted to get another ride in." Bobby watches Josie trot by.

Clark watches Josie for a few strides, "She looks great. That little mare could give them a run for their money. She can rack her butt off."

There are four additional horses in the class and after watching them trot the first direction, Bobby and Clark quickly agree that Spy Master had the best trot the first direction.

When the announcer calls for the walk, Jennifer pulls Toreador to a stop on the rail near Bobby and Clark. She is obviously trying to catch her breath before beginning the slow gait. Bobby knows she can

261

hear him, so he says a few words of encouragement. "Take your time. You're doing great."

Jennifer doesn't look at him, but he can see her take a deliberate breath and she murmurs a few words to her horse.

The other horses in the ring are all moving, and Missy Phillips maneuvers Josie into a spot on the rail near Toreador. When the announcer calls for the slow gait, Josie is perfectly positioned and is the first horse to slow gait by the judge and she looks perfect. As she slow gaits towards the pavilion, she alertly watches the crowd but shows none of the hesitancy at approaching the noise that she showed on Wednesday night. Her head and ears are up and she looks eager and happy.

Bobby's eyes return to Jennifer. Toreador's gait is too fast, but he suspends each front foot in the air a fraction of a second longer than any other horse.

By now, it is apparent to the crowd that the top three horses are Spy Master, Toreador and Josie. The onlookers begin to yell encouragement to their favorites as the horses speed around the ring.

Bobby keeps his eyes on Jennifer. Toreador is much faster than the other horses and Jennifer has to pull him off the rail as she passes the other horses. This makes her corners tighter and Bobby can see they she is starting to struggle to keep her horse under control.

"Man! That little mare gets BUSY!"

Bobby hears Clark's comment and tears his eyes away from Toreador to focus on Missy as she and Josie flash by. Josie looks phenomenal. With a smaller frame, she is not covering ground as quickly as most of the other horses, but her step is quick and crisp.

Bobby watches Spy Master next. He is still on the rail and looks distracted as he racks by the screaming crowd. He sees Spy Master's rider nod as she rides by Kenny Rivers. He must have told her to get off the rail, as she moves her horse a few feet towards the inside of the ring. The horse relaxes almost immediately, and his rack improves.

The canter is next and Toreador has built up steam. He gallops around the ring, and Jennifer works to keep him clear of traffic. Bobby breathes a sigh of relief when the announcer them to walk and then to reverse and trot.

262

The horses repeat the gaits going the same direction, and once the horses are lined up, Bobby asks Clark, "What do you think?"

"Toreador won the first direction but I think Spy Master won the second direction. He was more consistent. But that little mare is the horse I'd like to take home. She's solid in all her gaits. She's probably the most well-rounded horse in the class."

The announcer begins, "I think you'll all agree that this was an excellent class. Please give our riders and horses another round of applause to let them know how much you liked their effort." The crowd responds enthusiastically. "Unfortunately, we can only have one winner. Please welcome…" He pauses dramatically and then continues, "SS Toreador to the winner's circle!"

The crowd erupts, and Bobby yells "Yes!" Jennifer flashes a huge smile and racks Toreador to the end of the ring near the pavilion while the announcer describes Toreador's pedigree and ownership, and then proceeds through the rest of the awards. "Our reserve champion tonight came all the way from California!" The crowd cheers as Spy Master's name, pedigree and ownership are announced.

"The third place ribbon goes to Josephine's Dream." Missy is clearly pleased with this outcome and smiles as she racks Josie out of the ring with her ribbon.

On their way back to the barn Bobby asks Clark, "Do you they'll show that mare in the Open Class in Louisville?"

"It's no secret that Missy Phillips wants to win the Open Stake and she can certainly ride well enough to get it done, but it would be hard for that little mare to beat those bigger horses. I think they'd have to screw up. And the chance of that happening in Louisville is slim." Clark shrugs, "I guess we'll have to wait and see. I imagine she's tempted."

Before leaving the fairgrounds that evening, Bobby goes to Jennifer's stalls to congratulate her. After making his way through a large group of Marianne Smithson's family and friends, he gives her a hug. "Congratulations! Nice ride!"

"Stand back! I'm sweaty and gross." Then, more quietly, "Thanks, but moments of it were terrifying. There were a few times when I wasn't sure I'd stay in control."

"Maybe so, but this is a big confidence builder."

"True, it's just what we needed before Louisville."

CHAPTER 63

"Damn." Jennifer mutters to herself. She is standing in her office, looking hopefully at the door on Eduardo's trailer. Her assistant is late to work this morning. As she watches, the door opens and she sees Eduardo trot down the stairs and jog towards the barn. Jennifer breathes a sigh of relief, as he is clearly sober.

She returns to the stall of one of her young horses and is in the middle of rewrapping the colt's legs when Eduardo comes to the door of the stall. "Good morning."

"Hi Eduardo." Her relief at having him arrive in the barn suddenly changes to concern as she sees his distraught expression. "What's wrong? What happened?"

"My sister called. My mother is dying."

"Oh no. Eduardo, I'm so sorry." Jennifer gives her assistant a hug. She knows that he has a very close family. Eduardo's mother lives with his sister in southern California. "You need to go to California. Let's get you on an airplane."

"No. I cannot leave now. We have too much to do." Eduardo shakes his head.

"Yes. You can. You have to see your mom before it is too late."

"Who will help you with Toreador? There are only two weeks left."

"I'll get the other grooms to help. Don't worry. It will be okay." Jennifer attempts to reassure Eduardo.

He hesitates and runs his hands through his hair. "Maybe I should go for just two days. But I will come right back."

"Stay as long as you need." Although she is saying all the right things to Eduardo, Jennifer's heart sinks. She needs his help but she knows that he will be distracted and upset if he does stay. "I'll go get you an airplane ticket. Go home and pack."

Within two hours, Jennifer is dropping Eduardo off at the airport. "Stay as long as you need to. Don't worry about the horses. We'll be fine." She then says, "And promise me you'll stay away from the booze. When you come back, I'll need you to be clear-headed. I can't win Louisville on Toreador without your help. And you won't be any help if you're drinking."

He solemnly promises her and then disappears through the sliding doors.

On her way back to the farm, she dials Bobby's number. She expects to get his voice mail since it is in the middle of a work day but is surprised when he answers.

"Hey there. How are you?"

"I'm on my way home from the airport. Eduardo's mom is ill so he just left for California."

"Oh no. That's not good." Bobby understands immediately that this will disrupt the routine of the barn, and more importantly, is likely to impact Toreador's training schedule. "What can I do to help?"

"Thanks so much for asking, but I think it'll be okay. You have plenty of your own work to do. You guys must be taking about 16 horses to Louisville, right?" Jennifer knows that a breeding and training operation like Kiplenan's is particularly busy at this time of year, as they will be showing so many young and inexperienced horses.

"Yeah. We have plenty to do, but I could help you in the evenings if you need it."

"Would you be willing to help me with Toreador? He's the only one that I don't really want to work by myself. I really don't need to have a wreck on him at this stage in the game." Before he can answer, she goes on, "And I really want to try a different bit like you suggested on Sunday. I'd sure like another pair of eyes to make sure it's a good change."

"Absolutely. I can be there by six each night. Will that work?"

"That'll work great. He has to show in the evening anyway, so moving his workouts to late in the day is probably a good thing." Jennifer's dark mood has suddenly lifted and she adds, "I'll need to find a way to reward you."

"Oh, I'm sure you'll think of something," he teases.

CHAPTER 64

Johnnie is long-lining Night Train when he notices the four-year-old is slightly stiff in his back legs. He stops working the horse immediately and runs his hands down his hind legs. He can't detect heat or swelling but puts the horse in his stall and goes directly to his office to call his veterinarian, Dr. Rice.

When the vet answers the phone, Johnnie begins, "My nice four-year-old gaited horse is a little stiff in his hind legs this morning. I can't feel any heat or swelling, but he's sure not moving quite right. And it looks to me like it might be in multiple joints. So I don't think it's a specific injury."

In response to the vet's queries about whether he has given him any medications, Johnnie answers, "Nope. Thought I'd wait for ya'll to come look at him first." For almost any other horse in his stable, he probably would just administer one of the pain medications he has on hand and rest him a couple of days. But Night Train shows in exactly two weeks and he needs every possible opportunity for training.

Once the vet arrives and watches Night Train move, he examines the horse's hind legs. "There is a slight amount of heat and swelling in the fetlock joint. I probably wouldn't have noticed it if we weren't trying to explain why he's a little lame in the back." The vet continues his examination, "While he's young to be showing joint inflammation, I'm guessing that you've been working him pretty hard all summer to get him ready for Louisville, right?"

When Johnnie answers, "Yep. And I showed him in Shelbyville in the mud."

The vet goes on, "Ah. He might have just strained something. He's young and I hope he's not already showing joint problems."

The vet takes the horse's temperature and checks his pulse and respiration rate. After making notes, he says, "Everything else is on the high side of normal." Dr. Rice stands back to look at Night Train and says, "As you know, we have three choices. We can try to do something intramuscular, intravenously or we can inject the joint directly with an intra-articular medication. If it were an older horse or

267

we had more time, then there wouldn't be much question. We'd inject the joint directly. But you already know the risks. "

Johnnie and Dr. Rice discuss this treatment for a few moments. It is a commonly used method of improving joints in performance horses, much like a physician would give a human patient a cortisone shot to ease joint pain. It is a procedure that must be done by a veterinarian since it is important to remove any excess joint fluid first and to avoid scratching the cartilage surface with the tip of the injection needle. Dr. Rice says, "I'd add an antibiotic to the injection just to reduce the likelihood of any infection. He'd have to go on stall rest for three days or so after we do it, so you'll want to keep that in mind."

"Okay. What else can we do?"

"Well, we could give him some Legend in an IV. Typically, we'd give him three doses, each a week apart. But that won't be possible here because of the show schedule. He has to be drug free within 12 hours of the show, so he's probably just going to have to make do with a single dose. It might or might not work."

Johnnie shakes his head. "And it has possible side effects, right? I tried it once and my horse quit eating."

"Yes. Some trainers have noticed lethargy and depression. You might also notice some fever."

"Shit. What's the third option?"

"The last option is the simplest. We use a version of the same drug we use in a joint injection and we give it in the muscle. We'd typically give it every four days over an entire month. So the timing isn't good for Night Train."

To Johnnie, the choice is clear. "It sounds like we need to inject the joint directly. Would you also put him on Bute?"

The vet stands back and looks at the horse and answers, "We definitely want to give him a non-steroidal anti-inflammatory, but we need to be careful because of the Louisville Show. They will definitely drug test him." Dr. Rice continues, "As you know, we typically give Phenylbutazone, or Bute. It works by inhibiting the COX enzymes. There are two COX enzymes. COX 2 is the inflammatory one. COX 1 is actually a good enzyme and is important."

268

Johnnie can see that Dr. Rice may have an alternative to Bute, so he asks, "Do you have a drug that just blocks COX 2?"

"There's a drug called Equioxx. Theoretically, it only blocks COX 2. And you can only use it for 14 days." Dr. Rice then says, "It will show up in the drug test."

"Yeah, but as long as he hasn't had a dose within 12 hours of showing, he'll pass the drug test."

"He should."

"Okay. Let's inject the joint and give him the Equioxx. I won't work him until Thursday and I'll take his temperature a couple of times a day. What other Equioxx side effects do I need to watch out for?"

"Well, beyond the fact that it is more expensive than Bute, you mean?" the vet asks. "You need to watch him for signs of colic or lethargy. But the biggest problem is probably ulcers. That's why we won't use it for more than 14 days. Also, since it is a paste, we need to watch carefully that he doesn't get any sores in his mouth. That would make it impossible for him to wear a bit comfortably and could stop him from eating."

Johnnie asks a few more questions to make sure he understands the drugs and the vet prepares the medications.

Before giving the injections, Dr. Rice offers one last reminder. "Now, you need to resist giving him Bute since we're giving him the Equioxx. We wouldn't recommend giving both drugs anyway, but the rules say you can only be using one NSAID within three days of showing. And you can't use any NSAID within 12 hours of showing."

"How will they know? Won't just one show up in his system?"

"As you know, the drug tests get more sophisticated all the time. You have to assume that they could detect them since they're chemically different."

Once the vet is finished and packing up his equipment, Johnnie asks, "Did you see the Stake in Shelbyville?"

"I did. I thought that horse from California was going to win it. It was the first time I'd seen Toreador since last year. What'd you think?" He knows that Toreador was Johnnie's horse and he is curious what Johnnie will say about Toreador's performance.

"I think he's gone straight to hell. He's nothing like he was last year. And he's nothing like he could be if he was still here. Night Train could have beat him easily on Saturday Night."

CHAPTER 65

"You've watched the video of Saturday Night's Stake Class, right?" Holly's voice comes over the speakerphone in Kenny's office.

"Several times. And I also was there to see it live and in color." He attempts to make a joke, but she completely misses it.

"What do you see? Tell me honestly. What beat me?"

"I haven't changed my mind from what I told you after the class. I believe Spy Master won the second direction. He was rock solid. I believe he was too tentative the first direction. You came in as though you were trying to avoid making a mistake."

There is silence on the phone as she processes his comments. "Yes. I agree. I should have pulled him off the rail right away to get his attention and keep him fresh. Instead, I dawdled along."

"Well, I wouldn't beat up on yourself. You didn't get beat by some hack. You got beat by the defending World's Champion. And I wouldn't exactly call it dawdling, either."

"True. But I ruined Spy Master's perfect record." Holly had been very proud that Spy Master was unbeaten going into his class on Saturday Night.

"Yes. But he's in the big leagues now. This is a whole different thing. Until this year, he was only competing against horses his own age. Now, he's up against seasoned veterans and reigning world champions." Kenny softens his voice, "But, that being said, I think Spy Master can beat Toreador. His trot is better by far. He just needs to quit looking like the kid at school that sits in the front row and dutifully does his homework and can answer every question the teacher asks."

Holly finally laughs, "Like I was, you mean? Are you saying he needs to be more like the kid who shows up late, ball cap pulled down low, who never even bought the book they are supposed to be studying?"

"Hey, come on now! I wasn't that bad." But Kenny has succeeded in lightening her mood so he goes on. "Toreador is the bully that sits in the back row and shoots spit balls at everyone. He also happens to

271

be the handsome and athletic captain of the football, baseball, hockey and track teams."

"Okay, so how does the kid in the front row beat the bully?"

"By acting like a bit of a bully himself. I think you have to play his game. You have to come into the ring like you're on fire. Stop worrying about making a mistake that will beat you." Kenny knows he has her attention so he goes on. "There's no need to panic here. You'll ride a qualifying class on Monday night. Then, you don't show again until Saturday night. Toreador doesn't qualify until Wednesday night with the geldings. So Spy Master will have more rest before the Championship."

"True. We'll need to keep his workouts light and keep him fresh. I'm glad our stalls are not in the big main barn. They leave the lights on all the time and it's hard for a horse to get any rest. I'm glad we're out back."

"Yeah. Me too. Let's talk about the week and make a schedule, ok?" His anxious to iron out the details of the show. "Let's start at the beginning. When do you get here?"

"I arrive with the rest of my horses on Friday before the show. About a week and a half from today. I'll come in on the plane with them."

"Okay. When do you want me to bring Spy Master over to the fairgrounds? I could do it as early as Friday, or we could wait until Monday and do it in the afternoon before he shows."

"What do you think?"

"I'd be tempted to wait until Monday. I don't have any other horses going, so I'll be here and we can treat it just like any other show. He'll get good rest here."

"You know, I hadn't considered that. I guess I just assumed we'd move him over on Saturday, but I like your idea." After a short pause, she continues, "I need to think about it a little more, but let's assume that we'll do that."

"Then, I think I'd be tempted to bring him back here after the show on Monday night. Let him spend the week here at the barn, getting light workouts. You can come ride him on Wednesday, away from the distractions of the show. I'd bring him back to the fairgrounds on Saturday afternoon."

272

After a long pause, Holly replies, "I like your idea for a couple of reasons. First, it reduces the risk of him colicking because he's in an unfamiliar environment, even though I'm starting to believe that's behind him anyway." Holly goes on, "Second, he'll sleep and train better."

Kenny stays silent, giving her a chance to think.

"I need to think about it, but I like it. So, let's start talking about his training schedule between now and then. Tomorrow is Tuesday. Normally, he'd get long-lining…"

Kenny starts to write on his calendar as Holly talks, and they settle into a conversation about the details of preparing Spy Master to win the World Championship.

CHAPTER 66

1:00 PM August 16, Kentucky State Fairgrounds

"Eduardo! I'm so glad to see you!" Although her assistant called last night to say he would be returning to Kentucky this morning, Jennifer is relieved and happy to see him. "How are you? How's your family?" She looks at him with concern. He seems to have aged several years since she last saw him, although it has been only 12 days.

"I am okay. My family is sad."

"The funeral was yesterday wasn't it? I'm sorry you couldn't have stayed with them longer. Maybe you can go back next week." She is relieved to see his tired eyes are clear and he appears sober.

"Yes. Maybe I can go back soon." He looks around him and sees that the stall area is already completely decorated and ready for the week ahead. There is a sitting area for clients and visitors with several chairs and a small wooden side table filled with glossy horse industry publications. The front door of each horse's stall is covered with a green and purple curtain and contains a brass plaque with the horse's name and a hook holding a leather halter. A rectangular tack trunk, painted in the barn's colors, sits in front of each stall. The aisle is neatly raked and the entire area looks clean and neat. "The stalls look nice."

"The grooms worked hard yesterday and I think we're ready to go." Jennifer had brought four horses from Beech Tree. In addition to Toreador, three of her clients are showing their pleasure horses throughout the week.

"How was Toreador this week?" Eduardo is looking into the horse's stall.

"Pretty good. I changed his bits so I can take a better hold of him. I rode him Wednesday and Friday. Since he shows on Wednesday in the gelding's qualifier, I thought we should ride him on Monday and long-line on Tuesday. Do you think we should work him on Sunday? Or should we let him rest like he would at home?"

Eduardo is slow to answer and says distractedly, "He did not work today, right? Then I would jog him tomorrow."

274

This is exactly what Jennifer thinks as well, so she agrees and then says, "You must be tired. I got you a hotel room so you wouldn't need to drive back and forth from the barn or bunk with the grooms in the sleeping area. Why don't you go over and take a nap?" Jennifer hands him a key, but he shakes his head and heads toward the tack room.

"I would rather be busy. I will clean tack."

Jennifer hears laughter from the stalls next to hers that are inhabited by horses from Big View Farm in North Carolina. She is glad to have neighbors that she knows, since it is sometimes necessary to borrow equipment or get assistance from other trainers. As she looks down the aisle toward their stalls, she recognizes Missy Phillips and wonders whether the young woman will buy Toreador. She would use the commission to fund some improvements at Beech Tree. Selling Toreador will also make it more likely that Marianne and Blair will give her Vendome Copper to train after Louisville.

Thinking about Vendome leads her thoughts to Bobby and she takes a moment to text him. "*Whassup?*"

It only takes a few seconds for his answer to come back. "*Not much. Did Eduardo make it back?*"

"Yep. Got time 4 a soda?"

She has about given up on getting a response when she sees his tall, thin figure coming towards her down the aisle. "You're the only guy I know that texts using full sentences, capitalized letters and punctuation."

"Really? Then you need to start hanging out with a classier crowd. Are you buying?"

As they walk toward one of the vendors that is set up in the parking lot, she asks, "How many horses do you show tomorrow night?"

Sunday night is the first night of the horse show and includes several futurity classes for young Saddlebreds as well as championship classes for horses that have been competing all summer on the Kentucky County Fair Circuit.

"Six. We'll be busy."

"Wow. There are only 14 classes, so you'll be busy. I'm not showing anything at all tomorrow night. Do you need any help?"

275

He looks at her, "You know, we might. Maybe you could help us get a horse or two back to the stalls when we've got back-to-back classes. We'd usually ask the grooms to do it, but I'd feel better if they stayed close to the ring in case we need help down there."

"Of course. Just let me know what you need."

"I'll see what Clark thinks. I imagine he'll be grateful for the offer." They exchange a bit of gossip about who is at the show and how their horses look while they return to the barn. He gives her a quick hug, "Better get back to it. See you later."

CHAPTER 67

"Look Mom. Mrs. Clancy-Mellon is sitting in the next box over.
I'm going to go say hello and wish her good luck." Blair and
Marianne are sitting in their box seats in Freedom Hall.

"Okay. Wish her good luck for me, too." Marianne stands slightly
to let her daughter squeeze by her to greet Vendome Copper's current
owner. She adds quietly as her daughter passes by, "Make sure she
isn't going to increase his price if he wins. We already made a deal."

"Oh Mom." Blair doesn't bother to hide her eye roll from her
mother, and she smiles widely as she approaches Vendome's owner.
"Mrs. Clancy-Mellon, good evening! I wanted to wish you luck in
Vendome's class."

The older lady immediately puts her at ease. "Please call me
Louise. And wish us BOTH luck, you mean. I have a good feeling
about this."

"I do too!" Blair responds. "I'm so excited about the opportunity
to have such a sweet and talented horse." She pauses and then says,
"Good luck to us both, but mostly, good luck to Vendome. I know
he'll do well."

"Yes! Good luck to Vendome."

"No worries. She acknowledged that Vendome is ours after the
show." Blair says quietly when she returns to her mom. She perches
on the edge of her seat and then asks, "Do you think there was anyone
in the Junior Mare Class we just saw that can beat him?"

"Now let's not get ahead of ourselves. He needs to qualify for the
finals to meet any of the mares. And it's hard to tell. I don't yet have a
feel for what these judges like," her mother answers thoughtfully. "I
think the top four or five were all really nice. I especially liked the
second horse, though."

"Isn't that the one that was just imported from South Africa?"
While the Saddlebred breed originated in America, several horses
were exported around the world after World War I. The first
Saddlebred in South Africa arrived in 1917 and was a black stallion
named Myer's Kentucky Star. Today, the American Saddlebred breed

is quite popular in South Africa, with several top-notch trainers and breeders and more than 4,000 registered horses.

"Yes. She was bred over there. She sure is a high-headed mare and you can tell that she loves the show ring. It was hard for me to look at anything else." Marianne is making notes in the large catalog that contains the show information. In addition to identifying each horse, rider and owner in every class throughout the week, it also includes pedigree and breeding information. After consulting her book, Marianne goes on. "She sure comes from a long and distinguished line of racking horses. I don't know why the judges put her in second place. I thought she was a clear winner."

"They'll post the judges' cards later tonight. Then we'll know if they agreed with each other." Blair is referring to the cards that the judges fill out when they place the top ten horses in the class. These rankings are made public soon after each performance and are a major source of conversation and speculation throughout the week. She adds, "I looked at last night's cards and the judge from up north seems out of step with the other two. In a couple of classes, the horse they both placed first ended up fifth or sixth on his card."

Marianne looks at her daughter, "That's interesting. I imagine that he'll start agreeing with them more as the week goes on. He's not going to like being a maverick. It is too easy to be criticized."

They continue talking quietly while they watch a Fine Harness Class in the ring. Blair mentions, "Lee Kiplenan's horses sure did well last night. I hope it's a positive sign that they'll like Vendome tonight." Blair looks anxiously towards the gate through which the harness horses are leaving the ring with their ribbons and the qualifying class junior five-gaited stallions and geldings are next.

The bugler sounds the call and the ring starts to fill up with high-trotting four-year-olds. Marianne and Blair scan each horse that comes down the ramp, looking for Vendome. Finally, Blair says, "There he is Mom!" She has been holding her breath and exhales as he begins his first trot up the rail. She watches as Bobby looks over his shoulder, and then pulls his gelding off the rail and out towards the judges to avoid getting screened from their view. Blair keeps her eyes glued on Vendome as he goes deep into the far corner and Bobby

278

positions him to make another trotting pass. "Wow. This is a big group."

"Yes. It's always one of the most competitive qualifying classes. It's too bad that only the top eight qualify for the Friday night four-year-old championship."

The announcer tells the riders to walk and Blair notices that Johnnie Stuart's bay stallion, Night Train, is tossing his head and snorting, interfering with several other horses as he dances down the rail. When the announcer tells the riders, "Set 'em up and slow gait. Slow gait your horses, please." Night Train begins the four-beat gait immediately and passes directly in front of the judges before many of the other horses have even begun the gait, earning cheers from the crowd.

As Vendome passes in front of them, Blair hears a familiar voice, "Good Bobby. He looks great. He's perfect. Don't change a thing." Blair cranes her neck to verify that Jennifer Hornig is coaching Bobby on the rail. She wonders briefly about their relationship but is distracted by the announcer's direction for the riders to "Let 'em rack!"

The watching crowd erupts in whistles, shouts and cheers of encouragement for the riders as the horses increase speed. Marianne leans towards Blair and says, "Here's where we separate the men from the boys."

Blair smiles at the truth in her mother's statement as several horses are clearly having trouble keeping the gait steady and balanced at the higher speed. Her eyes are glued on Vendome and she begins to yell encouragement to Bobby as Vendome racks by in front of their seats. "Go Bobby! WHOOO!" The chestnut gelding looks phenomenal. His head is up and his knees are pumping as he flies down the side of the ring. As he goes deep into the end, she notices that Johnnie Stuart's horse, Night Train, is slightly to the inside and is gaining on Vendome. She watches as Night Train cuts the corner on Vendome and leads him up the straightaway. As they pass in front of the judges, Night Train is clearly racking faster than Vendome and Blair notices the judges making notes on their cards as the four-year-olds flash by.

"I think Johnnie Stuart won that gait." Marianne voices Blair's fears as the announcer directs the riders to canter their horses.

"Yeah, maybe. But Bobby is probably saving something for the second direction." Blair's voice is hopeful as they watch the young horses careen around the ring. Her eyes are again drawn to Night Train as he nearly collides with several other horses and Johnnie works to keep him as close to the rail as possible. Blair struggles a bit to find Vendome in the crowd of cantering horses and finally locates him on the rail. He looks calm and steady, but unremarkable.

When the horses reverse direction, Bobby has Vendome perfectly positioned. He makes a sweeping cut across the center of the ring, directly in front of a judge and his horse looks fresh and focused as he lengthens his stride. "Mom! Look at Vendome!" Blair grins and begins whistling as Vendome leads the large group of horses through the reverse and down the ring.

"He's really stepping up. Some of them look tired already." Marianne adds her yells to the crowd.

By the time the horses are racking in the second direction, it is clear that Vendome is one of the top horses in the ring and Blair is having trouble containing her excitement. She is yelling encouragement to Bobby on every pass and leans forward on her seat as she checks to make sure the judges are also watching the horse. On the final racking pass, she notices that Night Train and Vendome will pass in front of the judges together. She holds her breath as the horses rack around the end and head down the side of the ring. They are neck and neck, with Vendome on the rail, giving him a slight disadvantage as he must cover a longer distance than Night Train. As they speed down the rail, Vendome passes Night Train and Blair yells with approval.

"I'm glad we agreed on a price for Vendome before this class. I think it's between Night Train and Vendome." Marianne smiles as they watch the final canter. "It looks to me like Night Train is out of gas."

Blair follows her Mom's gaze and notices that Johnnie Stuart's horse is now galloping with his head down. His neck and chest are lathered with sweat. As the horses complete the canter and make their final pass to the line-up, the people sitting around them begin talking about who should win. As she eavesdrops, Blair realizes that she wasn't watching the class very carefully at all and that there are three or four horses that the people around her have noticed in addition to Vendome and Night Train. As the crowd waits for the top eight horses to be announced she crosses her fingers.

Several minutes pass before the announcer begins the awards. He begins with remarks about the quality of the class and reminds the crowd that the top eight horses have earned the right to show back in the Four-Year-Old Championship on Friday night. "The winner of the four-year-old Stallion and Gelding Five-Gaited Class is…" he pauses dramatically, and then finally continues, "Vendome Copper."

Marianne and Blair both leap to their feet to cheer as they watch Bobby rack Vendome to the end of the ring to pose for a photo and receive his championship ribbon. Blair glances over to Mrs. M's seat and sees that she is also standing to cheer and is receiving congratulations from those around her. They briefly make eye contact and share a happy smile. Blair hugs her mother and says "I'm going to go congratulate them! I'll meet you at Vendome's stall." As she steps around her mother and heads out of the seating area, she barely hears the announcement of the other ribbon winners, only noticing that Night Train was second.

Blair waits to meet Bobby and Vendome after his victory pass in Stopher's Walk, the long and narrow covered alley through which the horses enter and leave the ring. As she waits, Johnnie Stuart passes directly in front of her, still riding Night Train. His horse is still heaving, and he is responding to people who are congratulating him on his second place finish. "Thank ya'll, but I don't know what those judges are looking at. My horse can out-rack and out-trot that horse any day of the week."

As she watches Johnnie pass by she hears a soft voice at her elbow. "Some guys just can't admit they got beat fair and square."

Blair turns to see Jennifer just behind her and says in agreement. "Vendome was great, wasn't he?"

"Yes. He was great. You've got a great horse there. He's going to be perfect for you. Did you see how level-headed he was? Even on his last pass?"

281

"I'm so excited to have him. I can't wait to get him moved to your place and start riding him."

Jennifer stands back and looks at her client. She asks Blair to confirm what she's just said, "Really? Did you decide to bring him to Beech Tree?"

Blair nods and smiles broadly. "Yes. Mother agreed. We'll take him back to Beech Tree as soon as the show is over and we've handed over a big check."

"Oh wow! That is fabulous news!" Jennifer and Blair's conversation is interrupted by Bobby's approach on Vendome. Bobby is smiling broadly while he pats his horse, accepting the congratulations of people as he proceeds down the congested Stopher's Walk towards Kiplenan's stalls. Jennifer and Blair both yell their congratulations as he goes by and turn to follow him. Jennifer quietly says to Blair. "If you don't mind, let's wait awhile to tell Bobby that Vendome is going to move, ok? He's totally in love with that horse and he'll be sad to see him go. Let's just let him enjoy the victory for a bit, if you don't mind."

"Of course. We won't say anything until the show is over." Blair is tempted to tease her trainer about her interest in Bobby but decides to stay quiet.

CHAPTER 68

10:00 PM August 18, Kentucky State Fairgrounds

"It's time." Kenny Rivers has just heard the announcer mention that the class before theirs will be entering the ring in two minutes. Kenny leads Spy Master from his stall and puts blinkers on the horse so that he will be less distracted during his warm-up. Holly carefully mounts the chestnut stallion and gathers her reins as Kenny reaches back to straighten the skirt on her coat. Holly looks nervous and Kenny attempts to calm her. "Holly, it's just another show. He's in fabulous condition. He won the four-year-old championship here last year so you know he likes this ring. You're going to kick some ass in there tonight."

"We need to win so that the judges will be looking for him on Saturday night." Holly smiles nervously.

He pats her leg as he uses a towel to clean the dust off her boot. "It's a small class. There are only seven. This is easy pickings for Spy Master. Go win this class so that everyone knows the horse from California came to play."

Kenny assists Holly in the warm-up ring and by the time the announcer calls for the class to enter the ring, she is relaxed and ready. As she trots down the ramp and onto the green shavings of Freedom Hall, he yells encouragement "Go get 'em!"

He flashes his colored wristband that identifies him as a trainer to the security guard and hurries to the rail to watch. He eases into a vacant spot and cranes his neck to see Holly. She and Spy Master are already rounding the far end of the ring and trotting back towards him. There are only seven horses in the large ring, so it will be easy to stay clear of the traffic.

When Holly trots by where he is standing, he encourages her. "Good speed. He looks great right where you have him." They have discussed Holly's strategy and have decided to try to keep Spy Master on the rail the first direction until he is comfortable. As the class continues through all the gaits in the first direction, Spy Master shows well, looking confident and strong. Kenny watches the judges and begins to worry that the stallion isn't standing out from the other

283

horses. As Holly canters by he tells her, "You need to step it up and catch their eye."

She nods slightly to indicate she's heard him and he can see her looking around the ring to assess the traffic and pick a place to reverse. When the announcer tells the class to change directions, Kenny watches Holly break into a trot and cut across the center of the ring. She straightens Spy Master before he reaches the rail and keeps him slightly away from it as she makes her pass. She trots deep into the corner and Kenny can hear her cluck to Spy Master as she turns to make another pass up the side. He watches her speed up the side of the ring, passing two horses on her way, and notices that the two judges watching that side follow her carefully. Kenny knows that she has now caught their attention. The next time she passes by, he says "Good! They're watching you now. Stay with it."

The stallions work through all the remaining gaits and Spy Master continues to gain momentum. By the end, there is very little doubt in Kenny's mind that he should win. When the horses have lined up, he moves to where Holly can see him and gives her a thumbs up and says, "He just kept getting better and better."

Holly pats her sweating horse. "Every time I asked for more, he gave it to me."

Before long the announcer begins, "We saw an exceptional group of Stallions this year to close out the Monday night performance of the World Championship Horse Show. Ribbon winners in this class are qualified to come back in the Gaited Stake on Saturday Night. It is now time to congratulate the winner of this year's Five-Gaited Stallion Stake." He pauses dramatically, and then continues, "In a unanimous victory, please welcome a horse that came all the way from California..." The remainder of his announcement is drowned in cheers and Holly's face erupts in a broad smile as she turns Spy Master and racks to the end of the ring to receive her awards.

Eileen meets them at the stalls. "Well done! He was awesome!" She hugs Holly and pats Spy Master's sweaty neck. She excitedly says, "When you reversed, he really turned it on. There wasn't a horse in there that could touch him. I've never seen him so good!"

Holly laughs at Eileen's excitement and stands back as Kenny leads the young stallion into his stall. "He felt perfect the entire ride. If we can get a performance like that on Saturday, he'll be tough."

"I was worried that bringing him to Kentucky so far before the show was a bad idea, but it was a brilliant move. He looked so comfortable and happy." Eileen pauses and then says to Kenny, "I really appreciate the amazing care you've given him. Thank you!"

Kenny responds, "It has been my privilege to work with such a talented horse. But our work is only half done. We need to get him ready to win on Saturday."

"Are you still going to take him back to Riverside until Saturday?" Eileen directs her question to Holly.

"Yes. I think that trailering him in this afternoon clearly worked well for him. He's obviously happy at Kenny's place and it will help him rest and relax to go back to his stall there. We'll bring him back on Saturday afternoon before the show and follow the same routine we did today."

"Sounds like a good plan." Eileen begins unwrapping peppermints for her horse. "I'll just give him a reward or two and get out of your hair."

It takes nearly two hours for Spy Master to cool and for Kenny and Holly to prepare the horse for the trip back to Riverside. As they load him carefully in Kenny's trailer, they review the plan for the rest of the week. "I'll hand walk him tomorrow and make sure he's recovering okay. And then we can jog him on Wednesday, ride on Thursday, and just line him on Friday." Kenny says.

"Yep. I'll keep an eye on him tonight. I can watch him through his stall camera on my laptop and I'll set the alarm so I check him every hour." Holly continues to worry about Spy Master's previous issues with colic.

"He looks good but I know what you mean. Better safe than sorry. I'll be in the barn with him after six AM, so don't worry about it after that. I'll call you right away if he even twitches."

"Thanks Kenny. I really appreciate it." Holly gives her friend a big hug.

"My pleasure. I think you can win this thing."

285

CHAPTER 69

When Missy Phillips approaches Big View's stalls on Tuesday evening, she is happy to see several ribbons already hanging on the curtain above the tack room. It is clear that Annie's riders have done well in the early sessions and Missy knows that the entire barn can benefit from the extra confidence and energy that nice ribbons in early classes provides. Big View has three horses performing in this evening's performance. Missy's mare, Josie, is the first of the three to go, and her class won't begin for another hour or so.

Despite the available time, Annie is standing near the tack room looking over the schedule, compulsively checking her watch. The grooms are all busy and several trunks are open in the aisle between the rows of stalls. Missy ducks into the dressing room to hang her riding coat and to recheck her hair and makeup.

"You look nervous," Missy jokes. "That's my job."

"If you screw up, you only let yourself down. If I screw up, I let my clients and their families down. And I'm as competitive as the next trainer. I want people to appreciate my work and my horses."

"I guess I didn't realize that you have as much on the line as I do," Missy says.

"Yeah. It doesn't matter how well the rest of the show season has been if you have a bad Championship. It makes it harder to sell horses and attract new clients and without that, a barn can get stale." Annie yawns.

"How much sleep are you getting?"

"About four hours a night. I get here at 6 AM so everyone is ready for the morning session that starts at 9. I usually sneak back to the hotel around 2 and catch a couple of hours of sleep, and then come back to prepare for the evening performance. We start working horses after the evening performance and finish around 2 AM. I should be used to it after all these years, but by the end of this week, I'll be ready for a good sleep!" Annie continues, "But enough about me. Let's talk about your strategy tonight." Annie focuses completely on her rider. "You need to remember that this is an amateur class. Josie loves this ring, and she is going to want to be fast and wild, but you'll need to contain all that energy until the last couple of passes."

Missy nods to show that she has heard Annie.

"We're going to put you on your mare here at the stalls. I want you to walk to the warm-up area, and while you're doing that, I want you to start a conversation with her mouth. Just keep moving the bit back and forth gently so that she starts to soften and bend to it."

Missy continues nodding as Annie talks through the warm-up sequence. "Once they call your class, I want you to go into the ring somewhere near the end. She'll be wound up, and the longer she is in the ring, the more excited she'll be."

Annie pauses and when Missy nods, she goes on. "Be very careful going down the ramp. Make sure you keep her head up and keep her slow until you get into the ring. Once you're in, be calm and thoughtful about your transitions. Take your time. If you can move to the rail between gaits, then do it so that the other horses might screen any fussiness she shows." Annie again makes sure that Missy understands and then keeps talking. "She isn't going to be the biggest horse in there but she will definitely have the best rack in the class. For your slow gait and rack, I want you on the inside, near the judges so that they can't possibly miss you. Now don't run them over but go deep into the ends and come out towards the middle." Annie finishes with, "You're going to be one of the best riders in the ring and you have one of the best horses in the whole show. You can win this thing. Just keep thinking and keep working every step of the way."

Less than an hour later, Missy and Josie have finished the class and are in the line-up, waiting for the ribbons to be announced. Missy scans the group of faces lining the rail to find her trainer. She thinks the ride has gone well, and she finally sees Annie making her way through the crowd in front of where she and Josie are standing. Annie confirms Missy's feeling by flashing a broad smile and pointing up with both thumbs. Missy smiles back and shrugs subtly as if to ask whether the ride was good enough to win. Annie returns the shrug, communicating that she is unsure of what ribbon Missy will receive.

It takes the judges and the show staff a few long minutes to compile the result, and then the announcer begins. "These amateur mares were exceptional. The top eight are invited back to compete in the Amateur Five-Gaited Championship on Saturday night. We congratulate our winner from the state of Missouri…"

Missy works hard to hide her disappointment, and watches with a forced smile as the winner rides his mare towards the end of the ring to receive his blue ribbon. She tries to find Annie again in the crowd but is still searching when the announcer continues.

"The second place mare is certainly a dream… Josephine's Dream that is…" Missy feels a rush of relief and happiness as she trots forward to receive the red ribbon and then turns Josie to the gate and racks her out of the ring and up the ramp to meet Annie.

On the way back to the stalls, Annie walks next to Josie and pats Missy's leg. "It was close. I think you had that first place mare beat the second direction, but she beat you the first way. Perhaps we were a little too conservative."

"I can definitely turn it up a notch. I made a small mistake on the first canter. I was in a bad position and didn't make a good decision about where to ask her for it."

"True. But there wasn't too much to pick on during that ride. I'm real proud of you. You did exactly what we wanted."

When they reach the stalls, Missy dismounts and pats Josie. She asks Annie, "Would you be able to watch the Open Five-Gaited Mare Class on the rail with me tonight?"

Annie hesitates to answer, and Missy knows that her trainer suspects that she is still tempted to show Josie in the Stake Class rather than in the Amateur Championship on Saturday night. Missy is relieved when Annie finally nods and says, "Sure!" I've got two more horses to put in the ring, but I'll definitely be down on the rail for the final class. Let's meet there."

It is nearly 10PM when Annie squeezes into a spot next to Missy on the rail. The class in which the mares will qualify for the Open Stake is about to enter the ring. Missy greets Annie and asks, "Did you watch the stallions last night?"

"Yes. That horse from California won it easily. He might be just five years old, but he has the body and mind of a seasoned show horse. I thought he was on the money. If he comes back on Saturday night looking as strong as he did last night, he'll be tough to beat."

This is consistent with Missy's opinion as well. "Who do you think will be his big competition?"

"It's hard to say. There might be a mare or two from this class that challenge him, but I imagine his big challenge will be Toreador if they can get him in the ring and get him around without any disasters."

Missy looks at Annie with interest. "He's here then?"

"Yep. I saw them working him last night. He looks good but he also acts like he's looking for an excuse to throw a tantrum." Annie goes on to ask, "Are you still considering buying him?"

"I change my mind daily, to be honest." Missy thinks back to her ride at Beech Tree in late June. "Riding him is like riding dynamite. He feels twitchy, if you know what I mean. I've never ridden anything like him before. It was mentally and physically exhausting."

Annie nods and looks around to make sure no one can overhear her before saying, "I know what you mean. I think he's had a tough go of it. Johnnie Stuart's horses are always edgy. The gal that has him now seems like a good trainer, and I imagine the people on the rail will be three-deep watching the Gelding qualifier tomorrow night. Half of them will want to see her win, just to spite Johnnie's trash-talking about how he's the only one that can handle Toreador. The other half will be jealous and will want to see her fail so they can feel superior. Personally, I'd like to see her kick some ass. It is about time the younger generation of trainers started making some noise."

They are interrupted by the bugler, sounding the call for the Open Five-Gaited Mares.

Later, as they walk back to the Big View stalls together, Missy asks, "What did you think?"

"There were some nice horses in there, but I don't think any of them will win on Saturday." Annie then asks the question she has been avoiding, "Are you still tempted to show Josie back against the Open Horses on Saturday?"

"I am still tempted, but I am trying to make sure I'm making the best decision for Josie," Missy admits. "I can improve on tonight's ride. I'm going to watch tonight's video before I make a final decision. What's your honest opinion?"

289

"Well, I think you can win the Amateur Stake. It will be very tough, but I think you have a good chance. We can give her a bit more freedom in the finals, turn her loose a little going the second direction. I really think you can win it." She looks intently at her client, "I'm less sure about the Open Stake. Even if you have a perfect ride, Spy Master and Toreador are going to give her everything she can handle. They are bigger and stronger. But I think she can get a good ribbon. Maybe even top three. You need to decide whether you prefer a possible win in the Amateur Championship, or a top three in the Stakes."

While it is hard to hear that Annie doesn't believe Josie can win the Stakes even with a perfect ride, she appreciates her trainer's honesty. "I'm going to watch video tonight and make the decision in the morning so that we can plan the rest of her week."

"It won't really matter, Missy. Both classes are on Saturday night so you can wait to watch the gelding qualifier tomorrow night before you decide. I'm on board with either way you want to go."

CHAPTER 70

10:00 PM August 20, Kentucky State Fairgrounds

Bobby arrives at the rail just before the bugler calls the geldings into the ring and the announcer introduces the class, "Tonight is the final qualifying class for Saturday's main event. The stallions qualified on Monday night and the mares qualified last night. Tonight, we see the best five-gaited geldings in the country. Please sound the call." With this, the bugler summons the horses and the gate to Freedom Hall swings open.

Bobby looks back toward the gate to watch the horses enter and sees Clark, leaning back against the wall. He catches his eye and Clark immediately heads his direction and sliding into a spot next to him in the crowd of trainers lining the rail.

"Hey Bobby," Clark greets him. "Is she going to get him into the ring?"

There is no doubt that he is talking about Jennifer and Toreador. "Yes. He's a handful, but she seemed to be getting along with him alright. I noticed Johnnie Stuart out there watching the warm-up. I wonder what's going through his mind."

"I can tell you what Johnnie thinks," Clark responds quietly. "He thinks that he should be the one riding that horse and nothing would make him happier than to see Toreador get beat." As he speaks, the crowd cheers and Toreador enters the ring. Jennifer keeps him far off the rail as she makes her first pass and he looks stunning. His chestnut coat is gleaming and his blond tail is streaming behind him as he strides down the ring. Jennifer takes him deep into the end and pulls out of the corner to make the next pass, still staying away from the rail. The big gelding is moving much faster than most of the other horses, and it is clear the crowd is watching him as they cheer and applaud the defending World Champion.

"He looks good." Clark directs his comment to Bobby, but several trainers around them overhear and there is a general murmur of agreement.

Bobby watches Jennifer tensely. She maneuvers Toreador around the ring two more times before the announcer asks for the horses to walk. Jennifer stops Toreador in the corner near where Bobby is standing and Bobby takes the opportunity to talk to her. "Looking good. Stay ahead of him."

She keeps her eyes on Toreador's head and talks quietly to her horse. When the announcer calls for the slow gait, it takes several strides before Jennifer has him working in a steady frame. She manages to keep him under control as they work around the ring, and when the announcer finally calls for the class to rack, she swerves off the rail and loosens her hold on the gelding. Toreador racks down the ring, easily speeding by several other horses and the crowd gets louder as they encourage the horses and riders.

"He's getting a full head of steam now," Clark says. "I hope she ate her Wheaties this morning."

"Yeah. Me too." It is all Bobby can say as he watches the class complete the first rack. When the announcer calls for the walk, Jennifer allows Toreador to jog down the ring slightly off the rail, maintaining some momentum and keeping Toreador occupied while they wait for the announcer to call for the canter. As soon as he does, Jennifer turns him to the rail and he immediately begins the gait, his huge strides causing her to work hard to avoid collision with the other horses.

Bobby continues to watch carefully and doesn't realize he is holding his breath until his boss nudges him and jokes, "You're going to pass out if you don't start breathing. She's doing fine. I think she's winning it so far."

The rest of the class passes in a blur for Bobby. He watches Toreador get more agitated with every gait. When the horses and riders are finally stopped and lined up waiting for the judges to complete their cards, he asks Clark. "What do you think?"

"I think she won it," Clark answers without hesitation.

"Do you think she can beat the stallion from California?"

"Well, she beat him in Shelbyville, so it's possible. But I think he's got a taste for this ring now and he'll be hard to manage on Saturday night. That California horse looks like he's a lot easier to show because he's got a better disposition. That could be her Achilles Heel."

As they talk, the announcer tells the class that the judges' cards are in, and they leave the line-up to await the results. Bobby watches

Jennifer as she jogs Toreador toward the rail at the end of the ring, and he notices her assistant Eduardo waiting for her there. Bobby works his way through the crowd towards them. "Nice ride!" He compliments Jennifer as soon as he is close enough for her to hear him.

She beams at him. Her face is sweaty and red from exertion, and she reaches down to pat Toreador on the neck. "Thanks! He was awesome."

Just then the announcer begins to speak. "This was a great group of gaited geldings, and it is now time to find out who is going to be back on Saturday night. Last year, SS Toreador won this class. This year..." After a pause that seems to Bobby to go on forever, the announcer finally completes his statement, "SS TOREADOR MAKES IT TWO IN A ROW!" Eduardo whoops and Jennifer yells "YES!" as she wheels Toreador and racks him towards the end of the ring. Eduardo rushes to the gate, squeezes into the ring, and follows her at a run, carrying a towel so that he can help her pose for her picture. Bobby hears cheering from some of the box seats near the center of the ring, and looks up to see Toreador's owner, Marianne Smithson, on her feet, smiling and cheering.

Bobby and Eduardo have to walk quickly to keep up with Jennifer on the way back to Toreador's stall. Stopher's Walk is congested with people leaving the show and horses coming in for the evening's training session. "That was so much fun!" Jennifer is half turned in her saddle, looking back at them when Bobby hears yelling. He looks around Toreador and sees the crowd parting as people scramble to the sides of the narrow, fenced area. A panicked young harness horse is racing toward them, dragging an overturned buggy. Several people are yelling "WHOA" at the oncoming horse, but the noise of the dragging buggy hitting the fences of the narrow space contributes to the pandemonium. Toreador rears and whirls away from the oncoming disaster. Jennifer struggles to get control and keep Toreador from trampling the people nearest him, but it is obvious that the panic of the oncoming horse has infected him. He continues to rear and Bobby and Eduardo avoid his hoofs as he threatens to fall over backwards. Bobby yells at Jennifer to bail off to avoid being crushed by Toreador and she pushes herself off the gelding, ending up on the ground, directly in the path of the oncoming horse.

CHAPTER 71

Jennifer uses crutches to lever herself off the waiting room chair when Marianne and Blair enter the lobby of Urgent Care. "Thanks for coming to pick me up." Jennifer has a black eye and her left leg is encased in a brace that runs from her upper thigh down to her ankle. The young trainer grimaces as she slowly achieves a standing position.

"Didn't they give you any pain killers?" Marianne asks.

"They did, but I don't want to take them." Jennifer sways slightly and Blair spontaneously reaches for her arm to steady her. "I can't take pain killers and be around horses."

"Be around horses?" Marianne says it too loudly. "What are you talking about? We're taking you straight to your hotel to put you to bed. We're going to jam a couple of pain killers down your throat if we have to."

"I have to go to the barn. We have horses to show today."

Blair interrupts her. "We just stopped at the stalls. Eduardo has everything under control. Bobby is helping him. Bobby said that he was here last night and told you that he had you covered."

Jennifer takes an awkward step towards the exit. "He did say that, but it's my responsibility."

"Jennifer. I'm not joking and we're not going to negotiate. We're taking you to the hotel. We'll come get you later this afternoon and take you over to the stalls, but you're in no shape to sit there now. You have a concussion and a broken leg. You're lucky it wasn't more serious."

On the way to the hotel Jennifer broaches the subject that is at the top of her mind. "I'm so sorry this happened. I'm just thankful Toreador wasn't hurt."

"There isn't a scratch on him." Marianne replies. "The vet came back this morning to make sure he hadn't missed anything last night and Eduardo lunged him. He's totally fine."

"Well that's a huge relief. Was anyone else hurt?" Jennifer grimaces again as she tries to get more comfortable.

295

"No one else was hurt as seriously as you. That poor filly that was pulling the buggy is all skinned up." Blair sighs and then says, "It was truly a miracle that it wasn't worse. What a wreck."

Jennifer says, "I've been thinking about how we're going to show Toreador back since I can't ride him."

Marianne glances at her in surprise. "What do you mean?"

"Well, he was so good last night that he could win this thing like he did last year. We can't miss the chance."

"But you clearly can't ride him." Blair leans forward from the back seat, "We've already talked about it and we'll just have to miss the chance to repeat last year's win."

Jennifer begins to shake her head but stops immediately, in obvious pain. "I've had all night to think about it and I've spent a good share of it feeling sorry for myself. But this is about Toreador, and I think we have three choices."

Marianne is stopped at the light waiting for it to turn green. "Go on."

"First, we could ask Johnnie Stuart to ride him."

"That's a horrifying idea. He is despicable." Marianne hadn't planned to tell Jennifer that Johnnie had already offered to take Toreador back for the remainder of the show season, but now she can't avoid it. "In fact, he had the gall to call me last night. He didn't even ask how you were. He told me that he supposed he could do me a favor and take Toreador back." She shakes her head, "As if I'd even consider giving that crook the satisfaction of showing Toreador. It would be taking a step backward. I'd rather not show."

Jennifer hides her relief. "Our second option is to ask another trainer like Bobby Acton to ride him. I could coach him. We could practice tonight and let Toreador rest tomorrow, so at least they could get one ride in before the Championship."

Blair leans forward from the back seat. "Wouldn't it be hard for someone that hasn't been around him to ride well? What's the chance that it would be a real disaster?"

"I won't lie. It would be really hard. Which brings me to the third option." She takes a deep breath. "Eduardo could show him."

"Eduardo? Are you serious?" Marianne looks away from the road to make eye contact with Jennifer.

296

"I am. Eduardo has been helping me all year. He knows Toreador as well as I do. Toreador likes him and trusts him."

Blair interrupts Jennifer, "I guess I hadn't thought about Eduardo."

"He's a great rider. He first learned by riding all my Dad's young horses. The problem is that he doesn't have any show ring experience and he hasn't ever ridden Toreador. But he's been with me every step and he's more familiar with Toreador than anyone else." Jennifer interprets Marianne's silence as a willingness to consider the suggestion and she goes on, "Here's what I think we should do. I think we should put Eduardo up on Toreador tonight to see how it goes. If it goes well, then we should let Eduardo show him."

Blair asks, "Does he even have a suit?"

"I hadn't thought of that. I don't think so."

"That's the least of our worries. We can get something off the rack from one of the vendors at the fairgrounds if we need to." Marianne speaks decisively. "Your idea is probably worth a try. But first things first, let's get you to the hotel and put you to bed. We'll come back and get you at six o'clock. If we decide that Eduardo can handle Toreador, Blair and I will figure out how we can get a suit and hat."

They continue the rest of the ride in happier conversation, replaying Toreador's win from the previous night.

Once Jennifer is in her room at the hotel, she makes a quick call to Eduardo. After reassuring him that she is going to be fine, she tells him about her idea. "I think you should show Toreador on Saturday night in the Stake Class." Before he can protest, she rushes on. "You know Toreador and you can ride as well as I can. I know you can do this."

Eduardo begins, "But I have never ridden him. I do not even own a riding suit."

"I know, but we can fix the suit thing. Marianne will help. I'll be over at the stalls this evening. We'll talk about it then and you can get in a practice ride after the show tonight. I know you can do this. You understand horses better than anyone I know, other than my Dad. You've watched a million gaited classes and you've broken thousands

297

of colts." She repeats her words, "I know you can do this. Are you willing to give it a try?"

Eduardo is silent for a moment, and then says, "Yes. I can try."

CHAPTER 72

"Here. Let me help you for God's sake." Bobby has agreed to drive Jennifer back to her hotel in the Kiplenan Stables' golf cart, and she is struggling to swing her leg brace into the area between the seat and the dashboard of the small vehicle.

"Thanks. I don't mean to be prickly. I just have a lot on my mind." She runs her hands through her hair and gives him a small smile of apology.

"It's no problem. But it seems like everything went okay tonight, right? Eduardo is going to show Toreador on Saturday and I heard Marianne telling him that she had talked to one of the vendors this afternoon and that she can get a suit fitted in the morning." Bobby carefully puts the golf cart in motion, and merges onto the street that will take them back to Jennifer's hotel.

"Yeah, he rode well tonight. It was hard to watch because his reactions are a bit slower than they'd be if he had more time to practice. He was being more tentative than he'll need to be in the ring, when Toreador has a full head of steam. I really tried to keep my mouth shut and only focus on the big stuff. It was hard, too, because there were so many people watching. He's not used to being the center of attention." While the practice session went well, Jennifer knows that she and Eduardo will need to spend several hours talking about the upcoming ride so that he is as prepared as he can possibly be for the Stake.

"He seemed pretty quiet tonight." Bobby is concentrating on avoiding pot holes in the road that might jar Jennifer. "He's usually pretty happy and jokes around but he seemed withdrawn. Do you think he's nervous? I know that I would be."

"It isn't just that. When I got to the stalls this evening he told me that he's decided to move to California after this show is over."

"Oh no! That's bad news. I know how well you get along and how much you depend on him."

"Yeah." Jennifer swallows hard to quell her emotions and replies, "He's a good friend and I'll miss him. But he's been sad and lonely since he came back from his mom's funeral."

299

"Do you think the move is temporary? Maybe he just needs to spend a couple of months with family and then he'll be ready to come back."

"I asked him that, but he insists that he needs to take care of his dad, so I think he plans for it to be permanent."

Bobby waits to see if she will go on, but when she is silent he gently asks, "What will you do?"

"Well, I need help. I've got several new horses coming this fall."

"I've been afraid to ask, but is Vendome one of them?"

Jennifer hesitates and then admits, "Yes. Marianne and Blair told me that they will move him to Beech Tree after the show. I was going to wait until after the show to tell you."

"Look. It's not like it's a surprise. I assumed that tomorrow night would be my last ride on him. But I'll definitely miss him. Vendome has been my favorite."

"Well then, why don't you consider coming over to Beech Tree with him?" Bobby turns to her in surprise and the cart hits a pothole in the road. She gasps and grabs the seat tightly and hurries to finish her thought. "I don't mean as an assistant. I mean as a partner. I think we have similar styles and I think we get along. We could build a good business."

"Wow." Bobby starts to speak and stops, then starts again. "Wow. I wasn't expecting this. It's an interesting idea."

"Don't answer now. Give it some thought. Maybe we can talk about it after the craziness of this show is over." Jennifer talks quickly to relieve the awkwardness of the situation. "Just think about it, okay?"

"I'll do that. I'll definitely consider it." He takes a deep breath and repeats. "Wow."

CHAPTER 73

9:30 PM August 22, Kentucky State Fairgrounds

It is Friday night and the bugler is sounding the call for the Junior Gaited Championship. Mrs. M has invited Blair to sit with her during Vendome's class.

"Look! There he is!" Blair points toward the gate unnecessarily, as Mrs. M has already spotted the tall chestnut gelding. He is the fourth horse in the gate, and both women's eyes follow him up the rail as he trots by them. Mrs. M yells encouragement at Bobby as he goes by, "Ride hard!" After a quick scan, Mrs. M glances at Blair and says, "Fifteen horses. One is missing. Johnnie Stuart isn't in the ring."

"Right. I don't see him. I wonder what happened."

"Maybe he decided to show Night Train in the Stake Class tomorrow night." Ribbon winners from the qualifying classes have earned the right to show tonight in the championship, but also have the option to show in the Saturday night Open Championship.

"That's a big step for a four-year-old." Blair watches Vendome as he trots around the far end and says, "Well, I guess I'm relieved. I thought he would be Vendome's toughest competition."

"That liver chestnut mare is making a show, though."

Blair follows Mrs. M's line of sight to a big-strided mare with a nearly black mane and tail that is trotting down the far side behind Vendome. "Who is she?"

"I don't recognize the woman riding her. We'll have to check her number when she comes around." Both women are silent as the mare passes by, making the number on the back of the rider visible.

Blair quickly turns to the index in the back of her program that lists all the horses by their back number. "She's from Texas. Her name is Texas Beauty Queen. I love that name. But I guess that's why we don't recognize her. We don't often compete against horses from Texas." She keeps her eyes glued on Vendome through the slow gait, and when the announcer tells the riders to rack, she joins the rest of the crowd in shouting encouragement to the riders.

"Wow! Look at Vendome go!" Blair remarks, but Mrs. M is already focused on her gelding. Vendome's head is up and his front knees are pumping up to his chest with every long stride. The crowd

301

has begun to pick their favorites and the cheers swell as Vendome makes a pass down the ring.

Mrs. M's attention is drawn back to the bay mare as the crowd reacts equally enthusiastically to her racking pass. "That mare is giving him a run for his money, though."

By the time the horses have reversed and shown at all five gaits the second direction, it is clear that the crowd has identified Vendome and Texas Beauty Queen as their favorites. When the four-year-olds line up, the announcer calls for the attendants to enter the ring to assist in stripping the horses. The gate at the far end of the ring opens, and 30 people jog into the ring, two attendants for each horse.

"Oh. I forgot that they strip this class." Blair says, as the announcer explains to the crowd that horses' saddles are removed during the championships on Friday and Saturday night so that the judges can more easily assess conformation. Occasionally, this reveals a horse with a serious conformation fault that causes the judges to place a horse at the bottom of the class, even though they performed all their gaits well and earned a high ribbon in the qualifier.

Once all the horses have been evaluated, the riders and attendants replace the saddles and remount to wait until the judge's cards are complete. Blair leans over to Mrs. M and says, "He should win, don't you think?"

"I don't know. That bay mare was very nice. He's prettier than she is and has a nicer trot, but her rack was phenomenal. I imagine we'll hear a lot more about her in the next few years."

After what seems like a very long delay, the announcer begins. "This was a very competitive class…"

Mrs. M. growls quietly, "Get on with it."

"… but there can only be one winner. Tonight the win goes to… Vendome Copper!"

Mrs. M. and Blair leap to their feet, cheering loudly as Bobby removes his hat and wearing a broad grin, racks Vendome to the end of the ring.

The announcer describes the horse's pedigree and names Mrs. M. as owner. He then says, "I've also been asked to announce that as of tonight, he will have a new owner. Miss Blair Bartlett will be showing

302

Vendome Copper next year!" The crowd claps and several people around Mrs. M and Blair congratulate them.

"Our reserve champion is a beautiful mare from Texas..." the crowd erupts again, as they anticipate the rest of his announcement. "...it is Texas Beauty Queen!" The crowd continues clapping, clearly pleased with the judges' choices.

CHAPTER 74

9:00 AM August 23, Kentucky State Fairgrounds

Johnnie Stuart takes a quick glance at his watch and looks up and down the alley to make sure no one is around. He then enters Night Train's stall with two syringes. Johnnie injects the clear liquid into the horse's neck. After withdrawing the second needle, he looks carefully at Night Train's neck to be sure the injection site isn't bleeding, detaches the cross ties and removes the horse's halter.

He returns to the tack room and quickly puts the bottles of Phenylbutazone and Equioxx back into his medication cabinet and locks it. He is safely outside of the 12-hour window but has violated the rule about giving two NSAIDS within three days of competition. The likelihood of Night Train receiving a drug test is fairly high if he wins, but he is confident that his horse will metabolize the drugs quickly enough that the drug test won't detect that he has been given two.

CHAPTER 75

"Do we have time to stop and see Dad and give Spy Master a peppermint for luck?" Jeremy and Angela Rivers are getting out of her car. She misjudged the traffic and the final night of the horse show begins in just 10 minutes.

"We'll need to hurry. We don't want to miss the beginning of the show." Angela locks the doors and she and Jeremy hurry across the parking lot toward the stalls for Riverside Stables. Her heels make walking difficult in the shavings, and she has a moment of regret that she didn't wear her sensible flats. But she has been looking forward to this evening's outing with Jeremy and has taken a lot of time with her appearance. A girlfriend helped her highlight her hair and do her makeup earlier in the day, and she has borrowed a short black cocktail dress. The unfamiliar glamour has made her self-conscious.

As they turn into the barn door, they maneuver around people that are streaming the opposite direction, going to take their seats in Freedom Hall. As they stand back to let a chattering group of well-dressed people slowly walk by, Angela sees Kenny and his friend Holly at the end of the aisle. They are hugging, and Kenny is facing away from her. As she hesitates in confusion, Jeremy spots them and yells "Dad!"

Angela watches as Holly quickly steps away from her husband, and Kenny turns to greet his son, "Hi there. You made it I see. I thought you'd probably gone directly to your seats." He looks at Angela and says, "Wow! You look great!"

Angela replies frostily, "Jeremy wanted to come and wish you luck, but we need to hurry."

Kenny notices her tone and looks at her quizzically, but is distracted when Jeremy asks Holly, "Can I give him a peppermint for luck?"

She laughs and says, "Of course."

"Jeremy, we need to go!" Angela pivots and begins walking away from the stalls, leaving Jeremy to hurry in order to catch up.

Holly waits until they are out of earshot before saying quietly, "She saw us hugging."

"But we have no reason to feel guilty about that."

"I know that and you know that, but maybe she doesn't know that." Holly looks at Kenny. "Maybe you should go talk to her."

"I wouldn't be able to find her in the crowd. She has no reason to be jealous and I don't really want to deal with it now, anyway."

He ducks through the curtain into the tack room and she says to his back, "Well, at least send her a text or something."

CHAPTER 76

The first ten classes of the night are complete, and ten World's Champions have been crowned. Only one class remains. The crowd quiets expectantly as the lights in Freedom Hall are dimmed, and a video begins to play. To the strains of "All That Jazz," it highlights Five-Gaited World Champions that have been victorious on previous Stake Nights, focusing on the most famous performance horses in the Saddlebred breed, including Imperator, Sky Watch, My-My, and Onion. Many in the glittering crowd have seen the video before, but everyone cheers and claps for their favorites. As the video fades to black, the organist plays 'My Old Kentucky Home' and the ringmasters and judges take their places on the green shavings and the crowd settles into their seats to await the horses.

The horses in this final class are introduced individually, in an order that roughly equates to the standing they have earned from their show records and the qualifying classes.

The announcer begins, "There are a total of eight horses showing tonight and we are certain to see a very tough competition. Our first horse is from here in Kentucky and was second in the gelding stake. Please welcome…"

Mr. Lee Kiplenan is watching carefully from his box. He is seated next to his long-time friend, Michael Vine. Attending Stake Night together has become a tradition for the friends, and they have not missed a Saturday Night performance in more than fifteen years. They are both dressed in jackets and colorful ties and are sipping bourbon as they begin to talk about the horses in the final class as they enter the ring.

Michael says, "Who's your money on this year?" Michael and Lee typically have a friendly bet about who will win.

"Well, the easy bet would have been Toreador. He's the returning champion. But his trainer broke her leg after his qualifier the other night so her assistant is going to show him. His name is Eduardo Muñoz." Lee answers. "The assistant trainer at my barn is dating the gal that got hurt. He told me that Eduardo rode Toreador for the first time on Thursday."

307

"You can't be serious." Michael looks at his friend in astonishment.

"What's more, I don't think he's ever ridden in a show before. He came up through the grooming ranks. I think it might be a disaster."

"I'm surprised they couldn't find a better catch rider than that," Michael shakes his head. "So that probably takes him out of the running. Who's your next pick?"

While the friends have been talking, the announcer has introduced the first two horses. Both are veterans of the Stake. He continues, "The next horse was Reserve Champion in the Four-Year-Old Stallion and Gelding Class, with wins in the Junior Five-Gaited Championship at Shelbyville, Rock Creek and Asheville. Please welcome SS Night Train to the ring."

As Johnnie rides Night Train down the ramp and onto the green shavings, Michael leans toward Lee and says, "We don't often see a four-year-old in this class. I'm surprised that Toreador's owner didn't ask him to catch ride Toreador since that trainer got hurt."

"They had a serious falling out after last year's show. Do you remember how he didn't give the owner, Marianne Smithson, any credit or acknowledgement in his victory speech? It was the last straw for her and that was his last ride on Toreador. That probably fueled his fire to win this again on a horse that he owns himself. A lot of people don't like Johnnie, but he's successful and he's got a very nice horse."

The announcer continues, "The fifth horse in our class tonight was the unanimous winner of the Amateur Mare gaited class and placed third in last year's Stake. Please welcome Josephine's Dream to Freedom Hall."

The crowd cheers for Josie and Lee says to Michael, "That's Senator Phillips' daughter riding."

Michael responds, "Why didn't she stay in the Amateur Class? It seems like she would have had a better shot at winning that class than this one. I remember that mare from last year. She's got a helluva motor, but the boys out-muscled her."

"Yes. Annie Jessup showed her last year. She's a racking machine, but she just doesn't have the big stride that some of the other horses in this class have." Lee pauses and says, "Riding in this class is a life-long goal for our industry, amateurs and trainers alike. I imagine Missy Phillips has won enough ribbons in her life that she'd rather win any ribbon in this class at the World Championship than get a first place ribbon in any other class. And if she rides well, that mare won't embarrass her."

By now the announcer is continuing, "We only have two more horses to introduce. This next entry won the Four-Year-Old Gaited class last year. He was the unanimous winner of the Stallion qualifier and was Reserve Champion in the Stake at Shelbyville. His name is Spy Master."

Lee and Michael both watch Holly trot Spy Master into the ring. Michael quickly says, "He's my pick!" Spy Master is breathtaking. His four white feet emphasize the crispness of his gait as he strides down the ring.

Lee and Michael both watch him carefully as the announcer completes the introductions, "And now our final entrant is the defending World Champion. Please welcome SS Toreador to the ring. The class is now underway."

As Eduardo rides Toreador into the ring, the entire class begins working at a trot going counter-clockwise. Lee watches Eduardo, dressed in a black suit and hat, maneuver Toreador around the far end of the ring and then says to Lee, "I'm going to bet on Toreador. They wouldn't have put that guy on him if they didn't think he could handle him."

"True." Michael is also watching Toreador, "But he looks a little tentative to me. I'm going to stick with Spy Master."

The class quickly starts to sort itself out as the horses work through the first trot, slow gait and rack. By the time the horses canter and reverse, Lee and Michael have formed some strong opinions.

"Well, there are the top four and then there are the bottom four, do you agree?" Lee asks Michael.

"Yes, but I'm not sure Toreador fits in the top four. He's always in a bad position, he isn't getting free of the traffic, and it looks to me like Johnnie Stuart is deliberately cutting him off every chance he gets."

"I agree," Lee replies. "His rider needs to make some better decisions, but the horse looks good."

309

These sentiments echo Jennifer's, as she watches from the rail. She is leaning on her crutches while attempting to coach Eduardo each time he passes by. When the horses pause before cantering, Eduardo stops Toreador on the rail next to her and she says sharply, "Eduardo. You need to step it up. You're riding the best horse in the ring and you're letting him get beat on every pass. Settle down and act like you want to win this class. I know you can do it, damn it. Now lighten up on his mouth and get busy!"

Eduardo glances at her. She sees a mixture of annoyance and hurt flicker across his face, then he cues Toreador for the canter and is gone.

Lee Kiplenan has been watching the interchange and although he cannot hear what was said, he can see the expression on Jennifer's face and he points her out to Michael. "Down there on the rail, see that young woman in the black shirt on crutches? That's Toreador's trainer. Her dad started Beech Tree Stables and she's taken it over. It's really a shame that she got hurt. In the qualifier it looked like she had Toreador in good form. A nice ribbon in this class would have meant a lot for her business."

"Yeah. Toreador is getting dusted." Michael looks back at the class as the announcer tells them to reverse and trot.

The noise and energy in Freedom Hall escalates, now that the class has reversed. Missy pulls Josie off the rail and stays toward the inside of the ring so that she won't get blocked from the judges' views by the larger horses in the class. Michael notices her strategy and comments to Lee, "That chestnut mare is looking good. She might be an amateur, but she's holding her own in this class."

Lee watches Josie's next trotting pass and agrees, "Yes. She is. And her best gait is the rack. But she's got to get by that Stallion from California."

Michael smiles as the horse he chose as his favorite in the beginning of the class follows Josie. Spy Master is working on the rail and it is clear from the roar of the crowd that he has fans. As Michael watches him, he hears another roar, and quickly looks at the opposite rail to see what is causing it. Toreador is making a trotting pass and has just passed Night Train as though the four-year-old was standing still. "Well, it looks like Toreador finally came to the party!"

310

Lee has a small smile on his face as he watches the defending champion sweep around the end of the ring. Eduardo steers the horse out of the corner and gives him his head. Toreador reacts to the new freedom and the crowd's encouragement as he quickly overtakes two other horses and gains ground on Josie, even though he is on the outside of her. "Yes. I agree. It looks like he might make a show after all. I just hope it isn't too late."

When the announcer calls for the horses to slow gait, Josie is the first horse to make a long pass in front of the judge. Michael says, "With those white legs, it is hard to tear your eyes way from her. And that amateur is riding as well as anyone else in the class."

Lee agrees and then he notices that Johnnie Stuart has pulled up his horse and is motioning to get the ring master's attention. "Looks like we have a time-out."

Michael says quietly, "It seems a little convenient, doesn't it? I was just going to say that it looked like he was starting to fade."

Johnnie's groom has jogged into the ring and is adjusting the chin strap on Night Train's bridle. It seems to be taking him a long time to get it right, and Lee says, "Yes. It will give everyone a breather, though. Not just Night Train." He notices that Toreador is stopped next to where Jennifer is leaning on her crutches. She is clearly giving Eduardo encouragement and instructions and he straightens his posture and adjusts his reins as he listens. Lee's gaze shifts to Spy Master, who is also stopped on the rail near Toreador. His rider, Holly McNair is talking to Kenny Rivers as she gives her horse a chance to catch his breath.

It takes nearly three minutes until the announcer finally calls the class back to order and they are slow gaiting again. Very shortly after that, the announcer calls for the horses to rack and the crowd is fully engaged. The roars swell and fade as the favorites make passes down the long sides of the ring. Night Train and Toreador are making most of the passes together.

After watching one of these passes, Michael says to Lee, "Is it just me, or does it look like Johnnie Stuart is intentionally crowding Toreador?"

"Yes. I've been watching him. He'd be better off to just worry about his own ride instead of trying to sabotage someone else." He watches closely as the two horses finish a racking pass. Toreador is on the rail, with Night Train right next to him. They are close enough so that Lee realizes that their stirrups must be rubbing. As they near the end of the ring, he watches as Eduardo pulls back on Toreador so that he hesitates, letting Night Train pass him. At first, Lee thinks that Eduardo's hesitation is an error, but as soon as Night Train passes, Eduardo moves Toreador to the inside and accelerates past Night Train for the next pass. The crowd yells its approval and Lee laughs. "Did you see that?"

Michael is also laughing, "He gave Johnnie Stuart a bit of his own medicine. Suddenly, I'm a big Toreador fan!"

When the announcer finally tells the class to walk, Spy Master makes one final, perfect racking pass. Michael elbows Lee and says, "That pass just won it."

"It ain't over 'til it's over, my friend." But Lee agrees that Spy Master has established himself as a front runner.

The horses canter and then line up. The attendants jog into the ring to assist the riders in removing the saddles and preparing their horses to be presented to the judges for the conformation judging. The announcer individually introduces each horse as they approach the judges, pose, and return to the line-up to be re-saddled. The crowd shouts encouragement to their favorites throughout this process.

"Who is going to make the work out?" Michael asks Lee. Nearly everyone in the crowd is anticipating that the judges will request a workout between the top horses before they make a final decision. The judges have full discretion over how many horses they select for extra work.

"I think I'd call back Toreador and Spy Master. You have to call Toreador back out of respect for his win last year. And if you call Toreador back, you almost have to include Night Train, because I think Night Train had him beat, especially going the first direction."

The crowd waits in anticipation until the announcer finally says, "Ladies and Gentlemen. We will have a workout." The audience reacts with pleasure and he then says, "The judges have selected four horses to return to the rail." The announcer calls out Toreador, Spy Master, Night Train and Josephine's Dream to begin a trot going the first direction.

Lee and Michael watch as the four riders spread themselves out around the ring. "They look spectacular," says Michael.

Lee agrees, but his eyes are drawn to Toreador. "Toreador looks the best he has looked all night. I think his rider is taking charge." Eduardo's face and posture are determined and focused as he trots Toreador around the ring.

As the class works, it is apparent that Night Train is tired. The bay stallion is lathered, and he appears to be struggling to maintain the pace of the other three. The judges watch as the horses work through all the gaits in both directions. By the time they are lined up again, all the horses and riders are covered in sweat.

"I'll give you a chance to change your bet if you want it," Michael says to Lee.

"None of them left anything in the tank, did they?" Lee replies. "That is one of the best gaited Stakes we've seen recently. It's a tough call. If there hadn't been a work out, I think Spy Master and Night Train were the top two. But the work out changed everything. Toreador came on strong, Josephine's Dream showed that she was up to the challenge, and Spy Master maintained. I guess I'll stick with my pick, though."

The crowd doesn't have long to wait before the announcer begins by congratulating all of the competitors and introducing the many people who are assembling at the end of the ring holding the trophies and awards. He finally says, "But we can only have one World Champion and winner in our $100,000 Stake. This year, that honor goes to…"

It seems that the entire audience is holding their breath until he finally completes his sentence, "… SS Toreador!" The crowd erupts as a broad smile creases Eduardo's tense face. He looks uncertain as to what he should do next, but Bobby enters the ring at a run and motions for him to go to the end of the ring to receive the trophies. The announcer then explains to the crowd, "This win is exceptional because I'm told that this is not just the first time that Toreador's rider has shown in Freedom Hall, it is the first time he has ever shown a gaited horse in front of a judge! I think that we can all agree that he did a great job! Before we go on, we've provided a little assistance for Toreador's trainer and usual rider, Jennifer Hornig, to join him in the

313

winner's circle." The gate at the end of the ring swings open and admits a golf cart driven by a ring steward and carrying a beaming Jennifer and her crutches. As they make their way to the end of the ring, the announcer continues by describing the trophies and awards that will be received by the second place horse. "Our Reserve World Champion came all the way from California… Spy Master!"

Holly smiles and racks Spy Master up to where a group is waiting to present the Reserve Championship trophy and ribbon. Kenny Rivers hurries into the ring with a towel to help her pose for the picture, and they exchange a high five when he reaches her.

"Third place goes to the only amateur rider in our class. Congratulations to Josephine's Dream and Missy Phillips!" Missy happily wheels Josie away from where she is waiting on the rail, and picks up her ribbon. She waves it over her head and leaves the ring at a rack as the crowd applauds.

"Our fourth place award goes to SS Night Train…" Johnnie Stuart doesn't smile as he accepts the ribbon and leaves the ring. His fourth place ribbon was the lowest ribbon he could receive after being selected for the four-horse workout, and it is obvious to those nearest him that he is disappointed.

After the remainder of the eight ribbons are distributed, the announcer moves to the end of the ring to conduct the traditional rider interview. Eduardo has dismounted, and stands next to Jennifer. Jennifer offers him the microphone but he shakes his head and steps back so she begins, "First of all, I want to thank Marianne Smithson who owns Toreador and has believed in him from the beginning. I appreciate that she stuck with the Beech Tree team this year as we figure out her talented horse." She pauses and takes a deep breath. "Second, I want to thank my parents. I know my Dad was watching over us tonight and I'm so thankful to bring a World Championship back to his beloved Beech Tree Farm. And you may not know this, but it was my mom's brilliant idea to lure Eduardo back to Kentucky when I needed help with Toreador, which brings me to Eduardo." She looks directly at her assistant, "I'd like to thank and congratulate Eduardo. He has helped me with every step of preparing Toreador for this night. And it's a testament to his skill and determination that he rode this challenging horse to victory. On Wednesday night after my

314

accident, we thought we might have to put this dream on the shelf for this year, but he stepped in and I couldn't have ridden Toreador any better than he did." Eduardo and Jennifer exchange a hug, and she continues in an emotional voice. "Finally, I want to acknowledge the talent and grit of this great horse. Toreador was never easy. We had some scary moments, some confusing moments," she laughs lightly and then admits, "Well maybe a LOT of confusing moments." The crowd laughs too as she goes on, "And then some exhilarating moments like this one. Toreador works hard every moment that he is awake. He came to the ring ready to go every day. I imagine he wondered how long it was going to take us to figure out how to speak his language, but we finally did." She takes another deep breath, "When I broke my leg earlier this week, I thought I'd missed my chance to feel the joy that I feel right now. Thank you to my friends at Kiplenan Stables for pitching in and helping make this possible." With that she hands the microphone back to the announcer and watches proudly as Eduardo remounts and guides Toreador through a victory pass.

Made in the USA
Coppell, TX
21 October 2020

40042769R00187